Liars Like Us

MORALLY GRAY BOOK 1

J.T. GEISSINGER

Published by J.T. Geissinger, Inc.

ISBN-13: 979-8-9853168-8-9

Editing by Linda Ingmanson

Cover design by Lori Jackson

Cover photograph of Eric Guilmette by Michelle Lancaster @lanefotograf

www.jtgeissinger.com

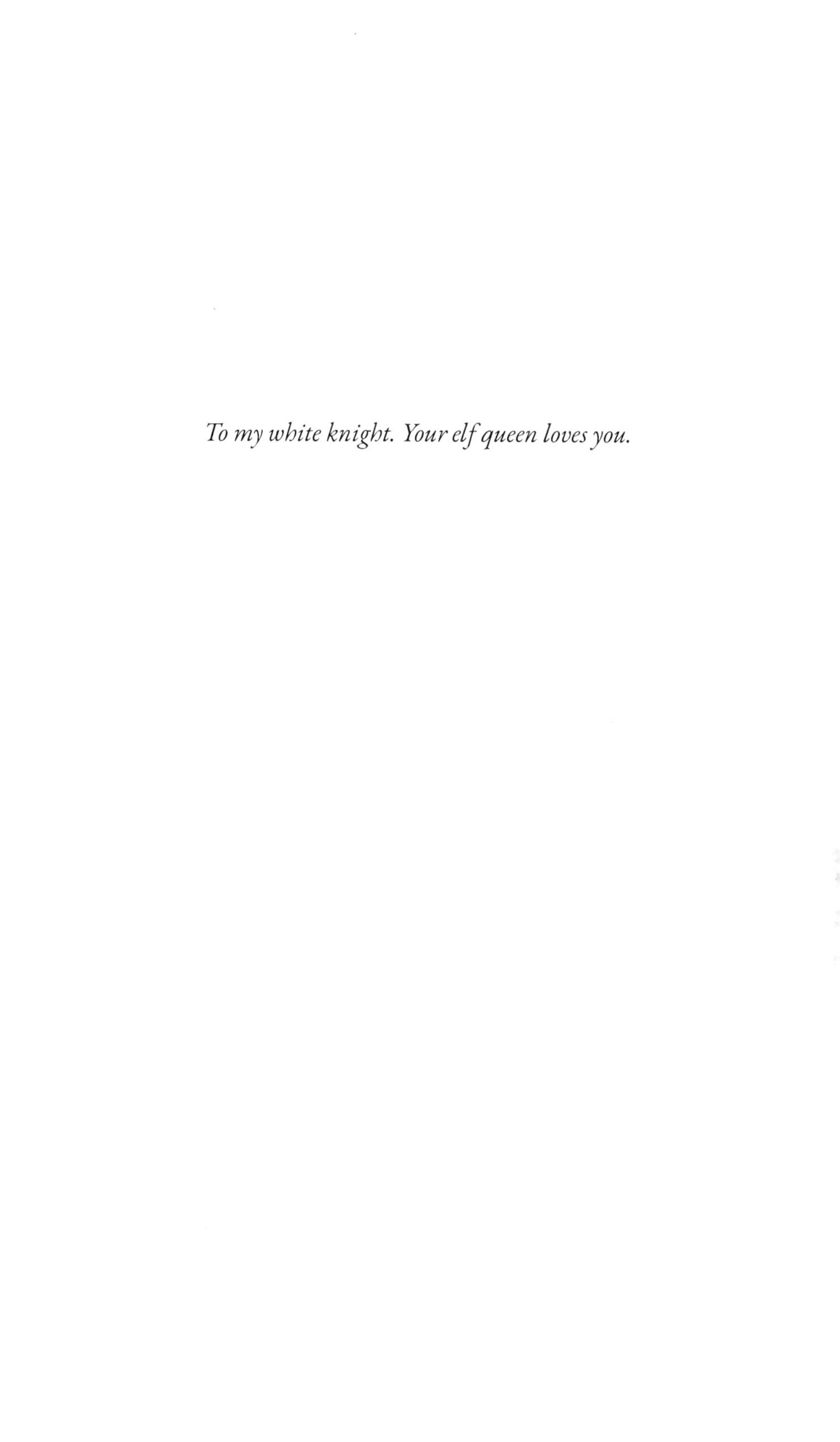

To my white knight. Your elf queen loves you.

Find what you love and let it kill you.
~ (Falsely attributed to) Charles Bukowski

Playlist

"Killer" Valerie Broussard
"Big Bad Wolf" Roses & Revolutions
"I Want To" Rosenfeld
"Devil Devil" MILCK
"Animal" AG, MOONZz
"Devil I Know" Allie X
"Bad Guy" Billie Eilish
"Secret" The Pierces
"Lunatic" UPSAHL
"Watch Me Burn" Michele Morrone
"Choke" Royal & the Serpent
"Monsters" Ruelle
"Joke's on You" Charlotte Lawrence
"A Little Wicked" Valerie Broussard
"SHE" Winona Oak
"Goddess" Jaira Burns
"Wicked as They Come" CRMNL
"Trustfall" Pink

One

The yellow balloons bob in a cheery arch over the open glass doors of ValUBooks as a steady stream of customers passes through on their blissful way to kill my soul, my family's legacy, and every dream I ever dared to dream.

"It's not that bad," says Viv brightly.

My sweet employee, she of the freckles and strawberry-blonde hair, stands beside me at the window of my shop as we watch the throng of people outside make their way to fatten the already fat bank account of my arch nemesis.

I'd say competitor, but there's no competition. ValUBooks is a Fortune 500 company with over a billion in assets, operating more than 1,000 successful retail outlets across the country, and employing over 30,000 people.

My company, Lit Happens, has one location, five employees, and "assets" that include an assortment of feral cats that wander in and out and an ancient espresso machine possessed by a fire demon that once burst into flames just as the city health inspector arrived to conduct the annual inspection on the tiny café inside the store.

I mutter, "Sure. In the same way a brain tumor isn't that bad."

Viv shoots me a glance, examines my expression, then turns back to the view of the sunny July morning and continues trying to reassure me.

"Don't sound so depressed. It's opening day. They're bound to be busy today. I bet tomorrow, it will be slower. Then next week, it will be totally dead."

Dead like my business. Dead like my future. Dead like my love life, which came to a screeching halt six months ago when my boyfriend Ben suddenly declared it was over between us. Then he blocked my number as if I were a bill collector he was trying to avoid.

I still have no idea what happened. When I went to his apartment to try to talk to him, his neighbor across the hall said he'd moved.

He didn't leave a forwarding address. He didn't even give the landlord notice. He just cleared out like a criminal on the run from the law.

He probably had a premonition that my life was about to end, and he didn't want to get dragged down into the depths of bankruptcy and self-loathing with me.

"Oh God. It's Channel 4 News!" Horrified, I point to the blue-and-white van with the satellite dish affixed to its roof that's pulling into the parking lot.

Viv says hopefully, "Maybe there's a gas leak."

I scoff. "Thanks for that, but the news doesn't show up to cover a gas leak. They're reporting on the grand opening."

"Maybe it's a *big* gas leak. Maybe the building is about to be evacuated. Maybe ValUBooks is going to explode!"

That's Viv in a nutshell. Little Miss Sunshine, always looking on the bright side, even in the face of imminent disaster.

I could point to a gigantic asteroid entering the atmosphere directly over our heads that was about to obliterate all life on the planet, and she'd say something chipper about how at least there are no income taxes or internet trolls in the afterlife.

"Nothing is exploding around here except my sanity. I need a drink."

Despondent, I turn away from the window and cross the store, stopping behind the counter where the register sits. From beneath it, I pull a bottle of whiskey. I unscrew the cap and take a slug right from the bottle as Viv watches me, her pretty face pinched.

She says tentatively, "Isn't it a little early for a drink, Em?"

"Don't judge me. My life's falling apart. Liquor is the answer."

"Liquor is never the answer. Especially at ten o'clock on a Friday morning."

"Ha! Says the infant with no problems."

She looks insulted. "Twenty isn't an infant."

"Pfft. Get back to me in a decade and we'll talk."

I take another swig from the bottle, cap it, then put it back under the counter. Because although I'd never admit aloud that my young and unjaded employee is right, she's right. Ten o'clock is much too early to drink.

I'll wait until noon to really get started.

The front door of the shop swings open. A tanned brunette wearing a gold USC hoodie, cutoff jean shorts, and flip-flops bursts in, looking panicked.

"Emery! OhmyfuckingGod the *news* is out there! Did you see the van? Did you see the crowd? Did you see how many cars are in the lot? I had to park down the *street*, it's so packed!"

"Maybe tone down the hysteria," suggests Viv, sending an uncharacteristic frown toward Harper as she charges at me, tossing her Louis Vuitton handbag onto the counter.

Harper ignores her. She grabs me by the shoulders and gives me a shake.

"I can't lose this job, Em. You know my financial situation.

You know Chad wiped me out. You know I could never find another job because I have no work ethic!"

"What I know is that you're giving me bruises and making me want to give you a friendly little slap in return." I reach under the counter and grab the whiskey. "Here. This will help."

As Harper unscrews the cap on the whiskey and takes a drink, Viv throws her hands in the air in exasperation.

"Doesn't anyone around here have healthy stress management skills?"

"They didn't teach that back in the dark ages when we went to school. Now make yourself useful, Vivienne. Go next door to the enemy camp, have a look around, and report back."

"What am I supposed to be looking for?"

"Anything we can send as a code violation to the county to get those bastards closed down."

"What if I don't find anything?"

Harper pipes in, "Pretend to slip. Fall and break a bone. Make a scene. And make sure there's blood! News reporters love it when there's blood."

Viv sighs and shakes her head.

"She's joking," I say.

"No, I'm not!" insists Harper. "This is life or death, girls! I'm a thirty-year-old single mother with no marketable skills, forty grand in credit card debt, and a child who visits the emergency room at least once a month because he's allergic to everything. I *can't* lose this job. And if we don't do something drastic, ValU-Books will be the end of us."

She turns toward the front window, waves an arm in the air, and wails, "Just look at that crowd!"

Harper always gets dramatic when she's upset. She was a theater major in college before she dropped out to marry the star quarterback, have a baby, and discover that her husband's idea of monogamy included a rotating roster of perky coeds.

I take the bottle from her and put it back under the counter. I'd let her have more, but I need it.

Over the sound of Harper hyperventilating, a gruff male voice calls, “Good morning, ladies.”

Mr. Murphy stands in the front door, nodding a curt hello to all of us.

He’s a retired English teacher originally from the Bronx whose wife passed away last year. He was a long-time customer of the shop before I owned it, and the first employee I hired after my father died.

In my opinion, every good bookstore has at least one cat, several comfy chairs tucked away in hidden corners to curl up in, and a curmudgeon who knows how to find exactly the story you’re looking for.

Mr. Murphy is our curmudgeon.

“Oh, Murph,” cries Harper. “Did you see? We’re doomed!”

He closes the door behind him and surveys Harper with a look of distaste in his steely blue gaze. Nothing makes him more uncomfortable than displays of emotion.

Ignoring Harper’s outburst, he strides over to the espresso machine on the other side of the shop. In his crisp white button-down dress shirt, plastic pocket protector, and horn-rimmed glasses, he could be a rocket scientist straight out of the fifties.

His gray buzz cut and disdain for normal human feelings only add to the impression.

I say, “Murph, you’re not on the schedule for today.”

“Neither is Harper,” he replies stoically as he fixes himself an espresso. “Or Taylor, whom I spied in the parking lot, skulking around like a felon.”

Taylor is another employee, a gaming fanatic with tattoos of her favorite book quotes all over her body, lots of facial piercings, and a wicked sense of humor.

She’s probably here for the same reason the rest of us are.

To commiserate with our fate.

As if on cue, the front door opens again, revealing Sabine.

Sabine is one of those quintessential California beach girls, all shiny gold hair and big blue eyes and teeth like the star of a

Colgate commercial. In contrast to her sunny appearance, however, she radiates the kind of dark intensity usually associated with cult leaders.

It's an irresistible combination. I can't count how many men I've seen fall lovestruck at her feet.

She steps inside and fixes me with a piercing stare. "Hey, Em. How are you?"

I smile. "Who, me? Just in the middle of a minor breakdown. Nothing to worry about."

From over his shoulder, Murph calls, "Good morning, Sabine."

"Morning, Murph. Viv, Harper. What's everyone doing here?"

Murph turns to peer at her over the rims of his glasses. "Isn't it obvious? We're on the deck of the *Titanic*, listening to the musicians play before we sink into the freezing water and drown."

He's always good for a depressing metaphor.

"Nobody's drowning!" says Viv with a huff. "You guys are overreacting. Lit Happens has been a mainstay of this community for forty years. I mean, that's like..." She struggles for a comparison, then points at me. "Practically as long as Emery's been celibate!"

"Excuse me, but six months is hardly forty years."

Sabine chuckles. "Maybe for you, it isn't."

The phone rings. I rush to answer it, hoping it's a customer with a big special order or maybe a long-lost relative calling to inform me of the billions I've just inherited from an eccentric great-aunt I never knew I had. But when I pick up, I'm disappointed to hear a familiar voice.

"Oh, good, I caught you," says my landlord in his distinct Boston accent.

"Hi, Bill." I sneak a furtive glance behind me to make sure nobody's too close, then turn back to face the wall and lower my voice. "The rent check cleared, didn't it?"

"Yes, it did. After I put it through twice."

I wince, then start to chew my thumbnail. "Shit. I'm so sorry. It's just been a little tight lately, what with the economy and inflation and still trying to get over the pandemic downturn—"

He interrupts, "No, no, I understand completely. It's been hard times for everybody in retail, that's for sure."

I'm relieved for half a second, until he says, "Which is actually why I'm calling."

There's something in the tone of his voice that makes my pulse jump. "What do you mean?"

He clears his throat. "Well, your current lease term will end soon..."

Oh no. Oh God no, don't you dare do this to me right now.

"...and as you know, we haven't raised the rent in several years..."

Don't say it, Bill. Please don't say what I think you're about to say.

"...but with ValUBooks moving into the complex, those smaller spaces like yours are going to command a much higher price per square foot. So I'm afraid there's going to be an increase."

When my silence becomes too much for him to bear, he says sheepishly, "Your rent will double starting September first."

"Double?" I shout, startling the chubby orange cat dozing on the countertop nearby. "You're telling me you want me to pay *twenty thousand dollars a month* for rent?"

At least he has the decency to sound embarrassed. "You haven't had an increase in five years. And before that, it was another five. It's only fair that we bring things up to current market value."

I want to say that if things were fair, my father would never have died in the first place.

If things were fair, my mother wouldn't have succumbed to breast cancer when I was only ten years old.

If things were *fair*, for fuck's sake, I wouldn't have had to skip college to help run the family business. The business currently gasping its last breath.

But I simply close my eyes and draw a slow breath. "I have people who rely on this business for jobs, Bill."

"And I have people who rely on my business for theirs. I'm really sorry, Em. This isn't personal."

My face flaming, I retort, "Actually, this is about as personal as it gets."

"Look. You're a businesswoman. You know how it goes. Only the strong survive."

"That's not business, it's a Bruce Springsteen song."

"Same thing."

"You could've given me a little more notice!"

"Would it have made any difference if I did?"

I close my eyes and exhale in defeat. We both know he could give me a year's advance notice, and I still wouldn't be able to make the new rent.

At that moment, the marching band I didn't know had assembled in the parking lot launches into an enthusiastic rendition of "Start Me Up" by the Rolling Stones.

"What's all that racket?" says Bill.

"The sound of my life ending." I slam the receiver down with a curse, making the orange cat on the counter glare at me in outrage for disturbing him.

Taylor bursts through the door, knocking Sabine aside in her rush.

"Hey!" Sabine says, aggravated. "I'm standing here!"

Without acknowledging her, Taylor crosses to me in a few long strides and slaps her hands down on the countertop.

Leaning in, she says hotly, "They have a Starbucks. A fucking *Starbucks*, those twats!"

In addition to her fondness for piercings and tattoos, Taylor also has a vulgar mouth. It's one of the many things I love about her.

"We knew that, Tay. It was announced in the paper."

Murph says, "Taylor, make yourself useful and go find something next door to light on fire. Preferably the romance section."

Harper snaps, "Don't diss romance novels, Murph! They're the only thing that's gotten me through the last year!"

Taylor smirks. "Yeah, that and your battery-operated toy collection."

Harper props her hands on her hips and glares at her. Sabine laughs. Murph's face turns red. And I reach for the bottle again, because this is going to be a very long day.

It's just as I'm swallowing around the burn of the whiskey that I catch a glimpse of a man through the shop windows.

Partly hidden by the bobbing arch of balloons, he's standing still outside the entrance of ValUBooks. A head taller than everyone else, he ignores the crowd and the blaring band as he stares in the direction of my shop.

His arms are folded across his broad chest. Despite the July heat, he's dressed all in black, including a leather jacket and cowboy boots. His mirrored sunglasses reflect the morning light.

He's too far away for me to see his face clearly, but there's something familiar about him. His stance, maybe, or his height. I think I've seen him somewhere before but can't place where.

Narrowing my eyes, I look closer.

The man in black turns and vanishes into the crowd.

Two

Several weeks later, I'm sitting across a desk from a nice lady at the Small Business Administration office, listening to her list all the reasons why my business doesn't qualify for a loan.

I've already heard the same thing from my bank.

And my credit union.

And the only rich person I know, my childless, elderly neighbor Maude, who still lives like a pauper despite winning millions in the lottery a few years ago. I have no idea what she does with all the money, but, like everyone else, she's not interested in giving any of it to me.

I thank the SBA lady for her time and leave the office in a daze. Then I drive to the beach, park, and walk out to the sand, where I sit and stare blankly out at the shimmering blue Pacific, trying to figure out how the hell I'm going to save Lit Happens.

I've already looked all over the city for a new space to lease. I didn't find anything I could afford. Besides, I'd need first, last, and a security deposit to get into a new place, which might as well be a billion dollars for how out of reach that amount is.

Unless a ten-year-old VW Jetta counts, I have no assets I can sell to scrounge up some cash. I lease my apartment, which takes over half my salary because LA is an expensive place to live. Dad left me a little money when he died, but most of it went to funeral expenses and a rainy-day fund for the store.

Which has now been depleted.

A seagull lands near my feet. I say sadly to it, "I'm screwed, birdie."

It stares back at me with zero sympathy before waddling off in search of someone less depressed.

After another hour of racking my brain for possible solutions, I give up. Using the app on my cell phone, I check the business bank account.

There's enough in it to make payroll, plus about a thousand dollars left over.

I get up from the sand and walk back to my car. My head is spinning with thoughts, but one thing is clear: I need to tell my employees as soon as possible that Lit Happens is closing its doors.

Jameson's in Beverly Hills is the kind of swanky steakhouse where a six-ounce steak with no sides costs eighty bucks and every server looks like a cover model.

If I have to fire these people I love, at least I can give them a beautiful meal and surroundings while I'm doing it.

That grand left in my bank account should just about cover the cost.

Seated around the table are Harper, Vivienne, Taylor, Sabine, and Mr. Murphy.

Dressed in heels and a slinky red dress that had everyone's head swiveling when we walked in, Sabine is acting as if she can't see the group of middle-aged businessmen at the bar salivating in her direction.

Next to her, Taylor restlessly taps out a staccato beat on the tablecloth as she looks around.

Murph examines the leather-bound menu with his eyebrows raised.

Harper, meanwhile, is twirling a lock of hair and batting her lashes at the big blond stud seated at a nearby table.

And to my left sits Viv, who just rested her hand on my jittering knee and gave it a reassuring squeeze.

A handsome young waiter walks up to the table and beams me an insincere smile. "Can I get some cocktails started for everyone?"

"Murph, will you order a few bottles of wine for the table, please? Maybe a red and a white."

He glances up at me. "There's nothing on the list under three hundred dollars."

Taylor whistles. I try not to fall off my chair.

Seeing my stunned expression, Viv says brightly, "I'll just have a sparkling water."

"And I'll have a vodka martini," says Murph, snapping shut the menu and setting it aside.

"Make it two," says Harper.

"Three," chimes in Sabine.

"I might as well have one, too," says Taylor, leaning back in her chair. With her choppy black hair flopping over one eye and the silver rings in her left nostril and brow winking in the light, she glares at the waiter, daring him to ask for her ID.

Surely disappointing her, the waiter simply says, "Very good, miss. And for you?"

"The same. Thank you."

When he leaves, we all look at each other. The sound of other guests talking in the dining room and the elegant piano music piped in through the hidden speakers overhead seems very loud.

I take a deep breath, gather my courage, and begin.

"I'm sure you're all wondering what this dinner is about. As you know, Lit Happens has been struggling. ValUBooks has taken all the foot traffic we had. And they have the Starbucks. And the floral section. And the incredible breakfast café. And that amazing selection of books. Their inventory is just so huge..."

I glance down at my clammy hands, which I'm wringing together in my lap. Inside my chest, my heart is shriveling. I clear my throat and continue.

"When my dad started the company decades ago, it was a different time. There was no internet to buy books from. There were no giant retail chains. There weren't any tablets or cell phones to read on. And though I had faith that a small local store with real people who loved books more than anything would be something that customers would always want, it turns out I was wrong."

I glance up to find everyone staring at me silently. I see sadness and resignation in their faces. Except for Harper, who looks panicked.

They already know.

My throat closes. Water wells in my eyes. Of course they'd know, they're not stupid.

I'm the only stupid person here.

I'm such a failure.

"I've held it together as long as I can. I've tried everything I could think of to raise capital. I've tried every kind of advertising and looked for cheap space to rent...but the reality is, I can't keep it going any longer. I'd give anything to stop it. I'd literally cut off my own arm if it would help." My voice breaks. "But Lit Happens is closing its doors."

A tear escapes my eye and slips down my cheek. Embarrassed, I dash it away with my knuckle. "I'm sorry, guys. I know how much all of you count on your jobs. I'm so sorry I failed you."

"That's bullshit," says Taylor forcefully.

Startled, I glance up to find her scowling at me.

"This isn't your fault. It's the fault of that big asswipe, ValU-Books. Why the fuck would they move right next to another bookstore? It's like they *wanted* you to fail!"

I shake my head. "It wasn't personal. The location is great, and they've been expanding aggressively for a few years. To be honest, I'm surprised we didn't get one nearby sooner."

"But right next door?" she insists. "That's fucked up!"

In a small voice, Harper asks, "What about our health insurance?"

Sabine sends her a withering look. "There's continuation coverage we can buy until we find other jobs."

Harper gazes beseechingly around the table. "That's like double the cost, though, right?"

Murph says, "Will you be able to pay us our final checks?"

He's expressionless, but I know he's worried about his finances. His social security income isn't much, and he's on several medications, none of which are cheap.

"Yes, of course," I say, getting choked up. "And I'll give all of you glowing references, letters of recommendation, whatever you need. ValUBooks is probably still hiring..."

Viv squeezes my knee again and says gently, "None of us would ever go to work for them, Em."

The others agree, but I shake my head again. "You should. They'll probably be able to pay you more than I could. And you're all qualified. It's the obvious choice."

Rescuing me from having to continue, the waiter arrives with a tray of cocktails and a sparkling water for Viv.

He distributes the drinks with silent efficiency as I fight the urge to burst into tears. When everyone has a drink in hand and he's gone, I raise my glass for a toast.

"To the future. May it be as bright as you all deserve. From the bottom of my heart, thank you for being such wonderful friends. Actually, you're more than my friends. You're my family. I love you all."

When I lift the glass to my lips, my hand trembles.

Taylor says, "To the death of soulless corporations. May they all rot in hell." She takes a gulp of her martini, then swallows and makes a face. "Fuck, that tastes like ass. I should've ordered a beer."

Everyone else takes a sip of their drinks. Then Murph sets his glass on the table and looks at me. "What about you, Emery? What are you going to do?"

I draw a shaky breath. "Honestly, I don't know. I've been too focused on keeping the shop afloat to worry about what happens to me."

Like where I'm going to get money for my food, rent, gas, utilities, credit card bills, and all the rest. The thought of it is overwhelming.

"I'll figure it out," I say, trying to sound optimistic.

Mr. Murphy nods understandingly. "It won't be easy, but you'll find a way. You're a resourceful person."

I force a smile, grateful for his support and hating myself for putting everyone in this position.

The conversation moves on, but I can't stop the overwhelming feelings of guilt and shame. If only I'd been more aggressive with advertising or been more prepared for the unexpected, then maybe we wouldn't be in this situation.

I try to push those thoughts out of my mind and focus on the present, but I can't shake the weight of responsibility I feel. It's suffocating.

This is all my fault. If only there were *something* I could do...

But I already know there isn't.

This is the end.

The next morning, I'm alone in the back of the shop, slumped over my desk with my eyes closed and my cheek pressed against the overdue bills scattered all over the surface, when I hear someone come through the front door.

Disoriented, I sit up. An invoice stuck to my cheek falls off and flutters to the floor.

After a moment, a deep male voice calls out, "Hello? Is anyone here?"

I smooth my hands over my hair and stand. Due to the bottle of cheap wine I drank in the dark while crying myself to sleep on my sofa last night, I'm hungover and a little unsteady on my feet.

Trying to compose myself as I walk to the front of the shop, I take a deep breath and smile.

My smile falters when I see the man standing near the register.

He's tall and well-dressed, wearing a beautiful gray suit fitted snug across his broad shoulders. His white dress shirt is open at the collar, revealing a strong, tanned throat. His hair is dark and so are his eyes, and his square jaw is shadowed with scruff.

He's the sexiest man I've ever seen. The cloud of testosterone surrounding him is probably visible from space.

His dark gaze rakes over me, head to toe. I swear I think he can see my naked body right through my clothes. Or maybe that's just wishful thinking.

"Hi?" I say uncertainly.

"Good morning."

His voice is low and husky. He holds my gaze without blinking. He doesn't smile.

My vagina wakes up from her six-month nap and screams at me that though this man looks like the emotionally unavailable type with major control issues, she would very much like to be wrecked by him.

"Yes, it is a good morning. A very good morning. It certainly is." *Don't babble, idiot!* I clear my throat and smile wider to mask my self-consciousness. "How can I help you?"

He tilts his head to one side and considers me. It's like being hit with a spotlight. My entire body heats, scalp to toes. Then he looks around the shop, scanning it with interest.

"I was hoping we could help each other. I have a proposition for you."

He turns his attention back to me and pins me in a stare so intense, it rocks me back onto my heels. Because my mouth has gone dry, I can only whisper, "Proposition?"

Then I suffer a lethal brain aneurysm and drop dead on the spot.

I know I must because of the next words I hear the gorgeous stranger speak, which could only happen in another dimension where all my mental functions had permanently ceased.

Gazing deep into my eyes, he says, "I want you to marry me."

Three

For a few moments, my mind is blank.

If he asked me my name, I wouldn't be able to remember it. Sex hormones scream through my veins at lightning speed, vibrating all my sub-atomic particles at such high frequency, I'm probably glowing like a neon sign.

Then all the gears in my head start up again, and I laugh. "Very funny. Good joke. Who put you up to this? Sabine?"

He looks like her type. The beautiful people always stick together, those selfish bastards.

"It wasn't a joke."

He says it with irritation, as if I've insulted him. He gazes at me in tense silence, a muscle flexing in his jaw.

I cross my arms over my chest and say sarcastically, "Sure. And next you'll tell me you're a billionaire book lover who wants to help save my store."

"That's correct."

We stare at each other as I try to decide if I should play along with this ridiculous farce or tell him to get lost. But if he leaves, I won't be able to drink in all that overpowering sex appeal dressed up in an expensive suit.

Maybe I'll indulge him for a minute or two. If only for the sake of my poor, neglected vagina.

"I see. Well, if we're going to be married, I suppose I should know your name."

"So you're accepting my proposal."

His unblinking intensity is intimidating. I can't decide if this hot supermodel has a side gig as an assassin or if he just has no personality other than a good staring game.

"Just tell me your name, please."

"Callum McCord."

"Great to meet you, Cal. And should I call the police now to report a criminally bad comedian, or are you leaving?"

That muscle flexes in his jaw again. "It's Callum," he says in a low voice, holding me captive in that dark, powerful gaze. "And you're not going to call the police."

There's something unusual about the intensity of his stare. Something unsettling. The faintest stirring of fear tightens my stomach.

When I glance nervously at the front door, he says, "You're not in danger."

Unnerved that he can read me so easily, I look him in the eye and lift my chin. "I don't know what kind of game this is, but I don't want to play. Unless you're here to buy a book, I'd like you to leave now."

"I'm not here to buy a book. I'm here to offer you a deal. Marry me and I'll make sure your bookstore stays open, no matter what."

Stunned and trying to process what's happening, I take a step back. "What do you mean? Why would you want to marry me? And how could you possibly keep my store open?"

"I have the means to make it happen. As for why I want to marry you..." A wolflike hunger flickers in his gaze. "Let's just say I find you interesting."

If my vagina could detach from my body and fling itself right onto his face, it would.

Despite the absolute ludicrousness of the conversation and the distinct possibility that this guy is out of his mind, I feel like a lit stick of dynamite with a short fuse.

But I still have my dignity. I won't drop to my knees and latch on to his dick like a lamprey, no matter what my vagina has to say about it.

"Interesting? You don't know me. We've never met before."

"But I know your situation. And I know you'd do anything to solve it. I believe your exact words were 'I'd literally cut off my own arm if it would help.' Sound familiar?"

I gasp in horror and humiliation. This bastard eavesdropped on me at the restaurant yesterday! "That was a private conversation. You had no right to listen in on it."

"I was seated at the table behind you. I couldn't help but overhear. And you should seriously consider me as an alternative to amputation."

"This is crazy."

"No, this is a solution to a problem. For us both."

"Oh, really? What kinds of problems does a guy like you have?"

His gaze sharpens. "A guy like me? Meaning?"

I'm starting to get really annoyed now. I'm all for playful banter, but this is getting ridiculous.

"If you need an ego stroke, you came to the wrong place. But I'm sure ValUBooks has a large selection of novels on narcissism that might be helpful to you. Now, if you'll excuse me, I have to get back to work."

I turn away and start to walk back to my office, but then Callum calls out, "I'll give you ten million dollars," and I stop dead in my tracks.

My heart starts to pound. My hands start to shake.

This crazy son of a bitch actually sounds serious.

In a daze, I turn slowly and squint at him. "I'm sorry, did you just say...?"

"Yes. Ten million dollars."

"To...save my store."

"Yes."

"And...marry you."

"Yes."

A long, tense pause follows, during which I blink rapidly and he burns holes into my head with his eyes. Finally, I say, "Pardon my manners, but are you fucking nuts?"

He answers without hesitation. "Depends on your definition. But I am serious about my offer. Why don't I tell you more over lunch?"

He gestures toward the window.

Idling outside at the curb in front of the shop is a black luxury sedan, something sleek and futuristic-looking. Standing at attention beside the rear passenger door is a man in a black suit wearing dark sunglasses that hide his eyes.

"Is that your car?"

"It is."

"You have a driver?"

"I do."

I glance away from the window and focus on Callum. He stands motionless under my scrutiny, still and calm, but I get the strange sense that under his outward control, he's waging an internal war with himself.

If I'm being honest, it freaks me out. *He* freaks me out.

Who is this guy?

"I'm not getting into a car with a complete stranger."

"Afraid of being kidnapped?"

How irritating that he nailed it. It's like he's inside my head. I say, "Don't mock me."

He says mildly, "I wouldn't dare."

"Now I know you're mocking me."

His left brow drifts upward into a sardonic arch, as if he's thinking my sense of self-preservation is childish and overly dramatic, but when he speaks, his voice is still mild.

"Why don't you take a picture of the license plate and send it to a friend? That way if your dismembered body is discovered in a dumpster tomorrow morning, the police will know where to start looking for your murderer."

"You could change the plates after you dump my body."

"Hmm. Good point."

"FYI, that was pretty much exactly the wrong thing to say. I'm not getting in the car."

When he doesn't respond and only stands there looking at me with an inscrutable expression, I grow self-conscious. "What?"

"It's just that people don't often say no to me."

"Meaning never."

"Exactly."

I say flippantly, "If I'm going to be your wife, you'd better get used to it."

His dark eyes burn. He says softly, "Is that a yes?"

I throw my hands in the air. "Of course not! I met you ten seconds ago!"

"Just let me take you to lunch. Let me explain everything. Then, if you're still not interested, I'll return you here and you've lost nothing but an hour of time." His gaze grows even more penetrating. "Or did you have something more important on your schedule?"

Yes, the man is all sorts of hot, but I can already tell he'll be getting on my last nerve regularly.

Not that I'll be seeing him regularly. Because his proposal is crazy, and so, most likely, is he.

But lunch can't hurt. And I am hungry. And broke. And I don't have anything more important to do...

Decision made, I say, "Bring me the registration from the car. I'll need your driver's license, too, so I can text pictures of both to my girlfriend. And grab that glass of water on the counter. Make sure to get your fingerprints all over it."

When he lifts both brows, I smile. "If my body shows up in a dumpster somewhere, Mr. McCord, you'll spend the rest of your life in prison."

~

The drive to the restaurant is spent in awkward silence. I stare straight ahead while Callum stares at my profile. At every stoplight, I consider jumping out of the car and running away screaming. It's only my overpowering curiosity that keeps me in my seat.

"I want you to marry me."

He actually *said* that.

I can't wait to tell my best friend, Dani. She'll die.

"You're tense."

Startled, I jump and turn to look at Callum. He sits beside me in the back of the sedan with his long legs spread open and a predatory expression on his face, as if he's about to lunge at me.

My eyes widen. My pulse flutters. A flash of heat burns between my thighs.

Dammit, pull yourself together!

I clear my throat, then say tartly, "If the large and intimidating stranger who walked into your bookstore and proposed marriage were looking at you as if you were his next meal, you might be tense too."

A note of darkness creeps into his voice. "If I were looking at you like you were my next meal, you'd already be eaten."

Wow. This guy is something else. Vagina, settle down and stop moaning.

"Is that supposed to make me feel better?"

Instead of answering my question, he asks his own. "Intimidating?"

I give him a sour look. "There you go fishing for an ego stroke again. I already told you, Cal, you came to the wrong place for that."

His gaze drops to my mouth. That muscle in his jaw flexes again. "And I already told you, it's Callum. Don't call me anything else."

I know it's only my imagination that adds an unspoken threat that if I do, I'll be punished.

Or it could be that look in his eyes, the shiver-inducing dark disapproval.

Fighting to maintain my composure, I gaze at him coolly. "I realize you don't often hear the word no, but I don't take orders. If you want me to do something, you'll have to say please."

He gazes at me in weighted silence for a moment. Then in a low, stroking voice, he murmurs, "Please."

My panties erupt into flames. My nipples harden, and my lungs stop working. I gape at him, helpless to respond coherently.

How am I'm going to get through an entire lunch with this man without having a spontaneous orgasm?

It's impossible. I might have multiple orgasms just sitting next to him. His sexual magnetism is astonishing.

Holding my gaze, he says, "Why are you looking at me like that?"

I'd rather die than admit my panties are on fire, so I deflect. "It's just that you have something between your front teeth. It's green. Could be spinach."

"You're funny. How unexpected."

"No, I'm serious. It's a big clump of green stuff. You should find a toothpick before we get to the restaurant and everyone starts laughing at you."

"And you should find a cold compress. Your face is bright red."

I lift a hand to my cheek. Sure enough, it's burning. Embarrassed, I blurt, "I'm still trying to get over that plague I caught last month."

His expression remains the same, but his eyes sparkle with amusement. "Plague? Sounds serious."

"It was. It is, I mean. I'm highly infectious. You could break out in boils any minute."

I have no idea what the hell I'm saying, but one thing is clear: my brain has melted under Callum's scorching-hot proximity. If I don't get away from him soon, my entire body will liquefy into a pile of goo and ruin the upholstery.

The car slows to a stop at the curb. A valet in a red vest opens the door for me. Breathless and disoriented, I climb out of the car. In a moment, Callum comes to stand beside me.

Taking me by the elbow, he gazes down into my eyes.

He says, "It's only lunch. There's nothing to be afraid of."

It's chilling how strongly I suspect both those statements will turn out to be lies.

Four

It's a good thing this gorgeous stranger and I aren't married, because the way the pretty hostess swoons when he approaches her and asks for a table is exasperating.

I mean, it would be. As it is, I'm simply considering this an interesting education in the power of a charming smile.

"R-right this way, Mr. McCord," she stammers, reddening.

When she turns and starts to walk away, I say drily, "Come here often?"

"Something like that."

He steers me through the restaurant by my elbow, nodding at people here and there as we pass by. He's obviously well known around the place, which makes me relax a little.

If he were a murderer, he probably wouldn't be so popular.

The hostess leads us to a table in the back of the restaurant, next to a window overlooking a tree-lined courtyard with a fountain in the middle. Callum pulls out my chair, makes sure I'm comfortably seated, then takes the chair across from me. He snaps open a white linen napkin and elegantly settles it over his lap.

Without looking at the hostess, he says, "I'll start with the usual, Sophie. And the lady will have a vodka martini."

"Yes, sir." Gaze downcast, Sophie turns to leave, but I stop her.

"Actually, I'd like an iced tea, please."

Startled, she looks at me with wide eyes. Then she glances at Callum, wanting permission to change my order.

When he inclines his head, I laugh in disbelief.

Sophie scurries away before I can ask her if she's ever heard of the feminist movement.

I catch Callum looking at me and say, "Don't mind me. It's just that I've grown so accustomed to making my own decisions that it's a huge relief to discover I no longer have to."

He leans back in his chair, rests one hand on the edge of the table, and considers me thoughtfully for a moment.

"You're being sarcastic."

I have to resist the urge to roll my eyes. "How gratifying to know that your brains equal your—"

I bite my tongue. Heat rises in my cheeks. Mentally hitting myself over the head with my chair, I remain silent.

Leaning in and clasping his hands together, Callum stares intently at me.

"My what?"

I cast around for something that will sound reasonable. "Your...um...I forgot."

Congratulations, Em. Your brain has left the building.

"You forgot?"

There's a trace of humor in his voice, but his expression is serious. The tips of my ears begin to burn.

"Let's talk about something else."

"Tell me what you were going to say first."

"No."

His stare is unwavering. The heat in my cheeks burns hotter.

"I mean, no, thank you."

I want to cover my face with my napkin, slide under the table, and hide, but won't give him the satisfaction. I remain stiff and embarrassed in my chair, staring back at him with what I hope is convincing confidence.

Holding my gaze, he commands softly, "Tell me what you were going to say, Emery."

Whew. If I'm going to have to beat my vagina into submission every time this man says something sexy and commanding, my arms will fall off.

I blow out a hard breath and decide to go with the truth. What the hell, this whole thing couldn't get any weirder.

"Beauty. There you have it. I was going to say that your brains equal your beauty. Now let's talk about how you know my name."

"I overheard your employees say it at the restaurant. Then I researched your business. Don't change the subject."

"You researched my business?" I repeat, surprised.

"I had to find out where it was located so I could come and make my proposition to you. Don't change the subject."

His intensity is alarming. It's also arousing. I don't believe I've ever been looked at with such perfect focus in my life.

My voice faint, I say, "What was the subject again?"

"You said my brains equal my beauty."

Honestly, at this point he could tell me I said I'd like to throw a saddle on him and go for a ride, and I'd believe it.

"Yes. I suppose I did."

"So you think I'm beautiful."

Put off that he's hunting for more compliments, I scrunch up my nose. "I take it back. Narcissism is never pretty."

If that insulted him, he doesn't show it. He simply says, "I'm many things, but a narcissist isn't one of them."

"Which is exactly what a narcissist would say."

That earns me a smile, his first of the day. To say it's gorgeous would be a massive understatement. It is, in fact, dazzling.

My palms start to sweat.

Sophie returns with our drinks. As soon as she sets the glass of iced tea in front of me, I turn to her and say, "You know, I think I will have that martini after all."

When she looks at Callum for approval, I sigh in disappointment.

"Give Miss Eastwood whatever she wants, Sophie," murmurs Callum, dark eyes burning as they consider me.

"Yes, sir," she whispers before walking away.

Seriously, what is it with that girl? She's as meek as a mouse!

"You don't approve."

Pulled from my thoughts, I glance at Callum. He's looking at me with an indecipherable expression, his smile gone.

"Of what?"

"Of Sophie."

"What do you mean?"

"Exactly what I said. You don't approve of her."

I think for a moment, not understanding where he's going with this but wanting to be truthful nonetheless. "I suppose it's just uncomfortable for me to see a woman be so..."

"Submissive?"

That wolflike glimmer has resurfaced in his eyes. Is he laughing at me?

Equal parts annoyed and unsettled, I say, "Yeah. Exactly. It's like she's afraid of you."

"But you're not."

I lift my brows and stare at him straight on. "I never said that."

"You're not. If you were, you never would have gotten into the car with me."

"Maybe I'm mentally incompetent."

Honestly, it would explain a lot.

But he doesn't think so because he shakes his head. "You sent pictures of my driver's license, registration, and license plate to your friend. And you made me leave my fingerprints on the water glass."

"Maybe I'm *carefully* mentally incompetent."

"Or maybe you're intrigued by my offer." He pauses. "Or by me."

When I don't answer, he gifts me with a small, mysterious smile.

It irritates the hell out of me. Smugness is one of my least favorite personality traits in people.

I take a long drink of my martini, set it back onto the table, and gaze into Callum's gorgeous dark eyes.

"Look. I'm in the middle of one of the worst times of my life. I'm losing my business. I'm disappointing my friends. I'm failing my father's memory and betraying the legacy he worked his entire life to build. By this time next month, I'll be crashing on my girlfriend's sofa because I'll no longer be able to afford my apartment. I don't have any interest in indulging some rich stranger's ego on top of all that. So let's get to the part where you tell me about this ridiculous offer of yours or reveal the whole thing is being filmed for a reality show, because otherwise, I'm gonna get drunk on your dime, then call myself a cab and go home."

He stares at me.

I stare back.

It goes on and on until my ears are scalding, and I'm forcing myself to sit still in my seat and not squirm.

But I'll be damned if I'll look away first or cower like Sophie, so I maintain eye contact and suffer through it, even though it's excruciating.

Gradually, a strange expression settles over Callum's features.

If I didn't know better, I'd swear it was pride.

He begins without preamble, his voice stroking soft and his dark eyes impossibly bright.

"My family owns McCord Media, the largest private corporation in the world. Our revenue was three hundred billion dollars last year alone. My father built it from the ground up when he took over a small newspaper in New York in the seventies. Then he bought more papers, both domestic and international, then a television station, then a cable network, then a film studio. It grew from there. We're now considered one of the most successful and influential businesses on the planet. In addition to operating the media empire, we're heavily invested in real estate. We own this building, in fact. Along with most of Beverly Hills. And Manhattan. Hong Kong is a big part of the portfolio too."

He pauses to take a drink of whiskey. At least I think it's whiskey, I have no godly fucking clue because I'm too busy being stunned.

No wonder poor Sophie is so scared of him.

"My father is extremely old-fashioned. He's been married to my mother for more than forty years, and he believes marriage is the foundation of civilization. Literally. He thinks men would still be hunting with spears in the jungle if it wasn't for women domesticating us."

Here he pauses again to look me deeply in the eyes.

"Women are lion tamers, he says. Can you believe that?"

What I can believe is that my underwear is no match for the throaty tone of his voice. What remained from before that didn't already burn up dissolves in a puff of smoke, leaving me bare and throbbing, clenching my thighs together so I don't drench the seat of my chair.

I manage to say, "He sounds like quite the character."

"He is. He's also stubborn. Once his mind is made up, there's no changing it. Which is where my proposition to you comes in."

I almost spit out the sip of martini I just took. "Your father told you to propose to me?"

"No. He told me that he put a condition in his will that if I didn't marry by December of this year, I'd be disinherited, fired from the company, cut off from all contact with the family, and discredited so badly in the international business community that I'd find it impossible to work again."

Callum's smile is grim. "In other words, he'd make it his mission to ruin my life. Which he can do quite easily. One of his rivals in business who crossed him is currently living in a tent on Skid Row."

Shocked, I gape at him. "Really?"

"Really."

"Wow. So on top of being a super successful family man, he's also super vindictive."

"Yes. When he dies, we'll need an entire cemetery to bury him along with all his grudges. Which brings us back to you."

I don't like being mentioned in the same sentence with his mean, grudge-holding Dad, so I sit back in my chair and drink more of my martini.

Maybe it will kill the rest of my remaining brain cells. They haven't done much for me lately anyway.

Callum leans over the table and rests his forearms on the edge. His tone grows urgent.

"I need a wife. Not want but need. I'm willing to pay a considerable sum to make that happen, because if I don't marry, I lose everything. Income, lifestyle, family, property, investments, opportunity...it all vanishes. For good. I'd be left with only the clothes in my closet and what I've saved in cash, which isn't enough to fund a single one of the many vacations I take a year."

I swallow a sarcastic *boo-hoo* and simply look at him. And think.

Sophie returns to ask if we'd like to place an order for food. Callum dismisses her with a royal flick of his wrist.

When she's gone and I've collected my thoughts, I say, "Okay. I have some observations to share. Don't interrupt, please. I have the attention span of a puppy, and I'll forget what I was saying."

I wait for a sign from him that he's agreeing, which arrives in the form of a curt nod. Then I say, "Assuming this information about your family's business is true—"

"It's true," he says forcefully. "Look it up right now on your phone."

When I stare at him in disapproval, he settles back into his chair, crosses one leg over the other, and folds his hands in his lap. "My apologies," he says, his expression impassive. "Please proceed."

"Thank you. As I was saying, a few observations. Here's the first: it's odd that you would ask a complete stranger to help you out with this problem of yours. If I were in your shoes, I'd ask a friend. Some other rich person in your social circle. Not some random girl you eavesdropped on at a restaurant. For all you know, I could be a serial killer."

After a moment of silence, he says, "Is that pause an invitation for me to speak, or should I wait until the end of these interesting little observations of yours?"

"You should wait till the end. And don't be sarcastic. There's only room for one smartass at this table, and it's me."

This time, his smile is amused. He inclines his head in that kingly way of his, granting me permission to continue.

It's amazing how someone I find so attractive can also make me want to bash him over the head with my shoe.

"Observation number two: you're not good with money."

His brows shoot up.

I've insulted him. Good. He could use getting taken down a notch or two. But I give him a smile to take some of the sting out of my words.

"If your father can literally boot you out onto the street and leave you with nothing, you've done a terrible job adulting. If I were a rich playboy with access to billions and such a shaky grip on my own fate, you can bet I'd have plans A through Z set up in case I needed a parachute. But you've been riding Daddy's coat-tails instead. Shame on you."

Callum lowers his brows and proceeds to glower at me.

"I won't let that face derail me, but nice try. Observation three: December is only a few months away. Assuming you've known about this plan of your father's to cut you off if you don't marry, you've procrastinated an awful lot for a guy with every-thing to lose. Which suggests that in addition to being bad with money, your self-motivational skills leave a lot to be desired. Observation four: maybe that's because being stinking rich isn't good for building character."

I can tell he wants to say something, but he keeps his jaw clamped shut and merely gazes at me in silence. Blistering hot, unblinking silence.

I think I might be starting to have fun.

After another sip of my martini, I continue. "You admitted you don't want to get married, which means that you'd probably make a terrible husband."

He folds his arms over his chest and exhales a hard, aggravated breath.

"Sigh all you want, it's true. Which brings us to observation number..." Thinking, I wrinkle my forehead. "What number was I on?"

"It feels like a thousand."

Ignoring his deadly tone, I say, "Five, I think. Or six. Whatever, it doesn't matter. But you mentioned the amount of ten million dollars back at the shop. If you have that much cash to throw at a total stranger, you don't have to listen to your father. You could live comfortably the rest of your life on that."

He slow blinks, as if incredulous. I understand that he thinks I've said something stupid.

"You're telling me you *couldn't* live comfortably on ten million dollars?"

"Of course I could. For a month."

I mutter, "I knew you were bad with money."

"For the record, I'm an excellent money manager."

"Sure. You just don't have any of your own. And I didn't tell you it was time for you to talk yet."

Staring at me, he moistens his lips.

That simple gesture is so sexy, I lose the rest of what little composure I had to begin with and blurt, "The final observation is that this is all too convenient."

"What is?"

"This. You. Your ridiculous offer of marriage and a pile of money to save me right when I need it most."

He shrugs, the picture of nonchalance. "Maybe you're lucky."

"Ha! No, I'm not, I promise you. There has to be something else going on here." I look suspiciously around the restaurant, trying to spot the hidden cameras.

"All right, Emery. You caught me. I'll tell you the truth."

I glance back at Callum to find him gazing at me with that same cool nonchalance, a small, mysterious smile playing around his sculpted lips.

His tone gently mocking, he says, "I've been obsessed with you for years. I've watched you from afar, planning, scheming, waiting for exactly the right moment to make you mine. Now all my planning has paid off, and the moment is here."

His mysterious smile grows wider. "Hello, little lamb. Welcome to the lion's den."

I roll my eyes. "Your sense of humor is as bad as your money management skills."

I spot Sophie staring at us from the hostess stand across the restaurant. She's wringing her hands, looking on the verge of a panic attack. I gesture for her to come over, because I need another drink.

When I look back at Callum, he's holding his whiskey, swirling it slowly around in the glass as he gazes at me with half-lidded eyes.

He's still smiling.

Five

When Sophie arrives, I order another martini and a chicken salad. Callum orders a dozen raw oysters, a terrine of foie gras, a ten-ounce wagyu steak with black truffle sauce, lobster mashed potatoes, and a side of steamed asparagus wrapped in bacon.

Without batting an eyelash at the size of his order, Sophie says, "Should I bring a bottle of Peter Michael as well, sir?"

"Yes. The 2012. Along with a glass of Sancerre with the oysters and Sauterne with the foie gras. And a large Pellegrino."

"Very good, sir. Thank you."

Perplexed, I watch her leave, wondering how many other people will be joining us for lunch. From the sound of it, a crew of construction workers will arrive any minute.

"Do you always eat like it's your last meal?"

He replies in a husky voice, "I have a big appetite," then takes a swig of his whiskey. His burning dark eyes meet mine over the crystal rim of the glass.

My smile is small and nervous. I'd better get him talking about something else other than his appetite or my vagina will seize control of the rest of my body and stage a coup. I'm liable to jump onto the table, grab his head, and grind my crotch into the poor man's face.

"You look flustered," he observes, eyeing me. "Everything all right?"

"Absolutely!" I thunder. Then I cough in embarrassment and lower my volume. "It's just not every day that a billionaire with an eating disorder proposes marriage to me. I mean, it's happened before, *obviously*"—my laugh sounds crazed, like someone's holding a gun to my head—"just not this week. Oh, that reminds me."

"Of?"

"You don't know if I'm already married or in a relationship."

"Don't I?" He chuckles and takes another sip of whiskey.

"Blech. There you go being smug again. How annoying."

When he raises his brows and stares at me, I blush. "I have a tendency to say inside thoughts out loud. Sorry."

"Don't be. It's refreshing."

I examine his expression for a moment. "Having people kiss your bossy billionaire ass all the livelong day gets boring, hmm?"

He laughs.

It seems to surprise him in an unpleasant way, because he stops abruptly and sets his whiskey on the table with a jarring thud, then looks around, as if to make sure nobody heard him.

His reaction makes me smile. At least I'm not the only uncomfortable one.

"Don't worry. I won't tell anyone you let that slip. It'll be our little secret."

He meets my eyes again. His gaze grows assessing. "Are you good at keeping secrets?"

"No. That was just a figure of speech. All my friends know not to tell me anything they don't want repeated because everyone else I know will hear about it within twenty-four hours. Are you?"

"Yes. Very."

When I stare at him in silence with my lips pursed, he says, "Don't overthink it."

"Telling a woman not to overthink something is as dangerous as telling her to calm down when she's angry."

A faint smile lifts the corners of his lips. "I only meant that I have to be good at keeping secrets because of business. I was raised to hold my cards close to the chest. With the position my family is in, we never know who we can trust. So we don't trust anyone."

"What, like, nobody?"

"No one outside the family, no."

I think about that for a moment. "Sounds like a miserable existence."

"It's not."

"I'll have to take your word for it. So I guess this means I'll have to learn to keep secrets. I mean, since I'm going to be family and everything." I laugh and swallow the last sip of my martini.

"You still don't think I'm serious. I assure you, I am."

I want to roll my eyes again, but he looks so intense, I don't chance it. I've decided he isn't a murderer, but there's a ton of gray area between killer and good guy. Besides, anyone who'd ask a stranger to marry him is at least a teensy bit off in the head.

Inside my purse, my cell starts to ring. When I ignore it, Callum says, "I don't mind if you need to take that."

"I can talk to her later."

He looks intrigued. "How do you know who it is?"

"We have a psychic connection."

He stares at me, narrowing his eyes.

"Just kidding." I'm not, but I don't want to sound insane. There's enough of that going around already. "It's my girlfriend Daniela. When I sent her the pics of your driver's license and other stuff, I also told her to call me in exactly thirty minutes to make sure I wasn't dead."

"You have an overactive imagination."

That makes me smile. "Guilty. Comes from reading too many books."

He chuckles. "So if you don't pick up the call, she'll think I've done something awful to you and call 9-1-1?"

"You don't seem terribly worried about the idea."

He casually lifts a shoulder. "I know the chief of police."

"You're saying he wouldn't care if you murdered me? That's a little insulting."

"I'm saying he knows I wouldn't murder anyone. He'd assume it was a prank."

"Wait, this is confusing. Just because you're rich doesn't mean you wouldn't murder anyone."

"It means I wouldn't have to do it myself."

I can't tell if that was a joke or not, but I'll think about it later. "What if you snapped?"

His gaze steady, he says, "I'm not the snapping type."

I knew it. He's totally a control freak.

Just to prove it, he says, "Go ahead. Answer the call. You have my permission."

"Your *permission*," I repeat, my tone dry. "What a relief."

Without breaking eye contact, he reaches out and touches the fork next to his plate. He strokes the tip of his finger slowly down the handle. Then, because he clearly wants me to faint, he moistens his lips again.

The phone stops ringing. Callum and I stare at each other. The phone starts to ring again.

"Answer it," he commands softly. He strokes his finger back up the handle of the fork, caressing it like a lover's skin.

Never before in all my life have I been jealous of a piece of silverware. What the hell is he doing to me?

I fumble for my handbag hanging off the back of my chair. Then I fumble around inside it, looking anywhere but at the burning-hot hunk of machismo sitting across from me.

Phone in hand, I start to rise, murmuring, "I'll just take this outside."

"Sit," he orders, his voice low and dark.

I plop back down into my chair so fast, my head spins. Then I sit there, stunned, as Callum's small smile grows wider.

It must be the martini. It's gone to my head. There's no other reasonable explanation as to why I'd obey him so unthinkingly.

I raise the phone to my ear and say something. Pretty sure it's a hello, but I wouldn't swear on it.

"Callum McCord?" hollers Dani over the line. "*Callum fucking McCord?* Are you kidding me?"

"Yes, I'm still alive, thank you very much for asking."

Blasting right past that, she launches into a series of rapid-fire questions.

"How did you meet him? Is he as hot in person as he is in photos? Does he smell as good as he looks? I bet he smells like a fucking candy store. Where are you right now? What exactly are you doing? And what about the BDE? I bet he's got major big dick energy, am I right? Jesus Christ, Emery, why aren't you saying anything?"

She's shouting so loudly, I'm sure half the restaurant can hear. Callum definitely can, because from the corner of my eye, I see him smirking.

"Good to know you're so concerned for my well-being, Dani. Remind me to text someone who cares next time I think I'm about to be kidnapped."

She scoffs. "Oh, please. No kidnappers would ever be able to withstand hearing you go on and on about Jamie Fraser from *Outlander*. They'd return you in five minutes."

I say sourly, "You're too kind. I'll call you later."

"Okay, but do you even know who Callum McCord *is*? He's a huge deal, Em. Like, a *really* huge deal. He's pretty much the most eligible bachelor in the world right now!"

I glance at Callum. He winks.

"Gotta go. Thanks for checking to make sure I wasn't murdered."

Snickering, she says, "Not yet, anyway. If you're lucky, that stud will murder you with his giant, throbbing—"

I hang up before she can finish and shove the cell back into my purse.

"What an interesting friend you have," says Callum, his mild tone underscored with amusement.

"Yeah, she's a keeper. I wonder if your police chief buddy can get me off on felony charges?"

"Why's that?"

"Because I'm going to kill her later."

A waiter arrives, bearing a tray of food. Behind him follows Sophie holding two wineglasses filled with golden liquid.

"Good afternoon, sir," says the waiter to Callum, setting a platter in the middle of the table. "Kumamoto oysters on ice and Hudson Valley foie gras with fig compote."

He doesn't glance in my direction or acknowledge me in any way. It feels purposeful, but is probably only my imagination. Then he gives Callum a slight bow and retreats without another word.

Sophie sets both wineglasses on the table to Callum's right. He hands her his whiskey glass and says, "The Pellegrino?"

She looks stricken. "Oh, my goodness. I'm so sorry, sir! I'll be right back."

Bemused, I watch her run away as if being chased by wolves. "Why is that poor girl so terrified of you? Does she think you'll beat her if she screws up your order?"

I can tell he finds something about that question extremely funny, but doesn't allow himself to show it with anything more than a faint smile.

"Oh, no," I say, furrowing my brow. "Don't tell me you're one of those guys."

"Which guys?"

"One of those rich assholes who likes to shout at people because it makes him feel important."

He reaches for one of the wineglasses, takes a sip, then looks at me in silent contemplation.

"Why aren't you saying anything?"

"I'm trying to remember the last time someone called me an asshole to my face."

"And?"

"It's never happened."

"Probably because everyone's scared of you...because you're an asshole."

When he only studies me without comment, I send him a winning smile.

"Regretting asking me to marry you already, aren't you? I could've told you I was a pain in the butt back at the shop, but watching you figure it out for yourself has been so much more fun. Would you mind if I tried a sip of that? Sophie forgot my martini, and as she's probably sobbing into your mashed potatoes at the moment, I doubt I'll see it any time soon."

Without waiting for his answer, I grab the other wineglass from the table and lift it to my lips. Then I swallow a mouthful of something so rich, delicious, and decadent, my eyes widen.

"Holy shit," I breathe, astonished. "What is this?"

"Chateau d'Yquem," comes the amused reply. "It's a French white. Do you like it?"

I laugh. "*Like* it? I want to have its babies! This stuff is incredible!" Just to make sure, I drink more, then nod. "Yep, it's the best thing I've ever put into my mouth."

When I realize how that sounded, heat rises in my cheeks.

The heat grows hotter when Callum murmurs, "I'm sure we can find something better for you to put in your mouth, Emery."

I have to brace both feet flat against the floor so I remain upright in my chair. "Okay, you're gonna have to turn it down, Mr. McCord, because I'm not emotionally equipped to deal with all of this before I've even had my chicken salad."

Lifting his brows, he says innocently, "All of this?"

I sigh. "There you go again, hunting for praise. You know exactly what I'm talking about. All of *that*." I wave a hand in his direction, indicating his face, body, and general hotness overload.

"Are you trying to pay me a compliment? Because if so, you're failing miserably."

"Grin at me like that again, and I'll kick you in the shin."

Laughing softly, he tilts his head back and drinks from his wineglass. I watch in helpless fascination as his Adam's apple bobs as he swallows.

How is such a simple thing so devastating? If I had even a smidgen of this man's looks, I'd never step away from a mirror.

I finish the rest of the delectable wine in a few big gulps, then set the glass back onto the table with a flourish. A nice buzz is setting in, which should help me navigate the rest of this conversation.

Considering my brain checked out a while back, I've got to rely on something.

Sophie arrives with a large glass bottle of overpriced water. She twists off the cap with shaking hands. She pours for Callum first, then me, her gaze lowered and her face red.

I say gently, "Thank you, Sophie."

She jerks, looks at me with wide eyes, then swallows. "Oh. Um. You're welcome." She turns to Callum. "I-is there anything else I can get for you, sir?"

"Just the wine with the main course."

"Yes. Of course. I won't forget."

She turns to go but turns back when I say her name.

"Yes?"

My smile is genuine. "I just wanted to tell you that you're doing a great job."

She couldn't look more shocked if I smacked her right across the face.

She says tentatively, "Really?"

"Yes. I know the restaurant business is tough, what with having to deal with so many assholes." I feel Callum's glower without looking at him but ignore it. "I have to deal with the public in my job, too, so I get it. But just remember that you're the one in charge, not them."

She glances at Callum, pales when she sees his expression, then looks back at me. It appears to take all her courage to ask, "How am I in charge, exactly?"

"Because all these rich people would starve to death if they didn't have people like you bringing them food." I gesture to Callum. "You think this guy knows how to boil an egg? No. He doesn't even drive his own car. So don't underestimate your value. And don't let anybody push you around. In this economy, you could get a job anywhere. Every business owner I know is hurting for good employees. In fact, you should ask for a raise. You deserve it."

She stares at me with her lips parted, blinking as if in a dream. Then she murmurs, "Thank you," and drifts away from the table.

I beam at her retreating figure, satisfied that I did my good deed for the day.

"Bravo. What an inspiring speech."

Callum's approving words are the opposite of his tone, which is bone dry.

"It really was, wasn't it?" I enjoy his disapproval. I don't know why, but it gives me a charge to think I might be the only person in his universe who'd dare to do something so revolutionary as irritate him.

"Maybe next you should march into the kitchen and spearhead an effort to unionize."

"I would, but my blood sugar is low. Where *is* that salad?"

"You seem more excited about your salad than my offer."

"I am. In fact, that reminds me of something you should be aware of if I'm going to be your wife. Sitting down for a proper supper every night is nonnegotiable. In formal wear, preferably. I'm sure you have a tux, right? I'll wear all my diamonds."

His steady gaze turns smoldering. "Still don't take me seriously, I see."

My confidence bolstered by the liquor, I laugh at him. "Oh, come on! This whole thing is so ridiculous, you can't expect me to take you seriously. If you really needed a wife, I'm sure there are a million girls in the world more suitable than me."

Callum's heated stare burns darker and hotter. He reaches into his jacket. From an inside pocket, he pulls out a small black velvet box. He places it on the table, pushes it across the white linen cloth toward me, then sits back in his chair without a word.

My heart thudding, I stare at the box. "Please tell me that's not what I think it is."

"Open it and find out."

I hear the smirk in his tone, but can't rip my gaze from the little black box. It might as well be a bomb for how dangerous it seems.

Callum commands softly, "*Open it.*"

My hand obeys him before I can decide not to. I pick up the box, flip open the lid, and gasp.

Nestled inside is an enormous diamond engagement ring, sparkling with cold fire.

Six

"It's eight carats, in case you're wondering." says Callum, reaching for an oyster.

I look up in time to watch him lift the shell to his mouth, suck the oyster out, and swallow. He licks his lips and makes a small sound of pleasure low in his throat, then sets the empty shell back onto the platter. He picks up another one and holds it aloft.

"Oyster?"

"Hang on a sec. I'm trying to locate my brain."

He repeats the ritual with the second oyster, then says, "Kumamoto is an excellent variety. Quite sweet. They're flown in fresh from British Columbia every morning."

The little black box in my hand weighs ten thousand pounds. The light all around us is searingly bright. My heart throbs, my stomach churns, and all the tiny hairs on the back of my neck stand on end.

Meanwhile, Callum makes casual conversation about seafood.

"The lobster here is incredible too. Do you like lobster? I love it, myself. There's an island named Anegada in the Caribbean that has an unusual type. Very briny and delicious. The locals barbecue it on top of cut-open oil drums. I visit the

British Virgin Islands every May. It's one of my favorite places to sail."

"Sounds fab."

"It is."

Exasperated with his composure, I say, "Can we please return from vacation to talk about this rock I'm holding?"

"That rock is your engagement ring, darling. Care for a bite of foie gras?"

I blink for a few moments, trying to reconcile the absurdity of the situation with Callum's offhand use of "darling," as if he's been saying it to me over lunch every day for years.

Then my temper kicks in.

I snap shut the box and place it atop an empty oyster shell. Looking him dead in the eye, I say, "Okay. This is where I get off the crazy train. Great to meet you. Have a nice life."

I stand, grab my purse, and stalk off toward the entrance of the restaurant, passing by Sophie on the way.

"Remember what I said about that raise, girlfriend," I say as I stride by.

Out at the valet stand, I stop to order an Uber. The app says the driver is two minutes away. I pace until the car arrives, then jump into the back, half expecting a big beautiful madman in a gray suit to jump in behind me.

But the car pulls away from the curb with me as its only passenger.

I call Dani first thing. She answers, demanding, "Seriously, what the fuck?"

"Ha! You're asking me? I have no idea what just happened."

"Start with how you met Callum McCord, you lucky bitch!"

"He came into the shop."

"*Your* shop? The little bohemian bookstore with all the stray cats and shabby furniture? Why the hell would a billionaire go in there?"

"Oh my God. Thanks for the support. Why are we even friends?"

"Listen, just tell me the damn story, starting from the beginning and ending at the part where you're on your knees somewhere with his big billionaire dick down your throat."

The driver's gaze meets mine in the rearview mirror. He looks eager for a juicy story.

I say to both of them, "That didn't happen."

Looking disappointed, the driver glances away.

Dani demands, "So what *did* happen? Tell me everything!"

I heave out a heavy breath, then start from the beginning. When I'm finished, there's silence on the other end of the line.

"Are you still there?"

"Still here. Except I think my brain is broken."

"Yeah, join the club."

After another moment, she says, "So we've got a few possibilities. The first is that you were being filmed for a reality show."

"That's what I thought!"

"Except the producers would've given you a release to sign. I don't think you can be on TV without your consent."

I ponder it. "Maybe they were going to approach me with the release afterwards. To make my reactions more realistic in the moment."

"I mean, I guess? But what's the show about?"

"Maybe like *The Bachelor* meets *Married at First Sight*?"

"Hmm. Maybe. But with a total opposites-attract trope. Billionaire and the beast."

I'd be insulted that she's saying I'm the beast in this scenario, but unfortunately, I agree with her. I'm hardly Frankenstein's monster, but compared to Callum, I might as well be.

"Did you see any cameras?"

"No."

"Okay, so maybe it's something else."

"For instance?"

"Well, if he already had an engagement ring ready to go and it wasn't for television, he must've had a fiancée at some point, right?"

"Makes sense."

"So maybe they split up. Maybe it was a bad breakup. Maybe she broke his heart." I can tell by her excited tone that she's warming up to the idea. "So now he wants to get back at her and make her jealous by getting engaged to *you*!"

"If he was engaged to anyone, she'd be a supermodel. How the hell would I make a supermodel jealous?"

She pauses, then says, "Don't take this the wrong way, but if you're Gisele Bündchen and Tom Brady left you for, say, Hermione Granger, wouldn't that drive you absolutely batty?"

She has a point, the witch.

"Your logic is flawed, Einstein, because he didn't leave anyone for me. I never laid eyes on the man before this morning."

"You know what I mean. He's trying to drive her nuts figuring out what you have that she doesn't."

I laugh at that. "Gisele wouldn't lose a wink of sleep over me. She'd just assume Tom had been hit one too many times in the head and move on with her glamorous life."

"Hey, give yourself some credit. Gisele doesn't have your body."

I snort. "Which is why she's a supermodel and I'm not."

"I meant your curves, idiot."

"You're still losing this argument. We both know that I'm five-feet-two inches of bad attitude, high anxiety, and no filter. Nobody's jealous of that. And by the way, why can't we come up with another word than 'curves'? I'm not a mountain road, for fuck's sake."

"Lady lumps?"

The driver snickers. I'd like to give that eavesdropper a proper smack, but I'm only violent on the inside. Plus, I don't want to go to jail for assault.

Not all of us have the chief of police on speed dial.

Just then, a siren blares out from behind us.

"Fuck," mutters the driver, glancing in the rearview mirror. I turn around, look out the back window, and see the pair of motorcycle cops following us with their lights flashing.

Then I spot the sleek black sedan following behind them and start to panic. "Oh no."

Dani says, "What's wrong?"

"I think Callum called the cops on me."

"*What?* Did you steal his watch or something?"

"Just because I'm broke doesn't mean I'm a thief!"

Except now that I think of it, he was wearing a very expensive-looking watch. It's actually not a bad idea.

"Then why would he call the cops on you?"

"Maybe running out on a billionaire in the middle of lunch is against the law."

"You ran out on him? You didn't tell me that part! What the hell is the matter with you?"

I groan. "Literally everything."

The driver pulls to the side of the road and kills the engine. The motorcycle cops park behind us, and behind them parks the black sedan. One of the cops swings his leg over his bike and walks toward us. I take the opportunity to slide down low in the seat and hyperventilate.

Dani says, "Why are you quiet? What's happening? I'm dying over here."

"I'm gonna FaceTime you so you can see everything. If I get arrested, call that attorney friend of yours."

"He's an immigration attorney. Are you being deported?"

I don't bother answering her sarcastic question before disconnecting, then calling her back on FaceTime. When she answers, I tell her to shut up and point the screen toward the driver's window.

The police officer taps on the window. The driver rolls it down. The officer looks at the driver, then looks at me hiding in the back seat like a fugitive. "Miss?"

"Um. Yes?"

"Are you Emery Eastwood?"

After swallowing around the rock in my throat, I nod.

"Step out of the car, please."

Though tinny because it's coming over the phone, Dani's voice is still perfectly audible. "Ask him why he pulled you over! He can't pull you over without cause!"

The officer removes his mirrored sunglasses and stares at me. I slide a little lower in the seat.

"Miss Eastwood, step out of the vehicle. Now."

The way he says those words sends a chill straight down my spine. I imagine years of orange jumpsuits, bad food, and communal showers in my future and whimper.

He opens the back door of the car and stands aside. The driver cranes his neck around and looks at me with obvious fear, as if he just recognized me from the FBI's Most Wanted Fugitives list.

Dani shouts over the phone, "This is the United States of America! She has rights!"

The officer leans down and pins me in a ferocious glare. "I'll give you five seconds, Miss Eastwood. Then I'm coming in to get you."

With Dani shouting at the top of her lungs and the driver staring at me in horror, I slide across the bench seat and climb out of the car.

The officer gestures toward the black sedan. "Mr. McCord would like a word with you."

We gaze at each other as the midday traffic zooms past on Santa Monica Boulevard until I regain the power of speech. "So… he called you to come get me?"

He glances at the phone in my hand, which I'm holding beside my head so Dani has a front-row seat to my imminent arrest. Then he says, "You can't film me."

Dani hollers, "Oh, yes, she can! The Constitution guarantees it, buddy!"

The officer sighs heavily and looks up at the sky like he'd

rather be anywhere else on earth doing anything else but this. Against my better judgment, I feel sorry for him.

"Okay, fine. I'll talk to him. But if I wind up dead in a ditch somewhere, it's your fault."

Without waiting for a response, I march over to Callum's car, purse slung over my shoulder and phone in hand.

Callum's driver opens the back door for me. I can't tell for sure because his sunglasses hide his eyes and he's got a good poker face, but I think he's trying not to laugh.

I sit next to Callum. The driver shuts the door behind me, then strolls over to the police officers and lights a cigarette. I watch through the windshield as the three of them start to chat and laugh like they're having an impromptu get-together of fraternity bros.

"Hello again," says Callum.

Pretending I'm accustomed to having billionaires use the local police force to kidnap me from taxis, I smile blandly at him. "Hello. Are you going to tell me why the cops snatched me from the back of my Uber?"

"You left before you got your salad."

He gestures to the brown paper bag on the floor beside his feet, then laces his fingers together and rests his hands in his lap, right over a big bulge that I am definitely not looking at.

Then he says, "What's that shouting?"

"That would be my girlfriend Dani. I've got her on FaceTime on my phone."

He glances at the phone in my right hand, which I'm hiding next to my thigh.

Dani chooses that moment to holler, "I can't see anything! Emery, what the fuck is happening? Are you riding his dick or what?"

If a person could die of embarrassment, I'd already be six feet under.

I lift the phone and point the screen in Callum's direction. When he smiles, Dani inhales sharply.

"Hello, Dani."

"Uh, er...hi."

"It's a pleasure to meet you."

"Um...uh-huh."

Honestly, the power this man has to render women speechless is astonishing.

I turn the screen toward me so I'm looking at Dani's slack-jawed face. "I'll call you back in a minute, okay?"

With her eyes wide and her nose pressed to the screen, she mouths *Holy shit.*

"Indeed." I disconnect and turn back to Callum.

Somehow, he's grown even more handsome in the short interim since I last saw him. I'm tempted to ask him about his skincare routine but get distracted by the way he's looking at my mouth.

Why is he looking at my mouth?

Now I'm a cliché, because butterflies explode in an ecstatic, fluttering burst in my stomach. I'd give myself a bracing slap across the cheek, but don't want to look like a lunatic.

"Your face is red again."

"And you've got more spinach stuck in your gums."

"You also forgot your engagement ring."

"If you reach into your suit pocket right now, I can guarantee I'll draw blood."

His intense gaze drifts up from my mouth to my eyes, where it electrocutes me. He murmurs, "Are you threatening your fiancé, darling?"

"Yes. And if you call me darling one more time, you can say goodbye to your two front teeth."

Amused by my attitude, he breaks into a smile so dazzling, I nearly suffer a heart attack on the spot. I stare at him breathlessly, my pulse pounding, at a loss for words.

"What would you like me to call you?"

"My first name will do just fine, thanks." I can't remember it at the moment, but hopefully, he does.

"How about..." He pauses to moisten his lips. His voice drops an octave. "Baby?"

When I only stare at him in disbelief, he chuckles.

"We can leave that for the wedding night."

"I am *not* marrying you."

"So you don't want to save your business?"

I glare at him. Unflinchingly cool, he gazes right back at me.

"And you don't care that all your employees will be left jobless? Or that you have no other work experience that might interest an employer? Or that your father's dream of a generational family bookshop will go up in smoke?"

I demand, "What do you know about my father's dreams?"

"There's a whole page devoted to the subject on your company website."

That deflates me. "Oh. Right."

He examines me for a moment, then says, "What are your primary concerns?"

"About what?"

"About marrying me."

Fighting the urge to break out into hysterical laughter, I huff out a breath instead and say sarcastically, "I'll mail you a list."

"No, tell me right now."

Groaning, I cover my face with my hands. "Can someone sane please tell me what's going on?"

Callum pries my hands away from my face and holds my wrists firmly as he stares into my eyes.

With quiet intensity, he says, "It's very simple. Listen carefully, because I don't like to repeat myself. I need a wife. You need money. I'm offering you a business arrangement that will solve both our problems. Say yes and you'll never want for anything again. You can open a chain of bookstores all over the country if you like. You can have whatever you desire, whatever you can imagine. The world will open up for you beyond your wildest dreams."

I topple headfirst into the endless abyss of his dark, powerful eyes and float there for what seems like an eternity. Eventually, I manage to pull myself out of the depths and back to reality.

"Callum?"

He leans closer. His eyes start to burn. "Yes, Emery?"

"Let go of my wrists."

For the longest moment, he remains still, staring at me with a crackling-hot concentration that sends a thrill through my blood.

Then something in his eyes changes. All his heat and intensity vanishes, as if a cage door has been slammed shut. He abruptly releases me and sits back.

Looking out the front windshield, he says stiffly, "I apologize. Sometimes my..."

In his unfinished sentence, a dangerous ocean of secrets churns. Resting on his thighs, his big hands curl to fists. He inhales a slow, controlled breath, closing his eyes and clenching his molars as he exhales.

It's like watching a T-Rex trying to convince itself it's vegan. I've never seen anything so unnerving in my life.

Time to run.

"I'm getting out of the car now and going back to my Uber. I'm just telling you that so you don't order the cops to tackle me on the way. Okay?"

He looks at me. Pressing his lips together, he remains silent.

"I'll take that as a yes. Bye now, Mr. McCord. Good luck finding your wife."

I lean across his legs, grab the brown bag containing my chicken salad, climb out of the sedan, and head back to the Uber.

Callum's gaze burns into my back every step of the way.

Seven

By the time the Uber drops me back at the store, the red marks around my wrists where Callum's hands gripped me have faded.

My shock, however, has not.

The first thing I do is go inside and lock the door. Then I hustle to the back, collapse onto my desk chair, and call Dani.

"Tell me everything," she demands. "And *don't* leave anything out this time!"

"First let me get into this chicken salad. I didn't have breakfast, and I'm about to pass out from hunger."

"Chicken salad?"

"Callum boxed up the lunch I ordered but didn't get to eat because I ran away. Oh good, there's a plastic fork."

As I pull the box and utensils out of the to-go bag, Dani mulls my words over in silence.

Then she says, "Let me get this straight. A gorgeous, single billionaire strolls into your failing business, proposes marriage and a one-time payment of ten million bucks to save said business, takes you to lunch, shows you the giant engagement ring that could be yours, calls for a police escort to pick you up after you ditched him at the restaurant...and *also* brings you the meal you left behind when you ran away."

I speak around a mouthful of salad. "Why do you sound most impressed about the last part?"

"Because if nothing else convinced you to marry him, that alone should have."

"It's a chicken salad, not a declaration of undying love."

"It might as well be! He *fed* you, Em. Even after you rejected him. And we both know where food sits in your hierarchy of needs. If you say 'I'm hungry,' there's about twenty minutes before you turn into something that should be chained in a basement when the moon is full."

"Have I told you lately that I hate you?"

"Shut up. You love me. Now tell me why you said no."

I stop chewing to give the phone in my hand a look of disbelief. "Are you saying you think I should've said yes?"

"Sure. Why not?"

"Pfft. We could be here until next week if I listed all the reasons why not."

"Really? You have something more important to do?"

"Than marry a total stranger? Yes!"

She scoffs. "Like what?"

"Like everything! Listen to yourself, Dani. You sound just as nuts as he did. Besides, he wasn't serious. It was some kind of sick prank."

"Are you sure?"

"Oh my God. You've gone over to the dark side. Why would some random billionaire want to marry *me*?"

"Stop beating yourself up for a minute and consider the possibility that maybe you're more marriageable than you think."

I shake my head and chew another bite of my salad, giving her time to realize what she just said.

Finally, she sighs. "Okay, fine. It was a prank."

"Thank you."

"I'm only saying that so we don't get into a fight, by the way. I think there's a good possibility he was serious."

"I'm hanging up on you now."

Before I can, she says, "Remember how obsessed Ben was with you?"

"Before he abandoned me without an explanation and was never heard from again?"

"Well...yeah. He did do that. But *before* that, he was so pussy whipped, all his friends made fun of him."

I mutter, "This conversation is giving me a migraine."

Ignoring me, she goes on. "And Chris and Brandon were gaga about you too."

"Before they dumped me, you mean. Are you seeing the pattern here?"

"So you've had a couple of bad breakups in the past few years. That doesn't mean you're not amazing."

"Pretty sure that's exactly what it means, bud."

Sounding indignant, she says, "Well, *I'd* marry you. If I was a lesbian, I mean."

"How incredibly comforting. Thank you."

"Don't be snotty. I'm giving you a compliment."

The shop phone rings as I'm rolling my eyes. "Gotta go. I'll talk to you later."

"Come over for dinner Friday night."

"What are you making?"

"Lasagna. See you at six."

She disconnects without waiting for a yes, because she knows I'll never say no to pasta. I set the cell on the desktop and pick up the shop phone. "Lit Happens, how may I help you?"

"This is David Montgomery from the California Department of Tax and Fee Administration. May I speak to the owner, please?"

Oh shit. The CDTFA. The only thing worse would be hearing from the IRS. My heart plummets to my stomach.

I say tentatively, "This is the owner."

"Ms. Eastwood?"

"Yes."

"Ah, excellent. I'm calling to discuss your sales tax account."

I already know on a gut level that this is going to be extraordinarily bad. "What about it?"

"We've done an internal audit and discovered some anomalies in your returns."

Gulping, I repeat, "Anomalies?"

"Yes. Your earnings have been underreported for quite a few years. Ten, to be exact."

My heart beats so fast, I'm breathless. My voice comes out high and tight. "No, that's impossible. We keep records of every sale, even the cash ones. And we always file on time. My bookkeeper is an excellent—"

He cuts me off with, "There's a principal balance due on the account of one million, nine hundred sixty-four thousand dollars and seventy-two cents."

I gasp in horror and break out in a cold sweat.

Mr. Montgomery adds calmly, "Plus penalties."

"*Penalties?*"

"We can waive the penalties if you pay the principal amount within thirty days."

My grip on reality unravels, and I laugh hysterically. "Oh, how wonderful! How absolutely *generous* of you! I'm so *relieved*!"

He decides I'm being a pain in the ass and changes his professional tone to one of cold disapproval.

"Ms. Eastwood, this is no laughing matter. Tax fraud is a crime punishable by severe fines." His voice turns threatening. "Or prison time."

Leaping from my chair in panic, I start to pace. "Listen, there must be some mistake. We've paid every dime of the sales tax we ever collected. You need to go through the returns again."

"I assure you there is no mistake."

"There must be!"

"There isn't. Will you be paying by check or wire transfer?"

"I don't have two million dollars!"

He clucks. "How unfortunate. In that case, we'll proceed with collection efforts. Do you own your home?"

"Why?"

"We'll get a lien on the property."

"I rent an apartment! I don't own anything except my car!"

"Then we'll put a lien on that. And get a judgment against you personally so that any future earnings will be garnished until the total amount due is paid."

The way he's coldly discussing the ruination of my entire financial future makes me want to tear my hair out. Shaking and sweating, I stand beside the desk with one clammy hand clutching the receiver and the other clasped over my forehead.

"I haven't seen a bill or any kind of notice about this. How can you be starting collection efforts already?"

"We've mailed several invoices to your business address. You didn't respond."

"That's because I never got them!"

Sounding like he thinks I'm a big fat liar, he sniffs. "Nevertheless, the account remains overdue."

"How the hell am I supposed to come up with two million dollars?"

He says snippily, "I can't give financial advice, Ms. Eastwood. I'm not an accountant."

This guy. I swear to God, this guy is about to fuck around and find out.

"Listen to me, David. Someone has made a mistake. A huge mistake. You need to take another look and fix it."

He turns into a robot and recites a memorized script that sounds like it came straight from the company website. "If a taxpayer disagrees with a decision regarding their liability for taxes or fees, they can dispute that decision by filing an appeal within the time limits set forth by law."

Finally, hope! "So I can file an appeal?"

After a pause where I hear him shuffling paperwork, he comes back on the line with a smile in his voice. "Actually, no. The time limit has passed."

Over my aggravated groan, he says, "I'll give you my number so that you can get back to me with any questions."

I barely have the presence of mind to write it down, but I manage it, scrawling the 800 number on the pad beside the phone before throwing the pen down in disgust.

"Goodbye, Miss Eastwood. And good luck to you."

Sounding gleeful, he disconnects.

The prick.

It's as I'm standing there with cold sweat trickling down my temples that I see a small white card at the bottom of the brown to-go bag I took from Callum. I reach inside and pick it up.

It's his business card. His name, company name, and contact information are embossed on it in elegant black script.

I turn the card over to find he's written a note on the back in printing so precise, it looks engineered.

Thank you for the pleasure of your company. Please call me if you reconsider.

Staring at the card, I whisper, "Don't even think about it, Emery."

I toss it into the trash can and try not to cry.

The next morning, I'm online at the shop ordering a giant *Going Out of Business Sale* sign to hang in the window when someone comes through the door. When I get to the front, I find a shifty-eyed young man in a blue hoodie standing near the register, looking nervous.

"Hi there. How can I help you?"

"Are you Emery Eastwood?"

Something about his energy puts me on edge. I give him a good once-over so he knows I can pick him out of a police lineup if I need to. "Yes. Why?"

He pulls a folded brown envelope out of the pocket of his hoodie and tosses it onto the counter. "You've been served."

"*Served?* What do you mean?"

He turns around and quickly walks out the door.

I stare at the envelope with a sinking feeling in my stomach, then cross to it, rip it open, and withdraw a thick sheaf of papers.

With my heart in my throat, I scan the top page. Then I gasp.

It's a summons.

A civil lawsuit has been brought against me by someone I've never heard of who claims he was injured when he tripped and fell on a damaged floor tile.

Heat floods my face and chest. My hands begin to shake. I shout, "Fuck!"

Leaning my hip against the counter, I stand there trembling. How could this be happening? I've always made sure the store was safe for customers. And I *know* there's no broken floor tile. I know every inch of this shop like the back of my hand.

I take a deep breath and force myself to focus. I need to find an attorney and figure out what my next steps are.

Except attorneys cost money.

Which is one thing I definitely don't have.

Maybe I should sell pictures of my feet on the internet. I've heard there's a market for that. Looking down at my shoes, I mull it over for a moment before I catch myself and groan.

The shop phone rings. Disoriented and upset, I lean over the counter and pick up the receiver. "Lit Happens, how may I help you?"

"Emery, honey, is that you?"

I recognize my elderly neighbor's voice, except for one thing: the panic in it.

"Maude? What's wrong?"

"Oh, honey, it's awful. Just awful! Where am I supposed to go? I don't have anybody to take me in. What will I *do*?"

"Maude, calm down. You're talking so fast, I can barely understand you. What's happened?"

She drags in a hitching breath. "Our apartment building…it's been condemned. The police said we only have thirty minutes to pack our belongings before we have to get out!"

Someone invisible just hauled back and punched me in the throat. I make a faint sound of disbelief as all the blood drains out of my face.

"Oh! Here's one of the nice officers now. You talk to him, honey, see if you can get him to tell you anything."

Maude starts badgering someone in the background to take her phone. The person must decline, because she comes back on, groaning.

"Maude, please, can you tell me what happened? Why would the building be condemned? There's nothing wrong with it!"

"Oh, I don't know, honey. Something about repeated code violations." She sobs quietly. "I've lived in that apartment for fifty years. Where will I go now? What should I do?"

A police siren somewhere in the background wails in warning before abruptly cutting off. A man shouts curses at the top of his lungs. It sounds like another neighbor, Jim, a father of three young boys who's been unemployed for a year. His wife works the night shift at the hospital.

The only other tenant in the building, Anthony, is a sweet older man who lost his husband last year to Covid and one of his own legs to diabetes. He survives on social security and Meals on Wheels.

Now all of us are going to be out on the street.

"Don't move. I'll be there in ten minutes." I hang up and grab my handbag from under the counter. Then I run to my car, barely remembering to lock the front door because I'm in such a rush.

When I get to the apartment, my neighbors are milling around on the street outside, comforting Maude, who's crying. Two police cars are parked at the curb. Four armed officers stand in front of the building, glowering in the crowd's general direction.

A barrier of bright yellow crime scene tape crisscrosses the front entrance.

I march straight up to the officers and demand, "What's going on here?"

"Building's been condemned, miss. Move along, please."

"I live in that building!"

"What's your name?"

"Emery Eastwood. I'm in apartment 101, and I demand to know what's happening."

Two of the officers share a look, like they already know I'm trouble. The taller one says, "You have thirty minutes to pack up and get out."

"That's *ridiculous*! You can't just throw people out of their homes! I'm not leaving! You need a court order for something like this! You have to give proper notice!"

The shorter officer snaps, "Miss?"

I turn to look at him and his silly pointy moustache. "Yes?"

"Are you aware that failure to obey a police officer's order is a crime?"

I narrow my eyes at him, convinced he's stretching the truth. "What section of the criminal code is that under?"

He looks like he's two seconds away from wrapping his hands around my throat and giving it a long, hard squeeze.

Through gritted teeth, he says, "It's under the section where I tell you that you have thirty minutes to remove your personal belongings from your dwelling and leave the premises before I put you in cuffs, take you to the station, and charge you with obstruction."

Appalled, I stare at him.

This can't be real. I'm dreaming. Or I've fallen down and hit my head and am lying unconscious on the side of a road somewhere.

What the hell has happened to my life?

At that moment, my cell rings. I take the opportunity to turn away from the hard stares the group of cops are giving me to walk a few feet away and pull it from my purse.

"Hello?"

"Miss Eastwood, it's Callum McCord. I'm sorry to bother you. I just wanted to apologize for my behavior yesterday. I think I may have upset you, and that wasn't my intent."

He sounds detached and professional, with none of the rip-you-to-pieces carnivore energy he had before.

Giving the policemen a nervous glance over my shoulder, I move a few steps farther away. "You don't owe me an apology, but thank you. I should actually be apologizing to you for threatening to break your face."

"Are you all right? You sound anxious."

"Actually, this isn't a good time to talk. The police are throwing me out of my apartment."

Even though he's nowhere in sight, I feel his attention sharpen. His voice lower, he demands, "Tell me exactly what's happening."

I suppose it could be because I'm emotional, or because he sounds so concerned and I need a shoulder to lean on, but I blurt out the entire story, telling him every awful detail.

When I'm finished, he orders, "Give your phone to whichever officer is in charge."

"Why would I do that? These guys already want to arrest me!"

"Emery. Do exactly what I told you to do. And do it *now*."

His voice is so commanding. So soft yet utterly in control. It slides over all my nerve endings like poured silk, smoothing their jagged edges and giving me a little boost of confidence.

At least somebody around here knows what they're doing.

I take a breath and turn back toward the policemen. "Which one of you guys is in charge?"

Nobody says anything, but the short officer darts a glance toward the tall one.

Bingo.

I walk up to him and hold out my cell phone. "Callum McCord wants to talk to you."

Speaking that name has an immediate effect on the group of men. Everyone tenses. The air goes electric. One of the cops takes a single step back, looking as if he's about to turn and break into a run.

The tall officer reluctantly takes the phone from my hand. He lifts it to his ear and clears his throat. "Officer Anderson speaking."

Then he listens to whatever Callum is telling him with an expression like he's attending his own funeral.

After several long moments, he hands the phone back to me. He says stiffly, "Sorry for the inconvenience, miss. You can go ahead and go inside." He turns to his men. "Take down the tape. We're done here."

Dumbfounded, I watch as two of the officers go to the front doors of the building and tear down the tape. Then all four of them head to their patrol cars.

Into my phone, I say, "Boy, it must be really great to be a billionaire."

"Are they leaving?"

"Yes, and I'm deeply impressed. Do you actually own the police force?"

Callum chuckles. It's a sound so rich and sexy, it sends a tingle down my spine.

He says, "I'll get in touch with the city inspector to get this all straightened out. The city is notorious for overreacting to small infractions and levying fines so egregious, the building owners can't pay. The fight usually winds up in court, but in the meantime, they pull some power play like this to put pressure on the owner. I can't tell you how many times it's happened to us."

"Us?"

"My family. We own many rental properties there."

"I knew the building shouldn't be condemned!"

He chuckles again. "You were right. Buildings have to practically be falling down before that happens."

Heaving a sigh of relief, I watch the squad cars pull away from the curb and drive down the street. Over on the sidewalk, my gathered neighbors stare at me in open astonishment. I might as well be levitating for how shocked they look.

"I don't know what to say, Callum, except thank you. If you hadn't called, my neighbors and I would all be sleeping on the floor of my shop tonight."

"You're welcome. Anytime. And now I'll let you get back to your day. It was nice speaking with you."

"You, too. Thanks again."

He says goodbye and disconnects, leaving me standing in the street even more disoriented than I was before I pulled up.

He said nothing about his proposal.

He acted like a perfect gentleman.

He saved me and my neighbors from disaster with barely ten seconds of effort.

Most confusing of all is that I never gave him my cell phone number.

Eight

At Dani's Friday night, I update her on recent disasters as she puts together the salad to accompany the lasagna finishing up in the oven. Her husband, Ryan, tries to keep their screaming two-year-old daughter, Mia, occupied with toys on the living room floor while their dog, a rescue terrier with hyperactivity issues, tears around the house barking at invisible squirrels, and Ryan's partially deaf father watches *Jeopardy* with the volume cranked. At regular intervals, he shouts out incorrect trivia answers, then hollers, "Bullshit!" when he's proven wrong.

I love this family, but after a week living here, all my hair would fall out from stress.

Which makes my current situation even more terrifying. If I can't afford rent anymore and wind up couch surfing at Casa Chaos, I might never recover my wits.

Or my hearing.

"I can't believe someone's suing you. It's not like you have any money they can get," Dani says, calmly tossing dressing into a bowl of salad greens like her home is an oasis of tranquility instead of the circus it actually is.

"Pretty sure they don't know that, or they wouldn't have

bothered. Everybody seems to think business owners are rolling in dough."

"Did you hire an attorney?"

"And pay him with what? Tears?"

"I don't know, but you better get someone soon. If you don't answer the summons, the other guy gets an automatic judgment, and you're screwed."

Dejected, I mutter, "I can't imagine being any more screwed than I already am."

I set the table while Dani takes the lasagna out of the oven. As we sit down to eat, Mia starts banging her fork on the table and the dog jumps up, knocking over a glass of water. Ryan's father, who has now switched over to *Wheel of Fortune*, yells out a guess, then cackles when it turns out to be right.

"Dad, it's time to eat!" Ryan shouts from the table. "*Dad!*"

I can already feel the headache starting to pulse at my temples.

"So I spent some time stalking your future husband all over the internet. Want to hear what I found?"

I give Dani a stern look. "No. And he's not my future husband."

Ryan chuckles. "I'll marry him if you're not interested."

Smiling, Dani says, "Excuse me, pal, but you already have a spouse."

"Yeah, but think about it. I'd get the ten mil, file for a quickie divorce, then move you, me, and our terrorist spawn out to that little ranch in Montana that we saw on Zillow that had the guest cottage for Dad and the horse stalls."

Mia bounces in her high chair and shrieks, "Horsie! Horsie!"

"You guys aren't allowed to move away from here," I say, helping myself to a big chunk of lasagna from the casserole dish in the middle of the table. "We're all gonna grow old together and throw ragers at the nursing home, remember?"

When Ryan and Dani share a quick look, I get nervous. "Oh God. What is it? What's wrong? Is someone sick? Who's dying? Hurry up and tell me before I pass out."

Dani hands me the salad bowl. "Nobody's sick or dying, maniac. It's not always the end of the world. Hurry up and eat something before your blood sugar crashes and you turn into a gremlin."

I say drily, "If you'd had the month I've had, trust me, you'd assume every little thing was the end of the world."

Serving Ryan a piece of lasagna, Dani says, "We actually might need to move, though. We've started looking at places out of state."

Shocked, I set the salad bowl down with a clatter and look back and forth between her and Ryan. "Why?"

"I got laid off," admits Ryan quietly, staring at his daughter.

"No! Oh, you guys, I'm so sorry. I thought the job was going well?"

Dani sighs. "Yeah. It was a complete surprise. Apparently, the company can do without middle managers."

Ryan conducts appraisals on commercial properties for large corporations investing in real estate. Business had been booming until the economy took a downturn, but I had no idea things had gotten so bad.

He says, "We've got equity in the house. Since home prices are so much higher here than in other parts of the country, if we sell, we'd be able to afford to pay cash for a place. Which would be necessary, since I couldn't qualify for another mortgage if I'm out of work."

"But can't you look for work here? I'm sure something else will come up. Someone with your skills is bound to find another position quickly!"

Ryan shakes his head. "I'll be forty this year, Em. I'm competing with recent college grads for jobs now, and they'll work for practically nothing. Nobody wants to pay my salary."

When Dani glances guiltily at Mia, I decide it's time to change the subject. "Don't give up just yet. I have faith in you. And now let's talk about something cheerful. Who has good news?"

The three of us look at each other while the dog races around the table, barking at nothing, and Ryan's dad throws the remote control across the room at the television.

I sigh heavily. "Okay, fine. Tell me what you found out about Callum McCord."

Instantly, Dani perks up. "*Lots.* He's thirty-five, never been married, and lives in this gigantic mansion in Bel Air that used to belong to Jennifer Lopez. He's the oldest of three brothers who all work for the company. You have to check out this family photo."

She jumps up, grabs her laptop from the kitchen counter, and returns to set it on the table next to me. Opening a browser, she clicks on a saved link. A photo appears on the screen.

Impressed, I say, "Wow. Talk about good genetics. Those people all look like they were created by AI."

It's a formal picture, the posed kind where everyone's gathered stiffly together in front of a hearth wearing their best smiles. Except for the dark-haired man standing next to Callum. He's scowling as if someone just told him his dog had been shot.

"Who's the one with the pissy face?"

Dani takes her seat again, saying, "The middle brother, Cole. He looks like that in every picture. Handsome and murderous."

"And the one with the dimples?"

"Carter, the youngest."

"And that must be his grudge-holding dad sitting in front of them all like King Charles."

"Isn't his mother beautiful? Guess how old she is?"

"I dunno. Fiftyish?"

"Sixty-four."

Callum's mother stands directly behind her seated husband. A slender redhead wearing a blue dress with a plunging neckline, she gazes out from the photo with a serene smile, radiating the kind of tranquil confidence that comes from sleeping on piles of money every night.

"They're all beautiful. It's unnatural. I bet they made a pact with the devil. Pass me the Parmesan."

Dani slides the jar across the table while Ryan wolfs down his food and I sprinkle more cheese over my plate.

"Okay, but you want to know the really interesting thing?"

Looking at her sly smile, I'm nervous all over again. "What?"

"Not only has Callum never been married, he's never been engaged. So that rock he waved in your face never belonged to anyone before."

"He didn't wave it. He set it on the table. And how do you know he's never been engaged?"

"There's no mention of a girlfriend in any of the articles about him. No pics of him at charity functions with models on his arms. Nary a mention of anyone he's been linked to on his Wikipedia page or in the tabloids, and those things *always* have the dirt. For such a rich and good-looking guy, he doesn't seem to date."

"He said he had to keep secrets because of his family's position. That he couldn't trust anyone. So it was probably a private engagement. Some people like to keep their business out of the tabloids."

"Or maybe he bought that ring for *you*."

I shake my head in amusement. "Oh, sure. He overheard my sad story at dinner one night, and the next morning, he marched directly into the nearest Harry Winston store and bought the biggest rock he could find."

"Hey, stranger things have happened."

I look to Ryan for support. "Please tell your wife she's hallucinating."

Feeding Mia a bite of pasta, he says, "I would, but she's within swinging distance."

Dani insists, "Just consider the possibility, Em."

"That man could marry any girl he wanted. I know I'm a sparkly explosion of fucking awesomeness, but I'm not his type."

Waving her hands in the air, Mia shrieks, "Fuckie!"

In the living room, Ryan's father shouts, "Bullshit!" at Vanna White.

Dani says, "Okay, then, how about this? What if Callum's father really did give him that ultimatum? And Callum was so pissed off about the whole thing that he decided to get back at his father by marrying someone..."

She looks me up and down, then scrunches up her nose. "Inappropriate."

"You're lucky you make good lasagna, lady, otherwise this fork would already be embedded in one of your eyeballs."

"C'mon. You know what I mean. Daddy Dearest probably expected his son would run to the nearest socialite named Cordelia who owns polo ponies and wears cashmere sweater sets with her Mikimoto pearls, right? But *instead*, Callum decides to get a little payback and rebel against his dad's stupid ultimatum by getting engaged to Wednesday Addams."

I look at Ryan again. "Remind me why I like your wife?"

He smiles at her. "Because she's beautiful and funny."

"No, that's why *you* like her. I think she's about as funny as a suspicious rash."

Dani says, "There's only one way to find out if he's serious, Em."

I warn, "Don't even say it, cuckoo bird."

With a flourish of her fork, she pronounces, "Say yes."

I sigh and look at the ceiling.

Ryan agrees, the traitor. "It's worth a try. If somebody were offering me a boatload of money to save my whole life, I'd definitely consider it."

That makes me laugh. "Really? You'd sleep with a total stranger for ten million bucks?"

Ryan glances at Dani, then looks at me. "Before I got married, I would've slept with a total stranger for nothing at all."

Dani smacks his arm affectionately. "Slut."

"Former slut, now happily married. Besides, from what I'm hearing, this guy never said anything about sex, right?"

Frowning, I think about it. "No...but doesn't it go without saying that sex is expected?"

"Not if it's a business arrangement. Maybe the dude already has his side chicks that he keeps on the downlow, and he just needs a wife for the formalities to satisfy Daddy Warbucks. Maybe all he'd expect of you would be to show up at family functions and annoy the shit out of everyone with your awkward social skills and lack of an Ivy League education."

I stare at Ryan in outrage. "Awkward social skills?"

He grins at me. "You burped in my dad's face at our wedding reception."

"I'd been drinking champagne all afternoon. It makes me gassy!"

Dani says, "And let's not forget the time you laughed at your grandma's funeral."

"I was *eight*. And corpses are funny!"

Ryan says, "Or the time the security guard at the mall wished you a Merry Christmas and you politely answered 'No, thank you.' And the time our neighbor Jenny put her baby in your hands and you said the same thing and set the baby on the ground."

Indignant, I demand, "Well, what kind of a mother goes around shoving her newborn at strangers? What was I supposed to do, stick it on my boob and start to nurse?"

Ryan laughs at that. "Don't forget the time we were at that Halloween party and that guy in the wolf mask came up to you and asked who you were, and you stuck your hand on your hip and said, 'I'm the one your mother warned you about, that's who.'"

"I was in a mood, okay?"

They keep going, the heartless jerks, telling each other my greatest hits until they're crying with laughter. I say without heat, "You guys suck."

Wiping at her watering eyes, Dani says, "Let's face it, girl, you march to the beat of your own drum."

"I'm glad I'm such a source of amusement. Now be quiet until I finish my dinner, or I might accidentally stab one of you."

Feeding Mia another bite of pasta, Ryan says, "Not that you'll take my advice, but I'm gonna give it anyway. Ask this rich guy what the conditions of his offer are. Even if you don't believe he's for real, call his bluff. See what he has to say. And if it turns out he's serious..."

He wipes Mia's mouth with a napkin, then turns back to me. "Negotiate."

"Pardon me, but I'm not livestock. I'm not about to haggle over my purchase price."

"You don't have to. He's already named the price. What you haggle over are the terms."

Leaning in, Dani says excitedly, "Ooo, yeah, I love that idea. Tell him he has to buy you at least ten carats of diamonds a year."

Ryan says, "No, I meant like how long you have to stay married before you can keep all the money, stuff like that." He pauses to think. "Actually, what you should do is tell him the money gets put into a trust in your name first or you don't walk down the aisle at all."

"Listen to you. What a mercenary."

"Hey, it's business, not love. The rules are different. You have to make sure you get everything you want up front and in writing or no deal."

What *I* want. Now there's a concept. I can't remember the last time someone asked what I want. In fact, now that I think about it, I'm not sure anyone ever has.

My parents always taught me to be grateful for what I have, to not ask for more. But what if Callum *was* serious about his offer? What if, like Dani said, he wanted to choose someone who wouldn't fit in with his family, just to spite his father?

And what if, just once, I was in a position to get anything I dreamed of?

As I sit there, I seriously consider the possibilities for the first time. Ten million dollars is a fortune. The things I could do with that kind of money...

Not only could I keep the store open, everyone would keep their jobs.

I could hire an attorney to fight that ridiculous lawsuit.

I could pay off the stupid tax bill from the CDTFA.

I could go back to school and get that degree I never had the time or money for.

I could figure out what I really wanted to do with my life. Who I actually wanted to be, aside from the person I was always expected to be. The good girl. The dutiful daughter. The person who took on the identity her parents wanted for her. The hard-working, self-sacrificing, loyal-to-the-family-before-all-else child.

The heir to her father's dreams.

It hits me with a shock that Callum and I have that in common. We're both products of our fathers' making, of their inflexible ideas about how things should be. Callum with his dad's insistence on marriage or disinheritance, me with my dad's insistence that a literary life is the only one worth living.

"And how strange that we both work for the family business," I murmur aloud, eyes glazed over as my mind works in a frenzy.

"Earth to Emery. Come back from Mars, girl, your lasagna's getting cold."

When I look at Ryan, he grimaces. "That face you're making is scary."

I shake my head slowly, feeling wobbly and disoriented, like the room has started to spin. "This isn't my scary face. This is my negotiating face."

Dani sits bolt upright, clapping. "You're going to do it? You'll see if he's for real?"

I hesitate before nodding. "Yeah. You're right. What have I got to lose?"

I glance at Ryan. After that irrevocable trust he mentioned, I know the first thing I'll be asking Callum for.

A billionaire whose family owns as much property as his does could most likely use a good real estate appraiser.

As soon as dinner's over, I grab my purse off the sofa. With

Ryan's dad hollering curses at the television in the background, I send Callum a text to the number he called me from.

Hi. It's Emery.

I send that, then stand there thinking for a moment, wondering what would be the least whorish way to tell a man you'd like to meet to discuss the terms of your own acquisition. But before I can send anything else, I get a text in return.

Tell me where you are. I'll be there immediately.

Surprised both by the speed of his response and the brusque tone of it, I type back.

I didn't invite you anywhere. And how about a hello?

His answer comes so fast, he must be using the microphone to dictate it.

Hello. Now tell me where you are.

When I just stand there frowning at the phone in my hand and don't answer, another text comes through.

Emery.

That's it. All he sends is my name. But in that single word, I feel every ounce of his impatience. He somehow managed to convey that clearly, along with supreme frustration that I'm disobeying a command.

I mutter, "Are all rich people so bossy?"

I'm at a friend's having dinner, but I was hoping we could talk tomorrow.

I wait, but he doesn't reply.

Unsettled by the exchange, I go back to the kitchen and help with the dishes. As Dani and Ryan continue to discuss things I should negotiate for, I think about what exactly bothers me about Callum's text messages.

It isn't until I pull into the driveway of my apartment building later that I stop worrying about it. Now I have something more important to focus on.

Wearing a black suit and a glower to match, Callum stands outside my front door.

Nine

I park and take a moment to give myself a silent pep talk and let my pulse settle. Then I take a deep breath and open the door.

When I turn around, Callum stands five feet away next to the trunk.

"Oh. There you are." Startled, I glance nervously at the door of my apartment. *How did he get over here so fast?*

"Here I am," he agrees, his voice low and his eyes piercing. "Invite me inside."

We stare at each other while I listen to crickets sing and worry that maybe this bossy billionaire is actually undead. In addition to possessing superhuman speed, didn't Dracula always need an invitation before he could enter someone's house?

"You're overthinking again."

"Yes. And how annoying that you noticed. What are you doing here?"

"You wanted to talk. I came to talk."

"I wanted to talk tomorrow."

"I was in the neighborhood."

"This neighborhood?" I say doubtfully.

"Yes."

"Why?"

"Why wouldn't I be?"

"Oh, I don't know. Maybe because you live an hour away with all the other gazillionaires in Bel Air, and funky little beach towns don't seem like your thing."

His eyes sharpen. "I see you've done some research on me."

"No, I haven't."

"I'd appreciate it if you didn't lie."

"I'm not. Dani did the research. I was convinced you were playing a prank and was determined never to speak to you again. She talked me out of it."

The scent of him drifts to me on the warm evening air. Expensive cologne and a hint of musk, along with something crisp but undefinable. It's probably the smell of new hundred-dollar bills.

He suddenly commands, "Invite me inside."

I sigh. "Do you even know how to have a normal conversation?"

"No. Invite me inside."

Exasperated, I say, "Damn, you're relentless."

The corners of his lips curve upward. "You have no idea."

"Okay, fine. But first tell me how you got my phone number and know where I live."

His small smile grows slightly wider. "Did you really think I'd propose marriage to a woman I knew nothing about?"

I squint at him suspiciously. "The way you say that makes it sound like you hired a private detective to spy on me."

"I didn't have to hire a detective. I keep one on retainer."

"Riiight. In case you suddenly feel the need to know everything about the random woman you're eavesdropping on over dinner."

"Exactly. Now invite me inside. There's an old woman peering down from the second-story window who's five seconds away from calling the police on me."

I glance up to find Maude staring out her window at us. And he's right. She does look like she's about to call the cops.

Not that it would do any good, considering Callum probably has every peace officer in Southern California on retainer too.

I dig in my purse for my keys and head to the door, knowing Callum will follow, and also knowing it will irritate him that I turned my back on him and walked away.

He's not the only one around here who knows how to be annoying.

Once we're inside, I close the door behind him and watch as he prowls around the space like a caged lion, sniffing things out. He's got that predatory energy again. It's even more pronounced now that we're in my small, girly, messy place.

I look at everything through his eyes and wish we could go back outside.

He comes out of my kitchen and stands in the middle of my living room, taking up all the air. Then he pronounces, "I'd like a drink."

"Hooray for you. I'll notify the maître d'."

Tossing my handbag onto the sofa, I walk past him and head into the kitchen, where I open the fridge and pull out an open bottle of white wine. I pour myself a glass, go back into the living room, and sit down.

Callum stands there gazing at me with his inscrutable rich-person expression, the one that I know he thinks is intimidating.

"I'm not going to kiss your butt or wait on you like Sophie would. There's a Sauvignon Blanc in the fridge or a bottle of whiskey in the cabinet next to the sink. Glasses are in the same cabinet. Help yourself." I pause, then add cheekily, "Darling."

The signs of his restraint are small, but they're there. Now that I've seen him exercise his self-control, I notice the way his jaw tightens. The slow, controlled breath he draws. The way his hands, hanging by his sides, slightly flex.

Before, I found it all a little frightening. For some strange reason, now I find it quite the turn-on. What was it that he said to me at the restaurant? Oh yes.

"Hello, little lamb. Welcome to the lion's den."

Maybe he's not the only lion.

"Why are you smiling like that?" he demands.

I say innocently, "Like what?"

Gazing at me with lowered lids, he moistens his lips. It makes my pulse flutter and my stomach clench.

Okay, so maybe lion is a stretch. What's between that and a lamb? A fox? A raccoon?

Oh, who am I kidding? I might as well be a jellyfish for the way this man makes me quiver. How embarrassing.

Maintaining eye contact with me, Callum unbuttons his jacket and slides it off his shoulders. Beneath it, he's wearing a white dress shirt tailored so perfectly, the outline of his abs is visible. He drapes the coat over the back of a chair, then unbuttons his cuffs and slowly rolls them up his forearms, one after the other, all the while gazing into my eyes.

My mouth is dry. My armpits are damp. I try very hard to look casual and disinterested, but all I can hear is my uterus screaming OH MY GOD at the top of its lungs.

One of Callum's muscular forearms is tatted all the way down to his wrist.

He smirks, then turns and strolls into the kitchen, giving me a lovely view of his hard, perfect ass.

Though I'm a voracious little jellyfish, and I'd like nothing more than to rip those custom-made trousers off his body with my teeth, I refuse to be one of the many women I imagine fling themselves at his feet every day.

Let him have his harem of idolizers. I'll be the one he can't lead around by her clit. No matter how much it kills me to pretend he has no effect on me, I won't admit it.

I might not have much, but at least I have my pride.

He bangs around in the kitchen for a while to show his

displeasure at having to serve himself, then returns holding a glass of whiskey.

"Where do you want me to sit?" he inquires acidly.

"There's no need for that tone."

"I didn't have a tone."

"You totally had a tone, and you know it. Sit over there." I point to the chair on the other side of the coffee table, which is too small for him and also has a broken spring in the seat.

He looks at it for a moment. "If I sit in that thing, I might destroy it."

"You strike me as a man who enjoys taking risks."

When he turns his gaze to me, it's so scorching, it could light the whole room on fire. But I merely sit there and casually sip my wine as if this is all completely normal, and he's boring me out of my mind.

He walks into the dining room—it's six feet away—grabs one of the wooden dining chairs, and drags it across the floor back toward where I'm sitting. With his foot, he shoves the coffee table out of the way. Then he drops his chair in front of me and sits in it.

He leans forward to rest his forearms on his knees. Cradling his whiskey in his hands, he stares into my face.

Why does he have to be so handsome? And smell so good? God, he's awful.

Uncomfortable, I say, "This is too close for a conversation."

"I wasn't aware there were rules about distance."

"Haven't you ever heard of personal space?"

"Not a fan." He looks at my mouth and licks his lips.

Keep it together, girl. Keep that poker face. Look tough. Look bored. You're in control!

"Suit yourself," I say, and take another sip of wine.

He watches me with the focus of a man plotting a murder. Then he takes a swig of his whiskey and says, "The ten million will be deposited into an escrow account, which will be converted into an irrevocable trust in your name once the marriage license is signed."

I'm *this close* to spitting my wine in his face in shock but manage to control myself. I swallow and cough politely behind my hand. "Not one to mince words, are you?"

"I know that's why you texted me."

"Let's not get ahead of ourselves. I have questions. *So* many questions."

"Such as?"

"For starters, what about sex?"

He's so close, I see how fast his pupils dilate. Then, his tone husky, he says, "What about it?"

Shit. Leave it to me to blurt the most embarrassing thing first.

I shift uncomfortably in my chair but force myself to maintain eye contact. It feels important not to let him know how antsy he makes me. "I just...was wondering."

He gazes at me silently, waiting for me to open my mouth again to continue my assault on my self-esteem. Finally, I manage, "Is it expected?"

He studies me for a long moment, his eyes fierce. Then he murmurs, "The contract will have no mention of sex."

I try to parse that out to make sense of it but fail. "So you're saying we won't have sex?"

"I'm saying it won't be in the contract."

"Yeah, I heard that part, but what I mean is—"

"Do you want to have sex with me?" he interrupts.

My heart skips several beats. A rush of heat burns my cheeks. Then my mind unhelpfully provides me with a searing image of me naked, writhing, and crying out underneath him as he fucks me into next week.

Don't you dare break eye contact with him, you wuss!

I say airily, "Honestly, I haven't thought about it."

He studies my expression thoughtfully. Then his gaze turns amused.

"I'm serious," I insist, flustered. "It's not something that's been top of mind lately, what with all the fires I'm trying to put out in my personal life."

Eyes sparkling, he tips his head back and looks at me down his nose. "Hmm."

God, the smug is strong with this one.

"Listen, I'm sure you think you're all that, but you're really not my type."

"Oh? What is your type, exactly?"

He's mocking me. It's in his tone, his smirk, his body language. I go from uncomfortable to royally enraged and glare at him.

"Men who don't have resting rich face, for starters."

"Resting rich face?"

"The arrogant, entitled, contemptuous look certain wealthy people wear. That expression of exaggerated self-importance you have when you're going around being billionare-y all over the place and sneering at the common folk like me."

His eyes darken, and so does his energy. He gazes at me in silence for a moment, then says, "You're anything but common. And I'd never sneer at you, Emery. Never at you."

I was ready to throw my wine in his face, but now he's disarmed me. I stare at him, feeling frustrated, helpless, and confused.

"If I ask you something, will you be honest with me?"

"Yes."

His answer is quick and unequivocal. It gives me the little boost of confidence I need to continue. "Are you for real? Is this arrangement you're proposing legit?"

"Yes."

Again, his answer is firm. He maintains eye contact as he speaks. He doesn't blink, flinch, or make some strange twitch that I could pounce on with an *Ah-ha!* He simply looks like a man telling the truth.

I guzzle the rest of my wine, then clutch the empty glass in my lap and hope he doesn't notice how hard my hands are shaking.

"What else? Ask me anything," he says softly, still gazing into my eyes.

His voice is hypnotic. His eyes are mesmerizing. The scent of his skin intoxicates me. Or maybe that's the wine, but everything about this man seems designed to draw a woman in close. His face and body lay the trap, but it's his eyes that are the real snare.

The heat of his gaze is a velvet dark enticement that promises anything and everything and is both arousing and terrifying at once.

He's a force field, a powerful dark star slowly drawing me into his orbit and keeping me there with nothing but the sheer strength of his gravitational pull.

He says my name so quietly, it's barely a whisper. A tender, intimate whisper, the way a lover would say it close to my ear as he pushes inside me.

Which, of course, makes me completely fall apart.

I blurt, "I was just thinking about planets and gravity while having a little meltdown, will you please excuse me, I have to get more wine."

I jolt to my feet. Callum reaches out and takes my wrist. He pulls me back down into the chair and holds me there, gazing into my eyes with burning intensity.

He says, "I need you sober for this."

"Then maybe we should talk tomorrow, like I wanted to. Because right now, I'd like to get drunk."

"You shouldn't deal with stress by getting drunk."

"It's been working fine for me so far."

"No, it hasn't."

I close my eyes, draw a deep breath, then exhale. Then I open my eyes and look at him. "You're right. It hasn't. But that's really none of your business."

"Everything about you is my business."

"Since when?"

"Since you're going to be my wife."

Those words ringing in my ears, I sit there with my heart in my throat.

As if sensing I'm on the verge of total mental collapse, Callum releases my wrist, leans back in his chair, and takes a sip of whiskey. He thinks for a moment, then begins to talk in a low, soothing voice.

"I understand this is strange. If I were in your shoes, I'd be skeptical too. But my offer is real. The night I overheard you with your employees at Jameson's, I was having dinner with a woman I didn't like. She's a model, and very beautiful, and so self-centered and shallow, it physically hurt me to listen to her speak. Normally, I'd never date someone like that. But knowing the situation with my inheritance, my attorney suggested I meet Alexandra, a friend of his wife's. If you're wondering why I need my attorney to set me up on dates, the reason is that I find it difficult...*very* difficult to connect with most people, mainly because I detest small talk."

"And you're impatient and overbearing."

He glances up at me. I mutter, "Sorry," and chew on the inside of my lip.

After a moment, he nods. "You're correct. I'm both those things."

Surprised he's agreeing with me, I then start to feel like a jerk for pointing out his faults. "I mean, nobody's perfect."

He murmurs, "Almost nobody."

"I don't know what that means."

Looking contemplative now, he gazes at his glass of whiskey and swirls the ice slowly around. "You..." he begins carefully. He stops for a moment, then adds in a husky voice, "Are an unusual person."

On the outside, I'm perfectly still. But on the inside, I vibrate with an emotion I can't name because I've never experienced it before. I wait for him to continue with my heart—and other things—throbbing.

"You're sensitive, but you hate that about yourself, so you try to hide it. You want to be in control of everything and take care of everyone, but the effort exhausts you. You'd never ask for help, however, because your pride won't allow it. You're strong, so everyone relies on you, but you're also lonely, and you worry too much. And you've never had anyone ask you what you wanted to do with your life, because it was already decided for you before you were born. Which makes you resentful, yet also guilt-ridden for that resentment, because you know that all things considered, your life has been much better than most."

He glances up. Our eyes lock. I fight the sudden and unwelcome urge to cry.

"How close did I get?"

I lick my lips and swallow around the lump in my throat. "How do you know all that about me?"

"Because we're so much alike, I could have been talking about myself."

He lets me sit with that bombshell for a moment before continuing.

"And all it took for me to understand that was to listen to you tell your employees you were going to have to close your store. You were devastated. The only thing you could think about was how it would affect them. I sat with one ear on your conversation and the other on the trivial word salad coming out of Alexandra's mouth, and I realized that I wanted to know you. I wanted to help you. And if I was going to be forced to find a wife, that it would be good if she were someone I didn't find repulsive."

I blink. "Wow. You had me right up until the end."

"I said I *didn't* find you repulsive."

"I know this might come as a big shock to you, Romeo, but women don't find it irresistible to be told their best quality is not being repulsive."

"I never said it was your best quality."

We stare into each other's eyes. I'm pretty sure I'm getting ticked off again.

He smirks. "Oh, I see. You want me to tell you I think you're beautiful."

My face turns scalding. I snap, "Don't be an asshole," and jump up from the chair. Then I start to pace back and forth across the living room floor with my hands propped on my hips and my temper flaring.

Watching me, Callum chuckles. "That's one thing we don't have in common."

"Say one word about impulse control, and I'll light you on fire."

"Sit down, Emery."

I throw him a dangerous look. He pats the seat of my chair.

"No."

"Yes. Do it. Now."

I stop pacing and stare at him with my arms folded over my chest and my legs spread apart in full-on warrior woman, don't-fuck-with-me mode.

When he stands and faces me, drawing himself to his full, intimidating height, I take an unthinking step backward. Then I say crossly, "Wait, this is *my* house! You don't get to go all Tarzan on me. Now sit back down, we're not done with this conversation."

His eyes blaze. His jaw tightens. He gives the glass in his hand an aggressive little swirl. Then he walks closer, his burning gaze on mine.

He stops a foot away and stares down at me.

I refuse to step back or even move an inch. I glare at him with my chin lifted, letting him know I'm not one of his servants he can push around.

Just like when I defied him at lunch, into his heated eyes comes a look that I could swear was pride.

He leans down until his mouth is next to my ear. Then he says in a hot, rough voice, "You're something much better than beautiful. And when we're married, I'll tell you what it is."

He pulls away, grabs his suit jacket, and sets his whiskey glass on the table, then walks out my front door, leaving it open to the night.

Ten

A few days later at the store, I'm standing behind the front counter making a list of the pros and cons of marrying an arrogant, rich stranger who not only doesn't love me but whose idea of a compelling compliment is saying I'm nonrepulsive when Viv walks through the door. She's followed by Harper and Taylor, all of whom look like they spent the night crawling through a prison sewer frantically in search of the exit while dodging bullets and being chased by a pack of wolves.

"Holy shit. What happened to you guys?"

Taylor climbs up onto the counter, stretches out on her back, and closes her eyes. She has dark circles under her eyes and a deathly pallor that her all-black ensemble does nothing to improve.

"Girls' night. We hit it a little hard."

I wave the pad of paper over her head, fanning away fumes. "Yeah, I can tell. You smell like you slept in a tequila factory."

Harper says, "We haven't slept. We went from clubbing to an after-hours joint to Mickey Ds for breakfast to here."

Groaning, she collapses into the overstuffed chair near the front window and reclines with her bare legs splayed out and her head hanging over the back. In a miniskirt and flip-flops, her dark hair tangled and her lips chapped, she could be a shipwreck survivor who just washed ashore.

Vivienne, ever the ladylike one in a flowered summer dress that would be pretty if it wasn't so wrinkled and didn't have that big red wine stain down the front, burps politely behind her hand, then grimaces. She leans her elbows on Taylor's thighs and props her chin in her hands.

"Remind me never to mix red wine and fireball shots."

I snort. "And remind me never to go drinking with three amateurs."

From her chair, Harper says weakly, "Not everybody has an iron-clad liver."

"Or a death wish. Why would you girls be mixing alcohol like that? You know better."

There's a pause that feels heavy, then Taylor cracks open her bloodshot eyes and gazes up at me. "I'll tell you, but you have to promise not to freak out."

"Great. Now I *have* to freak out."

She sighs and sits up, crossing her ankles together and cradling her knees. "My mom and stepdad are getting a divorce."

Examining her unhappy expression, I say, "I would've thought that would be good news."

"It is. Except they're selling the house."

"Okay. And?"

"And my mom's moving to Florida."

"*Florida?* Why?"

She runs a hand through her choppy black hair and sighs again. "My grandparents. She's moving in with them to get back on her feet. And I'd rather die than relocate to Sunnyside Retirement Village in Tampa, which means I'm out of a place to live, effective immediately."

Harper chimes in, "Which wouldn't be such a biggie, but now that she's also out of a job—"

"Harper!" snaps Viv. "Be quiet!"

She listlessly waves a hand in the air. "Sorry, Em. I'm not trying to make you feel guilty."

Trying or not, I do. I feel awful that Taylor's in this position because of me. Setting aside the pad of paper, I say, "Don't you have any friends you can stay with while you look for work?"

All three of them stare at me like I've eaten an entire bag of THC gummies.

Taylor isn't exactly Ms. Popularity. In fact, she's probably the most antisocial person I know. The only reason she was so good at her job at Lit Happens is because she loves books so much and can talk to strangers about them. Pretty much all other topics are nonstarters.

Harper says, "I'd have her move in with me, except we don't have an extra bedroom. Even if we did, Cody's sick so much..."

"And I'm allergic to kids," Taylor finishes flatly.

Seeing my dismay, Viv says, "I told her she can stay with me if she wants, but she said no."

"Why would I want to stay with you? I'd be safer living on the streets!"

When Viv sends Taylor an exasperated look, Taylor turns sheepish. "Fuck. Sorry."

I demand, "What does that mean, Viv? You're having problems at your place?"

She scrubs her hands over her face, then drops them to her sides and nods. "Vandalism and stuff." She glances away, lowering her voice. "Somebody keeps throwing rocks through my windows and breaking into the garage. I've already filed a bunch of police reports, but they won't do anything."

Taylor says bitterly, "You have to be dead before the cops do anything. My mom stopped calling them when my stepdad would smack her around, because it would take them forever to show up. When they did, it was always the same pair of sexist douchebags who acted like maybe she had it coming."

I say, "That's awful!"

Taylor shrugs, as if injustice is the way of the world.

I sometimes can't believe that poor girl is only twenty-one years old. She has the air of someone who's been dealing with heavy shit for centuries.

Viv says, "So I need to find a new place. Only the place I'm in now is under rent control, so it's super cheap..."

When she bites her lip, I realize she didn't intend to reveal that. She didn't want to make me feel worse than I already do.

But of course I feel worse, considering I know that first and last month's rent plus a security deposit on a new apartment anywhere in LA that isn't rent controlled will run her at the very least ten grand.

Which I know she doesn't have.

And can't save up for because she's out of a job.

Because her boss is a fucking loser.

When my eyes well with moisture, Viv runs around to my side of the counter and seizes my hands. Sounding dismayed, she cries, "No! Don't be upset! None of this is your fault, Em!"

"Good fucking going, Viv," says Taylor in disgust. "You made her cry."

"You're the one who started it!"

Harper rises from the dead to shuffle toward us at the counter. "Nobody's crying without me. If anybody here has a good reason to cry, it's this girl. My cheap son-of-a-bitch ex-husband is taking me back to court to reduce his already miniscule childcare payments! What does he think I'm supposed to take care of my son with, my good looks?"

When Viv and Taylor glare at her in outrage, she stops where she is, makes a face, and pulls her shoulders up around her ears. "Oops."

So that's why they all had to go on a drinking binge.

I've ruined their lives.

Sabine and Murph have probably already carried out the suicide pact I imagine they made after that depressing dinner at Jameson's.

I'm about to cover my face with my hands and burst into

tears, but at that exact moment, Callum McCord walks through the front door.

He stops in the entry, looks at the one emotional and three bedraggled women staring at him, and produces a smile so blindingly gorgeous, we all suck in a collective breath.

"Good morning, ladies. Please pardon the interruption."

Vivienne looks him up and down, her eyes wide and her lips parted. Harper stares at him with obvious lust, as if he's a new Birkin bag. Even Taylor looks dazzled, blinking like a vampire in daylight.

Accustomed to stunning females into silence, Callum smiles wider. "I have some paperwork to drop off for Emery."

In no particular hurry, he swaggers toward us.

Today, he's in a deep blue suit that was probably handmade in Italy by a group of virgin monks and flown across the Atlantic on the back of a unicorn. His hair is perfectly combed. His beard is perfectly trimmed. His aura of sexual magnetism is perfectly devastating.

He stops on the other side of the counter and looks at Taylor sitting there. Noticing the tattoo on her exposed shoulder, he reads it aloud. "Whatever our souls are made of, his and mine are the same."

He looks into her eyes, then says softly, "Bronte's a favorite of mine too. Not that anyone could love a monster like Heathcliff in real life, but what's a good book if not an escape from that very thing?"

Taylor's tattoo doesn't include the name of the author who wrote that quote.

Which means that Callum not only knows one of the greatest works of classical literature—a novel written by a feminist before there was such a thing and considered by many to be the greatest love story of all time—*he knows it by heart.*

If the sound of ovaries screaming was audible, we'd all be deafened.

Two spots of pink appear on Taylor's pale cheeks. Her voice hoarse, she says, "Yeah."

Satisfied he's seared her frontal cortex so badly, she'll never be able to produce more than grunts ever again, Callum turns his attention to me.

"Hello, darling." He holds up the manila envelope in his hand. "The contract. I look forward to your feedback."

He sets the envelope on the counter, turns on his heel, and walks out.

When the door has closed behind him and the cloud of testosterone clears, my three friends turn to stare at me.

"Oh, stop gaping at me like that," I say, having gone from weepy to irritated by witnessing yet another Callum McCord slay-the-ladies performance.

Viv breathes, "Who. Was. *That?*"

"A super-hot super baller," says Harper. She lifts a hand to her cheek. "My face is tingling."

"My cooch is tingling," says Taylor, staring after him in wonder. "That dude knows *Wuthering Heights*?" She shakes her head in disbelief. "Maybe there's hope for humanity after all."

I snatch up the envelope and tear it open. "Everybody calm down. He's not that great."

They look at me as if I've lost my mind.

"You guys, seriously. Just because he's rich, attractive, dresses well, and has read *Wuthering Heights* doesn't mean he's all that."

Taylor says drily, "Pretty sure that's exactly what it means, dumbass."

"No, it doesn't, because he's also arrogant."

I get no response. Everyone continues to look at me like I'm speaking a foreign language. Obviously, they require more evidence.

"And impatient."

Nothing. Nada. Crickets.

I say louder, "And inflexible. Plus, he always thinks he's right!"

"Duh," says Taylor, laughing. "He's a man. He's still a fine piece of ass, though."

"Wait, don't tell me you *like* him? You don't like anyone!"

"I like him enough to peg him on the kitchen floor."

"What does 'peg' mean? Have sex with?"

Her smile is condescending.

"Forget it. I don't want to know."

"What's that contract he was talking about?" asks Viv, edging closer and eyeing the paperwork in my hands.

"Yeah," says Harper. "And why did he call you 'darling' if you hate him so much?"

"I didn't say I hated him. I just think he's a lunatic, that's all. As for the contract..."

I slide the sheaf of papers out of the envelope and look at the top page. "It's for our marriage."

Silence.

After a moment, Viv says tentatively, "You're getting married?"

Taylor says disbelievingly, "You're getting married?"

And Harper says loudly, "*You're getting married?* To *him*?"

"I haven't decided yet. He is offering me ten million dollars, though. And you should see the ring! It's bigger than my first car."

Three pairs of eyes bulge as they stare at me.

I sigh, flipping through the pages. "It's a long story."

"Fuck yes!" says Taylor, swinging her legs around so they dangle off the edge of the counter. "It's story time, girls."

I can tell by the way they're all salivating that I won't be getting off the hook until I give them something, so I grudgingly relent. "Fine. I'll give you the CliffsNotes version." I briefly sum up my encounters and conversations with Callum so far, then roll my eyes at the expressions on their faces.

"I know. It's totally weird, right?"

"Weird?" repeats Harper with a dry laugh. "No, Em. It's not weird. It's *amazing*."

"So you'd say yes?"

"Are you kidding me? I'd say yes, then climb that man like he was a tree and fuck him silly!"

"Same," says Taylor, nodding.

I look at Vivienne. Appearing disturbed, she thinks for a moment. "I admit it's tempting. But what about love?"

"What about it?" demands Harper, who's now draped over the countertop on the other side of Taylor. "Love is overrated, in my opinion, and an unreliable basis for something as serious as marriage. I was madly in love with Chad, and look where that got me."

Taylor nods. "My mom was madly in love with my stepdad too. All it got her was a broken heart and some broken bones to go along with it. The only love that works is in books."

Vivienne says, "You guys are wrong. Not all relationships end up like that. Love is the only thing that really matters."

Harper sighs. "Says the girl who's never been in love before. Call me in a few years after you've had your heart broken several times, and we'll have a good laugh about how naïve you were."

Vivienne crosses her arms and leans back against the counter. "Well, I still believe in love. And I wouldn't marry someone for his money."

I say, "So two votes for, one against."

"What does Dani think about all this?" Harper asks.

"She's on team Marry for Money."

Vivienne insists, "It's a bad idea. What happens if you marry this guy, then in a year you meet the love of your life?"

I look at the paperwork in my hands. "I don't know, but I'm sure there's something in here about that. Callum's nothing if not thorough."

Harper says, "The more likely scenario is that they'll get married, then she'll fall in love with *him*." She sends me a meaningful look. "And I think we can all agree that a guy that rich and good-looking could never be faithful. He has too many options."

I'm disturbed by the thought of being emotionally attached

to Callum. That would be like being in love with some exotic zoo animal that was always trying to escape from its cage and eat me.

"I'm not falling in love with anybody. And after what I went through with my last few relationships, I honestly hope I never will."

Harper's expression darkens. "That reminds me. We saw Ben last night."

Stunned, I stare at her. My heart starts pounding. "*My* Ben? Mr. Disappearing Act?"

"Yeah."

"Where?"

"At the club we went to, this new place in the Valley. He was there with a couple of his buddies."

I'm so shocked by this news, I can't form a coherent response.

After a serious year-long relationship, Ben broke up with me without a word of explanation, blocked my phone number, moved without telling me where he was going, and left me reeling in hurt and confusion, thinking maybe he was entering the witness protection program because that was the only logical explanation for his actions. And the whole time he's been living in the San Fernando Valley, not even an hour away?

"Did he see you?"

"Yeah, though it looked like he wished he hadn't. I could tell he didn't want to talk to me."

"You *talked* to him?"

"I wasn't about to let the opportunity pass to tell him what an ass he was for the way he left you! So yeah, I talked to him."

My heart pounds so hard, I have to press my hand over my chest to catch my breath. "What did he say?"

Harper straightens and runs her hands through her disheveled hair. "After I gave him a piece of my mind, he just stood there all weird and nervy for a minute. Then he said he was sorry, but he had to go."

I can tell there's more by the way she and Taylor exchange a fleeting glance. "What are you leaving out?"

She hesitates, but then says, "He turned around and walked away, but after a few steps, he turned back. And he said, 'Tell her to watch out.' Then he walked away again. I didn't see him after that. I think he left the club."

I'm flabbergasted. "He *threatened* me?"

Taylor says, "It doesn't mean anything. He's a lying piece of shit. He was playing games, that's all."

Vivienne nods in agreement. "Plus, he was probably drunk."

But Ben never drinks enough to get drunk. At least he didn't when we were together. And why would he choose to say that, of all things?

I think I might ask Callum if he'd let me borrow his private detective. I want to find out where Ben's living and go knock on his door.

No, I don't. What am I thinking? He left me! He broke my heart!

"Uh-oh," says Viv, watching me. "The gears are turning."

"I told you we shouldn't say anything about it," grouses Harper, who's also watching me worriedly.

They start to bicker, but I tune them out, my mind consumed with thoughts of Ben. I can't believe that after all this time, he was just a short drive away. And now he's warning me to watch out? What does that even mean?

I try to be angry, reminding myself that he was a jerk for leaving me without any explanation. If nothing else, he should've at least had the courtesy of giving me closure. The way he broke things off was cruel.

Despite all that, a feeling of unease settles in my stomach. For all his shortcomings, Ben wasn't a liar. And no matter what Taylor thinks of him, he also wasn't one for playing games.

I'm not sure what I'm going to do, but I know I need to do something. Sighing, I look down at the paperwork in my hands.

First, I have to decide whether or not I'm going to marry Callum McCord.

Eleven

After the girls leave, I conduct three hours of forensic research on Callum on the internet, but still don't have a solid view of who he is or what makes him tick. There's only so much information about a person's character you can glean from articles about charity donations and business mergers, product lines and expansion plans.

One thing I find peculiar is that in all the articles written about his family and their business, none includes a first-person account.

Not a single McCord has ever gone on the record about anything.

They don't speak to the press. They don't grant interviews. They smile for the cameras as they come and go from various parties and functions, but they never stop to chat with the photographers or reporters who call their names.

I mull over what he said to me at the restaurant about being good at keeping secrets.

"With the position my family is in, we never know who we can trust. So we don't trust anyone."

It would be impossible for the CEO of a publicly-traded firm to avoid commenting on the state of the company like that, but the privately-owned McCord Media isn't beholden to shareholders for reports.

They run their multibillion-dollar international empire in total silence.

Half of me admires that.

The other half wonders what they've got to hide.

When I finish data mining the internet, I review Callum's contract.

There's a lot of confusing technical legalese and Latin terms that I have to google, in addition to long passages concerning marital assets and financial arrangements. But the section that really grabs my attention is one ominously titled Irrevocability.

Boiled down, it says that the terms of the contract can't be voided after marriage, nor can they be challenged or changed by either party for any reason.

I suppose I could view it as an advantage. Callum couldn't back out on his financial promises to me, which is the only reason I'm entertaining the idea of this wacko deal.

On the other hand, there's something scary about that word.

Irrevocable.

It's disturbingly permanent.

The other odd thing is that there's no mention of what happens in the event of a divorce. I'm no expert on prenups, but it seems to me that's their main purpose.

As I sit at my desk pondering that, my cell phone rings. Distracted, I answer.

"Hello, darling," says Callum, his voice throaty. "What do you think of the paperwork?"

I groan in exasperation. "Stop calling me darling. And could you give me more than five minutes to go over it, please?"

"Why?"

"Because I'm not familiar with all this legal terminology. I've got to find an attorney who'll work for bookmarks to help me understand it all."

"No, I meant why do you want me to stop calling you darling?"

I lean back in my desk chair, close my eyes, and rub my temple. "Please try not to aggravate me already. It's only been ten seconds. And by the way, where's all the stuff about what happens in the event we divorce? I think you forgot a few pages."

"Nothing was forgotten."

I frown. "Then why isn't it in here?"

"Because there won't be a divorce."

I wait for him to laugh and tell me he's joking, but I should've known better. Callum McCord isn't a man who makes jokes. Which is probably because he doesn't think anything is funny.

Except me, when I'm telling him I haven't thought about having sex with him.

"You sound pretty confident, there, billionaire."

"I am."

"Pardon me for saying so, but that's just dumb."

"There aren't any clauses about abuse or adultery either. Can you guess why?"

"I see where you're going with that, but your logic is all wrong. Just because you leave something *out* of a contract doesn't mean it won't happen. Contracts are supposed to provide for all the contingencies, not pretend they don't exist."

In an amused drawl, he says, "I see. I didn't realize you were such an expert."

"Don't get sassy. I've got that covered for both of us. Let's go back to the part about abuse and adultery."

"What about them?"

I think of his intensity and the way he always has to stop to control himself when he's riled up in that unnerving way of his. "For starters, are you violent?"

His voice drops an octave. "Violence is a part of human nature."

I scoff. "Nice sidestep, billionaire. You just made me think you're a wife beater. Try again."

"I'm not a wife beater."

He's telling me what I want to hear, but somehow, it's still unsatisfying. "But you've never had a wife."

"Not yet, I haven't."

"Hold on, now I'm even more confused! Just tell me the truth. Do you smack women around or not?"

"No. Of course not. If I did, every news outlet in the world would've reported on it."

He makes a good point. Plus, that little huff of disbelief he made right before he answered was genuine. I can tell when he thinks I'm being ridiculous just by the tone of his exhalation.

It's like we're married already.

"I want sections about abuse and adultery."

"Why? Are you planning on beating me and cheating with the gardener, darling?"

Gritting my teeth, I say, "I can say with confidence that I won't cheat with the gardener, *darling*, but on the matter of beating you, the jury is still out."

I hear a noise that could be muffled laughter. Then he comes back on, sounding cool and composed. "All right. I'll have sections regarding abuse and adultery included. Anything else?"

"Yes. I want you to hire my best friend's husband to work for your company."

"Done. Next?"

I blink in surprise. "Don't you even want to know what he does?"

"I don't care what he does. We'll find a position for him. And we'll pay him double his former salary."

That's too important to go unchallenged. "Oh, yeah? What if he was making a million a year?"

Callum sighs.

"Okay, fine, he wasn't making a million a year. I just don't understand how you can promise to hire someone you don't know anything about."

In a hot, dark voice, he says, "Because my wife asked me to. And I'll give her anything she wants."

I sit there breathing unevenly and marveling at the gymnastics my heart is doing inside my chest, until he prompts, "Are you still there?"

"Most of me. My brain went on vacation."

"Why is it so hard for you to believe I'll give you whatever you want?"

I laugh. "Gee, I don't know. All the handsome rich guys who propose marriage to me over oysters say the same thing."

His tone sharpens. "Handsome?"

"Oh God. Here we go again."

"Don't sound so disgusted."

"Why must you always be hunting for compliments from me? Isn't having every other woman in the world constantly slobbering over you enough?"

The silence that follows is electric. Then, in a voice both soft and dangerous, he says, "No. I don't care what other women think of me. Because they're not you."

Damn, he's good at that. I swallow nervously and fidget in my chair. "I have something to say."

"You can just say it. You don't have to make an announcement first."

His reply is imperious. If only I could reach through the phone and strangle him.

"There's no need to try to dazzle me with the whole sexy smoke show. I'm under no illusions that this arrangement is anything other than a business deal, so you don't have to flirt."

Another electric pause. We're really starting to rack them up in this conversation.

"Emery."

"Yes, Callum?"

"Do you want to have sex with me?"

I groan and slump over on the desk, pressing my forehead to the wood.

"That's not an answer."

"No, that was the sum of my feelings about the question."

"Do you?"

"I can't believe you're asking me that."

"Why not? It's a perfectly reasonable thing for a husband to ask his wife."

"Yeah, except we're not husband and wife yet!"

He pounces on that like a tiger, saying slyly, "*Yet?*"

I sit upright and glare at the poster of the actor Sam Heughan as Jamie Fraser in the television version of *Outlander* hanging on the wall across from my desk.

"You know what we need to put into this contract? A section about mental health care. Because if I were to marry you, I'd need massive therapy on an ongoing basis to deal with the strain of being married to such a pain in the ass."

He chuckles. "That's another thing we have in common."

I say flatly, "Put in a clause about murder being an acceptable way for me to end the marriage."

"Darling," he purrs, "you're so adorable when you're angry."

"Stop being flirty. And stop calling me darling! It drives me mad!"

"I know it does. Why do you think I do it?"

"You know what? My blood pressure can't handle any more of this conversation. I'll call you back when I've stopped plotting ways to hide your dead body."

I disconnect, toss my phone onto the desk, and sit there seething until the urge to dismember a certain cocky billionaire passes.

Which is exactly when Callum calls again. His timing is uncanny.

I pick up with a terse, "What?"

He snickers. "You forgot to tell me you love me before you hung up."

I close my eyes and grip the phone so hard, it's a miracle the case doesn't shatter.

"All right, I'll be serious. Are you listening?"

I mutter, "Unfortunately, yes."

"There's nothing in the contract about divorce because if you agree to marry me, you also agree to never leave me."

"I want to leave every time I spend more than ten minutes with you. How am I supposed to promise I'll stay with you forever?"

"Simple."

When he doesn't continue, I say, "Waiting over here in nail-biting suspense, Hitchcock."

"Because you're going to make a vow," he says softly. "A very serious vow that includes the words 'Until death do us part.' And every time you think about leaving me, you'll remember those words and that vow, and it will stop you."

"I hate to break the news to you, but thousands of other couples make the same vow every day all around the world, and they end up getting a divorce later."

"We're not like other people. Our marriage won't be like theirs either."

He says that as if it's written in stone, like some bearded guy in robes descended from a mountaintop carrying a granite tablet with the words engraved on the front.

I demand, "What exactly makes you think we're so different from everyone else? I don't even know you! No, be quiet, that wasn't an invitation to speak. Now listen, Callum, I'm trying my best to take you seriously and not call the nearest asylum to try to get you committed, but you have to work with me here. Stop playing around with me and be straight."

"If you insist."

"I do!"

"Then here it is. I'm going to give you ten million dollars to do with as you wish. *Ten million dollars.* In return, you'll marry me *and* give me your word you'll never leave me. I require a wife to get my inheritance. If I divorce, that inheritance goes away. That's it. That's the bottom line. Everything else is just details."

"So your father's going to keep this inheritance thing hanging over your head forever, huh?"

"Yes."

"You didn't tell me that before."

"I'm telling you now."

"What else have you been leaving out?"

He sighs heavily.

"We might as well put it all on the table now. You can't expect me to make an informed decision if I don't know where all the skeletons are buried."

"You know what I find interesting?"

I mutter, "I can hardly wait to hear."

"Aside from your caustic under-the-breath comments, of course, is that you have any hesitation at all."

I laugh long and loud at that. "Gee, love yourself much?"

His voice hardens. "You misunderstand. This isn't about me. It's about the current position you're in. It's about the state of your life. Or should I say, the *sad* state of it. I've known felons with better prospects than you."

I grimace at the poster of Jamie Fraser. He smolders back at me, all Scottish and heroic. *He'd* never been such a dick.

"Wow, that was cutthroat, billionaire. I see you've been sharpening your knives."

Callum breezes right past that. "I also find it fascinating that if you find me so narcissistic, arrogant, and irritating, why you don't simply ask to have separate bedrooms so you won't be bothered by my presence at all."

Strangely deflated by the idea, I sit slowly back in my chair. "Separate bedrooms?" I repeat uncertainly.

"I told you I'd give you whatever you wanted. All you need to do is ask."

He's giving me an out on the sex thing. I can't decide if that's what I wanted or not.

Wait, does that mean I'm supposed to be celibate for the rest of my life just to pay my bills?

I'm outraged until I remember that he's not the one asking me to be celibate. He's saying I can have whatever I want, including separate bedrooms if I decide he's too aggravating to fuck.

I should test him.

"What if I asked to have a boyfriend on the side?"

"As I said, you can have anything you want. As long as you were extremely discreet, of course."

There's an unfamiliar edge to his voice that I can't identify, but he sounds sincere. More testing is in order to be sure.

I make my tone flippant. "I guess we don't need that adultery clause after all."

"Then I won't have the attorney include it."

His answer is crisp and businesslike, and I'm completely unsatisfied with all of it. What kind of man wouldn't care if his wife found herself a boyfriend?

A man who doesn't love his wife, that's who.

We've arrived at the biggest catch in the whole scenario.

If I marry him, my future will be free of financial worry, but also devoid of love. There won't be any hand-holding or romantic dinners, no date nights, inside jokes, or special songs. I'll be entering into a business agreement that will solve every one of my problems, with the price of admission being loneliness.

Which, let's be honest, I already am.

Except I could cry in my Lamborghini instead of my beat-up Volkswagen, which sounds a lot better.

I sit thinking for a moment, until Callum's patience comes to an end. He growls, "Emery!"

"Oh, hang on to your hat, Cal. I'm thinking."

A dangerous noise rumbles through his chest. "What did I tell you about calling me that?"

"Something I ignored, obviously. So would you have girlfriends on the side too?"

He hesitates. "I think it's best if we adopted a don't-ask-don't-tell policy about that. Just to keep things businesslike."

I say tartly, "Then I guess you won't be calling me darling after the wedding. You'll save that for your girlfriends."

"Is that a tone of jealousy I detect?"

"No, of course not."

Translated, that means yes, definitely. I'm giving myself whiplash over here. I'm about to set a personal record for number of lies in one conversation.

"You can rely on me to be discreet. I have no desire to embarrass you publicly, nor do I wish to cause any problems that might endanger my inheritance. As long as we conduct ourselves with respect for the other, we'll have no problems. Quite frankly, I think the arrangement is ideal for us both."

He sounds so confident. So clearheaded and logical, as if this whole thing makes perfect sense, and I'm the one being unreasonable with all my silly questions and concerns.

It makes me crazy, but if I'm honest with myself, I have to admit...

Maybe I am being unreasonable.

He's offering me everything I could want. Money, power, protection, a way to fix everything that's broken in my life and start over again. Not only for me, but for everyone I love.

Business? Saved.

Lawsuit? Settled.

Huge tax bill? Paid.

Dani and Ryan moving? Canceled.

My employees' problems caused by being out of work? Solved.

He's offering me a magic wand that would make all my problems disappear with one wave.

Bottom line, what he's really offering is salvation.

And never again would I have to deal with the anguish of heartbreak like I did with Ben. Never again would I get my hopes up and invest all my time and energy like I did with my two boyfriends before him before having my heart trampled when they left.

Never again would I get so horribly hurt.

I look at the papers spread over my desk, think hard about what I really want, and realize there's one important thing we haven't discussed that isn't in the contract.

"What about kids? Don't you want a family?"

"Do you?"

"No, I'm asking *you*. And I want you to be honest with me. This is important."

The silence that follows is long and loud. It makes me nervous. Finally, his voice strangely hollow, he says, "No."

"Oh."

"Your turn."

A wild mix of emotions rages through me. Thinking, I draw a slow breath and sit back in the chair as I fiddle with the edge of a page of the contract.

When I've gathered my thoughts, I say, "The truth is, I just always assumed I'd be a mom. I assumed I'd have time to think about it later. But I'm thirty now, so it's technically later. And if my own relationship history is any indicator, finding a father who'd stick around to raise his kids would be a miracle. I'd be better off going to a sperm bank. But I know how difficult being a single mother is, especially when finances are tight."

When I pause, I hear him breathing shallowly. I think I can feel his tension, too, the way he's hanging on every word, but I know that's only my imagination.

"Both my parents are gone. I'm an only child. The only real family I have is Dani and the people who work with me here at Lit Happens. They're what matters to me most, not some possible future baby who doesn't even exist."

As I speak those words, something crystallizes inside me.

These people I love, this family I've created and cherish above everything...I can help them. I can help them *all*.

But only if I marry Callum.

And let's be real. He can't force me to stay married to him. If it turns out to be a nightmare, I'll call one of those celebrity divorce attorneys. This town is so full of them, they're hanging from the palm trees.

I take a deep breath, then release it along with the last of my hesitation.

"Okay, billionaire. You've got yourself a wife."

Twelve

On the other end of the line, there's total silence.

I'm not sure what kind of response I was expecting, but dead air is definitely not it.

I say uncertainly, "Hello? Callum, are you listening?"

Nothing. I move the phone from my ear, look at the screen, see the call ended symbol, and am baffled. I look up at the *Outlander* poster on the wall. "What the fuck, Jamie? Did that smug asshole just hang up on me?"

My Scottish Highlander smolders unhelpfully.

Then an icy wave of horror washes over my body. I inhale sharply. "Wait. Oh God. Was this all some…some kind of…*test*?"

I sit with the phone gripped in my hand and my mind going a million miles per hour with all the awful possibilities of why Callum might have ended the call at the exact moment I agreed to marry him.

Was he only trying to get me to say yes all this time, but he never intended to actually go through with it? Did he make some sort of malicious bet with another rich person to see if he could convince the broke bookworm that he was swooping in like Superman to whisk me away? Was this whole thing just a game, a bit of entertainment, a way for a bored billionaire to pass the hours?

Could he do something like that?

Is he capable of such cruelty?

I recall all the times he smirked at me, how smug and self-satisfied he always seemed, and feel the phone grow hot in my hand.

I drop it onto my desk, then sit and stare at it with wide eyes, willing it to ring.

It refuses.

After twenty minutes of no callback, where I sit frozen at my desk with clammy hands and a pounding heart, I have to admit to myself that as much as I hate the thought of spending the rest of my life in prison, I better get used to the idea.

Because I'm going to kill Callum McCord.

I'm going to kill that arrogant, ruthless, game-playing son of a bitch in some grisly, agonizing manner that will headline the news cycle for months.

"Hello?" a man calls out from the front of the store. "Where are you, darling?"

I'd know that deep voice anywhere. The voice and that sarcastic nickname he insists on calling me. My blood heats instantly from simmering to a rolling boil.

My face hot, I leap to my feet and look wildly around the office for a murder weapon. Then I grab the stapler off my desk and march into the main room...

Where I find Callum standing near the front counter, flanked by two men.

"There's my bride," he says, smiling like a shark. "Why is your face so red?"

I brandish the stapler at him and demand, "Who are they?"

Without looking away from me, he gestures to the man on his left. He's middle-aged, tall and balding, wearing a navy pinstripe double-breasted suit and carrying a leather briefcase. "This is my attorney, William."

He gestures to the other man, a young, preppy-looking guy

who's dressed in beige slacks and a short-sleeved black polo shirt. "And this is Andrew."

Andrew beams at me. "I'm thrilled to meet you, Emery. Callum has told me so much about you."

The way he's smiling at me is disturbing. I suspect he's about to ask me if I have a personal relationship with Jesus.

I snap at him, "Who are you?"

"The McCord family chaplain."

Chaplain? Startled, I look at Callum. His sharky grin grows wider.

"Could you lower the stapler, darling? You look a little unhinged."

I drop my arm to my side, then look back and forth between the three men.

Standing between two mere mortals, Callum's physical beauty is even more pronounced. He's taller than them both, wider through the shoulders, with a more defined jaw and that stupid sculpted nose and those stunning eyes and that animal charisma that pulses off him like a heartbeat.

He's simply all-around, ridiculously gorgeous.

God, that's aggravating.

Everyone seems to be waiting for me to say something, so I go with a haughty "I'm confused. What's happening?"

His voice low and his eyes burning, Callum says, "We're getting married. Or did you already forget that you said yes?"

Married? Now? Is the man completely crazy? Rattled and sweating, my pulse haywire, I declare, "We are *not* getting married."

My outburst doesn't ruffle Callum's feathers. In fact, he seems to enjoy it. He says calmly, "No? Why not?"

I cast around for a reasonable explanation, but my head is spinning and I can't get it to stop. I finally end up shouting, "You hung up on me!"

Chuckling, Callum glances at his attorney. "It's fine. Everything's fine. She has a bit of a temper, that's all."

William gazes at me doubtfully.

"Would you gentlemen please excuse us for a moment? We'll be right back."

Callum crosses to me, takes my arm, and leads me into my office. He closes the door behind us and removes the stapler from my hand. Then he walks to my desk, sits on the edge of it, places the stapler next to the phone, and smiles.

Glaring at him, I say, "Don't you dare grin at me like that. What do you think you're doing?"

"Ah, you're right. Forgive me." He reaches into his suit pocket and extracts a little black velvet box.

The little black velvet box.

He cracks it open, displaying the Easter-egg sized diamond. "You should put it on before we say our vows."

I throw my hands in the air. "What's the matter with you? You hung up on me and left me sitting here thinking it was all a terrible joke!"

"Are you always this dramatic when you're angry? I'm only asking in case I should prepare myself for a lifetime of tiptoeing around the house."

"You're laughing at me."

He chuckles. "I wouldn't dare."

"You are! You just did! You hung up on me when I said I'd be your wife, then you show up a nanosecond later with an attorney and a priest!"

"Chaplain," he corrects matter-of-factly.

"I don't care if he's the damn pope. I can't believe the *nerve* of you."

Callum lowers his head and studies me through narrowed eyes. Then he snaps shut the box, puts it back into his suit pocket, and stands.

"You're upset I'm not giving you a proper wedding. You want a white dress and expensive flowers."

I exhale in aggravation, because not only is he outrageous and overbearing, he's clueless.

"No. I'm upset you didn't act like a normal human and communicate with me after I agreed to marry you. Instead, you hung up on me, then showed up not even half an hour later with your dream team without giving me a word of warning."

I pause to catch my breath and look at him suspiciously. "How did you get here so fast?"

"I was in the neighborhood."

I scoff. "For such a rich guy, you spend an awful lot of time cruising bad neighborhoods. Did your attorney and priest just happen to be in the neighborhood too?"

"Chaplain. No, I called them as soon as I got off the phone with you."

"And they both dropped everything to run to my crappy little bookstore in the middle of the day?"

"Of course. I'm Callum McCord. I could've called them at midnight on Christmas Eve and had the same result. And as soon as you have my ring on your finger, and you're sleeping in my bed, you'll have the same power."

Blood pulses in my cheeks. Only this time, it's not from anger. It's from hearing him say "sleeping in my bed."

I can't help but imagine it. Us, naked under the sheets together, his hands roving all over my body, his lips on my skin. What would he be like as a lover? Rough? Tender? Dirty? Sweet?

Probably all of the above, if my surging estrogen levels are any indicator.

His gaze sharpens. In a husky voice, he says, "What are you thinking right now?"

I clear my throat and attempt a disinterested expression. "Nothing."

Head cocked and eyes fierce, Callum moves slowly toward me. "Do I need to put a section in the contract about lying, Emery? Because I don't like it when you lie to me."

"Don't be ridiculous," I say nervously. "And go stand over there. You're crowding me."

"How odd. You've never seemed intimidated by me before. What could it be that has you so flustered?"

"I'm not flustered. Or intimidated. And why are you such a close talker, billionaire? That's far enough."

He's only about two feet away from me and showing no signs of stopping. I back up a few steps before coming into contact with the closed office door. Flattening myself against it, I watch in panic as Callum advances on me like the Roman army.

When he's inches away, gazing down into my eyes with the heat of his body warming mine, he murmurs, "I said 'sleeping in my bed,' and you melted."

"I'm not butter. I don't melt."

He leans closer until his lips brush the edge of my ear. "Do you want to sleep with me? Is that what has you so wound up?"

I stand there silently trembling for a moment, on the verge of shouting *Yes!* but then give myself a mental slap across the face.

If I'm going to sign a wedding contract that binds me to this man from here to eternity, I need to be clearheaded. For all I know, this is a ploy to get me to overlook some important clause in the paperwork.

I flatten my hands against his broad chest and push. When he doesn't budge, I look up at him and set my jaw.

He says, "What are you doing?"

"Pushing you away."

He glances down at my puny hands. "It doesn't seem to be working."

"Stop being horrible and stand back."

"Why would I want to do that? Watching you work yourself into a froth up close is highly amusing."

"I'm not frothing!"

"You're unusually weak for someone with such a hot temper."

"I'm not weak, and I'm not angry. Now *move*."

Smiling at me, he murmurs, "Say please."

I almost drop my hands right then and use them to tear all my hair out. Instead, I slide them up his chest on impulse and wrap them around his neck.

His big, warm, strong, stupid neck.

Gritting my teeth and staring into his eyes, I say, "I don't care how many people you can summon at midnight on Christmas Eve to do your bidding, demon spawn, I'm not one of them. And if you don't move away right now, we'll see exactly how weak I am, because I'm gonna start squeezing. I won't stop until you're passed out on the floor."

Into his eyes comes a look of such hot excitement and pure animal savagery, I almost pee my pants in terror.

He grips my hips, yanks me against him, and growls, "You better make sure you squeeze hard, schoolgirl, because if I'm not passed out in five seconds, I'll throw you onto that desk, tear off your panties, and give you what we both know you need."

Stunned, I stare at him with my mouth hanging open, my heart racing, and my nipples growing hard.

Against my pelvis, his erection throbs.

He drops his blistering gaze to my mouth. Breathing erratically, he licks his lips. His fingers dig deeper into the flesh of my hips. I'm either about to burst into flames or be devoured.

I say breathlessly, "Here's where I remind you that you said you'd give me anything I wanted. Remember that?"

Still staring hungrily at my mouth, he growls, "I remember."

"Good. Because what I want right now is for you to step back."

His hot gaze flashes up to mine. "You scared of me, little lamb?"

"Call me a farm animal one more time, and your testicles pay the price. Step back."

Instead of doing that, he resumes staring at my mouth like it's a ripe apple he's dying to sink his teeth into. The heat of his body burns me right through my clothes. He's huge, hot, and immoveable, and if I don't get away from him within seconds, I'm liable to crack and crush my mouth to his.

That can't happen.

Despite the heat pulsing between my thighs, I can't kiss Callum. If I do, and it's as good as I suspect it would be, I'll end up liking it. And if I like it, I'll want it to happen again. Multiple times. And what starts out as kissing turns into me catching feelings, which inevitably winds up with me having a broken heart.

The last few times I tripped and fell in love, it ended in disaster.

This time I'm going to keep my head straight, keep my panties on, and stay on the safe side of love by marrying a man for his money.

I look into his eyes and enunciate each word. "Step. Back. Or the deal. Is off."

He says hotly, "You don't want me to move."

"I really do."

"Don't fucking lie to me!"

Why does he have to smell so good? Why does he have to feel so good? And why, oh why, does he have to pester me to tell him the truth when we both know this will all be so much easier if I lie?

Oh, yeah. Because his bloodthirsty ego demands every woman within shouting distance throw themselves at his feet and beg to have his pretty, rich, entitled babies.

I smile sweetly up at him. "For every second you stand in that spot, I'll add a million dollars to the contract."

Thunderclouds descend over his head. He glowers at me, his jaw muscle popped out and his brows drawn together.

Oh, the thrill it gives me, making him mad. It's perverse, but it's good for him. The man needs someone in his life who doesn't cower or swoon in his presence.

In fact, I'm probably doing a public service. I should get a tax credit for this.

"I could do this all day, billionaire. I'll just keep on counting my money until you decide to move."

A low, dangerous sound rumbles through his chest. It rumbles louder when I whisper, "You're up another ten. Darling."

He wrests himself away from me, whirls around, shoves his hands into his hair, and stands with his back to me and his hands on his head. He exhales hard.

The loss of his body heat chills me. Unsteady, I wrap my arms around myself and try to shake off the fog of sexual desire clouding my vision.

It's a good thing I wore a bra today, because otherwise the front of my blouse would be shredded by my nipples. The damn things are so hard, they could etch glass.

When Callum turns back to face me, he's got himself under control. His expression is placid. The fire in his eyes has cooled. The only thing that remains of his unexpected excitement is his disheveled hair, sticking on end where he tugged on it.

He says calmly, "Twenty million it is. Now let's go sign the paperwork before one of us does something we'll regret."

He grabs my wrist and doesn't let go of it until I'm standing behind the counter in the front of the shop with the contract in front of me and a pen in my hand.

Thirteen

With Callum, William, and a beaming Andrew standing on the other side of the counter, I gaze down at the contract, hesitating.

A man walks through the door. Before he can say a word, Callum crosses to him, shoves him back out, slams the door in his face, and locks it.

"Hey! That was a customer!"

"Not anymore. Sign the fucking paperwork."

Exasperated, I look at William. "I need to add a few things to this."

William opens his mouth to answer, but Callum snaps, "You'll get your money. Just sign it."

Undeterred, I say, "I can see living with you is going to be a laugh a minute. What about the job for my friend's husband?"

Callum glares at me from across the shop. His jaw clenched, he says, "It's in."

"Really?"

"Yes. Look on the last page."

I flip to the last page. Sure enough, he's already updated the contract to include a job for Ryan, his salary to be double that of his last position.

When the hell did that happen? On the drive over?

Before I can ask, Callum snaps, "Satisfied?"

Looking at his glower, I say, "I know you're desperate to secure that fat inheritance of yours, but why are you so angsty all of a sudden? And by the way, don't we need a marriage license for this thing to be legal?"

"I already got the license! Everything's handled! All you have to do is *sign*!"

I sigh and look at William again. Since Callum's throwing a temper tantrum, I need to deal with an adult.

"What about the escrow account? I'd like to have some proof this money I'm signing my life away for actually exists."

William nods in approval. "Of course. Let me pull it up."

From the briefcase on the counter he produced the new contract from, he withdraws a laptop. After clicking around on it for a moment, he turns it to face me.

The screen shows a brokerage account with a balance of ten million dollars.

When I glance up at him, lips pursed, Callum says tersely, "William, transfer another ten to the account."

I have to give the attorney credit. If I were in his shoes, I'd either laugh or cry at my client's whimsical approach to money. Throw ten million here, toss another ten million there, no big whoop. But William simply nods and does as he's instructed, turning the computer toward him again and clicking around efficiently.

"Complete, sir."

"Show her."

William turns the screen to face me. I look at it for a moment, then say, "But how do I know this is even for me?"

Callum closes his eyes and stands with his face turned toward the ceiling, eyes closed, breathing deeply with his hands clenched to fists by his side.

William says gently, "At the top right side of the screen, you'll notice the account says FBO Emery Eastwood."

"So it does. What does FBO mean?"

"For benefit of. The account is being managed in a custodial capacity only until you sign the contract. Then the funds transfer to an irrevocable trust, of which you are the sole beneficiary."

Just to make sure I'm understanding correctly, I press him. "Meaning once I have the money, he can never take it back?"

Callum thunders, "For fuck's sake, woman! *Sign the contract!*"

William and I grimace at each other. Andrew is beginning to look pale.

Leaning closer to William, I whisper, "Could you cross out the dollar amount on this line here and write the new one in? Just so we're all on the same page about everything."

"Very good," he whispers back. He takes the pen from me and scribbles the number twenty over the ten he scratched out.

"And where are the trust documents? Don't I need to sign those?"

In the background, Callum groans. William grimaces again. Andrew looks as if he's about to make the sign of the cross over his chest and start tossing around holy water.

Apparently, these two have never seen their boss lose his temper before.

Or maybe they have, and that's what they're really afraid of.

Sweat beading his forehead, William whispers, "No, but I have a copy of that for you here."

He withdraws a thick sheaf of papers bound with a blue cover from his briefcase and hands it to me. I flip open the cover, review the first few pages, then glance at Callum standing in obvious agony near the door.

Without saying anything, I tap a finger on the part of the page where it describes the trust's assets. William sees where I'm indicating and nods. He scratches out the ten, writes in twenty, then initials above his change.

I have no idea if that's legally binding or not, but as it appears Callum is about to explode with impatience, it will have to do. If I push him too far, he might change his mind and call off the whole thing.

Plus, if we wind up in court, I've got Andrew as a witness. I doubt a chaplain could lie under oath, what with him being a personal assistant to God.

I close the trust binder, inhale a deep breath, and say a silent prayer. "All right. I'm ready."

Callum stalks over to me, rips the velvet box out of his pocket, pulls the diamond out of it, and tosses the box over his shoulder. Grabbing my left hand, he jams the ring onto my ring finger.

"Ow!"

"You can complain all you want later," he says darkly, keeping my hand in a death grip when I try to pull away. He turns to Andrew and snaps his fingers. "Let's do this."

After that, everything happens so fast, it's a blur. Andrew says some words. Callum and I repeat "I do" when necessary. Another document is shoved in front of me—the marriage license, I think —and Callum jabs his finger on the line where I'm supposed to sign.

Then it's over, and we're married.

"Congratulations, Mrs. McCord!" says Andrew. "How do you feel?"

Dazed, I say, "Like I just got run over by a truck."

Callum growls, "Give it a few minutes, it'll get worse," and grabs me. This time, instead of shoving fine jewelry on my hand, he swings me up into his arms.

Yelping in surprise, I try to wriggle away and escape, but he holds me tight against his body as he strides toward the door.

"What are you doing?" I cry, panicking.

"Taking my wife home."

He makes it sound as if a dungeon and a pair of shackles are in my immediate future.

"William! Andrew! Help me!"

They stare after me with matching expressions of apprehension as Callum somehow manages to unlock the front door while carrying a squirming woman in his arms. Then we're out in the heat of the summer day, moving toward his sleek black sedan, which is pulling up at the curb.

The driver jumps out and opens the door for us as we reach it. Callum stuffs me inside the car and follows, slamming the door shut behind us.

He turns to me, smiling that lethal smile of his, every inch of him predatory.

Holding up a hand, I say, "Stop!"

It works like one of those harsh commands a professional dog trainer shouts at a Doberman. Callum freezes in place, bristling.

My heart pounds so hard, I can't catch my breath. I'm disoriented and shaky, and will probably be diagnosed with PTSD after that clusterfuck of a wedding I just endured. And now I'm trapped in the back of a car with the crazy billionaire who wifed me and who seems as if he's about to gobble me up like the wolf that ate Red Riding Hood's grandma.

On the best of days, my brain works at about ten percent capacity. Today, that wimp quit for good and left anxiety in charge.

The car pulls away from the curb as my new husband and I sit in the back seat, staring at each other in crackling silence.

I manage to say, "What's happening?"

"We're going home."

"Your home?"

"Our home."

"But...I'm working."

"Not anymore, you're not."

His breathing is irregular. His eyes are burning. Every atom of his energy is focused on me.

I swallow nervously. "Why are you acting so weird?"

His smile is beautiful and terrifying. "Because your favorite word in the English language is no. But I just got you to say yes."

"Oh, I get it. You think you won, huh?"

"Whose ring is that on your finger?"

"Don't be smug. You know I absolutely *hate* it when you're smug."

"And I hate it when you pretend you don't want me, so we're even."

"I don't want you. You're the worst!"

Low and utterly pleased, his chuckle sends tingles up my spine. He drawls, "Darling wife, you have no idea."

Then he sits back in his seat, smooths his hands over his hair, and chuckles again, as if he's enjoying some delicious secret.

It freaks me the fuck out.

"Callum?"

Without glancing my way, he says, "Yes?"

"Am I going to regret this?"

"If you do, I'm sure you can console yourself with your bank balance."

"That's not funny."

He chuckles again. "I thought it was."

I shoot a nervous glance toward the driver. He's got his damn black sunglasses on again, so I can't see his eyes. I can't tell if he knows I'm about to be thrown into a gator pit that Callum has in his backyard or if he knows Callum's idea of fun is terrifying broke bookstore owners.

Except, wait. I'm not broke anymore.

I'm rich.

I just married a billionaire, which makes *me* a billionaire too.

My imagination marinates in that bizarre new reality until Callum says, "Wait until you see the house. You'll feel even better then."

I huff out a breath, lean back against the seat, fold my arms over my chest, and mutter, "It would be great if you could stop reading my mind."

"But then how would I know what you're thinking? Considering half of what comes out of your mouth are lies, I need some way of getting the truth."

"I'm not lying."

Another chuckle, this one scarier than the others. He turns his head and pins me in a heated stare. "The next time you lie to me, there will be consequences."

I narrow my eyes at him and pretend I'm more angry than nervous. "Yeah? Like what?"

His voice throaty, he says, "Try me and find out."

My cheeks flush with heat. "Is that a threat?"

He holds my gaze and merely smiles.

I'm beginning to think I might have jumped out of the frying pan right into the fire. *Did I just legally promise myself to a psychopath? Oh God, what have I done?*

"It's not as bad as all that," Callum says, turning away. After a beat, he chuckles again. "Actually, it is."

My heart palpitates madly. My hands shake, my skin is clammy, and my stomach tightens to knots. If I didn't know better, I'd think he slipped something funny into my drink.

But I haven't been drinking. This is just what happens when a mouse realizes it has wandered into a trap. That cheese looked *soo* tasty, didn't it? Yes. And now look: there's a metal bar snapping down to crush my back.

I say faintly, "This might have been a mistake."

At that, Callum bursts out laughing. I'm so surprised by his reaction, I sit with my mouth open, watching him, until he recovers his composure and turns to me, his dark eyes sparkling with mirth.

"It's not a mistake for me. For you..." He shrugs. "Probably."

"*Seriously?* That's your answer?"

His tone innocent, he says, "I'm sorry, did you want me to lie?"

Panicking all over again, I demand, "I want you to tell me it wasn't a mistake! And mean it!"

"And I want you to tell me you want me and mean it, so I guess we'll both be disappointed."

That voracious ego of his. He married me for the sole purpose of making sure he'd stay rich, but he still needs me to flatter him. Unbelievable.

I glare at him. "I swear to God, Callum McCord, if you turn out to be some kind of woman abuser, or even anything more irritating than I already know you are, I'll leave you so fast, your head will spin."

His dangerous smile makes a reappearance. "We'll see. In the meantime, there's one last thing we have to do to make the marriage legal."

Suspicious of his tone and this new curveball, I say, "What?"

"Consummate it."

Reaching over, he grabs me and drags me onto his lap.

Fourteen

The man can kiss, I'll give him that. He might be the single most aggravating human to ever walk the face of the earth, and he clearly has control issues and a boatload of secrets, but he sure can kiss.

What an unfortunate development.

With one hand wrapped around my jaw, he delves his tongue into my mouth, sliding it against mine with delicious friction. His lips are soft. His body is hard. The arm he has wrapped around my back cradles me tightly. He holds me captive between his spread legs and drinks from my mouth as if from a well of water he's been crawling over miles of burning sand to reach.

And for all the sniping I've done and the annoyance he causes me, I've never felt such sweet relief.

Though it pains me to admit it, I've been wanting this since I first met him.

Might as well enjoy it while I can, considering I'll never let it happen again.

I arch into him and slide a hand up around the back of his strong neck, twining my fingers into his hair. He makes a sound of pleasure low in his throat and kisses me deeper. When I whimper softly, he moves his hand down from my jaw to encircle my neck.

"Sweet little lamb," he murmurs against my lips. "Hungry, aren't you?"

"Why do you have to ruin everything by talking?"

He chuckles. I open my eyes to find him gazing down at me, his eyes dark and hazy. A small smile plays over his mouth.

I frown at him. "Don't look so pleased with yourself."

"I can't help it."

"If you say one word about how much you think I liked that, I'll commit an act of unspeakable violence."

"But you *did* like it." He lowers his head to nuzzle his nose against the tender spot beneath my earlobe. Then he whispers into my ear, "You'll like it even more when I fuck you."

Hearing him say that makes every one of my body systems slam into red alert. Heat flashes over my skin. My heartbeat takes off like a rocket. My thighs clench, and my nerves stand on end and start screaming.

Which is all very inconvenient, considering I've already decided there will be nothing between us but paperwork. This is a business arrangement, nothing more. The sooner I get my hormones on board with it, the better.

Besides, who knows how many other women he's already sleeping with? The line is probably so long, it circles the city.

When I make a move to escape, he tightens his hand around my throat and holds me in place. His voice gruff, he says, "Here's where you tell me how you want it."

"No, here's where I tell you my temper goes from zero to life in prison faster than you can blink. Let me go."

"Oh, I know all about that temper of yours. For someone so bookish, you're surprisingly hotheaded."

"Calling me bookish isn't an insult, but nice try. *Let me go.*"

Ignoring that, he says, "The longer you pretend you don't want to fuck me, the more punishment you'll have coming, so you might as well admit it."

"Stop saying the F word! And you can lay off on the punishment thing too. If you put a hand on me, I'll murder you in your sleep."

"You don't want to murder me. You want to ride my big stiff cock until you come so hard, you pass out."

His language makes me gasp in disbelief.

"Admit it."

"No. Because I don't!"

My denial does nothing to dent his confidence. His smile is so self-satisfied, it makes me want to rip off his face.

"Let me go. I'm serious."

"I'm never letting you go, wife. Get used to it."

The way he said "wife" is so possessive, it makes my face hot. Other parts of me are hot, too. In fact, my entire body is feverish. Desperate to escape, I squirm in his arms.

"Emery, stop wriggling and look at me. No, not at the fucking roof. At *me*."

He said that in his commanding tone, the one he uses when he's trying to intimidate me. He should know by now that it doesn't work.

When I continue to fight to get away, he says hotly, "Keep fighting me, and I'll spank your pussy."

Shocked, I fall still and stare up at him with wide eyes, my heart hammering.

"Good girl," he murmurs, pleased. He kisses my forehead. Then he groans softly. "God, I can't fucking wait to do that. I want to spank your pussy until you squirt all over my hand."

My face burns, as do my nether regions. "Callum!"

He growls, "Yes, baby. You're gonna say my name just like that when I'm fucking your sweet wet cunt nice and hard."

He releases me abruptly, setting me aside on the seat. Then his cell phone rings, and he starts a casual conversation with someone on the other end, as if he didn't just shatter my entire perception of reality.

I collapse against the door, press a hand over my pounding

heart, and hyperventilate until I see stars. Then I close my eyes and try to convince myself I imagined the whole thing.

It doesn't work. Every cell in my body has it on replay.

His words echo on my skin, in my head, through my veins. And especially between my legs, where a pulsing, repetitive beat of *please please please* has started. I squeeze my thighs together, which only makes the ache worse.

The rest of the ride is spent the same way, with Callum on the phone and me attempting to piece myself back together.

But no matter how attracted to him I am, I can't allow myself to be another one of his conquests. I can't risk getting my heart involved.

I already know I'm nothing to him but a means to an end.

We turn off Sunset Boulevard and pass through the massive gates that mark the entry to Bel Air. It looks like a movie set with the towering palm trees, carved limestone blocks, and elaborate ironwork. After following the road for a few miles, we turn into a long, curving driveway, at the end of which is a closed wooden gate. The driver rolls down his window and punches a few buttons on the black box on the pole standing beside the gate. With a creak, the gate slowly opens. We drive through.

"Home sweet home," says Callum, disconnecting his call. "What do you think?"

"I think I'm about to shit myself is what I think. That's your house?"

"No, that's our house."

I look away from the enormous chateau looming past the windshield and stare nervously at Callum's handsome profile.

Looking straight ahead, he says, "Don't be scared."

"That sounds like bad advice."

He turns his head and gazes at me. After a thoughtful pause, he says, "You never have to be afraid of anything again. If you have a problem, I'll fix it. If you need something, I'll give it to you. If anyone bothers you, I'll make them wish they hadn't. Whatever you want or need, you tell me, and you'll have it. You're mine now."

He reaches out and caresses my cheek. His voice drops, and his eyes start to burn. "You belong to me."

His intensity terrifies me. So does the *you belong to me* stuff.

"I feel like it's important to mention at this point in the conversation that I'm not your property. Just because we signed some paperwork—"

"You're mine," he interrupts firmly. "And if you ever start to doubt that, look at the ring on your finger."

I search his face. A sickening feeling of fear takes root under my breastbone. "I need to be honest with you about something now."

"What is it?"

"You're scaring me."

"What did I just tell you about that?"

"It feels important to reiterate."

He gazes at me for a moment, then says in a softer voice, "When I said you don't have to be afraid of anything again, that includes me. I'll never harm you, Emery. And deep down, you know that, or you'd never have agreed to become my wife."

I lick my dry lips and swallow, darting a glance at the driver before lowering my voice.

"It might be all the sex talk that's got me so worried. Especially this consummate-the-marriage thing. You never mentioned anything about that before. In fact, you promised I could have my own bedroom if I wanted. I've decided to take you up on that."

Callum's smile comes on slowly. He seems to be amused by a thought, but doesn't say it aloud.

"What's that face you're wearing?"

"Why? Is it making you nervous?"

"Yes."

His smile grows wider. "It should."

I want to thump him on the shoulder, but don't. Who knows

how he'd retaliate? I could be over his knee getting my bare ass spanked in five seconds flat.

I'm not sure if I hate that idea or love it. I'm also not sure what it says about me that I can't make up my mind.

"I'll ignore that to head back to reality for a moment. Will you please call William and ask him to lock up the shop? The spare keys are under the—"

"It's handled," he interrupts.

Confused, I furrow my brow. "How?"

"I gave him instructions before we arrived."

All the creaky gears in my brain struggle to make sense of that new piece of information. They don't have much luck. "You told your attorney to lock my store before you even knew we'd be going to your house today?"

"*Our* house. And everything I do is planned carefully in advance, so yes, I told him before I got there to lock up the shop when we left."

I'm still confused, but now I'm frustrated and annoyed too. "So you just assumed I'd agree to marry you on the spot?"

"I didn't assume. I knew."

"How?" I demand, growing angrier.

With a trace of darkness in his voice, he says, "Because I know everything about you, wife. Including where you hide your spare set of keys."

I stare at him for a moment, my mind and my pulse both racing. "You really did hire a private investigator to spy on me, didn't you?"

His small smile is the only answer I need.

We drive down a sloped driveway and pull into an enormous underground garage. A few dozen luxury vehicles in various models and colors line each side. As the driver parks, I look around, taking in the sheer size of the place. Soft overhead lighting makes the cars and floors gleam. It's immaculate, like a showroom.

Callum exits the car, then comes around to my side and opens my door for me. Looking up at him in growing alarm, I stall by saying, "I left my purse at the store."

"Do you want it?"

"Yes."

"I'll have someone bring it here. Give me your hand."

I look at his outstretched hand, telling myself not to be a coward, that everything is going to be okay, and that if it isn't, I'll deal with it.

I've made it this far in life. I'm sure I can handle a bossy billionaire who apparently has a predilection for spanking tender body parts.

"Give me your hand."

His command is spoken in a gentle tone, but there's steel underneath.

Trembling, I glance up at his face. Then I chew on my lip, undecided.

Callum reaches in, grasps my hand, hauls me out of the car, then lifts me and tosses me over his shoulder. I squawk in panic and grab his suit jacket for balance as he starts to walk away from the car.

"Hey!"

"Yes, wife?"

"Put me down!"

"Soon."

When I kick my feet in frustration, he gives me a sharp smack on my behind to settle me down. It does the opposite.

"Do that again, and you'll regret it!"

My threat does nothing but earn me one of his annoying, self-satisfied chuckles.

He carries me through a door at one end of the garage with the ease of a man accustomed to abducting adults from their places of business, scrambling their brains with some unexpected, filthy sex talk, then speeding away with them to his bachelor pad in the hills.

I barely have time to wonder if his backyard is full of buried bodies before we're moving through a lavish marble foyer with a staircase on one side. Sparkling chandeliers hang from the ceiling, casting a warm glow over the space.

I'm starting to get dizzy.

"May I please not be upside down anymore? I don't like this."

He stops midstride and sets me on my feet, then steadies me with his hands on my shoulders when I sway to one side.

I thank him breathlessly. He smiles, then bends, lifts me into his arms, and starts walking again. I gaze up at his handsome face and try to figure out what the hell this crazy person thinks he's accomplishing by this.

Noticing my expression, he says, "Don't overthink it."

"I'm going on the record right now to inform you that the next time you say that, I'll hit you in the head with something heavy. Put me down."

He smirks. "And you say I'm bossy."

Then he's taking the stairs, two at a time.

Pretending I'm not impressed—or freaked out, or in shock, or any of the other things I currently am—I say calmly, "Your home is lovely. A bit gargantuan for one person, but I suppose you need all the extra space for your ego. I wouldn't have pegged you for the French country décor type."

He slants me a look, warm and full of secrets. "I'm not."

"I'd ask if you could be any more irritating, but I already know the answer. Why are you carrying me?"

"It's traditional for the groom to carry his bride across the threshold."

I'm about to argue with him about the absurdity of that statement when we reach the top of the staircase and he makes a sharp left turn down a corridor. It's lined with gilt-framed portraits of people who all look like they need more fiber in their diets.

"I'm afraid to ask, but I will. Where are we going?"

"To bed."

I stare at his profile. He doesn't smile, so I have to assume he's not making a joke.

"I'm not sleeping with you."

"Who said anything about sleeping?"

"I think you should put me down now."

"And I think you should admit that you'd like to have sex with me so that we can dispense with the bullshit once and for all."

He strides through an open set of carved wooden doors. We're in what looks like the master suite. It's elegantly decorated in shades of cream and gold, with floor-to-ceiling windows on one side of the room and a cozy sitting area on the other. Complete with gauzy white panels of fabric and too many plush ivory throw pillows to count, a king-size antique canopy bed dominates another wall.

Callum heads straight for it.

"Whoa, cowboy!" I say, panicking.

His sideways glance is so hot, it sears me. He grins and chuckles darkly. "Oh, I'm a cowboy all right. Just wait until I show you my pistol."

He stops at the edge of the bed, drops me onto it, then flattens his body over mine. I try to roll out from under him, but the man weighs a thousand pounds. With his forearms braced on either side of my shoulders, he holds my head in both huge hands as he gazes down into my wide eyes.

He smiles.

I swallow nervously and dart a glance toward the door. He lowers his head and inhales deeply against my neck. His beard tickles my cheek. He smells like soap and clean skin. When he exhales, it's with a low groan that vibrates all the way through me.

This feels like something very different than a business arrangement.

The rock-hard erection pulsing against my hip especially doesn't feel very businesslike.

Lying stiffly beneath him with my pulse screaming through my veins, I whisper, "Will you please let me up?"

"Yes."

"Thank you."

He sucks on my earlobe, then opens his mouth over the throbbing pulse on the side of my neck and softly bites me.

My nipples harden. Heat spreads throughout my lower body, belly to thighs. I shiver involuntarily, which encourages my captor to flex his hips into mine. Then he's kissing my throat down to my collarbone as I lose my breath and a big chunk of my mind.

"Should I have asked when?"

As an answer, he rubs his cheek against my chest, dragging it over my hard nipples. Then he cups my breasts in both hands and bites one of my nipples right through my blouse and bra.

When I cry out and arch into his hands, he presses slightly harder with his teeth and firmly pinches my other nipple.

Pleasure ripples through me in hot, delicious waves. Sweat mists my skin. I grab the back of his jacket and try desperately not to give in to the growing need to rock my pelvis against his.

I already know that my panties are wet, because my clit is throbbing.

He breathes, "Tell me you want me."

He might as well have thrown a bucket of ice water on my head for what it does to my state of arousal. Flinging my arms out against the bed, I groan. "This again? Why is that so damn important?"

"Tell me."

"Are you really such a narcissist that you need every woman in your orbit to want to have sex with you?"

"No. Only you. *Tell me.*"

I'm so frustrated now that I pummel his back with my fists. I might as well be smacking a brick wall. He doesn't budge, but he does take my face in his hands and stares down at me in blazing hot intensity, his lips thinned and his nostrils flaring.

He growls, "You're getting your ten million dollars. Now I want you to—"

"Twenty."

He closes his eyes, breathes for a moment, then opens his eyes again and incinerates me with his gaze.

"Yes. Twenty. It seems like a very small fucking thing for me to ask you to tell me the truth in return."

"Maybe you should've put it in the contract."

Through gritted teeth, he says, "Goddammit, Emery."

"And by the way, what you're getting in return is your entire inheritance, right? All your billions and your lavish lifestyle? You can continue being Mr. Rich Guy and eating salty lobster in the Caribbean and terrifying poor hostesses in the restaurants in all the buildings you own all over the world. So what difference can it possibly make if I say I want you or not?"

"Admit you want to fuck me, and I'll give you another ten million dollars."

That stuns me into silence. I gaze up at him in confusion, searching his face. "You're serious, aren't you?"

"Yes."

The way he's staring at my mouth is thrilling. His heart beats raggedly against my chest. His breathing is uneven. His hands on either side of my head are hot and trembling, as is the rest of his body.

I realize with a shock like a slap across the face that this isn't about his ego.

This is about him needing the woman he wants to tell him she feels the same way.

He wants me.

Me, the girl he couldn't manage to find a better compliment for than that I wasn't repulsive. Me, the girl who rolls her eyes at him, and laughs at him, and defies him at every turn.

Me. His married-for-convenience wife.

He flexes his hips again, digging his erection into my thigh. My heart pounds impossibly hard. I can't catch my breath. I know we're on the verge of doing something incredibly stupid, but I'm not sure I could stop myself if I tried.

He lowers his head to kiss me, but then from inside his suit jacket his cell phone rings.

It's a creepy electronic version of the nursery rhyme "London

Bridge Is Falling Down," very different from the simple ringtone I heard in the car.

Callum closes his eyes and mutters, "Fuck."

He rolls off me, sits on the edge of the bed, and takes the call.

He takes the call.

"McCord." He listens in silence for what seems like a long time. Then he exhales heavily and says, "I'll be there."

He disconnects and stares at the wall as I lie crumpled and wet on the bed like a discarded tissue.

Standing, he puts his phone back into his pocket. He cracks his knuckles and smooths his hands down his lapels and over his hair. Then he turns and gazes down at me with distant eyes, his face expressionless.

"I have to go. I'll be back in a few days. Familiarize yourself with the house while I'm gone. If you need anything, Arlo will assist you."

Without further explanation, my new husband turns on his heel and walks out.

Fifteen

"Welcome to married life," I say in disbelief to the empty room. From somewhere down the corridor, a door slams shut in answer.

Sighing, I sit up and look around.

The suite décor is not at all what I pictured a man like Callum would choose. Spacious and airy, the room is elegant but distinctly feminine, right down to the soft pink-and-green floral pattern on the plush sofas and chairs in the sitting area.

There's an antique writing desk with an ornate gilt-framed mirror hung on the wall above it. The nightstands are distressed wood topped with brass reading lamps. Soft, billowy curtains filter the sunlight, providing a dreamy atmosphere, and the floors are rustic wide-plank hardwood covered by a vintage area rug in muted colors. A stunning crystal chandelier hangs from above, adding a touch of opulence to the overall design.

The focal point of the room is the beautiful antique armoire.

With carved details and a polished wood finish, it showcases a tantalizing collection of books through beveled glass doors.

Drawn to it, I slide off the bed and cross the room.

Up close, the armoire is so pretty, I'm almost afraid to touch it, but the gold-embossed spines of the books beg to be investigated. The doors are unlocked, so I open them and peer inside. When I read a few of the titles, euphoria expands in my chest.

Pride and Prejudice. Ulysses. The Great Gatsby. Madame Bovary. Wuthering Heights. Anna Karenina. The Grapes of Wrath.

Dozens more classics line the interior shelves. On impulse, I pluck the copy of *Pride and Prejudice* off a shelf and open it, then hold it to my nose and flip through the yellowed pages, inhaling that delicious old-book smell that's so unlike anything else.

Smiling, I flip back to the inside cover to see how old Callum's copy is.

The smile falls off my face when I see the copyright date of 1813 and the words First Edition printed beside it.

"Holy shit," I breathe, terrified.

I'm holding a literary treasure in my hands.

Very carefully, I close the cover and gently slide the book back to its home between *Gulliver's Travels* and *The Sun Also Rises*. Then I stand there quaking as my gaze travels over all the other titles in the armoire.

From a casual inspection of their spines, they all look as old as *Pride and Prejudice* does.

I suppose it makes sense. People with ungodly amounts of wealth like to collect rare things. Coveted, priceless things that others will envy them for.

But this kind of collection should be on display in a public space. A library or drawing room for instance, somewhere the lord of the manor could impress his guests as they smoked cigars and drank sherry after supper. A second-story master bedroom is hardly the place for these gems.

Frowning, I look over the books. Maybe that was a one-off. Maybe the rest of these are garage-sale finds or dummy copies for display with no printing inside.

I slowly slide *David Copperfield* from a shelf and gingerly open the cover.

1850. First edition. I'm gonna faint.

With shaking hands, I return the book to its nested spot between two other tomes from massive literary geniuses, then stand wide-eyed with my hands on my head, reviewing every glorious shelf.

When I spot the copy of *Outlander*, I clap my hands over my mouth to stifle a rapturous scream.

When I've recovered, I take it out and turn it over. The dust jacket is glossy perfection. The hardcover beneath is unblemished too. I know it's not nearly as valuable as some of the other novels in Callum's collection, but the existence of this book here immediately makes me forgive him for about ninety percent of his shortcomings.

Then I open the cover and lose my breath.

In black pen on the title page someone has written the words, "To Emery."

Beneath that is a signature.

The *author's* signature.

One very famous woman by the name of Diana Gabaldon.

"Wait," I say. Then I say it again louder, because *what the actual fuck*?

I stand there with my heart pumping and sweat breaking out on my brow as I try to figure out how on earth Callum would have gotten my favorite book personalized by the author in the short span of time since I met him.

It has to be fake. That's the only logical explanation.

Except my gut tells me it's real. As real as the heavy diamond sparkling on my ring finger.

Cradling the book to my chest, I turn and look around the room with a growing sense of unreality.

Who is this man, really?

Eyeing the door on the other side of the room that I suspect leads to the closet, I decide to snoop around and find out.

Steeling myself, I cross the room and open the door. I was right: it's Callum's closet. Almost the size of the bedroom, it's filled with luxurious clothes, shoes, and accessories. In the middle of the closet is a large dresser topped with a rectangular leather-and-glass watch display case. Ignoring the rows of expensive timepieces within, I set the signed copy of *Outlander* on the top of the dresser, slide open one of the drawers, and peek inside.

Black briefs, folded neatly.

Another drawer reveals his socks.

Yet another holds silk pocket squares in every color.

Inside the bottom drawer, several hardshell black plastic cases of various sizes are fitted together like puzzle pieces. Each has a handle and two sliding latches. None of them are marked.

Curious, I kneel on the floor and remove one of the cases from the drawer. Balancing it on my knees, I flip open the latches and look inside.

The interior of the case is filled with small bundles of braided rope. The purple, green, and black rope bundles have a soft, synthetic sheen. A few of the light brown ones appear to be some kind of natural fiber. The gold looks most luxurious and is thicker and velvet to the touch.

I look at all the other cases in the drawer and wonder if they're all filled with rope too.

And if they are, why? How much home improvement does a billionaire do? If I had to take a wild guess, it would be zero.

So what does he need it for?

At lunch, he mentioned sailing. Maybe it's for his boat?

I try another case, but it's locked. So are all the others.

Stumped, I put the case back in its place and slide the drawer closed. Then I stand, curiosity thrumming through me like electricity.

I should look around for a set of keys.

From the doorway comes the sound of someone clearing his throat.

Gasping, I jump and spin around.

"Good afternoon," says Callum's driver, giving me a little bow.

"Oh God. You startled me." I press a shaking hand over my

chest. Then I realize I just got caught snooping through Callum's drawers, and my face goes hot. "I, um, was just having a look around."

If he knows what I was looking at, he doesn't show it. He merely smiles and holds up his hand. In it is a small black card.

"Mr. McCord asked me to give you this."

"What is it?"

"His American Express card. There's no limit on the account, so you can use it to purchase whatever you like."

My laugh is small and nervous. "Oh, good, I can get that jet I always wanted."

He nods, still smiling. "Yes."

He moves a few steps closer, holding out the card. I reluctantly take it from him. It's a heavy chunk of black metal, engraved with Callum's name and an account number. Turning it over in my hands, I say, "I couldn't really buy a jet with this, could I?"

"Of course."

He says it like I'm a moron for even asking.

Then he says, "I'm Arlo, by the way. Mr. McCord's driver and personal assistant. I'm happy to help you with anything you might want or need."

He put an emphasis on "anything." I suspect I could ask this guy to help me bury a body, and he'd say no problem, let me just go get the shovels, and we'll get started.

This is the first time I've seen him without his dark sunglasses, so I finally have a good look at his face. He's nice-looking, maybe mid-thirties, with olive skin and thick dark brows over unusual silvery-gray eyes.

Like his employer's, those eyes seem to hold a million secrets in their depths.

He says, "Your handbag will arrive soon, followed shortly by all your other belongings. Would you like me to help you unpack?"

Instantly suspicious, I say, "What do you mean, all my other belongings?"

"Your clothes and personal items from your apartment."

I'm momentarily stunned. "All my stuff is being brought here? Why?"

Arlo lifts his brows, then says gently, "Because you live here now, Mrs. McCord."

"Oh. Right." *Help.*

"Perhaps you'd like to give me your measurements and favorite clothing stores so I can send them to Mr. McCord's personal shopper."

When I stare at him in confusion, he adds, "For your new wardrobe."

"What new wardrobe?"

"The one Mr. McCord would like you to have."

I say hotly, "What's wrong with my old wardrobe?"

Bypassing that landmine, Arlo says, "The cleaning staff comes on Tuesday and Thursday. The chef arrives daily at eight a.m. and leaves at six in the evening. If you have any preferences for the day's menu, just leave a list on your writing desk"—he gestures to the antique desk across the room—"and I will deliver it to him. The masseuse is on call twenty-four hours a day, and if you'd like a lady's maid to assist you with dressing and keeping your personal possessions in good order, I'll have the agency send over candidates for you to interview."

He waits patiently for me to absorb all that, but the information bounces off my numb skull.

His voice gentler, he says, "I know it must be overwhelming. If you need anything, please don't hesitate to enlist my help."

From his suit jacket, he pulls a thin silver cell phone. "I'm also on call twenty-four hours a day. My number is already programmed in, as are the numbers of all your personal contacts."

I take the phone from him and hold it at arm's length between two fingers, as you might a small but venomous snake. "How are all my contacts already programmed in this thing?"

Arlo clasps his hands together and smiles.

Dropping my arm to my side, I sigh. "Look, Arlo. I know you think you're trying to be helpful, but that mysterious smile is freaking me out. Now answer my question, please—how are my numbers already programmed in?"

He thinks for a moment. "I realize you and Mr. McCord haven't known each other long, but you'll soon discover that he's always well prepared."

I say flatly, "Meaning he's been spying on me."

"Meaning he's exceptionally detail oriented."

"Meaning he's a control freak."

"Meaning that now that you're under his care, you'll never have to worry about anything again."

"The semantics are making me anxious. And the phrase 'under his care' makes me feel like a patient. I agreed to marry the guy, not let him treat my medical conditions."

After a thoughtful beat, Arlo says, "I'm sorry if I misspoke. I only meant that you'll be protected from now on."

"Protected from what? I run a bookshop, not an illegal gambling ring."

He doesn't answer. He merely smiles and walks out.

Just like his boss, Arlo is aggravating.

Sighing, I inspect the phone he gave me. Almost as thin as the black Amex card, it has no buttons on the sides. When I tap the screen with my thumb, nothing happens.

I doubt Arlo would give me a phone with a dead battery, so I set aside the credit card on the dresser and turn the phone over in my hands, inspecting it. In addition to having no buttons, it also has no holes where a charger would go or any other markings of any sort.

It's sleek, blank, and slightly menacing.

On impulse, I hold it close to my mouth and say, "Call Dani."

The screen lights up. *Calling Dani* shows in white type against a plain blue background. Then the sound of a ring fills the air.

"Hello?"

Holy shit. It worked.

"Dani, it's me."

"Emery?"

"Yeah."

"Why does my phone show caller unknown?"

"I'm using this freaky batphone Callum gave me. I don't even really know how the thing works. Voice command, it seems like. He probably had it custom made by Elon Musk."

Her tone turns excited. "Callum gave you a phone?"

I look around the sumptuous closet and sigh. "Yeah. He gave me something else too."

"Oh God. If you say herpes, I'll kill him."

"No, idiot! Why would you think that?"

"Because you sound like you just went to a funeral."

"Close. A wedding."

There's a pause, then she says flatly, "You did not."

"I did."

The shriek that comes over the line is so loud, I blink. Then she screams, "*You did not marry Callum fucking McCord! Oh my God, bitch, tell me you're joking!*"

"I'm not joking. I'm standing in the middle of his ginormous closet in his gargantuan master bedroom in his castle of a house as we speak."

Hyperventilating, she says, "*How?* When you left after dinner, you said you texted him. What in the fuckity-fuck happened between now and then that ends up with you married?"

She pauses to take a breath, then demands, "And why didn't you invite me to the wedding, asshole?"

Rubbing my forehead, I say, "It was more like a shotgun wedding, only without the pregnancy."

Thinking about the whirlwind day makes me tired. And, honestly, a little depressed.

I've never been one of those girls who dreams her whole life about the big white wedding she wants, but having a ring jammed onto my finger by a controlling stranger, then getting thrown over his shoulder and into his car wasn't exactly what I expected either.

"It all happened so fast. He showed up at my house unannounced, we had a really strange talk that didn't solve anything, then he came to the shop this morning with a contract and gave Harper, Viv, and Taylor spontaneous orgasms when they saw him. Then he called a while later to go over the details of the paperwork, and we had another strange conversation that didn't solve anything except that I agreed to marry him. Then he hung up on me and showed up not even half an hour later with his attorney and, get this, a fucking chaplain. And then, basically…we said our vows."

That muffled thud I hear is probably Dani collapsing into the nearest chair.

I say drily, "If you think that was interesting, wait until I tell you what he said to me in the car after the ceremony."

"What?"

"That he wanted to spank my pussy until I squirted on his hand."

After a moment of silence, Dani breathes, "There *is* a God."

I groan. "All I know is that I'm standing in a stranger's closet with nothing but a signed copy of *Outlander*, a weird cell phone, and a black American Express card to keep me company, and I'm pretty sure I'm having a nervous breakdown. Can you please come over here and hold my hand?"

"Back up. Did you say black American Express card?"

"Yes."

Her voice thrilled, Dani says, "Oh, honey. I know the perfect way to cure a nervous breakdown."

"What?"

"Therapy."

When I blow out a breath, she laughs. "*Retail* therapy. You just married a billionaire, Em. Let's go shopping."

I think for a moment, then smile. "And this is why I love you."

"Should I come pick you up?"

"No, I've got a better idea." My smile grows bigger. "What's your favorite color for a Ferrari?"

Sixteen

It turns out the answer to that question is red.

When I pull up in Dani's driveway in the Ferrari Daytona SP3 that Arlo gave me the keys to and honk the horn, she runs out of the house as if it's on fire, screaming and waving her arms.

"I can't believe this shit! Oh my God, this isn't happening! *You have a Ferrari!*" She stops shouting and stares at my left hand, resting on the steering wheel. "And a giant hunk of ice. Is that thing real?"

"At this point, I don't think anything is real. Get in the car."

She frowns at the door. "How? There's no handle."

"Lean down. It's tucked under the swoop in the door. But watch out when you press it, because the door opens up, not out."

Dani leans over and presses the handle, then jumps back in surprise when the door does exactly what I said it would.

She leans in to inspect the interior with wide eyes. "This thing is like a spaceship! How fast does it go?"

"I don't know, but Arlo said it's got a V12 engine with more than 800 horsepower, so I'm thinking pretty damn fast."

When she hesitates, looking doubtfully at the contoured seat with the shoulder belt straps like a race car has, I say, "I won't go over the speed limit. Promise."

"That's exactly what you said that time we got pulled over on PCH and almost got thrown in jail for doing over a hundred."

"Yeah, but I was nineteen."

She purses her lips. "You say that like you've matured in the last eleven years."

"Get in the car, Dani."

She climbs in, figures out how to get the door closed, then buckles the seat belt and shoulder straps. Then Ryan walks out of the house, mouth open and eyes bugging, holding a squirming Mia in his arms.

"Holy shit," he breathes, gazing reverently at the Ferrari like he sees an image of the Virgin Mary in the paint. "Do you have any idea how much this car costs?"

"No, and I don't want to."

"Over two million dollars."

Dani says, "Oh my God, Ry! What did she just say? And how do you know how much it cost, anyway?"

"It was featured in *Car and Driver* magazine last month. They said only five hundred of these were made."

Two million bucks for a car. What a waste of money.

"I guess that means we shouldn't have cocktails after shopping. A fender bender would probably cost a hundred grand. I'll have her back in a few hours, Ryan."

We pull out of the driveway, then head out of Dani's neighborhood toward the 405, where I realize how dumb it is to own a car that can probably move faster than the speed of light when you live in a city with the most congested freeways in America.

We crawl along in traffic, waving at all the other motorists gawking at us, until we exit on Santa Monica Boulevard and arrive in Beverly Hills.

Then I have my Julia Roberts in *Pretty Woman* moment, going from one expensive boutique to the next while every salesperson looks at me in horror as if I'm wearing a dress made of fresh turds.

In each case, it's incredibly satisfying when I slap that black Amex down on the counter.

I have to call Arlo on the batphone for the address of the house to have all the packages sent to because the damn Ferrari doesn't have a trunk.

By the time we're finished, it's dark. We hit the same restaurant where Callum took me to lunch, and lo and behold, Sophie's working the hostess stand. She brightens when she sees me walking up.

"Miss Eastwood! Welcome in!"

"Hi again, Sophie. How are you?"

"Just great, thanks!"

"You seem great."

She blushes, clutching a pair of menus to her chest. "I got a raise, thanks to you."

"Thanks to *me*? How?"

"Because you told Mr. McCord I deserved one. Right after you left that day, he asked to see my boss. The next thing I know, my boss tells me I'm getting an increase."

"Wow." I don't know what else to say. I'm happy for her, but also surprised. I suppose I shouldn't be, considering I already know how generous Callum is.

But this is more than generous. It's thoughtful.

It's kind.

As he did when he sent the police away from my apartment building, he once again used his rich-person superpowers for good.

If only he wasn't so irritating the rest of the time.

Sophie seats us, and we have an amazing meal. We talk over everything that's happened, including what Callum put in the contract about a job for Ryan.

Dani can't believe it. She also can't believe Callum said I could have a boyfriend if I wanted.

"I mean, it's a dream come true. You should buy a lottery ticket. Your luck is incredible."

"I would, but I don't need one. I've got twenty million in a trust in my name."

We stare at each other across the table for a moment. She says, "I have to admit, for someone who self-medicates with liquor like an eighties rock star, you're handling this whole thing extremely well."

"Only on the outside. On the inside, I'm winning a gold medal in the Panic Olympics."

"So how long is he going to be gone?"

"No idea."

"Was it for business?"

"He didn't tell me. He just left and gave Arlo his credit card."

She shakes her head in disbelief. "It's the perfect relationship. He gives you twenty million bucks, tells you that you can do whatever you want, then goes out of town and leaves you a credit card with no limit and a garage full of luxury cars."

I chuckle, taking a sip of water. "And a whole bunch of rope."

Dani looks up from her plate of pasta with furrowed brows. "Rope?"

"Yeah, I was snooping around in his dresser drawers and found all these bundles of pretty colored rope in a black case."

Leaning forward over the table, she says, "You found bundles of *colored rope* in his dresser drawer?"

"Congratulations. Your ears work. Why do you look so weird?"

She gazes at me in silence for a moment, then starts laughing.

"What the hell is so damn funny?"

"You are."

"Why?"

"Because you're not that clueless."

It's my turn to furrow my brow. "What are you talking about?"

She sighs, wipes her mouth with her napkin, then throws it

on the table in disgust. "Honey, think. What would a *man* be doing with *rope* in his *bedroom*?"

After mulling it over for a moment, I blanch. "Oh shit."

"Oh shit is right," she says, cackling.

My heart palpitating, I go over the conversation Callum and I had in the car, thinking of his surprisingly filthy language and how he said he'd punish me. The idea that he also has a bondage kink makes me squirm in my chair.

But it's not as if I need to worry about it, since we won't be sleeping together.

This marriage is for convenience only. For both of us.

Sex is off the table.

Except I'm pretty sure we both want it, which is going to be a problem.

Dani laughs harder at the expression on my face.

At that moment, the batphone rings. Lying beside my water glass on the table, the strange little thing launches into a sly saxophone rendition of the main theme from *The Pink Panther*. Then the screen lights up. A single word appears on the pale blue background.

Daddy.

I know immediately who it is.

"No," I say forcefully, glaring at it. "No way am I calling you Daddy."

Dani leans over and looks at the screen. Then she snickers. "Maybe it's your father calling from beyond the grave."

Aggravated, I lean closer to the phone. "Decline call."

The screen goes blank. *The Pink Panther* theme falls silent. Dani and I stare at it for a moment until it starts to ring again.

We look at each other. She shrugs. I sigh heavily and reach for the phone.

Holding it next to my ear, I say, "Hello, Callum."

Sounding as smug as ever, he says, "Hello, darling. Enjoying dinner?"

I glance around the restaurant, but don't spot anyone

peering out from behind a corner with a telephoto lens. "I'd ask why you're spying on me, but I already know you're a freak like that. Thank you for the credit card. I've been making good use of it."

He chuckles. "I know you have."

"Of course you do."

"And I'm gratified that you're not one of those silly girls who'd be offended or refuse to use it on the grounds of your feminism or some such."

"My brand of feminism is too smart to turn down free stuff. By the way, I borrowed one of your cars."

"Yes, I got a call from the police chief about that. Apparently, you were speeding on Rodeo Drive."

"Why am I not surprised you've got the police chief spying on me too? And nobody can speed on Rodeo Drive. It's a short street with a million stop lights."

"Yet somehow, you managed it."

I grudgingly admit, "I might've been trying to discover its zero-to-sixty speed."

"You could've just asked me."

"That wouldn't have been nearly as much fun. Why are you calling me?"

"Maybe I miss you."

Rolling my eyes, I sit back in my chair and shake my head.

His voice darker, Callum says, "Don't roll your eyes at your husband, darling. That will earn you a spanking."

I sit bolt upright and look wildly around for some clue of how he's seeing me, but find nothing out of sorts. Chewing a mouthful of pasta, Dani watches me with interest.

Callum says, "Look up and to the right. See that security camera on the ceiling? No, that's a speaker. Farther right, over the potted palms."

I squint at the small black glass orb protruding from the ceiling over the plants in the corner. A red light inside flashes on and off as if it's signaling hello.

When I remain silent, he prompts, "Why aren't you saying anything?"

"I'm too busy patting myself on the back for how well I'm adjusting to being married to a psychopath. I'm not even crying or anything."

He chuckles again, pleased. "I have mobile access to all the security cameras in the buildings I own."

"Bypassing how wrong it is that you think it's kosher to watch someone remotely through a ceiling camera, how did you know I was here?"

"The GPS on the Ferrari."

"Ah."

"I know what you're thinking, but you're wrong. I won't do this all the time."

"Somehow, I find that extremely hard to believe."

"I promise I won't. But when I'm out of town..." He pauses for a moment, then comes back on sounding far more intense. "I need to know you're safe."

I sense layer upon layer of hidden meanings in that short sentence, a whole world of secrets I know nothing about. The hairs on my arms prickle.

When he speaks again, his tone has returned to normal. "I won't keep you. I just wanted to let you know that the transfer from the brokerage account has gone through. The trust was fully funded an hour ago. The documents will be waiting on the kitchen table when you get home, along with instructions for accessing the money."

Slightly dazed by the conversation, I can only think to thank him again.

"You're welcome. Oh, and Emery?"

"Yes?"

"Be a good girl and don't snoop in my drawers."

The line goes dead. I slowly set the phone down and meet Dani's eager eyes.

She says, "So?"

"I don't even know where to start. Every time I have a conversation with that man, he turns my brain into mashed potatoes."

"I can't wait to hear about it when he turns your vagina into ground beef."

"That's not gonna happen, girlfriend."

"But you want it to, don't you?"

Shooting a glance at the ceiling camera in the far corner of the room, I say loudly, "No."

When the camera's red light blinks on and off again, I can almost hear Callum growling that I'll be punished for lying.

For the rest of the night, all I can think about is what kind of punishment that might be.

Seventeen

True to his word, the documents Callum said would be waiting for me on the kitchen table are there when I arrive back at the castle.

Referring to it as a house would be insulting to the architect, whoever they were. And I still don't believe this is actually my home, so I won't call it that either. So for the time being, it's "the castle."

I should look on the internet to find out how Marie Antoinette referred to Versailles and use that.

I spend a while wandering around the place, looking into room after sumptuous room. Arlo is nowhere to be seen, so I climb the big curving staircase to the second floor and poke my head into more rooms until I find a modest guest bedroom that doesn't look like somewhere King Louis XIV would sleep.

Exhausted, I kick off my shoes, crawl under the covers of the queen-sized bed fully clothed, and fall into a deep sleep.

When I open my eyes in the morning, Arlo is standing bedside, smiling down at me.

"Good morning, madam."

"Good morning, Arlo. Please don't call me madam, I don't own a brothel. Emery is fine. Also, what the hell are you doing?"

"I wondered if you'd like to take breakfast in bed?"

I sit up and rub my eyes. Thank God I didn't sleep naked, or Arlo would be getting an eyeful. "No, thanks. I'll just have coffee."

"Mr. McCord prefers that you eat something in the mornings."

I frown up at him. "And I would prefer that Mr. McCord mind his own business."

Ignoring that, Arlo says, "If you'd like something light, we have a selection of fresh seasonal fruit, organic yogurt, and steel-cut oats. I can also have the chef prepare eggs any way you like them—"

I cut in sarcastically, "What, the lord of the manor doesn't already know?"

Arlo clasps his hands at his waist. "He indicated you enjoy them poached, but I didn't want to presume."

I close my eyes and sigh.

Arlo says, "Poached it is. How do you take your coffee?"

Opening my eyes, I send him a death glare. "Don't pretend like it's a mystery."

Unmoved by my murder face, he smiles. "Two poached eggs and coffee with whole milk and brown sugar coming right up." He turns and walks out, leaving me to stew in annoyance.

My new husband and I are going to have a serious discussion about personal boundaries when he gets back.

I get up, use the toilet, and wash my face. Then I realize I don't have any cosmetics or toiletries here. *Then* I remember Arlo saying my things were being brought from my apartment, so I head out to investigate.

Sure enough, all my clothes have been hung up in the master bedroom closet. My cosmetics are in a drawer under the bathroom sink. My shampoo and conditioner are on the shelf in the cavernous white marble shower, along with my razor and the loofah thing I use to scrub my face.

I suppose other women might find this show of dominant

caretaking endearing. But I don't know any of those women. As for me, the thought of a bunch of strangers packing up my apartment and personal things at the behest of Callum doesn't feel like a romantic gesture, it just feels like an invasion of privacy.

It's impossible to reconcile the two sides of him.

On the one hand, he's incredibly generous and thoughtful. On the other, he's incredibly controlling. And his fanatical knowledge of my habits, preferences, and whereabouts is flat-out disturbing.

Irked, I change into fresh clothes and emerge from the closet just as Arlo is coming in the bedroom carrying a tray.

"Ah, there you are. Should I lay everything out on your writing desk?"

"Sure. Might as well eat the breakfast I didn't want on the desk I didn't buy in the bedroom I didn't decorate in the house I don't own. Sounds fantastic."

Setting the tray on the desk, Arlo turns to me. His tone gentle, he says, "You're having a hard time adjusting."

I snort. "Who, me?"

"I think once you get to know Mr. McCord better, you'll find him to be an excellent companion."

"Thanks, but you have to say that. You're on his payroll."

I pull out the chair and sit. Arlo hands me a white linen napkin.

"Give him a chance. I know he can be...difficult. But he's an exceptional man. And having known him as long as I have, I can tell you with total confidence that he'd do anything to make you happy. It's all he wants."

Startled by that, I look up at him. His expression is passive, but his silvery-gray eyes are warm.

"I'm pretty sure all he wants is his inheritance."

He frowns and opens his mouth as if he's about to say something, but must think better of it because he closes his mouth again and doesn't respond.

I say, "What's been done with my furniture and books?"

"The furniture has been put into storage. Your books are in the library on the first floor. There are several boxes of personal items in the garage—photo albums and whatnot. If you tell me where you'd like them, I'll have them unpacked."

"I can do it."

"Mr. McCord would prefer—"

"He's *your* boss, Arlo, not mine," I interrupt, growing more irritated by the second. "I'll unpack the rest of my things. Where's my car?"

"In the garage."

"Good. Thank you. Now if you don't mind, I'm going to rage eat these eggs so you won't be in trouble with Callum, then I'm going to work. Which I'm only telling you so you don't get into trouble when he asks where I am, which I know he will."

"You didn't like the Ferrari?"

"I didn't like its GPS."

"Ah."

"Yeah."

He hesitates, then says, "I'll leave you to your breakfast," and walks out.

The moment he's gone, I take the eggs into the bathroom and flush them down the toilet. Then I take off my too-big diamond ring and leave it next to the faucet on the sink.

I drive my VW to the store, feeling strangely relieved to be out of the castle. It's beautiful, but way too huge for two people and a few domestic workers. I don't know why Callum bought it. Maybe billionaires are used to living alone in homes the size of Disneyland.

Not me.

When I unlock the shop and walk in, I'm overcome by a rush of emotion. I stand in the entryway and look around at the old-fashioned register, the displays of books, the faded, overstuffed chair near the window with the calico cat curled up on the seat, and have to fight back tears.

Lit Happens is still standing.

We don't have to close our doors anymore.

Everything my parents sacrificed for won't be in vain.

I gaze at the picture of them hanging on the wall behind the register. It's from right after they were married. Taken in front of the Ferris wheel on the Santa Monica pier, the picture shows them young and happy, smiling and carefree.

I miss them with a sudden ache that leaves me breathless.

My mom's been gone for twenty years, but I can still hear her voice in my head, always encouraging me. And my dad's big, unselfconscious laugh that would fill a room, I hear that too.

I don't know if they'd be proud of this decision I've made or not. One of my dad's favorite sayings was "If it seems too good to be true, it probably is."

Remembering that sends a little chill of foreboding down my spine.

Squaring my shoulders, I tell myself that what matters now is getting on with the important business at hand. With the paperwork I took from the kitchen counter, I go into my office, where I fire up the computer and have a look at the trust account.

It's all there. Twenty million in my name.

I stare at the number, letting it sink in.

Then I make myself an espresso and take it back to my desk, where I compile a list of everything that needs to get done.

The first thing on that list is calling my employees to tell them they're rehired.

And that they're all getting a nice fat raise.

Days go by. I pay the rent. I catch up on the overdue bills. I leave a message for the guy at the CDTFA to try to make arrangements to pay the tax thing, but he doesn't call me back, so I go online to check my account with them.

I can't find a balance due anywhere.

Typical government bureaucracy bullshit. The website probably hasn't been updated in years.

I expect some collections thug will come and try to impound my car, so I start parking blocks away from the store. Until I can clear that debt, I've got some hiding to do.

Then I find a local defense attorney and send him all the information about the lawsuit along with a big retainer check.

He informs me how the litigation process works and tells me to sit tight, because lawsuits can take years to settle. When I ask if we'll go to court, he laughs. Apparently, only a tiny percent of lawsuits ever go to trial.

In the meantime, I'll need to keep sending him cash on a monthly basis.

What a racket. The Mafia probably doesn't even have such a good money-making scheme.

I move my things into the modest guest bedroom at the castle, carrying my clothes from the master closet down the long corridor myself. When the packages from my shopping spree with Dani arrive, I put those into the guest bedroom too.

And because I'm vindictive and want revenge on Callum for weirdly knowing how I like my eggs and coffee, I make a game of ordering breakfast from the chef, but only unhealthy sugary things that come in a box.

One day it's Froot Loops. Another day it's PopTarts. Another it's Pillsbury cinnamon toaster strudel. I imagine the chef reporting back to Callum that he married a child.

Every night, I lie in bed and wonder what will happen when the lord of the manor returns.

I wonder about the rope in his drawer and the other locked cases.

I wonder if I'll be left alone like this most of the time and if that's a good thing or not.

I wonder if he's out banging some hot model and hate myself for even thinking about that.

I drive by my apartment several times after work, still in disbelief I don't live there anymore. There's already a For Rent sign in the front yard, so whoever came and collected all my stuff must've also told the management company I was moving.

Purely from curiosity, I call to ask what the balance is on my lease and if there's any penalty for breaking it. They tell me the whole thing has been paid in full, penalties included.

I don't have to ask by whom.

All the while, Callum McCord himself simmers on the back burner of my brain.

Then, in the dead of one sultry summer night, he returns.

Eighteen

I sense him before I see him, the way a storm brewing in the atmosphere can be felt long before the first drop of rain ever hits your face. I'm not sure if that's what wakes me up, but when I open my eyes to the darkness of the guest room, everything is still and quiet.

So quiet, the beating of my heart seems loud.

The air crackles with electricity. Some animal awareness deep in my brain warns me that danger is nearby. When I turn my head, I see Callum in the doorway of the room.

Silhouetted in light from the hallway, he stands motionless, his hands by his sides, his legs spread apart. He's barefoot and bare chested, wearing only a pair of jeans. His face is obscured by shadows, but I know he's looking at me.

I'm lying on top of the sheets in a thin cotton camisole and panties, my arms and legs exposed.

For a moment, nothing happens. Neither of us moves. I'm still in that hazy dream state between sleep and waking and am not entirely sure he isn't a figment of my imagination.

Then he steps into the room and an electrical current sizzles through me, alighting every nerve.

Quiet as a panther, he moves closer.

He stops beside the bed and gazes silently down at me.

Even in the shadows, the bulge under his zipper is unmistakable.

"You're back," I whisper nervously.

"So it seems."

He leans over, plants a hand on the mattress beside my head, and settles his other hand possessively around my neck. Staring down at me, his dark eyes glint silver in the shadows, like a cat's.

Trembling now, I wrap both hands around his thick forearm and stare up at him in growing anxiety. I want to say something, but I don't know what. The words are trapped in my throat.

But words become unnecessary when he leans down and kisses me.

He takes my lower lip between his teeth and bites it. Then he licks the sting away and kisses me again, this time until I'm breathless, squirming, and starting to sweat. My pulse is going wild now, thudding hard against my rib cage. My breathing is fast and shallow. My skin prickles with heat.

Sliding his hand from my neck down to my chest, he cups one of my breasts. When he breaks the kiss to suck on my rigid nipple right through my camisole, I gasp.

Then he bites it.

The pleasure is intense. The moan I make is loud and involuntary.

Kneeling next to the bed, he pulls up my camisole and drags his cheek over my chest, nuzzling my bare flesh with his beard, then his mouth. As I pant and cling to his shoulders, he sucks each of my nipples until they ache.

Then he slides his hand down my belly and between my thighs. He squeezes my pussy through my underwear, drawing another gasp from my lips.

"My sweet wife. You're already soaking wet for me."

His voice is so soft, but also hot and dark, with a thrilling edge to it.

I've never been this sexually aroused in my life.

I whisper, "We shouldn't be doing this."

"Oh, but we really should."

"I—I don't want to."

His voice hardens. "What did I tell you about lying to me?"

Pushing my thighs apart, he gives me a sharp, stinging slap between my legs.

I jerk and cry out in surprise, then lie there panting and disoriented as throbbing hot waves of pleasure spread throughout my body. Nose to nose, we stare at each other. His blazing eyes dare me to say I didn't like it, but I don't.

Because I did like it.

But this is the man I married for money, and I'm the girl he married for his inheritance. We shouldn't be muddying the waters like this.

Except I really want to.

Very softly, he says, "You need to learn to be my good girl. And your first lesson is in manners."

"You know manners aren't exactly my strong suit."

"Do you trust me?"

"Not even a little bit."

He chuckles. "Another lie. You'd have already screamed for help and gouged my eyes out if you thought you were in danger."

Trembling all over, I lick my lips and gaze up into his eyes. "I'm...I'm scared."

"No, you're not. You're excited."

He waits for me to deny it, but I don't. The evidence is too obvious. I've already started rocking my hips against his hand, desperate for him to shove his fingers inside me.

There's just something about this man. He's so damned attractive. I've never met anyone with such incredible magnetism.

He slides his other hand under the back of my neck and squeezes. "Say it, Emery. I want to hear the words."

Hyperventilating, I close my eyes and whisper, "Yes. I'm excited."

"Good girl."

As a reward, he softly strokes his thumb back and forth over my aching clit, petting me through my wet panties. He gives me that and nothing more, until I start restlessly moving my legs in the sheets, desperate to feel his mouth between my thighs.

He croons, "I know, baby. I know what you want. And as soon as you ask me properly, I'll feast on this pretty wet cunt, then fuck it. If you're a good girl and you ask very nicely, I'll spank your sweet ass, then fuck that too."

My pulse is flying. My entire body is shaking. I can't catch my breath. I've never had a man speak to me so explicitly, so I had no idea how arousing it would be.

I can't risk getting emotionally involved with him! I should be telling him to get lost! I should be doing anything other than lying here writhing in the bedsheets and letting him manipulate my body!

Attempting logic, I say, "What if we did it only once? To get it out of our systems."

"Everyone knows that doesn't work. Now ask me for what you want. And say please. You have five seconds."

His hands are hot on my flesh. His breath is warm in my ear. His husky voice just might be the death of me. He smells like pure masculinity—skin and sex, heat and power—and I'm so turned on, I can hardly think straight.

"Five."

I whisper nervously, "We should talk about this."

"Four."

"Like set some boundaries or something?"

"Three."

"I just...I just don't want things to get complicated, you know what I mean?"

Staring hungrily at my mouth, he growls, "Two."

"Okay, fine! I want you to fuck me, all right? Please fuck me."

His grin is devilish. "You sure? I don't want you accusing me of pressuring you when you wake up sore and bruised with my handprints on your ass and my cum all over you."

This asshole. He's rubbing my yes in my face for his own amusement.

"Have I told you lately that I can't stand you?"

"Yes, baby. But we both know you're a liar."

He kisses me like I've never been kissed in my entire life. It's devouring and all-consuming, an undeniable claim. Ten seconds in, I think I feel my soul leave my body.

Then he rips off my panties, shoves my legs apart, and falls on my pussy like he's been starving for it.

Shocked at the feel of his hot mouth, I cry out and dig my nails into his shoulder. He licks my clit furiously, strumming his thick tongue back and forth until I moan. Then he slides two fingers inside me and finger fucks me, plunging his fingers deep while he sucks hard on my clit.

I buck against his mouth like a madwoman. "Oh God, yes, *that feels so good*."

He reaches up and pulls on my hard nipple, then gives my breast a stinging slap.

I can no longer speak, so I moan my approval.

He keeps going until my clit throbs, my uterus contracts, and my back arches off the bed. I orgasm in his mouth, clawing his shoulder and groaning.

He holds me down with a hand flattened over my belly as I come hard, jerking and grinding my pussy into his face. Then he straightens and rains down a series of brisk slaps on my pulsating clit.

"Come for me, baby. Let the whole city hear who you belong to."

I scream his name.

He growls, "That's my good fucking girl. Now ask me to spank your ass."

When I do, he flips me over and spanks me, going back and forth between each cheek as I grind my pelvis into the bed.

Sobbing, I clench the sheets in my fists. He stops spanking me suddenly to push his fingers inside me again, hissing in approval when he feels how wet I am.

He demands, "You want my cock in that dripping cunt, don't you, sweetheart?"

"Yes!"

"Say please."

"Please! Pretty please! Hurry! I need you to fuck me!"

Hearing me beg like that drives him crazy. He quickly positions himself behind me, drags me to my knees, and rips open his fly. Gripping my hip in one hand, he uses the other to drag the head of his hard cock back and forth through my wetness until it's slippery. Then he grabs my other hip and shoves it deep inside, filling me.

I cry out his name.

"Yes, wife. I own you now. You're mine. Now take my dick like a good girl and maybe I'll let you suck me off when I'm ready to come."

Delirious, I squeeze my eyes shut as he starts to pound into me, unforgivingly hard.

Wetness slips down my inner thighs. His husky grunts of pleasure fill my ears. I feel high and unstable, a kite caught in a tornado.

He fucks me until I'm moaning loudly, on the verge of another orgasm. Then he sits back onto his heels, taking me with him with an arm wrapped around my body.

I drop my head back so it rests on his shoulder. Holding my back against his chest with my thighs spread open over his, he puts his mouth next to my ear.

His voice gravelly with lust, he says, "This belongs to me, doesn't it?"

He reaches around and down between my legs, sliding his fingers around the place he's sunk inside me.

I whimper.

Flexing his hips so his hard cock is seated fully inside me, he whispers, "Tell me it's mine, and I'll let you come again."

His thumb glides over my clit. My core contracts around him. I jerk, moaning. My nipples are hard and aching, and I can't catch my breath. I tilt my hips back, desperate for him to start thrusting again.

"So fucking perfect. This perfect cunt belongs to me, doesn't it, baby? Say it."

I whisper, "Yes."

"Yes, what?"

"Yes, it belongs to you. All of me belongs to you."

I hardly know what I'm saying, but it pleases him so much, he shivers.

Stroking my clit with the pads of two fingers, he thrusts into me again. I reach up and around the back of his head, digging my fingers into his hair. When I turn my face toward his, he takes my mouth in a deep, dominant kiss.

He's the most delicious thing I've ever tasted.

This is so good, but also so, so bad. I should've known he'd feel like this. I should've known we'd fit together this way. From the first time he walked into my store and our eyes met, I felt the chemistry between us.

I wanted him before I even knew his name.

He thrusts into me again and again, fondling my swollen clit. The open zipper of his jeans bites into my tender, throbbing ass with every motion of his hips. He moves his other hand up my ribs and squeezes my breast, then pinches my nipple.

"Ah!" I shudder in pleasure and beg him to do it again.

He pants, "Fuck, baby. You're even better than I imagined. You're everything I dreamed."

His words are rough. His breathing is rougher. He's getting close to losing control. He thrusts hard a few more times, then curses.

"On your hands and knees. Get ready to open that pretty mouth for me."

He releases me, withdraws, and stands at the edge of the bed.

Panting, I move to face him. He gathers a fistful of my hair and grips his erection in his other hand, pulling me closer to it.

He growls, "Now suck and swallow. And don't you spill one fucking drop of my cum, you understand me?"

Flexing his hips, he shoves his thick cock past my lips.

I take it eagerly into my mouth, using one hand to balance on the bed. The other I wrap around his shaft. I suck, lick, and stroke him until his guttural groans fill the room.

Gripping my head in both hands now, he whispers raggedly, "Here I come, baby. Ah, fuck, *here I come.*"

Jerking and cursing, he spills himself in hot pulses onto my tongue. I swallow, eyes watering as I struggle to breathe through my nose and accommodate his girth without gagging.

When his twitching and cursing are over and he's gazing down at me with lowered lids, his chest heaving, he slides a hand down to my neck and squeezes.

Gaze locked to mine, he exhales deeply, then whispers, "Perfect."

I'm unsurprised that his simple praise sends an involuntary shudder of pleasure though my body. It's why I've been so resistant to this. Why I wanted our relationship to be purely business, an emotionless transaction we'd both emerge from unscathed.

But now it's too late. We touched the fire. There's no going back from here.

The tragedy of it all is that I already know this man will ruin me, but even that isn't enough to make me want to save myself.

Now, I just want to jump into the flames and burn.

Nineteen

I wake in an unfamiliar room with an unfamiliar soreness between my legs and a feeling of dread hanging over me like thunderclouds. I look around in confusion. It takes a moment for my brain to kick into gear. When it does, I groan and close my eyes.

I had sex with my husband.

Rough, passionate, filthy hot sex, which I loved with every ounce of my being.

This has heartbreak written all over it.

"Good morning."

I tilt my head toward the husky voice near my right ear and look up into Callum's face. I'm lying against his nude body, tucked under his arm with one of my legs resting over his and an arm thrown over his broad chest.

We're cuddling? What a disaster.

Feeling embarrassed and a little shy, I say, "Good morning. Where am I?"

"Our bedroom."

"Right. I suppose I should've recognized the girly floral prints and dainty antique furniture. What am I doing here?"

"Why wouldn't you be here?"

"I should be in my own bedroom."

"You are in your own bedroom."

When I open my mouth to protest that my room is the green guest room, he adds, "End of discussion."

"Aw, that's cute. You actually believe that, don't you?"

Rolling me onto my back, he settles himself on top of me and stares down into my face.

"I'm not intimidated by that look, Callum."

"You should be."

"Annoyance always gives me courage. I can't breathe with you on top of me like this. You weigh as much as a small European car."

"That's the strangest compliment I've ever been given."

"It wasn't a compliment."

He kisses the tip of my nose. "I love it when you glare at me like that. Small evil things are my favorite."

"Get a Chihuahua. What are you going to tell your police chief buddy when I suffocate to death?"

He smiles. "That you died happy."

I close my eyes and sigh.

Lowering his head, he whispers into my ear, "Your mouth is heaven."

I feel my cheeks heating, but don't open my eyes. A Technicolor highlight reel of last night's fun starts to play under my lids.

"I have something to say."

He chuckles. "There you go with the announcements again."

"Be quiet. Okay, here it is."

When I hesitate, he says, "Are you going to open your eyes for this?"

"No."

"It's that bad that you can't look me in the eye?"

"Yes. I mean, no. I don't know. Be quiet!"

He drops his face to my neck and smothers a laugh.

Happy Callum is interesting. And confusing. How many personalities does this man have?

"So here's the thing. I enjoyed last night. A lot. Which you could probably tell by all the screaming. Anyway..." I clear my throat. "This is the strangest relationship I've ever had. Which is saying something, because my taste in men tends to run to walking red flags with good hair. But I don't do well with ambiguity, and mysteries don't intrigue me. They just make my anxiety worse. So I'm going to ask a question, and I'd appreciate it if you'd be brutally honest in your answer."

Inhaling a shaky breath, I brace myself. "I know we said don't-ask-don't-tell, but how many other people are you sleeping with?"

There's a moment of silence where I can tell he's looking at me. Then he rolls to his back, taking me with him and wrapping his arms around me. I tuck my head under his chin to hide. He strokes my hair, his chest warm under my cheek.

"None. You?"

"Don't pretend you don't know. And go back. None?"

"None."

"Are you sure?"

He says drily, "I think I'd remember."

"What I meant was, are you sure that's your final answer? Because I'm going to freak out either way. It's fine if you tell me the truth."

Grasping my chin, he forces me to look at him. Staring into my eyes, he says, "I'm not fucking anyone but you."

I can tell he's sincere. My toes curl in pleasure. The relief I feel is so sweet, I sigh.

I hate myself.

"Okay, next question."

"There are more? Wonderful."

"Don't sound so depressed. Next question: do you have any diseases I should know about? Of the sexual sort, I mean."

His stomach muscles clench. He presses his lips together. He's trying not to laugh and doing a shit job of it.

"STDs aren't funny, Callum."

"No, but your timing is."

"I couldn't exactly ask you in the middle of all the spanking and raunchy talk, now, could I?"

"I don't recall taping your mouth shut."

"Just answer the damn question!"

"Also no. Fuck, you're adorable when you're like this."

"Like *what*? And choose your words carefully, because my knee is within striking distance of your balls."

He decides to answer by rolling us over again so he's on top of me, smashing me with all his glorious manly weight. Not that I'll tell him I enjoy it, because he's already enough of a monster. Then he kisses me deeply, holding my head in his hands.

When we come up for air, he says gruffly, "I need to fuck you again."

"I like that plan, but we need to talk about some things first. No, don't flex your hips. That's distracting. And stop kissing my neck. I have more questions."

"So go ahead and ask them."

He bites my neck, then slides his hand down to my chest and starts to fondle my breast.

"I'll forget what I was saying if you keep doing that."

Pinching my nipple, he chuckles. "Hopefully."

I shiver in pleasure, loving the feel of his rough cheek against my neck and his rough hand on my body. I could get addicted to this very quickly.

Sliding my arms up around his shoulders, I say, "How did you get that signed copy of *Outlander*?"

"I'm me."

"You say that like it's a reasonable answer."

"It is."

He bends his head to my breast and sucks my hard nipple into his mouth. I stifle a moan and close my eyes, trying to concentrate.

"Um. Where was I?"

"Spreading your legs."

He reaches down and pulls my leg up next to his hip, so his erection is nestled between my thighs. It's huge, hot, and hard.

All the good words start with the letter H.

"Oh, I remember. Where did you go so suddenly after we got married?"

"Work."

He pulls my other leg up, so my thighs are spread open around his hips. He reaches between us, takes his stiff cock in his hand, and starts to rub the head back and forth between my legs.

"Work?" I repeat breathlessly. "You were gone for almost a week."

"I had to go to Prague."

I want to ask what's in Prague, but get distracted by the way he's nipping my nipple. When he slides the head of his cock inside me, I gasp.

Against my breast, he murmurs, "Be a good girl and ask for my dick."

"Or you could be a good boy and just give it to me."

He presses his teeth harder into my nipple, but if he thinks that's a punishment, he's crazy. I love how it feels so much, I moan. Then I wriggle my hips to try to get him deeper inside me.

He growls, "Do what you're told."

"You're not in charge of me."

"The hell I'm not."

He flexes his hips, giving me another inch, stretching me wider. Desperate for more, I moan again, pulling at his hair.

"See?"

"Oh, look, you're being smug again. What a surprise."

Grabbing one of my wrists, he presses it against the pillow above my head. Then he grabs the other one and traps it together with the first, clasping both in one of his big hands. Leaning on an elbow, he slides his other hand under my head and makes a fist in my hair.

His mouth close to my ear, he whispers, "Do as you're told, wife, or I'll fuck you, but I won't let you come."

Hearing him call me "wife" does strange things to me. Unsettling, emotional things. I squirm underneath him, trying to distract him long enough to get him all the way inside me without having to cave to his ridiculous demand.

I should've known it wouldn't work. The man's power of concentration is diabolical.

With sudden, shocking speed, he flips me over and starts to spank my ass.

When I cry out, he says, "I know you like this, so don't act like you weren't hoping it's what you'd get."

"I don't!"

"Yes, you do. Let me prove it to you."

He smooths his hand over my burning cheeks, then slides it between my legs and dips his fingers into my drenched pussy.

"Darling wife," he whispers, laughter in his voice. "You're such a shitty liar."

I bury my face in the pillow and gnash my teeth. When he swirls his fingers around my clit, lazily stroking it, I shudder, loving the way it feels.

"Do you want my mouth on this?"

"Isn't it obvious?"

"Say it."

"What's with this obsession with talking during sex?"

"It's called communicating."

"No, it's called distracting."

"You're the one doing the line of questioning. Now say what I need to hear."

I try to lift my head to turn and look at him, but he flattens me back down with a hand placed firmly between my shoulder blades and commands, "Say it."

We're both quiet for a moment as he works his magical fingers between my legs. My pussy is throbbing, aching to be filled. When I start to move my hips in time with the motion of his fingers, he warns, "Emery."

Squeezing my eyes shut, I say, "Please."

"Not good enough. You know better. Say it all."

He slides his fingers up, down, and all around, pausing every so often to rub my clit with the pad of his thumb until I'm panting.

He whispers, "Be my good girl. Come on, baby. Say it for me."

My skin burns. My nipples tingle. I rock my hips, chasing his fingers, until he makes a low, warning growl deep in his chest, and I give in.

I say breathlessly, "I want you to eat me. I want you to fuck me. I want you to make me come. And I want you to do it right now because you're *killing* me."

For my reward, he rolls me to my back and covers my pussy with his mouth. When I arch and moan, he shoves two fingers deep inside me and starts to pump them in and out.

I dig my fingers into his hair and rock my hips against his face.

When I groan loudly, he lifts his head and says, "You need to come?"

"Yes."

"Good. You'll do it choking on my cock, then again with it stuffed inside your pussy."

He falls onto his back, drags me on top of him, arranges me so my thighs are spread over his face and his jutting erection is inches from mine.

Then he smacks me on the ass and orders, "Suck until I tell you to stop."

Panting, I grip the base of his hard cock and lick the slit on the crown. Callum growls his approval and shoves his tongue deep inside me. I ride it, moaning, then take him all the way down my throat.

He grunts into me, digging his fingers into my bottom as he eats my pussy. Then he slides a hand between my ass cheeks and strokes me there, growling when I mewl and shudder.

When he sinks a thick finger into my ass, I come.

"Keep sucking that cock, wife," he hisses, thrusting his finger in and out. Then he sucks hard on my clit, making my whole body jerk.

I open my mouth as wide as I can and pull on his dick, working my hand up and down the shaft as I bob my head, mindlessly obeying him as pleasure floods through my body.

"Ah, good girl," he pants. "That's my good fucking girl. Come on my face."

I can feel how wet I am and know it's probably all over him, but can't stop myself from frantically rocking my hips, grinding against his mouth. Something about how explicitly he speaks to me makes me feel so uninhibited.

I keep sucking on him until my jaw aches and the contractions in my pussy have stopped. Then I'm manhandled into another position, lying on my back with my ankles hooked over his shoulders.

He thrusts into me with a savage snarl, then fucks me, bending over me with my breasts gripped in his hands. He's so impassioned, I have to hold on to his shoulders so I don't fly up and crash into the headboard.

All the while, he stares into my eyes with a look of feverish intensity, his gaze never leaving mine.

Another contraction makes me clench around him. I moan, bucking my hips and meeting every thrust of his with one of my own.

"You're gonna come again," he whispers, ecstatic. "That greedy little pussy loves to get fucked by her master's cock, doesn't she?"

"You're not my master," I protest weakly, eyes rolling back in my head.

As my orgasm hits, his dark laughter rings in my ears.

Callum pulls out of me, finishes on my stomach, then smears his cum all over my belly with his fingers.

Then he sits back onto his heels and surveys his handiwork, grinning like the devil.

Sated and sweating, I gaze up at him and wonder how deep in over my head I've gotten myself.

Probably a million miles.

Noticing the look on my face, he chuckles. "Don't worry. You're stronger than you think."

Then he picks me up and carries me into the bathroom.

Setting me on my feet beside the giant glassed-in shower, he turns on the spray, waits until he's satisfied with the temperature, then pulls me inside with him. He backs me up into the water and proceeds to shampoo my hair.

I close my eyes and stand motionless as he lathers my scalp and gently massages it with his fingers. He turns me around and massages my neck and shoulders, too, then squirts soap from a dispenser in a niche in the shower wall and washes my body.

His hands glide confidently over my skin as if he's done it a thousand times before. As if he knows every inch of me, every curve, crease, and tender spot that makes me shiver.

"Callum?"

"Hmm?"

"I'm feeling some kind of way about all this."

"The word you're searching for is good."

"I was thinking more along the lines of discombobulated."

"I love that word. Let's rinse your hair."

He maneuvers me back under the warm spray and tilts my head back so the shampoo runs down my temples. When he puts a bar of soap into my hands, I open my eyes and look at him.

He stands in front of me, wet and glorious, hot and smoldering, waiting in silence for me to wash him.

I let my gaze trail over his body, taking in all the planes and angles, all the muscles and manliness and the tattoos down his arm, and pinch my lower lip between my teeth.

Eyes aglow, he whispers, "That look will get you fucked again."

His thick shaft is already stiffening.

Staring at it, I say, "Your stamina is impressive."

He grabs my wrist and draws me closer, lowering his head. "Wash me, wife," he whispers, licking my earlobe. He curls my hand around his cock. "Do a good job, and I'll reward you."

"I'm not a circus animal," I retort crossly, going from hot and bothered to cold and stabby. "I don't do tricks on command."

He captures my mouth, kissing me deeply as he backs me against the shower wall. When I'm trapped between the marble and his big hot body, he wraps one hand around my throat. The other he slides between my legs.

Thrusting a finger inside me, he says gruffly, "Don't be disrespectful."

Swallowing a moan, I say defiantly, "Don't order me around."

He lowers his head and sucks hard on the side of my neck, pressing his teeth into my skin. I shudder and rock against his hand, wanting to push him away and slap him, but also wanting whatever else he's about to give me.

I've never met anyone so fucking sexy who I also wanted to kill with my bare hands.

Working his finger faster in and out, he leans down and sucks on my taut nipple. It feels delicious. I arch into his mouth. The bar of soap slips from my hands. When he uses his teeth, I yelp and clap him on the back.

Against my flesh, he chuckles. "My defiant little darling. Let's see how long you can keep defying me before you start to beg."

He turns me around, bends me over so my hands are flattened on the bench seat that runs along the wall, and starts to spank me, holding me in place by the scruff of my neck.

When I holler a curse at him, he slides his hand between my legs and strokes my pussy, tweaking my clit and making me cry out.

"Make another sound, and I'll give you something to keep you quiet," he growls, slapping my ass again.

Steam swirls around my face. Heat blooms over my bottom. My nipples harden. My breath catches, and my knees start to shake. The way he talks to me makes me furious, but also so turned on, I don't know which way is up.

He fondles my pussy again, rubbing his fingers back and forth over my clit until it's engorged, and I'm panting. Sliding his finger inside me, he hisses in approval when I flex my hips toward his hand.

"Oh, yes, wife. I know what you need."

He slides his finger out and starts fondling my ass, gently rubbing the sensitive knot of muscle until I think I'll collapse.

He says softly, "Beg for it, baby."

I grit my teeth and say, "No."

He slides his hand down and starts rubbing my pussy again, his strong fingers delving deep inside me, then swirling all around, paying special attention to my aching clit. Then he goes back up to my ass, petting it with gliding strokes until I'm helpless to stop the little moans slipping from my mouth.

I think I could climax just from this.

His voice low and dark, Callum says, "Tell your master which hole you want him to fuck. And tell me nicely, or I'll put you on your knees and fuck both rougher than you'll want it."

Dizzy from his words, their effect on my body, and the steam swirling around me like mist, I whimper his name. He responds by chuckling.

"You're testing my patience, wife. Let's try this another way. Cunt?"

He thrusts two fingers into my pussy. I jerk and moan.

"That wasn't a yes. How about now?" He pulls his fingers out. I feel pressure on my ass, then he slides a finger in up to the knuckle.

My moan is long and loud, echoing off the walls. My arms shake so hard, I fall onto my forearms on the bench to try to keep my balance.

Callum's laugh is gentle. "Sweet little ass it is. Now use your words and your manners. I won't give you what you want until you ask for it nicely."

How is he doing this to me?

How can he bend me to his will with nothing more than dirty talk and strong fingers?

I fight with myself for a moment, then decide. I whisper, "Please, Callum, I want you to fuck me in the ass."

He leans down, grips my jaw in his hand, and turns my face to his. Gazing deep into my eyes, he says in a husky voice, "Good girl. You're my perfect pet, and I adore you."

He kisses me tenderly, then releases my face, straightening. Keeping one hand resting on my lower back, he pumps a squirt of something into his other hand from a small metal container in the niche on the wall.

"Organic coconut oil," he explains, spreading it over my ass. Then he slowly slides his index finger inside me. When I moan and shudder, he whispers, "Goddamn, woman."

He adds another finger, crooning in approval when I gasp and arch my back.

My face is hot, my heart is pounding, and my body shakes all over. My eyes drift shut.

Callum works his fingers carefully in and out of my ass for several moments, until my clit is pulsing and my nipples ache. I can't take it anymore and hang my head, resting my forehead on my arms as hot water runs down my back and legs and everything inside me quivers.

"Please," I beg in a broken whisper. "I need you."

Exhaling with a groan, he says, "Ah, God, baby, I've waited so long to hear you say that."

He replaces his fingers with the engorged head of his cock and slowly slides it inside me.

I cry out.

He slides a hand around between my legs and strokes my clit, starting to pump gently in and out of my ass as he fingers my pussy. I'm stretched open wide around him, gasping with the kind of pleasure that walks the razor's edge with pain.

And as he begins to thrust more deeply, grunting words of praise and filthy expletives, I let go of any lingering hesitation, shyness, or fear I had and give myself over to him completely.

I sob his name.

He moans, grips my hips, and thrusts harder. "Get ready to take it, baby. Get ready to take it all."

I orgasm to the sound of those words echoing in my ears and our mingled cries of pleasure bouncing off the shower walls.

Afterward, I'm in such a daze, Callum towels me off and puts me back to bed.

He draws the covers over me and kisses me on the forehead. "I'll have some food sent up. In the meantime, rest."

He pauses, smoothing a hand over my damp hair. His voice an octave lower, he says, "And if I ever catch you without your ring again, darling, there will be hell to pay."

He gazes into my eyes for a moment to let the warning sink in so I know he's serious. Then he turns and strolls naked back into the bathroom, whistling *The Pink Panther* theme song.

I'll be annoyed at him later. Right now, I'm too wiped out.

I don't know how long I doze, but when I wake up, a tray of food and a cup of coffee waits for me on the writing desk, along with the big diamond ring in a porcelain dish.

There's also a handwritten note from Callum.

I want to tie your legs to the bed, bind your hands above your head, bite your neck, and bury my cock in your gorgeous body.

Looking around the empty bedroom, I wonder aloud, "What kind of vitamins does this man take?"

He left a black silk robe draped over the desk chair. I put it on, tying the sash around my waist and yawning. Taking a sip of the coffee, I'm surprised to discover it's piping hot.

It must have just been delivered.

I inspect the ceiling over the bed, wondering if there's a camera in it, but it's bare.

I debate with myself about whether or not I should eat breakfast, but decide I don't have the energy for a fight right now. My body is sore and aching, and my brain is cottage cheese. I'll take up my dining preferences with the lord of the manor the next time I see him.

After I finish the poached eggs and buttered toast, I pad down the corridor to the guest bedroom in my bare feet. I get dressed, wind my hair into a messy bun, and grab my handbag from the dresser. When I head downstairs, I find Arlo in the kitchen with the chef, a portly older man with a friendly sunburned face.

"Good morning, Mrs. McCord," says Arlo, looking up from his newspaper. He's sitting on a stool at the big island with a cup of black coffee but stands when I enter.

"Please don't stand up. I'm not royalty."

"Around here, you are."

Embarrassed, I wave that off. "Good morning to you too.

And I already told you to call me Emery. We don't have to be so formal." I turn to the chef and smile "Hi there."

"Good morning, Mrs. McCord. I'm Daniel. It's a pleasure to meet you. How was your breakfast?'

He seems so earnest and kind. I don't want to hurt his feelings by telling him I considered throwing it out the window, so I smile and tell him it was great.

Looking relieved, he beams. "That's good to hear. If you have any dietary restrictions or requests, just let me know."

"I will, thanks. Arlo, have you seen Callum?"

"Yes, he just left for the office."

Why am I disappointed? "And where is that?"

"The Wilshire Grand in downtown. McCord Media occupies the top ten floors of the building."

"Gotcha." I stand there awkwardly for a moment, aware of how strange it is that I have no idea where my husband works and unsure of what else to say. "Well, I'm off to the shop. Have a good day, guys."

Arlo says, "I'll follow you to the garage. You'll want the keys for whichever car you'd like to drive today."

I pat my handbag. "I've got the keys right here. I'm taking my VW."

When Arlo hesitates, looking at me sideways, my heart drops. "What?"

"I'm afraid Mr. McCord has had the Volkswagen disposed of."

"*What?*"

"Yes. I believe he thought it unsafe for you to drive. He had it removed from the premises early this morning."

I stand there with my heart pounding and my stomach twisting in disbelief. "But that was *my* car! He had no right to do that! He *can't* do that!"

The chef politely excuses himself and disappears behind the pantry door.

Arlo says quietly, "I'm sorry, Mrs. McCord, but it's already done."

I want to tear out all my hair. I want to break things. I want to scream. What I do instead is close my eyes and breathe deeply through my nose, reminding myself that this isn't Arlo's fault. Having a meltdown in front of him won't solve anything.

When I open my eyes, I say, "Arlo, I like you. But if you call me Mrs. McCord again, I'll have to change my opinion."

I leave the kitchen, breathing fire. When I get to the garage, I survey the rows of luxury sports cars with narrowed eyes, calculating which one would be the most fun to put a dent in.

Arlo strolls up beside me and holds out a set of keys. He says casually, "That black Bentley's one of his favorites...Emery."

We look at each other.

I take the keys and give him a humorless smile. "I think you and I are going to get along just fine."

When I pull out from the driveway and turn aggressively onto the street, I clip the curb.

I never imagined that the sound of concrete shredding expensive aluminum rims could be so satisfying.

Twenty-One

Sabine is already waiting for me outside when I arrive at the shop. I park, hoping the Bentley will be vandalized in my absence.

"Hello, gorgeous," she drawls, eyeing me. "You've got that freshly fucked look."

My face reddens. I unlock the front door. Still talking, she follows me inside.

"Which is interesting, since when you called to give me the news, you said that this thing with you and the billionaire was purely a matter of convenience."

"It was."

"What changed?"

I flip on the lights, stash my handbag under the counter, and turn to her, sighing. "In a nutshell? The man is a sorcerer. He entranced me with his dick. Now I know why it's called a magic wand. But let's never talk about it again. I'm pretending it didn't happen."

"Deal." She pauses. "Which means I'll ask again in ten minutes."

"I know. In the meantime, let's make a list of how we can spruce this place up." Propping my hands on my hips, I gaze around the shop in dissatisfaction. "It's starting to look like a feral cat shelter in here."

Sabine laughs. "*Starting* to?"

"Oh, be quiet. I never claimed to be Martha Stewart. Wait, you're the stylish one. *You* make the list. Here's a pen and a pad of paper."

Her eyes light up when I hand them to her. "Can I be in charge of the whole project, not just making the list?"

I shrug. "Why not? I've got the decorating skills of a raccoon on meth."

"Speaking of raccoons on meth, what are you wearing?"

Frowning, I look down at the outfit I'm in, then back up at her. "Clothes."

She wrinkles her nose.

"What's wrong with this outfit? I think it's interesting."

"Yes, if you're high on cocaine, it looks interesting. To the rest of the world, it looks like a cry for help."

"I'll have you know I got this on Rodeo Drive."

She arches a brow. "They opened a clown store on Rodeo?"

"You're fired."

She laughs, shaking her head and turning away. "I'll get started on the list."

I go to the office and work for about an hour before coming back up front just as a good-looking young guy is walking through the door. Wearing board shorts, a hoodie, and flip-flops, he looks around, smiling.

"Hi. Can I help you?"

"Yeah. I want to get a book for my girlfriend. I'd rather support a small business than those big corporate guys next door, so I thought I'd try here first."

This person is my new best friend.

"Great, thank you! Are you looking for something specific?"

He shoves his hands into his pockets and glances away. His cheeks turn ruddy. He clears his throat, then says, "Uh, yeah. Do you carry the uh, spicy stuff?"

Wiping down the counter near the espresso machine, Sabine looks over her shoulder at me and waggles her eyebrows. I know what she's thinking: the perfect man *does* exist.

I say warmly, "We sure do. I've got a whole section of erotica. Follow me."

I lead him to the romance section and point out different areas on the shelves. Each is tagged with a discreet white plaque with a number of red peppers, from one to five.

"So we've got a hotness rating that we use for an easy, at-a-glance gauge of spice. One chili pepper is the lowest spice rating. It's pretty much only kissing. Two chili peppers is kissing plus some foreplay or frisky talk, but no open-door sex scenes. When you get into the three-chili range, you're gonna get some lovemaking, but nothing too explicit. Four chilis will include explicit sex, probably multiple chapters of it, and five chilis"—I chuckle—"will get you some serious barn-burner sex. Anything goes with five chilis, which is probably why it's our most popular seller."

When I turn to him, he's staring at the shelves like he was just ushered through the pearly gates of heaven and is thrilled by the look of the place, but is also quite confused at how to find his way around.

I say gently, "Would you like me to make a recommendation?"

His relief is palpable. "Could you? That would be awesome."

"Sure. Which chili pepper are we looking at?"

His cheeks go ruddy again. He says sheepishly, "Five."

Smiling, I pat him on the shoulder. "Good man. She's a lucky girl. Try this one." I pull out one of Harper's favorites and hand it to him.

He looks at it doubtfully.

"Don't let the flowery cover fool you. This sucker will burn off your eyebrows."

To prove it to him, I take it back and flip to a chapter famous for its eloquent depiction of a woman stimulating her lover's prostate with a vibrator while performing fellatio on him in front of fifty people at a sex club.

I tap the page. "Here you go. Read that."

We stand shoulder to shoulder, reading the page together, until he exhales and says faintly, "Holy shit."

"I know. It's amazing, right? This author's a genius. She has this new series coming out at the end of the year about a woman who decides to explore her sexuality after leaving a stifling marriage and winds up having like ten different lovers, all devoted to her needs."

Appalled, he looks at me. "*Ten?*"

Great. I've traumatized him.

I'm about to reassure him that his girlfriend has no interest in having ten lovers—probably—but before I can, I'm interrupted by a voice from behind us.

"It does seem excessive, doesn't it?"

The tone is deadly soft and filled with menace. We turn.

Callum stands three feet away, staring at my customer with his nostrils flared, his fists clenched, and violence burning in his eyes.

Beside me, the young guy audibly gulps.

I say to him, "Go ahead and take that to the register. Sabine will help you check out."

I've never seen anyone run so fast. He sets a land speed record.

When he's gone, and I'm alone in the romance aisle with the T-Rex, I say, "What are you doing here?"

He demands, "Why haven't you been answering your cell phone?"

His furious tone takes me aback. "Why? Is there an emergency?"

"Yes," he says, jaw clenched. "I was trying to reach you."

When I cross my arms over my chest and stare at him with lifted brows, he adds, "I don't like it when I can't reach you. And your shop phone goes straight to voicemail."

My internal anger thermostat ticks up several degrees, but I keep my voice calm when I reply. "What's the emergency?'

"That *is* the fucking emergency."

He says it as if it should be obvious. As if not being able to get in contact with me after only a few hours being apart is the rudest and most inconvenient thing he's experienced in his entire adult life, and I should immediately throw myself at his feet and beg him for forgiveness.

"Callum?"

"What."

"Take a deep breath."

He glares at me, vibrating at a high, dangerous frequency that I bet only dogs can hear.

"Come on. Just take a breath. Do that Zen thing you do when you're aggravated. You're about to explode, and I don't want to spend the rest of the afternoon cleaning crabby billionaire bits off my bookshelves."

He closes his eyes, inhales slowly and deeply, and unclenches his hands. Exhaling through his nose, he rolls his shoulders. Then he cracks his knuckles as if he's preparing for a fistfight.

I watch him do all that, wondering what his childhood must have been like. I know he's privileged, but he acts like he was raised by wolves.

When he opens his eyes, he seems calmer. But then he opens his mouth and ruins the impression.

His voice even, he says, "Flirt with another man again, wife, and I'll send you his head on a platter."

He seems sincere about that threat, but I can't take him seriously. I can't get mad either. It's too ridiculous.

"How very Biblical of you," I say sweetly. "Will you also be sending plagues of frogs and locusts?"

He's about to snap some bossy Callumism or other at me, but gets distracted when he glances at my ring finger and realizes I'm still not wearing the giant diamond. Then he pulls his bull-pawing-the-ground impression again and bristles.

"Stop." I hold up a hand. He might be about to bite it off, but I continue. "I can't wear that thing. It's not safe."

"*Not safe?*" he hisses through clenched teeth.

I sigh in exasperation. "I should get a medal for dealing with you, you lunatic. I also think you need to reevaluate your caffeine intake. Yes, that's what I said, not safe. Look around, billionaire. This isn't Bel Air. They have a word for people who wear expensive, showy jewelry around the rest of LA. It's target."

When he frowns, I ask, "Don't you ever watch the news? People get followed home and robbed in their driveways for their Rolexes and diamond rings all the time."

I see it register. He opens his mouth, then closes it. He exhales and mutters, "Fuck."

Then he spins on his heel and stalks out, leaving me standing there wondering if I should start putting tranquilizers in his morning coffee.

For such a control freak, he loses his shit on the regular.

Sabine pops her head around the corner of the shelves. "Wow. I'm so impressed by how you handled him."

"You were eavesdropping?"

"Of course."

"You could at least sound apologetic about it."

"Except we both know I'm not. And where is all this new patience coming from, Em? I was expecting you to clobber him with the nearest copy of *Bridgerton*."

Sighing, I walk around to the other side of the shelves where she's standing. "He must've dicked all the anger out of me."

She snorts. "That must've been some good dick to calm you down so much."

"I told you, he's a magician."

"More like a warlock. That guy's wound so tight, you can hear his inner bomb ticking."

"Let's stop talking about him. I'll get a headache. What did you come up with for ideas on décor?"

"Lots. I'll show you. Let me make us an espresso first."

I pull up a stool at the counter while she prepares the coffees. Once they're made, she sits beside me and spreads out several sheets of paper on the counter between us.

"Okay, wow. That's a big list."

"This place needs big help."

After a cursory glance at one page, I say, "Were you planning on installing an Olympic-sized indoor pool as well? This is ridiculous."

"No, this is perfect. We need to draw customers away from ValUBooks, and as of now, there's no draw. Lit Happens needs more than a facelift, Em. It needs emergency surgery."

"God, you're dramatic. Harper would be proud. But fine. If we did everything on this list, what would it cost?"

Without a hint of hesitation, she says, "Five hundred thousand dollars."

I start to laugh. "Yeah, that's not gonna happen."

"Why not?"

"We don't own the building. I'm not making those kinds of improvements in a rented space."

"So buy the building."

I'm about to laugh again, but close my mouth and think about it instead.

She says, "Commercial real estate's always a good investment."

"I agree. I'm just allowing my brain a moment to remember that I've got a bunch of money now and could actually afford to buy a building."

She says drily, "Maybe you can invest in a stylist while you're at it."

"Oh my God. You're a jerk. What's so wrong with this outfit?"

"You look like a camp counselor who went off the rails and started murdering people in the woods."

"You're just saying that because *you* want to be my stylist, but I can't pull off the femme fatale look."

"Em, if you let me dress you, I could make you look like Marilyn fucking Monroe."

"Could we have a more current and less tragic reference? I don't want to look like a dead movie star. Plus, I'm not blonde."

"But you've got the red lips and doe eyes." She sizes me up and tries again. "Sophia Loren."

"She's too tall. And sultry. And you're still in the last century."

"Selena Gomez."

I stare at her. "If you can make me look like Selena Gomez, I will buy you a house."

"I've never understood how you don't think you're adorable."

"I'm as adorable as a wild boar."

"I wasn't talking about your personality."

"Have I fired you yet today?"

"Yes. Back to the list. Let's get this place looking sexy!"

Sighing, I say, "I don't know. I'll have to talk to the landlord to see if he's even willing to sell."

We go back and forth for another half hour, exchanging ideas and discussing possibilities, until the front door opens again.

A glowering Callum makes a beeline straight for me.

"Oh, look," says Sabine. "The warlock is back. And judging by his expression, you're about to practice all that fun new patience of yours."

Callum stops in front of us and stares down at me as if he's deciding what to bite first. Then he thrusts out his hand.

"Here."

I look at the small red velvet box he's holding. "What's that?"

He closes his eyes, clenches his jaw, and exhales.

"Oh for God's sake, Callum, take up yoga." I snatch the box from his hand as Sabine looks on, amused.

The box opens to reveal a simple and lovely eternity diamond wedding band.

He snaps, "Is it plain enough for you?"

I'm not sure what to make of this. On one hand, it's thoughtful. He listened to my complaint, respected my wishes, and went right out and bought a new ring.

On the other hand, what the fuck is the matter with him?

Deciding I don't want to argue, I slip the ring on my finger and hold out my hand to admire it.

"Yes," I say softly, pleased. "It's perfect. Thank you."

That sets him back on his heels. He was probably expecting a fight. He looks confused for a moment, frowning and blinking, then says brusquely, "Good."

The three of us stare at each other in awkward silence until Sabine says, "Hi. We haven't been introduced. I'm Sabine."

"I know who you are."

Rolling my eyes, I say, "The proper response is 'Hello, Sabine. I'm Callum. Nice to meet you.' Try again."

His look could peel the wallpaper off. Unaffected by it, I smile at him and gesture to Sabine.

He shifts his weight from foot to foot in agitation, then growls, "Hello, Sabine. I'm Callum. Nice to meet you."

"Good boy," I say. "Now, may I please get back to work?"

"Yes," he snaps. "But I want you home by five o'clock. And turn on your fucking phone!"

Watching him storm out the door, Sabine says, "Looks like you're not the only wild boar in this relationship."

"Did he really just tell me when I should be home?"

"He did. Five o'clock sharp, baby."

We look at each other, then she smiles. "Reservations for two at the Beach House at five thirty?"

"Perfect. Somebody's gotta teach that man who's in charge."

We high-five and go back to the list.

When I walk into the house later that night after dinner with Sabine, Callum is waiting for me in the dark like some nocturnal predator lying in wait for a meal.

Twenty-Two

At first, I think no one is home at the castle. The landscape lighting is on outside, but all the interior lights are off. I make my way through the kitchen, grateful for the subtle blue glow from the digital readouts on the appliances because I have no idea where the overhead light switch is.

Moonlight spilling through the windows helps me navigate downstairs. I go upstairs, listening for any sound, unnerved by the strange silence.

It's heavy and oddly tense, as if the air itself is holding its breath.

When I open the guest bedroom door, I find Callum standing across the room in darkness, gazing out the windows into the night. He's shirtless and barefoot again, wearing jeans and a palpable aura of danger.

His voice low, he says, "Where have you been?"

Electricity crackles along my nerve endings. A nervous flutter takes up space in my stomach, warning me to run.

But I don't. Instead, I take a breath and tell him the truth. "I went to the Beach House for supper with Sabine."

"I told you to be home by five."

"I know what you told me."

When he turns and looks at me over his shoulder, my heart stops.

It's the look a lion gives the poor creature it's about to tear to shreds with its teeth.

Forcing myself not to take a step back, I square my shoulders. "Don't do that."

"Do what?"

"Act like I'm responsible for your moods."

He turns around to face me, but stays where he is across the room. Despite the distance between us, I feel his dark energy. There's nothing subtle about it. He wields it like a hammer.

He says softly, "Do you enjoy defying me?"

Anger churns under my breastbone, but I hold it back and keep my voice calm when I reply.

"I enjoy this fun little thing called agency. Since you're not familiar with the concept, I'll enlighten you. It's when a person controls their own choices in life. I agreed to marry you, not hand you the keys to my autonomy."

His voice stroking soft, he says, "Oh, wife. If I wanted to take away your agency, I'd already have locked you in the basement and thrown away the key." After a pause, he adds darkly, "And believe me, I've considered it."

My heart races. We gaze at each other through the shadows. I'm not afraid that he'll harm me, but I don't know this man all that well, either.

In fact, I don't really know him at all.

I say, "I'd appreciate it if we could talk without all the tension. You know, communicate like adults? Maybe with the lights on?"

"You had the opportunity to communicate like an adult and call your husband to tell him you were going to dinner with your employee."

"I'm a little confused. What happened to 'this is just a business arrangement'? What happened to 'I can have a separate bedroom'? Most of all, what happened to the man who said he'd give me whatever I wanted? Because from where I'm standing, all that is starting to look like lies."

"Lies in the way you told me you don't want to have sex with me, you mean?"

I cross my arms over my chest and sigh.

He moves slowly closer. "Or how about lies like you saying you don't want to be spanked?"

"Come on. You know the difference between pride and entrapment."

"What I know is that you're my wife. The woman who promised to never leave me."

My patience finally snaps, and I throw my hands in the air. "Just because I went to dinner, it doesn't mean I'm leaving you! I did that to make a point!"

He walks even closer, his smoldering gaze never leaving mine. When he's a few feet away, he stops and stares down at me, crackling like a live wire.

I blow out a hard breath. "You have abandonment issues, is that it?"

"I have *you* issues. Do you have any idea how badly I want to throw you face-down onto that bed and spank you until you're begging for mercy?"

"I'm getting an inkling."

My sarcastic tone makes him clench his jaw. But he reins in his temper and answers calmly.

"I shouldn't have ordered you to come home like that. Especially in front of Sabine. For that, I apologize. It won't happen again. But I can't promise I won't be possessive, or worry about you when I don't know where you are, or want you to show me the simple courtesy of informing me of your whereabouts, because that would mean I'd have to become a different man. I know I'm not perfect, but you don't have to play games to try to get me to change my behavior. Tell me, and give me the opportunity to correct it myself."

That all sounded so reasonable and unlike him that I stand there stunned for a moment, unsure how to respond.

Finally, I settle on, "All right. I will. And I apologize for not calling you."

"Thank you. I need to fuck you now."

That's so unexpected, I start to laugh. "Oh my God, Callum. You're absolutely insane."

"Yes. Get used to it."

He picks me up and throws me over his shoulder, then strides down the hallway toward the master bedroom. I hang on to the belt loops in his jeans as he walks, my heart pounding uncontrollably.

He kicks open the bedroom door, strides over to the bed, and flips me over onto it. Breathless and wide-eyed, I stare up at him. The lights are off in here, too, but the curtains are open so moonlight fills the room. My eyes have adjusted to the shadows, so I can see how fiercely his own eyes burn.

Silent, he leans down and removes my shoes, dropping them to the floor one after the other. Then he peels me out of my clothes, rolling me around impatiently, then tossing it all to the floor to join my shoes. When I'm nude and trembling, he straightens and gazes down at me.

"Wife."

"Yes?"

"I want to restrain you."

Oh God. The rope. Swallowing, I say, "Will...will it hurt?"

"No. I'll be careful."

"Um. Okay, um. I believe you, but I'm still nervous. Why do you have to restrain me?"

Staring into my eyes, he says softly, "I need control. I crave it. When I don't have control, I feel...I don't know how to explain the feeling. Only that I hate it."

"It calms you," I whisper, suddenly understanding, though I don't know how.

Nodding, he moistens his lips. "Yes. Exactly."

I can tell he's getting more excited, though he's holding himself back. I think that's part of it for him too. He not only needs control over his external environment, he needs to control himself. His responses. His emotions. What he says and doesn't say.

But mostly me.

He needs to control me, especially in bed. He has to be the initiator and the executor, the one who decides what will happen, when, where, and how long it will take.

Unfortunately for me, the idea is appealing.

I say, "If I agree, I want us to have an understanding."

He shifts his weight from foot to foot but remains silent. The bulge under his zipper is growing rapidly.

"If I say stop, I expect you to stop immediately."

"Agreed." He licks his lips again.

"And I want you to ask before you do anything weird."

"Define weird," he demands.

"Like...I don't know. I haven't been tied up before. I don't want to be helpless and have you suddenly introduce a ten-inch dildo into my butt and dial the vibrate setting to max."

His breathing turns erratic. I think he just formed a vivid mental picture of doing exactly what I said I was afraid of him doing.

I warn, "Callum."

"Agreed. I'm sorry. When you talk like that..." He closes his eyes and slowly inhales. After he exhales, he opens his eyes and says, "I'll ask you for permission every step of the way."

His gaze drops to my breasts, then slowly moves down my body. He bites his lower lip. His breath shudders out of him.

This is when I realize *I'm* the one in control here.

I'm fully naked, lying on my back in bed, holding him in place with only my words. He could easily overpower me—he's far too strong to beat in a physical fight—but he won't do anything without my explicit consent.

I mean I *think* he won't. This is the T-Rex we're talking about.

Maybe I should test my theory.

Propping myself up on my elbows, I draw my knees up and press my thighs together. He stands perfectly still, except for his right index finger, which twitches.

I whisper, "I don't give you permission to touch me."

Then I spread my thighs.

A faint sound escapes him, but that's all. He doesn't move a muscle.

His eyes feast on my body as if it's the most delicious banquet ever made.

It's a thrilling sort of darkness that courses through my veins on seeing that look. It makes me feel bold and uninhibited, sexy and feminine, and honestly as powerful as fuck.

"Take off your jeans. But don't touch me yet."

He strips off his jeans, flings them aside, then stands before me nude with a jutting erection and breathing so ragged, it borders on a pant.

When I say, "Good boy," his eyes drift closed.

His voice so faint, it's almost inaudible, he says, "Wife. Please."

"Do you want me?"

"You know I do."

"And if I let you have me, will you promise to take care of me?"

He opens his eyes and pins me with a look of such ferocious desire, it steals my breath.

He growls, "I promise to take care of you in every way for the rest of both our lives. Now give me fucking permission to touch you before I die of need, you stubborn fucking woman."

"You're the only man I've ever met who can be so sweet and so annoying with so few words. Permission granted."

He grabs my thighs, drags me to the edge of the mattress, pulls me upright, grips my head in his hands, and kisses me hard.

Then he flattens his hand over my sternum and pushes me onto my back. Hovering above me, he commands, "Stay in this exact position. Move one inch, and you'll be punished."

He straightens and strolls away into the closet.

At least he isn't whistling *The Pink Panther* theme.

I lie still on the bed, fighting panic and trying to reassure myself that it might feel as if I'm having a heart attack, but I'm not.

My brain doesn't believe me. It's convinced we're also having a stroke in addition to a life-threatening cardiac emergency. Then, when Callum walks out of the closet holding a pair of handcuffs, I make an involuntary peep of terror and squeeze my eyes shut.

I hear a low, satisfied chuckle. "Nervous?"

"Extremely. Don't laugh at me."

"Put a please in front of that command, wife, or suffer the consequences."

I bite back a smart remark and whisper, "Please."

He kisses my thigh. The unexpected contact makes me suck in a startled breath.

"Hush, baby," he coos. "Now, open your eyes."

When I do, I find him smiling.

"Do you have to go to the bathroom?"

Wrinkling my brow, I say, "No. Odd question, but no."

"Good."

"Why is that good?"

"Because you're going to be here for a while."

He grabs my arm and snaps one link of the handcuffs around my right wrist. Then he pulls me toward the side of the mattress and snaps the other cuff around the bedpost.

Straightening, he crosses his arms over his chest and smiles wider as he gazes down at me with a look of utter satisfaction.

I look at my bound wrist in confusion. "What's happening?"

"I handcuffed you to the foot of the bed."

"Yes. Obviously. Why?"

"Oh, you want to know *why*." Chuckling, he rubs his jaw.

"Tell you what. I'll be back in the morning, and you can let me know what ideas you came up with."

Bending down, he retrieves his jeans from the floor. He drags them up his legs, stuffs his hard cock inside, pulls up the zipper, and turns and swaggers out.

Stunned, I sit on the bed in the darkness until my confusion clears. It's replaced by incandescent rage.

"Son of a bitch!"

From somewhere down the hall comes the faint but distinct sound of Callum's laughter.

Twenty-Three

That night is the longest of my life.

For a few hours, I'm in denial. I sit on the edge of the mattress in the dark, telling myself he'll be back any minute, and that this is all just a game. A little payback for not showing up when he ordered me to. Just a small time-out for me to reflect on my behavior, then he'll show up again, smirking and annoying as hell.

But sometime around midnight, cold, hard reality sets in, and I accept my fate.

I roll onto my back, scoot around on the mattress, and grab a pillow from the head of the bed with my feet. Drawing my knees up, I manage to grasp it with a hand, then settle it under my head. I pull the covers up from the bottom of the bed until I can wriggle under them one-handed, then I lie on my back in the dark and stare at the ceiling, vowing I'll find a way to make Callum regret this.

Finally, when the sky beyond the windows is lifting from deep sapphire to pearl gray, I fall into a fitful sleep.

I don't know how long I'm out, but when I wake up, I'm looking at an upside-down view of Arlo. He's leaning over me, smiling.

"Good morning. I trust you slept well. Coffee?"

I try to roll over, but am painfully reminded why I can't when I almost yank my arm from the socket.

I look at the handcuffs binding my wrist to the bedpost. Then I look back at Arlo.

I say calmly, "Yes, coffee would be wonderful, thank you. Right after you call the police to report a kidnapping."

He clucks. "You haven't been kidnapped. This is your own home, after all."

"Oh good. Then nobody should mind when I burn it to the ground."

From his shirt pocket, he produces a small silver key, which he holds up. "Shall I?"

Playing along with this polite insanity, I smile. "So kind of you. Thanks ever so much."

He unlocks the cuffs with a practiced twist of his wrist, then turns around discreetly as I sit up, pull them off, and angrily fling them against the headboard.

I suppose I should be embarrassed that I'm stark naked, but I've got more important things to worry about at the moment than modesty.

Rising from bed, I hold the sheet up to my chest and face Arlo. "Is my husband home, by any chance?"

Turning around to face me, he says, "He left for work early this morning."

"I see. But the chef is here, I presume?"

"He is. Would you like me to have him make you something to eat?"

"Yes. I'd like a Denver omelet, four pieces of bacon, a side of cut fruit, an apple juice, and coffee."

Revenge should always be carried out on a full stomach.

"Perfect. I'll be up with it soon." He inclines his head, then leaves.

I shower, blow-dry my hair, and dress, choosing an elegant red silk dress that Dani insisted I buy though I thought it made me look like a game show hostess. She said I'd need things like this for all the lunches I'd soon be having with wealthy society ladies or when I audition for the next season of *Real Housewives of Beverly Hills*.

I told her I'd rather live in the Ballona Wetlands than do either of those things.

She said I normally look as if I *have* been living in the Ballona Wetlands, so get the damn dress and shut up already.

Needless to say, she was right. I look respectable. Conservative, but with a hint of sex appeal. Stylish, but not flashy.

In a word, I look rich.

Satisfied, I slip on a pair of nude-colored high-heel sandals to complete the look, then come out of the master closet to find Arlo setting up my breakfast on the writing desk.

"Lovely. Thank you, Arlo."

He pulls out the chair for me, settles a napkin in my lap, and stands back, watching as I take the first bite of the omelet.

"Delicious."

"I'm so glad."

I take another bite, swallow that, then take a sip of coffee. The whole time, Arlo watches me as if he's a stray dog waiting for table scraps.

"Is there some reason you're lurking over my breakfast?"

"Mr. McCord instructed me to make sure you have everything you need this morning."

I smile at him. "Actually, I don't. Will you please bring me a hatchet? I'll need that for later, when my darling husband comes home."

I think I glimpse a fleeting smile cross his lips, but it's gone so fast, I can't be sure.

He says, "He was very concerned about your mood."

I say archly, "Was he? How thoughtful. And how odd that if he was so concerned, he wasn't here to gauge my mood for himself."

"I'm sure he wanted to be."

I snort and stab the omelet with my fork.

"It's just that he's extremely busy. He's under immense pressure at work."

I mutter, "That man hasn't seen immense pressure yet."

After a pause, Arlo says, "I shouldn't tell you this, but…" His sigh borders on melodramatic.

I look at him with raised brows. "What?"

He runs a finger along the carved edge of the writing desk, gazing thoughtfully at the wood. Then he taps it twice as if he's made a decision and looks up at me.

"He cares for you, Emery. In a way I've never seen him care for anyone before."

"If this is his way of showing he cares, God help me. The man requires a straightjacket."

He chuckles. "I know he's different."

"Different is an understatement. He's an alien species." After another sip of coffee, I ask, "How long have you worked for him?"

"Six years. Since he was first inducted into the—"

Stopping abruptly, he clears his throat. "Since he took over from his father as CEO of McCord Media."

Carefully watching his expression, I say, "Inducted into what?"

"I apologize. That was a wrong choice of word."

We gaze at each other. Both of us know he's lying. I decide to let it go because I know I won't get more out of him, but I tuck it into the back of my mind for further exploration later.

"If I wanted to have you drive me somewhere, is that doable? Or do you only work for Callum?"

"I'm at your service. I'll take you anywhere you want to go."

"Good. Meet me in the garage in twenty minutes."

My smile is dismissive. I can tell he wants to ask where we're going, but he doesn't.

He'll find out soon enough.

~

When we pull up in front of the Wilshire Grand in downtown, I get out before Arlo can open the door for me and strut into the lobby of the seventy-story building like I own it.

Which I suppose I might, considering whom I'm married to.

Smiling at the uniformed security guard seated behind the impressive black granite reception desk, I say cordially, "Good morning. I'm here to see Callum McCord."

The security guard, a nice young man with broad shoulders and a hideous bowl haircut obviously given to him by his archenemy, says, "Do you have an appointment, ma'am?"

"No, but I shouldn't need one."

His expression indicates otherwise. Before he can tell me to take a hike, I say, "I'm Emery, his wife."

He stares at me, blinking rapidly. The other security guard sitting next to him stares at me in shock too.

Apparently, my darling husband hasn't shared the blissful news of our marriage.

I say, "Tell him that if I don't see him within the next two minutes, I'm going to throw all his clothes into a big pile in the middle of Sunset Boulevard and set it on fire. And make sure you say that verbatim."

I walk over to the nearest chair and sit down to wait.

It doesn't take long. After only a minute, the security guard approaches me, looking nervous.

"Ma'am, Mr. McCord says to send you straight up. I'll escort you to the elevator."

"Thank you."

I rise, holding the brown paper bag I've brought with me, and follow him through the bustling lobby to the elevator bank. He uses his security badge to gain access to the floor, then presses the button for me when I get inside.

When the elevator stops and the doors slide open again, they reveal a beautifully decorated penthouse lobby with a floor-to-ceiling water feature on one side and a reception desk on the other. I approach the woman behind the desk. She's about my age, with wavy dark hair, a pretty, heart-shaped face, and an enviably glowing complexion.

"Good morning. I'm Emery. And can I just say I love that shade of lipstick you're wearing? A bold red lip is my favorite."

She looks up at me as if starstruck. "Oh my God. You *do* exist."

"You say that like I'm Bigfoot. What am I missing?"

Leaping to her feet, she comes around the corner of the desk and takes my free hand, shaking it vigorously.

"I'm so sorry, please excuse my manners! I'm Tracy. When Mr. McCord told me a minute ago that his wife was coming up, I almost keeled over. I mean, his *wife*?" She laughs. "A miracle! Nobody thought it would ever happen!"

I say drily, "Yes, he did wait right up until the last minute, didn't he?"

She stares at me quizzically for a beat, then shakes her head. "Please consider me your assistant as well. I'm here to help you with anything you might need, from travel arrangements to reservations to, well, anything. I'm just so excited to meet you. And congratulations! Oh, this is such unexpected, wonderful news—"

"*Tracy*."

The growled word cuts through the air like a knife. Tracy stops pumping my hand and freezes.

We look over to find Callum standing in his open office door, shooting poisoned darts at his secretary with his eyes.

Terrified, she drops my hand as if it burned her and scurries back to her desk, where she busies herself by frantically clicking around on her computer.

I send Callum a dour stare. "Good morning, Sunshine."

He presses his lips together and stands back to allow me to pass by.

Entering his office, I look around. It's impressive. The artwork, the furnishings, the view of the LA skyline—all of it screams money, power, and prestige.

I expected nothing less.

From behind me, Callum says, "This is a surprise."

"I bet."

I turn to face him. He's wearing a beautiful charcoal-gray suit that probably cost more than my annual employee payroll. He shuts the door, then glances at the bag I'm carrying.

"I brought you lunch." Sashaying over to his huge oak desk, I set it next to the telephone. Then I perch on the edge of the desk and smile at him.

He sends me a smirk in return. "You look well rested."

This arrogant prick. I hope he enjoys his fucking sandwich.

I say airily, "I am, thank you. That mattress is so comfy."

We gaze at each other as he slowly walks closer, his smirk growing with every step.

"I came to discuss my car. You remember it, don't you, darling? The VW you had hauled away for scrap?"

"It was a death trap."

"It was *my* death trap. You had no right to get rid of it. Just like you had no right to handcuff me to your bed."

"Our bed," he corrects, his gaze sweeping down my figure. Licking his lips, he says in a husky tone, "That dress is incredible."

"Oh, this old thing? I bought it with your ridiculous limitless credit card at some fancy boutique in Beverly Hills where the salespeople looked at me as if I'd given birth to Satan's scaly, forked-tongue baby and was dragging it around by its bloody umbilical cord. So *charming*, those boutique ladies. They made me feel as if suicide was my only viable option."

"Tell me which ones, and I'll have them all fired."

"A tempting thought, but I don't want to be responsible for the spike in the unemployment rate it would cause. And you can stop right there. That's close enough."

Only a few feet away, he stops and stares at me from under lowered brows.

When his hungry gaze drifts over my body again, I say succinctly, "I don't give you permission to touch me." Then I slide my butt onto his desk, lean back on my hands, and cross my legs.

Swinging one foot slowly back and forth, I smile at him.

His eyes flash. A muscle in his jaw flexes. He inhales slowly, his nostrils flaring when he exhales.

It's a dangerous game I'm playing, but holy hell, it's fun.

"My car, Callum."

He growls, "It's gone. I'll buy you whatever you want to replace it."

"Fine. I want the same make and model. The same year and color too. And I can tell by the way your nostrils are flaring you don't like that idea, but tough titties."

His heated gaze rakes over my breasts. "Careful, wife."

"No, *you* be careful. Because if you think you married a pushover, think again."

"I know exactly who I married," he says softly, his eyes piercing. "Do you?"

"Yes. A psychopath with too much money, too little patience, and too much confidence for his own good. When are you going to introduce me to your family?"

That muscle in his jaw flexes again. "When the time is right."

I laugh. "Oh, interesting! Will that be the same time you let literally *anyone* know that you have a wife? Because apparently, I've caused some shock waves just by showing up here this morning. I thought your poor secretary was going to need oxygen."

"I don't disclose my private life to anyone outside the family. I told you that."

"So, what, then? I'm supposed to hide in the castle and pretend I don't exist?"

He's getting more and more agitated. I'm not sure if it's my flippant tone or the way I'm swinging my leg seductively back and forth, but either way, I can tell his blood pressure is rising.

I hope his aorta bursts.

"No," he says through clenched teeth. "Now give me permission to touch you."

Twirling a lock of hair between my fingers, I say sweetly, "Dearest, darling husband, it will be a cold day in hell when that happens."

"Emery," he warns, eyes flashing.

I pretend to shiver in fright. "Ooo. So scary."

"Don't test me."

I giggle at the look of fury on his face. Winding him up might be my new favorite thing.

"Or what? You'll do your big bad wolf impression and growl? Sorry, but I've seen that routine before. You'll have to do better."

His expression hardens. His lips thin. He curls his hands to fists.

Electric and sweet, a thrill runs through my body. My pulse races, my nipples harden, and my breath catches in my throat. Reveling in my ability to piss him off and also in my newfound power of holding him in place with nothing but a denial, I laugh out loud.

I realize I've made a terrible miscalculation when he lunges at me.

Twenty-Four

He spins me around, shoves me roughly facedown onto his desk, and pins my wrists behind my back. Then he leans over and says hotly into my ear, "My mouthy little brat. You didn't come here to talk about your fucking car. You need what I didn't give you last night, don't you?"

He presses his hips against my ass so I can feel his erection.

"You wish," I hiss, struggling. "Let go of me!"

He fists his free hand in my hair, pulls my head back, and kisses me roughly, shoving his tongue into my mouth and biting my lip. Breathless, I wrench away, then glare at him.

"Oh, wife," he says, panting. "We really need to work on that attitude."

Shoving the hem of my dress up to my waist, he slaps me on the ass.

I yelp and suck in a breath, stiffening. Heat blooms over my skin where his palm struck me, followed by a wave of pleasure that settles between my legs and starts throbbing.

A faint moan escapes my lips.

Callum's chuckle is low and dark. Still holding my wrists captive behind my back, he yanks my panties down to the middle of my thighs, puts his hands between my legs, and fondles me.

"Sweet girl," he whispers, a thrill in his voice. "My dirty sweet girl. You were made for me."

He spanks me several more times until my ass is burning and my knees are weak. When he slides his fingers inside my pussy and starts to finger-fuck me, I close my eyes and bite my lip to keep from groaning.

"Oh God, so fucking slippery. You're ready for my dick already, aren't you, baby? Spread your legs for me."

I don't have a clue how we got here so quickly, but I let him kick my legs apart without resisting, feeling cool air on my heated skin and my blood rushing through my veins like wildfire. Hot, hard flesh nudges me from behind—Callum's stiff cock, seeking entrance.

He commands, "Ask for it, wife."

My eyes closed and my cheek pressed against the leather desk blotter, I whisper, "I'd rather die."

"Oh, I know. That pride of yours is so prickly."

He slides the engorged head of his cock up and down through my wetness, teasing me with it, but not sliding inside. Then he reaches under and rubs circles over my clit until it tingles, and I'm whimpering.

"Be a good girl and ask for it."

I resist as long as I can, lying there panting and exposed, my hard nipples rubbing against the desktop as he works his hand between my legs, until I can't take it anymore.

I whisper, "Please."

It's enough. Without demanding a more flowery invitation, Callum shoves inside me with a grunt.

Arching off the desk, I gasp as the huge, hard length of him fills me.

He releases my wrists, pulls my hair, and starts to fuck me, growling like an animal.

I grab the edge of the desk and tilt my hips back to meet his thrusts.

Through gritted teeth, he says, "Tell your master you love his cock."

"No."

As I hoped it would, that earns me a spanking.

I squeeze my eyes shut tight and decide to book an appointment with a reputable therapist first thing tomorrow morning.

Gripping my hips in both hands, he fucks me ruthlessly until my orgasm hits and I cry out, shuddering. "Harder! Do it harder!"

He leans over, grabs the back of my neck, and drives into me with savage force, sending wave after wave of pleasure rippling through me until I'm sobbing.

"Yes, baby," he pants. "Fall apart for me. Now be a good cum slut and get on your knees."

He withdraws, drags me off the desk, and pushes me down by my shoulders until I'm kneeling on the carpet in front of him. Then he grasps my jaw and forces his erection past my lips.

I grab on to his hips as he starts to fuck my mouth, gazing down at me with devilish dark eyes and a wicked grin.

My eyes drift shut. I go somewhere inside my head, a quiet, dark place where only the two of us and this rabid need coexist. It's a peaceful oasis where nothing else matters and I can lose myself, forgetting about what it all might mean.

When he climaxes, it's with a violent jerk and a shout, his fingers digging into my skull and his cock gagging me.

I swallow and swallow, tears streaming down my cheeks.

He drops his head back on a guttural groan. His chest heaves with his ragged breaths. We stay like that for a moment, his trembling hands around my head as I kneel like a supplicant, my jaw stretched open wide, all my senses reeling.

Finally, he inhales a deep breath, exhales it in a gust, and looks down at me.

Stroking my cheek, he whispers, "My sweet wife. You're so fucking perfect."

He pulls out of my mouth, drags me to my feet with his hands under my armpits, and hugs me so hard, I can't breathe.

My knees are rubber, so I sag against him for support. My

entire body trembles. My bare kneecaps burn, my jaw aches, and my ass stings where he spanked me.

And oh God, how I love it.

I love it all so much, it frightens me.

I must make some small sound of distress, because Callum strokes a gentle hand over my hair, shushing me. Then he kisses me deeply, holding my head and delving his tongue into my mouth.

When I open my eyes and look up at him, he's gazing down at me with a look of adoration.

"You taste like my cum."

"I can't imagine why."

He chuckles. "And you brought me lunch."

"Yes."

"I love that. Thank you."

"You're welcome."

He gathers me into a hug and rocks me until my trembling stops. Then he kisses my damp forehead and murmurs, "I ruined your lipstick, sweetheart. The restroom is through that door."

With a gentle push, he sends me in the direction of the bathroom. I wobble unsteadily across the room, go in the restroom, and close the door behind me.

When I see my reflection in the mirror, I'm not sure whether to laugh or cry.

My lipstick is smeared all around my mouth in messy streaks of red that make me look as if I've been gorging on crayons. My hair is disheveled, and so is my dress. My cheeks are flushed, and my mascara is running.

I look exactly like I feel: as if I've been fucked to within an inch of my life.

With a shaky laugh, I walk to the sink and splash cold water on my face. I dry my cheeks with paper towels from the dispenser, blot away the streaks of mascara, then attempt to smooth my flyaway hair.

It's when I'm thinking I should ask Tracy to borrow her

lipstick because it's the same shade as the one I always wear that it hits me how much the two of us look alike.

Same hair, same height, same lipstick, same complexion. She even has a figure like mine.

We look so similar, we could be sisters.

A sudden pang of jealousy sinks sharp claws into my heart.

Is Callum fucking his secretary?

I shove that thought aside, but it roars right back, despite me trying to reassure myself that I'm overthinking it.

Maybe he has a type. Short brunettes with hourglass figures and questionable taste in fashion. That orange jumpsuit she's wearing that I thought was so cute is definitely not something I could see any of my friends in. It's more appropriate for a women's correctional facility than the office of the CEO.

Maybe Callum appreciates more than Tracy's quirky sense of style. Maybe her efficiency with an Excel spreadsheet isn't her only valuable attribute.

Maybe he really likes her obvious terror of and deference to him.

Maybe he enjoys punishing her for disobedience the way he does me.

Maybe I'm not the only one he's calling his sweet cum slut and putting on her knees.

Queasy, I stare at my reflection in the mirror.

A sharp knock makes me jump. Through the door, Callum says, "You all right in there?"

"Yes. Be right out."

Heart racing, I toss the paper towels into the trash can and take a deep breath to steady myself. Then I don a brittle smile and open the door.

He eyes me warily. His spidey senses have obviously caught a whiff of disquiet in the air.

Avoiding his gaze, I say, "I should get to work." I try to brush past him, but he grips my upper arm and pulls me against his chest.

"Wife."

The word is a warning.

I know he's demanding an explanation from me, but I feel too unsettled and vulnerable. Too raw. I'm not sure what's happening between us, only that my emotions are all over the place.

Jealousy isn't a thing for me. It never has been. I don't know why it should be now, considering that my husband and I are strangers.

Except for our genitals, which are quickly becoming best friends.

Still avoiding his eyes, I say quietly, "I need to get to the shop."

"In that dress? I don't think so."

"I'll choose my own outfits for work, thank you."

"What's wrong?"

"Nothing."

"Bullshit. Look at me."

I send him a leery, side-eyed glance.

"What the fuck is wrong, Emery?"

"I don't like it when you say my name like that."

"Like what?"

"Like it's a weapon."

He's about to snap something, but before he can, a crackle comes over the desk phone intercom, and Tracy's voice interrupts.

"Mr. McCord, Cole is here to see you."

Callum mutters, "Fuck."

I remember the night I had dinner at Dani and Ryan's, and she showed me the picture of Callum's family she found on the internet. I remember the scowling, handsome middle brother whose name she said was Cole.

Guess I'll be meeting the family sooner than Callum anticipated. Or wanted, judging by the sudden storm clouds darkening his face.

He says, "That's my brother. I'll introduce you."

"And then will you jump out the window, like it looks like you're planning to?"

"No," he snaps. "And try not to disrespect me for the next five minutes."

I smile at his obvious discomfort. "Okay. But it'll cost you."

He gives me an evil glare that Satan would be proud of, then walks over to the desk and jabs his finger on a button on the phone. "Send him in."

Then he starts to pace behind his desk in agitation.

The door opens. Through it walks a slightly younger version of Callum dressed in black slacks and a pale blue dress shirt with the cuffs rolled up. He's as handsome as his brother, but his energy is even darker, if that's possible.

He stops short a few feet inside the door, looks at Callum, looks at me, then looks back at Callum and demands, "What the fuck is going on?"

If a lit stick of dynamite had legs and an attitude, it would be this guy.

Callum props his hands on his hips and glares at his brother. "Good morning to you too."

"Cut the shit, Callum. You're *married*? When the fuck did *that* happen? And why didn't I hear about it?"

Callum snaps, "I'm not obligated to tell you, that's why. And how did you find out, anyway?"

"Because when I came up to see you just now, your secretary informed that you were in here with *your wife*. What the hell kind of way is that for your own brother to find out about something so important?"

Callum scoffs. "We both know how important you think marriage is, Colton. Once again, cut the shit."

Oh boy. I think the McCord family skipped some much-needed family therapy sessions.

Bracing myself to have my hand bitten off, I walk forward and offer it to Cole.

"Hi. This is awkward, but your brother doesn't understand simple human customs like introductions, so I'll take it upon myself. I'm Emery."

He looks taken aback for a moment, but quickly recovers. "Hello," he says gruffly. He gives my hand a bone-crushing shake. Then he releases it, points at Callum, and demands, "You know this guy is a wild animal, right? You married an actual animal."

Callum barks, "Cole!"

Cole says dismissively, "Oh, shut up. You're a rabid gorilla, and everybody knows it."

I can't help myself. I start to laugh.

The McCord brothers stare at me as if I've lost my marbles.

"Sorry, guys, but it's been a morning. If I don't laugh, I'll cry. Cole, it's nice to meet you. And yes, I'm aware that your brother is a primate, though comparing him to a gorilla is actually an insult to gorillas. I like to think of him more as a baboon."

"Thank you, darling," says Callum drily. "That first insult didn't even take ninety seconds."

Cole's eyes bug at hearing his brother call me darling. He shakes his head, looking utterly confused.

"You two obviously have a lot to catch up on, so I'll get out of your hair. Cole, it was a pleasure. Callum..." Smiling, I look him up and down. "I hope you enjoy your sandwich. I made it especially for you."

I walk to him, go up on my toes, and kiss him on the cheek.

He looks at me with overt suspicion.

Gazing up into his eyes, I murmur, "Have a *wonderful* day."

I feel two pairs of eyes on me as I walk out of his office. I wave goodbye to Tracy, swallowing around the tightness in my throat when I see her smile, so much like mine.

Ten minutes later, when I'm back in the car with Arlo and we're on our way to the store, the batphone rings. I dig it out of my handbag and answer it with a bright and cheerful "Hello?"

Callum's furious voice fills the car. "I bet you think you're extremely funny."

I say innocently, "Whatever can you mean?"

"This will cost you, wife."

"Honestly, I have no idea what you're talking about."

"No? So you don't remember what the 'special' ingredient is in the sandwich you made for me?"

"Let me think. Was it baloney?"

Into his thundering silence, I start to laugh.

"Oh, wait! Now I remember. After I spent the entire night shackled to your bed, I stopped at my friend Dani's before coming over to your office. She has the sweetest little girl. Mia's her name. She's two. Just starting potty training as a matter of fact, but, conveniently, she's still in diapers."

He snaps, "You made me a baby shit sandwich!"

"With love, darling. With *oodles* of love." I sigh in satisfaction. "And the next time you think about handcuffing me to the furniture again, remember that an angry wife is a dangerous thing. Tread carefully."

I disconnect the call, then roll down the window and toss the batphone into the wind.

Twenty-Five

The rest of the morning passes uneventfully.

Murph is on schedule at the shop. We spend a few hours making a nursery out of an empty cardboard box for one of the strays who had a litter of six kittens underneath my office desk overnight, then transfer mama and babies to their cozy new home. I leave another message for the tax guy at the CDTFA about my outstanding balance. Then my attorney calls to talk about the lawsuit, and says I better sit down for his news, because it's something else.

My stomach drops. "Oh no. What's happened?"

Chuckling, he says, "The impossible."

"Don't tell me he brought another lawsuit against me?"

"No. He dropped it."

I'm sure I didn't hear him right. "What do you mean, dropped it?"

"His legal team filed a request for dismissal. I expect the judge will sign off on it this week."

"I'm confused. Why would they drop the case?"

A note of pride warms his voice. "Probably because our answer to the initial filing was so good, opposing counsel decided the case wasn't worth pursuing."

"Wow. I'm stunned. This is really good news. But what if he changes his mind?"

"They filed the motion with prejudice. Which means that when the judge approves it, they can't bring another case against you for the same thing."

I shake my head in disbelief. "Unbelievable."

"Sometimes the good guys win, kid. I'll let you know when the ruling is final. Shouldn't be too long."

"Thank you so much!"

"Anytime."

We hang up. I stand behind the counter looking at the receiver in my hand, still trying to process what the attorney told me, but get distracted by the flatbed truck pulling up at the curb outside.

Strapped to the long bed is a blue Volkswagen Jetta.

Carrying a clipboard, the driver of the flatbed jumps out of the cab. He ambles through the door, taps the brim of his baseball cap in greeting, and says, "Lookin' for an Emery Eastwood?"

"That's me."

"Got your car here for ya."

Well, well. Callum works fast. He's probably worried about what I might make him for dinner.

"Where do you want me to unload it?"

"Right where you are is great."

He asks for my ID and makes me sign a delivery sheet, then heads back out. When he's finished getting it off the back of the truck, he comes in and hands me the keys.

"Oh, and this came with it. Mr. McCord told me to make sure I handed it to you personally."

Grinning, he holds out another batphone, identical to the one I tossed out the window.

I take it reluctantly, knowing that if I don't, another one will only show up somewhere else, probably delivered by drone.

The driver pulls away as I'm saying to the cell, "Call Callum."

Nothing happens. The screen stays dark.

When I understand why, I sigh and shake my head. "Call Daddy."

As I knew it would, the screen lights up with *Calling Daddy.*

He answers after only one ring, his tone sarcastic. "Darling wife. What a surprise. I didn't think I'd hear from you until you started hollering when I kicked down the guest bedroom door tonight."

"So you *do* know which bedroom is mine. No such luck with your name, however."

"Meaning what?"

"Meaning I'll never, ever, not in a billion years, refer to you as Daddy."

"Why not?"

"You're not my father."

"It's not meant to be literal."

"I don't care what it's meant to be. And I'm not judging anybody who's into it, but it's not my thing."

He chuckles. "I know. I just like how much it annoys you."

I say sourly, "That must be why you keep breathing."

He doesn't take offense at that. He merely says, "Were you calling to insult me, or was there something else?"

"Actually, there is something else. I'm calling to thank you for the car. I know it must've taken a few years off your life to purchase a used Volkswagen."

"Don't thank me yet. I might change my mind and have it towed away in the middle of the night. It's hideous."

"It's reliable."

"So is an Aston Martin."

"No, that's ostentatious. You might as well drive around with a sign on the roof screaming 'Look at Me!' if you have one of those things."

"This from the woman who chose a two-million-dollar cherry-red Ferrari to go on a joyride through Beverly Hills."

"That was Dani's choice."

"At least one of you has sense. What time will you be home?"

The subtle change in the tenor of his voice on that last sentence makes me pause. "Why? Planning on tying me to the staircase banister as soon as I walk through the door?"

"No. I thought we could have dinner together."

"Your lunch didn't fill you up?"

"Careful with that smart tone, wife."

Smiling, I say flippantly, "Oh, please. You love my smart tone."

After a brief pause, he says in a husky voice, "Yes."

My heart skips a beat. A rush of heat prickles my skin. All of a sudden, I'm tongue-tied and breathless, unsure of what to say next. "Unless traffic is bad, I'll be there by six."

"Good. I'll see you then."

He disconnects, leaving me flushed and unsettled.

The afternoon passes in a blur. I keep myself busy organizing shelves and tidying up, but my thoughts are a chaotic mix of anticipation and anxiety. Every so often, when my gaze wanders to the Jetta parked outside, my heart races.

When the day winds down, I leave Murph to lock up the shop, and I head out to the car. Trying to calm my nerves, I take a deep breath before I start the engine. I tell myself it's only dinner, but the thought of spending a quiet evening alone with Callum is both exhilarating and terrifying.

I know I can't trust him not to punish me for the lunch I made him.

I also know I can't trust myself to resist if he tries.

I pull into the garage a few minutes before six and find Callum in the kitchen. He's standing at the stove, dressed casually in jeans and a button-down shirt, the sleeves rolled up his muscular forearms.

The sight of him is somehow both comforting and disturbing. My heart flutters at the thought of spending an intimate evening together.

"What on earth is going on here?" I set my handbag on the big white marble island and move closer.

He turns and smiles at me over his shoulder. "I'm cooking you dinner."

To cover my pleasure at that surprise, I say drily, "Uh-oh. Should I have the poison control center on speed dial?"

Chuckling, he turns back to the stove. "Not everyone in this marriage has quite the refined sense of vengeance you do."

I take a peek at what he's cooking, then stare in disbelief at the rich cream-and-mushroom sauce simmering in the pan alongside golden chicken cutlets.

"You're making chicken marsala? I *love* chicken marsala. It's probably my favorite..."

When I glance at him, he's smiling down at me, a genuine, warm smile that reaches his eyes.

"Meal. Which of course you know," I say, my voice cracking just a little.

"Does it bother you?" he asks softly, his gaze intense.

"Yes. It's strange that you know so much about me." Sighing, I add, "But also, weirdly, no. But I might have been dropped on my head a lot as a baby. My father was very uncoordinated. He was always bumping into the furniture and tripping over his own feet."

He murmurs, "I wish I could have met him. Your mother too. They must have been incredible to raise a daughter like you."

Our eyes lock. My stomach churns with nerves, and I blush. "Thank you."

He glances at my mouth, his gaze intense. "You're welcome," he says, his voice low and husky.

The moment stretches out until Callum turns back to the stove. I take a moment to reorient myself, then say, "So you cook. Guess I was wrong when I told Sophie you couldn't even boil an egg."

He chuckles, clearly amused. "I'm used to people misjudging me. Why don't you pour the wine, and I'll meet you in the dining room? The table's already set."

He gestures toward an open bottle of Pinot on the counter near the stove.

Feeling guilty over his comment about being misjudged, I nod silently and take the bottle of wine into the dining room. The table is set for two, with lit taper candles and an arrangement of fresh-cut flowers in the center.

I stop and take a moment to appreciate the view.

It's undeniably romantic that he went to all this trouble. Thoughtful too.

Especially for a man who shackled me to his bed and left me there overnight without batting an eyelash.

He walks in with two plates as I'm pouring the wine into crystal goblets. He sets the plates down, and we take our seats across from each other. Then he raises his wineglass for a toast.

"To my wife, the only woman I've ever met who uses infant shit as a condiment."

I pick up my own glass and smile. "Consider it a wedding present. Cheers."

Our gazes meet over the rims of our glasses as we drink, but I have to look away after a moment because the eye contact is too intense.

The food is delicious. I'm surprised, but probably shouldn't be. Callum seems to have more surprises up his sleeves than a magician. We make small talk for a while, chatting about our day, until I remember my misgivings about Tracy, and my mood sours.

"What?" he demands suddenly.

I look up from my plate. "Pardon?"

"Your face just dropped. What's wrong?"

Frowning at him, I say, "It's uncanny how you do that."

"Don't change the subject. What's wrong, Emery?"

I set my fork down slowly and admit, "I was just thinking about your secretary, Tracy."

"What about her?"

"How long has she worked for you?"

"About four years."

Four years. That's a long time. Definitely long enough to train her to be your obedient cum slut.

Inspecting my face, Callum drawls, "Dear wife. Are you jealous?"

"No."

He chuffs out a laugh. "You seem to forget I can tell when you're lying."

"Which is odd, isn't it? Considering you barely know me."

His voice drops, and his eyes start to burn. "I know all about you."

"Hmm. Your detective friend."

We gaze at each other across the table, the tension crackling, until he says, "I told you I wasn't fucking anyone else. That's the truth."

"That sounds like an equivocation."

"How so?"

"You said you're not fucking anyone else *now*. How about in the past? Did your dick accidentally find itself inside her?"

He licks his lips and grins at me. "No. But I wish I could say yes, just to see what your reaction would be."

"Don't start patting yourself on the back for your trust, billionaire. You nearly ripped the head off one of my customers just for standing next to me."

Without a hint of shame, he admits, "I did. And the same thing will happen with any other man you stand too close to. So do the male population of Los Angeles a favor and keep your smiles for your husband, or you might find yourself standing in a pool of someone else's blood."

When I gape at him in disbelief, he chuckles and takes another bite of his chicken.

I swallow a big gulp of wine, then set the glass down on the table with more force than necessary. "For a brief moment there, it felt like we were a normal couple enjoying a night in."

"Normal is overrated. And if you ever start to doubt that, go for another ride in the Ferrari."

"Let me just eat this meal in peace, please. My blood sugar is getting dangerously low. I could black out and forget murdering you."

I take out my aggravation with him on the poor chicken marsala, which doesn't stand a chance. Meanwhile, my husband watches me, his expression amused.

"Callum?"

"Yes, wife?"

"Stop staring at me."

"Never."

"Try."

"Even if I tried, I couldn't. It's my favorite thing."

Something in his tone makes me worry.

His look of amusement has changed to one of primal hunger, that predatory glint in his eyes that surfaces at random moments, always catching me off guard.

My breath hitches. My heart starts to pound. An electric charge shivers over my nerve endings. From one moment to the next, I go from being annoyed with him to feeling like a mouse who realizes there's a cat crouching right behind it, ready to pounce.

Holding my startled gaze, he says softly, "Sweet little lamb. I'll give you a five-second head start."

"No."

"Five."

I say sternly, "Don't you dare start that counting thing."

"Four."

"I'm not kidding. I won't run. I'll stab you with my fork."

"Three."

My voice comes out breathless from nerves. "Callum, stop it."

His smile could send every demon screaming in terror straight from the depths of hell.

"Two."

My mouth goes dry, my pulse goes haywire, and the hair on my arms stands on end.

"*One.*"

The air turns to fire. For a split second, neither of us moves.

Then Arlo walks into the room, and I nearly die of a heart attack.

"Excuse me, Mr. McCord, but there's someone here to see you."

"Send them away," Callum says, still staring hungrily at me.

"I would, but I'm afraid he insisted."

When Callum turns toward him, frowning, Arlo says, "It's your father." He glances in my direction. "He wants to meet your new wife."

Closing his eyes, Callum mutters, "Fuck."

"Should I pull the fire alarm to provide a distraction?"

Grim, Callum shakes his head. "No. Let's get this over with." He sends me a lethal look. "And let me do the talking, understood?"

"Whatever you say, billionaire," I reply, wondering what Callum's problem with his father is.

Whatever it is, I think I'm about to find out.

Twenty-Six

Taking me by the hand, Callum leads me into a quiet salon off the main living room, points at a seating area near an unlit fireplace, and orders me to sit. I bite back a smart remark about manners and watch him walk stiffly from the room, then wait in growing anxiety as the minutes tick by.

My mind swirls with questions. I mull over Cole's reaction to finding out about me and wonder if his father's will be the same.

Or worse.

Why is it such a big deal, anyway? Isn't this exactly what he was supposed to do? Find a wife?

Finally, his expression dark and his shoulders tense, Callum returns with his father.

He looks the same as in his pictures. Important is the word that comes to mind.

He's dressed in a double-breasted pinstripe suit. His watch is so big and gold, it could double as a choker. His dark hair is graying at the temples. His eyes are sharp and his bearing is regal, and I'm expecting him to launch into an interrogation about my relationship with his son that will leave me wilted and shame-filled, nursing my battered ego for weeks.

Remembering what Callum told me about how fanatically he holds grudges, I want to shrink into the sofa and disappear.

Which is why it's such a surprise when he strides toward me with his hands outstretched, breaking into a warm smile.

"Hello. I'm Konrad, Callum's father."

Feeling off-balance, I stand and take his outstretched hand. "Hi," I say shyly, glancing at Callum glowering at us in the background like a prison guard. "I'm Emery. It's nice to meet you."

Clasping my hand in both of his, he says enthusiastically, "Oh, my dear, the pleasure is all mine. I honestly never thought this day would come. When Cole called me to tell me the news this afternoon, I was overjoyed. I'm so, so happy to meet you. Welcome to the family."

Okay, this is weird. This guy doesn't seem at all like Callum made him out to be. I was expecting Genghis Khan, not Mr. Rogers.

"Thank you. That's very kind."

"I'm sorry to say that I haven't heard anything about you, because my son would rather have his fingernails pulled off with pliers than discuss his personal life with his parents."

Visibly agitated, Callum warns, "Dad."

Konrad waves him off as if swatting away a fly. "Let's sit, shall we, dear?"

Still clasping my hand, he draws me down next to him on the sofa, then takes me in from head to toe. He sighs.

"Just lovely. Although I must admit, I'm surprised you're brunette. He's always had a preference for blondes. The more dimwitted, the better. He once brought a young woman home to dinner who was such an airhead, his mother and I expected her to float up to the ceiling and bob there like a helium-filled balloon."

Unsure of how to respond to that, I say, "Um...thank you?"

Callum looks as if his head is about to explode. "That was fifteen years ago. I was in college."

"Yes, and the last time you brought home a date."

His tone dripping acid, Callum mutters, "Can't imagine why."

Arlo enters and gives the elder McCord a small, respectful bow. "Would anyone care for a drink?"

Callum snaps, "No. My wife and I were just about to go to bed."

Konrad looks at him as if he's lost his marbles. "Bed? It's not even seven o'clock. Don't be ridiculous." Dismissing him, he turns back to me and smiles. "I'm sorry to barge in on you unannounced like this, but I knew if I told Callum I was coming, he'd turn off all the lights and pretend he wasn't home."

"*Dad,*" Callum warns again, a vein in his temple popping.

His father ignores him. "I'll take a Grey Goose martini, Arlo. Thank you. What will you have, Emery?"

"That sounds great, thanks."

"Two Goose martinis, then." He shoots a glance at Callum, standing there looking like the poster child for repressed rage, and adds sourly, "And perhaps an enema for my son."

I think I love this man.

Completely charmed by him, I say, "I really appreciate you being so welcoming. I wasn't sure what to expect."

Konrad chuckles. "I'm sure my boy has told you some awful anecdote or other about me, but I can assure you, dear, I'm harmless."

"As a rattlesnake."

I'm shocked by the venom in Callum's tone, but Konrad acts as if he didn't hear it. He says, "So tell me, Emery. How did you two meet?"

Before I can even part my lips, Callum interjects, "At her bookstore."

Konrad looks interested. "You work at a bookstore?"

"I own it."

"An entrepreneur! How marvelous!" he cries, sounding as if I just told him I invented a cure for cancer.

His enthusiasm makes me feel bashful. "Well, I didn't start it. My parents did, back in the eighties. I've been running it since my dad passed."

Konrad is even more thrilled by this news. He glances at Callum. "She runs the family business," he says, sounding awed. "Just like you!"

It's a wonder that Callum's molars haven't yet been ground to dust.

Konrad turns back to me. "I'm sorry to hear your father's gone. Your mother is still with us, I hope?"

"No. She died twenty years ago."

"Oh no. Have you any siblings?"

"I'm an only child."

Distressed, he looks at Callum accusingly. "And you didn't immediately introduce her to your brothers?"

When seething silence is his only response, Konrad says sternly, "This poor girl doesn't have a family, son. She's an orphan. It's unconscionable that you've kept her to yourself."

Normally I would take offense at someone acting like I'm Little Orphan Annie, but this whole exchange is ruffling Callum's feathers so much, I can't. I laugh instead.

"Don't worry, Mr. McCord. I'm good. But thank you for that. And I can't wait to meet the rest of the family."

"Please, call me Konrad," he says warmly.

When we smile at each other, Callum snaps, "You haven't asked anyone to call you by your first name in the entire time I've been alive."

"I've never had a daughter-in-law before," he answers smoothly. Addressing me again, he says, "All my boys are bachelors, much to my dismay. If I've said it once, I've said it a million times, a man is nothing without the support of a good woman. We'd still be hunting with spears in the jungle if it wasn't for the fairer sex. We're basically wild animals who need to be tamed."

He's got some interesting ideas about masculinity, but now isn't the time to debate it.

Arlo returns with our drinks and a whiskey for Callum that he didn't ask for but obviously needs. After he distributes them and leaves, Konrad raises his glass to me.

"To my lovely new daughter-in-law. Thank you for marrying my son. And good luck." He chuckles, then takes a big swig of his martini.

Not the wedding toast I would have expected, but then again, what I've seen so far of these billionaires makes me think they're all a little nuts.

We spend another twenty minutes or so chatting and getting to know each other before Callum's patience finally expires and he declares, "That's enough for tonight."

In the middle of a sentence, Konrad looks at Callum, then back at me.

"I'm afraid the clock has struck midnight, my dear. Time for me to turn into a pumpkin. But promise me you'll convince Callum to come to dinner with us sometime soon. My wife is as eager to meet you as I was, but unfortunately, she's visiting her sister in Martha's Vineyard this week."

I smile at him. "I can't promise I'll get him to go, but I'll definitely be there."

"You're not going anywhere without me!" Callum barks.

Konrad shakes his head in amusement. "You see? Wild animals."

He rises, as do I. He clasps my hands again, holding them for a moment while gazing into my eyes, then he releases me and turns away.

"I'd like a word before I go," he says to Callum in a low voice, then walks out of the room.

I look at Callum with lifted brows. He growls, "Go upstairs and get ready for bed."

He turns on his heel and stalks out.

The man never learns.

I swallow the dregs of my martini, set the glass on the coffee table, then tiptoe after Callum and his father, stopping at the doorway to cock an ear.

Hearing the faint sound of voices coming from the direction of the front entry, I slip off my shoes and walk barefoot down the corridor, hiding around the corner when I get near. Leaning closer, I listen.

"Does she know?"

"No."

The first voice was Konrad's, the second, Callum's. I wonder what it is I don't know, but they're still talking.

"Are you planning on telling her?"

"No."

"You should."

"Why?"

Konrad's laugh is soft and disbelieving. "You have to ask?"

"She's not in any danger. I'm going to keep it that way."

"Son. You can't control everything."

"The hell I can't."

"That's reckless, and you know it. You can't always be around."

"I can't, but someone can."

There's a tense pause, then Konrad says, "You can't trust him."

"I don't have a choice."

"That man is—"

"I know what he is," Callum interrupts, his voice hard. "But I don't have a choice. You made sure of that when you got us into this mess."

"It isn't a mess. What we're doing is important. It's necessary."

"You can lay off the propaganda. I've heard it a million times, and I still don't buy it."

Konrad's voice grows impatient. "This family is in a unique position. You know that. We control the media. Our kind of power is indispensable to the cause."

A cell phone rings, interrupting them. The tune "London Bridge is Falling Down" plays, echoing eerily in the sudden silence.

"McCord," says Callum, his tone brusque. There's more

silence for several moments, then he says, "I can't leave again so soon." After another pause, he speaks again, his tone lethal. "I just got fucking married."

I stand there hidden behind the corner, craning my ears, my heart thumping like mad, until I hear Callum mutter a curse.

"Fine. But I need the usual." Pause. Then: "I don't give a shit if he's on the moon, get him here or I'm not leaving."

He must disconnect the call, because next I hear Konrad say, "You should tell her."

"She dislikes me enough as it is."

"That's nonsense. She wouldn't have married you if she disliked you."

Callum's laugh is low and dark. "She had incentive."

Konrad scoffs. "Not everyone is as mercenary as you."

"I have to go. This conversation is over."

When I hear Callum's footsteps approaching, I duck into another room and hide behind an overstuffed chair until the sound of his footsteps fades into the distance.

Then I rise, determined to discover what the hell is going on.

Callum McCord is hiding something from me.

And I'm going to find out what it is.

Twenty-Seven

I find him upstairs in the master closet, angrily opening, then slamming his dresser drawers. Leaning against the doorframe, I cross my arms over my chest and watch him for a moment.

"If you're looking for your patience, I think you lost it a good thirty years ago."

"Now isn't the time to be smart, wife."

He bangs around in the dresser drawers for a few more moments, shoving folded clothes aside and looking underneath, then mutters a curse when he doesn't find what he's looking for.

Recognizing his mood is black and I need to approach him as one would a cornered wolf, I keep my tone neutral. "So your dad's nice."

That observation earns me a blistering glare. Though it might be wiser to, I don't back down. I've got too many questions swimming around my head that require answers.

"I have to wonder, though, why he wasn't the first person you told about our situation." When Callum remains silent, I prompt, "Considering his ultimatum about your inheritance?"

"I know what you meant. But it's complicated."

"Seems like it."

Sensing I'm waiting for more, he adds, "We haven't always been close. There's...tension. History. Unresolved father-son shit."

"Yeah, I got that. What I don't get is what you're doing that he thinks is so dangerous."

He falls still for a split second, then glowers at me from under lowered brows.

"You listened in on our conversation?"

My smile is warm. "I know. It's rude of me. But I did learn from the master." I shrug, knowing he'll realize I'm referring to the dinner with my employees at Jameson's that started this whole thing.

He gazes at me in stone-faced silence for a moment, then snaps, "It's just business. Things you don't need to be involved in."

I look at him, so obviously upset but unwilling to give me even a clue as to why, and decide to jump right into the deep end of the pool.

Holding his angry gaze, I say softly, "I don't dislike you."

He seems taken aback, but quickly recovers. "You married me for my money."

"Yes. Guess what, asshole? You married me for your money too."

His expression sours. "Not the same thing."

"Oh, really? Explain how."

He clenches his jaw. "Why do you always have to test me? Is it a point of pride for you?"

"Let me take a page from your playbook and say don't change the subject."

His glare turns baleful. "I should've married someone less intelligent."

"Talk about a backhanded compliment. Well done. Don't change the subject."

Our eye contact is so intense, it's practically a physical thing.

We're standing six feet apart, but might as well be wrestling around on the floor for how rough it feels.

Finally, he demands, "Name one thing you like about me."

I tease, "Aside from your charming temperament, you mean?"

When he doesn't crack a smile, I relent. "Okay, sourpuss, I like your sense of humor."

He lifts one brow into a perfect, sardonic arch.

"Yes, it's true. When you're not busy being bossy and barking orders, you're actually quite funny. Don't give me that look. I also like how thoughtful you are."

He blinks, obviously surprised by that.

I enjoy catching him off guard, so I keep going.

"You're incredibly generous, too. For some reason, I always had this misconception that rich people were stingy, but you throw money around like it's confetti. Let's, see, what else? Oh, I like your taste in interior décor. And in books. That collection of first editions in the armoire is fucking amazing. Honestly, I should light some incense and a candle and make it into a shrine, it's that good. I also like your face. Which I realize is an odd thing to say, but if you knew me better, you'd know what a compliment it is. Sometimes, I look at a person's face and something about it is so irritating, I just want to throw a shoe at them. Personal quirk."

"You like my face," he repeats doubtfully.

"It's very symmetrical."

His expression of doubt turns to one of derision.

"Shut up. I'm not done with my list. You can think of witty comebacks while I'm talking. I like how you walk through the world as if you own it. You're comfortable in your own skin. I admit I'm a bit jealous of that, because I always feel like some alien who crash-landed on this planet and has to figure out how to blend in without getting shot at, experimented on, or stuck in a zoo. You're self-confident is what I'm saying. It's a very attractive quality in a person."

Callum is beginning to look baffled. It's so satisfying, I reach deep into my reserves of courage and continue.

"I like that you listen. You notice things. You keep track."

"Example," he demands.

"When I told Sophie she deserved a raise, you made her boss give her one."

He thinks about that, then lifts a shoulder as if it was nothing.

"It was a very generous thing to do."

"I didn't do it for her."

The instant it's out of his mouth, he looks as if he wishes he could take it back. He shifts his weight from foot to foot, glancing away.

I feel a strange softening in the center of my chest, as if a hard knot that has lived under my breastbone for years is slowly unfurling.

I say softly, "Then who did you do it for?"

He glances back at me, jaw clenched and eyes burning.

The knot loosens until I draw what feels like my first full breath in years.

"Callum, I know I give you tons of shit, but I honestly think you're an amazing person. Thank you for everything you've done for me."

He grimaces as if I kicked him in the gut with my words.

"Judging by that look on your face, I haven't done a good job communicating my appreciation. I'm sorry for that."

His expression cycles through a mix of different emotions, starting with shock and ending on frustration. He says gruffly, "Don't apologize. Don't ever apologize to me again for anything. If you knew—"

Whatever else he was about to say is bitten back when he clenches his jaw.

"If I knew what?"

"Nothing. I have to go."

"Right. The mysterious phone call. Are you off to Prague again?"

He gazes at me in tense silence, then orders, "Don't repeat that to anyone. And I mean *anyone*, understood?"

His manner is so odd and strained, it makes me nervous. My heart beating faster, I step closer to him. "Why? Tell me what's going on with you."

"I can't."

"Your father thinks you can."

"My father has a stale crouton for a brain."

"Really? The man who founded a multibillion dollar empire is an idiot? Somehow, I find that hard to believe."

"You find everything I say hard to believe."

"Not everything. Only the stuff that sounds like bullshit."

He closes his eyes and mutters, "Goddammit, woman."

"Hey, if you wanted a mouse for a wife, you should've married one. Talk to me, Callum. Please tell me what the hell is going on."

He scrubs a hand over his face, runs it through his hair, and sighs heavily. "What's going on is that I have to leave for work. I'm not sure when I'll be back. That's all I can tell you."

"All you want to tell me, you mean."

My hurt must echo in my voice, because he looks at me for a brief, intense moment, before closing the space between us and taking my face in his hands.

"You have to trust me," he says urgently, gazing deep into my eyes.

"My trust is earned, not dispensed on demand."

"Then at least cut me some slack until you *can* trust me."

"Why should I? Your dad obviously thinks I'm in some kind of danger, but you're refusing to give me an inch. And who's that guy he was talking about? And the mess you said your family is in? What the hell is happening, Callum?"

He drops his hands to his sides and blasts me with his most withering, he-man look, towering over me like Godzilla about to ransack a city.

I say flatly, "Yes, you're very scary. Happy?"

"No."

"What a shock."

We glare at each other in stalemate for an eternity, until he decides he's had enough of it and brushes past me, striding out of the closet without a backward glance.

I spin around and call after him, "You know what? I take back all that nice stuff I said about you. You're a monster!"

Over his shoulder, he growls, "Now you're getting it, wife."

He leaves me standing alone in his closet wondering which of his suits I should take the scissors to first.

I can't sleep that night. I lie alone in bed, staring at the shadows shifting on the ceiling, going over everything in my mind.

The McCord family is involved in something dangerous.

Callum told no one he got married.

He did something he thinks I'd hate him for if I found out.

It was the way he recoiled when I thanked him that clued me in. The way he ordered me never to apologize. Those bitten-back words after *"If you only knew."*

He's keeping secrets from me.

But why?

And what's with the mysterious phone calls? The sudden business trips? The man his father said they can't trust?

There was also something odd about the way Callum said I had incentive to marry him and Konrad's response. *"Not everyone is as mercenary as you."*

I can't make sense of that exchange, especially since the real mercenary is a man who'd force his son to marry to secure his inheritance.

I feel as if something important hovers just out of my reach. Like I'm missing the piece that will complete the puzzle, but I can't find it anywhere.

In the morning, I'm tired and on edge, preoccupied with thoughts of Callum. I head to work, but my anxiety grows as the day drags on. I can't shake the feeling that something is wrong, so I call Dani and ask if she can meet me for drinks after I close up.

"Not tonight, babe. Ryan called to say he'll be late at work, so he can't watch Mia."

"Oh God, I'm such a dick. I completely forgot to ask you how his new job is going."

She laughs. "It's not like you haven't had anything else happening in your life."

"I still feel awful about it."

"Don't. He's loving the new gig at McCord Media."

"Really?"

"They gave him a huge corner office with a view and doubled his salary. What's not to love?"

"I'm so happy for him!"

"All thanks to you, girl. All thanks to you."

I'm about to respond, but get distracted by the sight of a man standing outside the entrance of ValUBooks. He's leaning with his back on the wall and one foot kicked up against it, his arms crossed over his broad chest. Wearing a black leather jacket, black cowboy boots, and jeans, he looks vaguely familiar.

Though mirrored sunglasses obscure his eyes, he seems to be staring in the direction of my shop.

"Em? You still there?"

A frisson of fear runs through me, making me shiver. "I'm here."

"You okay? You sound weird all of a sudden."

"Let me call you back."

I hang up before she can say anything else and stare hard at the stranger in black, my heart thumping and adrenaline searing my veins.

I know I've seen him before. I *know* it. But where? When?

Has he been following me?

As if he can hear my thoughts, he pushes off the wall and disappears through the open glass doors of ValUBooks.

Viv glances up from the box of books she's unpacking and looks at me.

"What's wrong? You're as white as a sheet."

I barely hear her, because now I remember where I've seen the man in black before. It was the day of the grand opening of ValU-Books. He stood in almost the same spot, peering toward my shop from behind mirrored aviators.

Turning to look out the window, Viv says, "What are you looking at?"

I lick my dry lips and wipe my clammy palms on the front of my shirt. "There was a man...a guy who looked familiar."

She turns back and frowns at me. "Out in the parking lot?"

"Over by the entrance to ValUBooks. I think I've seen him there before, looking this way. There's something strange about him."

"What did he look like?"

"Tall. Built. Dressed in black, with mirrored sunglasses. Kinda looks like trouble."

After a beat, she says, "Like that guy at your dad's funeral."

Startled, I glance at her. "What?"

"You mentioned it once a while back. We were reading a list some critic put together about the best funeral scenes in movies, and Sabine said that when she's buried, she wants to hire someone to stand apart from the mourners under an umbrella, looking on from a distance, so everyone would think she was involved in something mysterious, and you said that happened at your dad's funeral. That there was a mysterious stranger watching from under a purple flowering tree. I remember because you said he had James Dean-meets-Wolverine vibes, and I could totally picture him in my mind."

James Dean meets Wolverine.

My entire body goes cold. My arms break out in goose bumps.

I remember it now in perfect detail, though up until this moment I'd forgotten. What struck me at the time was that the man looked so at ease among the crypts and headstones, as if he spent most of his time there.

As if he walked among the dead for a living.

As if maybe he was a ghost himself.

And though it's impossible, I'm convinced the man I saw outside is the same man I saw at my father's funeral.

The funeral that was four years ago.

Though my heart is racing and my stomach is in knots, I walk quickly toward the front door. "Viv, hold down the fort for a minute. I'm headed over to ValUBooks."

"Why? What are you doing?"

"Going ghost hunting."

Twenty-Eight

The moment I walk through the doors of ValUBooks, I understand why they're so successful.

It's not the delicate scent of vanilla and orange blossom piped through the AC system. It's not the gleaming white travertine floors or the elegant, modern furnishings. It's not even the huge coffee bar or the charming floral displays or the attractive, uniformed staff who all look as though they were recruited from a Ralph Lauren catalog.

It's how everything comes together into one seamless, elegant whole so beautiful, it could make a bibliophile weep with joy.

And the books. Sweet home Alabama, the sheer number of books displayed boggles the mind. This place could give the Library of Congress a run for its money.

I stand starstruck in the entrance, gazing around with dazzled eyes, until an annoyed customer brushes past me, muttering under her breath about idiots blocking doorways.

Then I shake off my awe and start to hunt.

Walking briskly, I make my way around the perimeter of the store first, peering down aisles and peeking around display stands. I don't catch sight of a tall man in black anywhere, so I keep looking, taking the glass elevator to the second floor to scan the travel, history, and children's sections. Still nothing.

I have no idea what I'll say to him if I do find him, but I'll worry about it when the time comes.

Maybe he went out a back door?

Growing agitated, I hurry through aisle after aisle until I round a corner and slam into an immoveable object blocking my path. It's young guy in a T-shirt and jeans, reading the book open in his hands.

"Oh shit! I'm so sorry!" Breathless, I stumble back.

Scowling, he turns to see who crashed into him so rudely. Our eyes meet, and we both freeze in shock.

It's Ben, my ex.

He looks exactly the same as the last time I saw him. Mussed brown hair that needs a trim. Denim-blue eyes fringed by long lashes. Boyish good looks made even more charming by the dimples creasing both cheeks.

We stare at each other for one long, frozen moment, until he says gruffly, "Hey."

Hey?

Fucking *hey*?

That's all he's got to say after disappearing without a word, breaking my heart, and leaving me with a permanent case of insecurity?

My pulse throbbing through my veins, I take a step back, inhale a shaky breath, and swallow around the rock in my throat.

"Hi, Ben."

Awkward silence. Ah, how excruciating. I might as well have jumped into a pool of hungry sharks for how this feels. My heart might just bleed out all over this nice shiny travertine floor.

For a man who dumped me in such a brutal fashion, his expression is curiously soft. He looks me slowly up and down, his eyes both warm and wistful, as if he's remembering something he once cherished that he lost.

But he didn't lose me. He threw me away like trash.

He ghosted me, the heartless prick.

Heat scalds my cheeks and ears. My heart throbs under my breastbone. He's lucky we're in a bookstore and not a hardware store, because I'd grab a hammer from the nearest shelf and have a go at his balls.

I should walk away, but I can't. I'm rooted to the spot as if I grew here.

He says softly, "How are you, Em?"

Fury washes over me in a hot, violent wave. I snap, "Oh no, you didn't. You did *not* just ask how I am."

Boy, that misty, sentimental look sure took a hike real quick. He frowns at me, shaking his head in annoyance.

"Wait. Just hold on a second before you start yelling at me."

"No, I don't think I will. I think I'll start yelling nice and loud so everybody way over in the checkout line knows what a dick I think you are. In fact, I think I'll scream it at the top of my—"

He grabs my arm and drags me around the corner into the aisle, then pushes me against a shelf of books and stares down into my face with a look of extreme concentration.

His voice hushed and urgent, he says, "I didn't want to do it, okay? I never wanted to leave you."

Caught off guard, I blink. "Are you saying *I* made you leave? I drove you away, is that it?"

Frustrated, he shakes his head. "No. That's not it at all. Listen, I've wanted to call you a thousand times. I never stopped thinking about you. I never stopped caring about you, Em."

Confused, upset, and sick to my stomach, I cover my mouth with my hand.

He draws a breath. "I wanted to tell you everything, and I should have, I know I should've. But—"

His eyes widen. His face turns the color of ash.

He's looking at my hand. The hand I've pressed over my mouth.

The hand with my wedding ring on it.

He takes an abrupt step back and swallows hard.

"Yes, I'm married. Did you think I'd wait around the rest of my life to see if you'd ever call me again?"

His silence is electric. I can tell he wants to say something, that he's fighting with himself about it, but whatever it is, he keeps it to himself.

He slowly sets the book he's holding on top of the others on the shelf beside my head, then turns his back and walks away.

I watch him go in disbelief.

Just before he turns the corner of the aisle, he stops. He hangs his head, seems to deliberate for a moment, then looks over his shoulder at me.

His eyes dark and his voice tight, he says, "It was good seeing you, Em. Take care."

He leaves me standing alone with the knife he buried in my chest, wishing I'd never set foot in this stupid place to begin with.

I spend the rest of the afternoon locked in my office in a gnarly funk. I know I shouldn't let it get to me, but seeing Ben so unexpectedly was a shock to my system. And not only did I get no answers that would help me understand what happened between us, I ended up with more questions than before.

Nothing about our encounter makes any kind of sense.

I go over and over it in my head, swinging back and forth between hurt and anger, until finally, I exhaust my emotional reservoirs and come out on the other side feeling numb.

Deciding to take my mind off the situation by throwing myself into work, I call the landlord to ask him if he'd be willing to sell the building. When I get him on the line, he sounds like he'd rather be getting a colonoscopy than talking to me.

"Hello, Emery," he says stiffly. "What can I do for you?"

"Hi, Bill. I wanted to float an idea past you to get your input."

After an oddly long pause, he says, "What is it?"

"I was wondering if you'd ever consider selling the building."

"Sell? To who?"

"To me."

Another strange pause ensues. I know my rent check cleared this month, thanks to Callum's trust fund, so I have no idea what his problem is.

He says carefully, "I...would have to think about that and get back to you."

My laugh is dry. "I'm good for the cash. I know you probably don't believe that, considering my payment history, but I've recently had what you could call a change in circumstances. Money is no longer a problem."

"I'm sorry, but I can't talk right now."

"Oh. Okay. Well, when do you think you might be able to tell me if you'll sell? Because I'm going to invest in upgrades, but I don't want to do it while I'm leasing—"

He cuts me off with, "I'll get back to you as soon as I can," and hangs up on me.

I sit at my desk, staring at the phone in my hand, wondering what the fuck is the matter with everyone.

Or is it all my imagination? Am I making mountains out of molehills? Am I creating drama where there isn't any?

After all, I am the queen of overthinking.

Maybe Bill wasn't acting strangely at all. Maybe he was just busy. And maybe the mystery man I saw outside ValU-Books was just some dude waiting for his wife shopping inside. Maybe I only *wished* Ben looked wistful and forlorn when he saw me, but what he actually looked like was embarrassed.

Maybe all that "I never wanted to leave you" nonsense was nothing more than excuses he made up on the spot to avoid a scene.

Which was a good call, considering I was about to do just that.

Aggravated with everyone and everything, including myself, I dig around in the bottom drawer of my desk until I find the whiskey bottle. I sit there taking swigs from it until Viv knocks on the door.

"Come in."

She opens the door, sees me sitting there with a bottle in my hand, and sighs.

"Don't judge me."

"That's what you always say when you know you're doing something stupid."

"Whiskey isn't stupid. It's a necessary food group. What's that envelope you're holding?"

She walks over to my desk and hands it to me. "A courier just delivered it."

The return address shows it's from the CDTFA.

Just what I needed today. Another disaster. The tax board probably doubled my fine.

But when I rip open the envelope and pull out the sheet of paper inside, I'm shocked to discover it's a letter from David Montgomery saying there was, in fact, an error on their end.

The current balance due on my account is zero.

"Everything okay?"

Smiling, I look up at Viv. "I can't believe I'm going to say this, but yes. This deserves a celebration."

"If you take another sip from that bottle, I'll hit you over the head."

"God, you're uptight for someone so young."

She leans over the desk, snags the whiskey bottle, then turns and walks toward the door, saying over her shoulder, "You'll thank me in the morning."

I call out after her, "You'll never know because I'll never admit it."

But as it turns out, she's right. I leave work early, go to bed early, and wake up with a clear head and a brighter outlook than I had the day before. I decide it was good that I ran into Ben, because now at least I know he's the same jerk he was when he left me all those months ago. No explanations, just another abrupt exit.

I'm lucky we never got engaged. He'd probably have stood me up at the altar.

I won't waste any more time thinking about him.

I won't waste any more time obsessing over whatever Callum's hiding from me either. Let the moody billionaire have his secrets. I've got my own life to worry about.

Two nights later, I'm awakened from a dead sleep when Callum picks me up from the guest room bed and carries me down the hallway to the master bedroom.

"You're back." Groggy, I rest my head against his shoulder. My legs dangle over the crook of his arm.

He doesn't respond. I feel the tension in his corded muscles, sense a certain heightened stress in his mood, and wonder if something's happened.

"You okay?"

"No. But I will be as soon as I'm inside you."

His voice is a low rumble of need that makes me shiver in anticipation. It also reminds me of something I neglected to tell him before.

"Hey."

"Hmm?"

"Remember when I was listing all the things I like about you?"

"No," he lies, a smile in his tone.

"Whatever. Anyway, I forgot to mention your voice."

"What about it?"

"It's incredible. All velvet, smoke, and honey, like expensive whiskey. If this billionaire gig of yours ever dries up, you could make a living as a spicy romance audiobook narrator."

"Did you get into the liquor cabinet tonight, darling?"

I smile at hearing my nickname and snuggle closer to his chest. "It's nice when we're not fighting. You should disappear for days on end more often."

He presses a kiss to the top of my head. "My mouthy little lamb. Fuck, how I miss you when I'm gone."

My pulse goes haywire. My body flushes with heat. A strange combination of hope and nervousness makes me hide my face in his shirt collar. "You do?"

"Yes."

His firm answer gives me the courage to ask, "Even though you only married me to save your inheritance?"

He squeezes me closer against his body. He doesn't answer, but the way his heart pounds against my cheek sets my soul on fire. I whisper, "I missed you too. This big old castle gets lonely without its bad-tempered beast."

"Why don't you call me when I'm away if you get lonely?"

"Because asking that stupid batphone to call Daddy gives me hives."

Chuckling, he strides through the door of his bedroom and heads straight to the bed.

"Where did you get that thing, anyway? I've never seen anything like it."

"I have a friend who gets all the latest techy gadgets."

"Like James Bond."

"He'd love it that you said that. Now be quiet and get ready to spread your legs for your master."

I groan. "Oh no. Not that master stuff again."

"Do you want me to make you come or not?"

When I grumble in annoyance, he says, "That's what I thought," and lays me down on the bed.

I stare up at him as he strips off his clothing. Moonlight spills through the windows, highlighting his hair and skin in a pale, ethereal glow. My chest grows tight with emotion as I watch him.

He's beautiful, this mysterious stranger I married. A beautiful enigma who walks through the world as if he owns it, wearing all his secrets like a second skin.

I don't know if I'll ever really know him, if he'll ever let me in to discover whatever he's hiding behind those gorgeous eyes, but in this moment, it doesn't matter.

All that matters is this addictive attraction we share, this strange passion that seemed to appear out of nowhere and burns hotter every time we're together, searing me down to the marrow of my bones.

"I love the way you're looking at me right now," he murmurs, staring down at me.

"How am I looking at you?"

"Like you're mine." Even through the shadows, his dangerous smile shines. "Now get on your hands and knees like a good girl and show me how much you missed me with that pretty mouth."

I sigh. "Callum?"

"Yeah, baby?"

"You don't really think you're the boss of me, do you?"

His laugh is low and sinister. "Tell you what. Let's find out."

He rolls me over onto my belly, holds me down by the back of my neck, and spanks me smartly on the ass until I'm breathless and squealing, his dark laughter the most heavenly music in my ears.

Twenty-Nine

Something shifts between us that night.

I don't recognize it at the time, but later, I'll look back and remember the feeling of yielding I experience. The softening that started before in my chest works in sinuous waves throughout my whole body as he fucks me, manhandling me in the most delicious ways, turning me as pliant as warmed putty in his hands.

If my mind still holds doubts about the man I married, my body trusts him instinctively.

He forces his hard cock past my lips as if it's his birthright. He grips my head with absolute dominance as he thrusts into my mouth. Grunting in pleasure, he holds me down and drives into my pussy as I cry out his name. He bites me and spanks me and pulls my head back using fistfuls of my hair. He comes inside me, licks it out as I sob, then fucks my ass and comes inside me again, the entire time calling me wife and baby and his perfect, beautiful pet.

I never knew sex could feel so transformative. That something so dirty could also be so pure. It's like we invented our own religion, a new way of worship involving not only heart and soul, but skin and breath, moans and sweat, frantic bodies and tangled sheets and complete surrender to something bigger than us both that's driven us from the moment we met.

It isn't love. I know that.

But it is divine.

No sermon ever preached could move my spirit more.

In the morning, I wake in his arms, feeling like I'm right where I'm supposed to be. Smiling and snuggling closer to his warmth, I whisper, "Hi there."

"Hi yourself."

"How did you sleep?"

"Like the dead. You milked every last drop of cum out of my dick. I'm completely dehydrated."

I press my face against his chest and laugh, ridiculously pleased with myself. "Are you complaining?"

"Hell no. You can drain me dry anytime, baby."

"God, it's sick that I found that statement romantic. How was your trip?"

In his pause, I sense turmoil. His voice comes low and tight.

"Aggravating."

I want to pry. I want to poke him in the ribs and demand he give me more than that. But I also understand that he'd tell me if he wanted me to know, so I console myself with the memory of him saying he misses me when he's gone and leave it at that.

"Well, I'm glad you're home anyway."

He pauses again, but this feels different. His attention sharpens, homing in on me like a laser beam.

Nervous, I peek up at his face. "What?"

He strokes a hand gently over my hair and murmurs, "You said home."

"So?"

"You could've said 'you're back.' Or 'you're here.' But instead you said you were glad I'm *home*."

I realize what he means by the emphasis he put on the word home. Slightly flustered by that, I backtrack. "Don't get all excited. It was a random choice."

He rolls me over onto my back, settles his weight on top of me, and stares down into my face, his eyes fierce with emotion.

"No, it wasn't random. You feel like this is your home. Admit it."

I already know that when he gets started with his demands, it's only a matter of time before I crack under the pressure, so I don't bother to put up a fight. I sigh and nod.

He's thrilled by the admission. I can taste it in his kiss, which is rough and passionate.

When we come up for air, I laugh. "You know, for a man who's only married to keep his money, you seem strangely invested in what I think about our situation."

He studies me in pensive silence for a moment. "Maybe you're growing on me."

"Ah. Like blight."

He makes a face, scrunching up his nose and curling his upper lip. "Blight?"

"Yeah. You know. Plant mildew. Soggy leaf rot."

"Who says that?"

"Someone who sells books for a living. Don't tell me you've never heard of blight."

"Of course I've heard of it. I've just never heard of anyone who'd refer to themselves as plant mildew when they're naked in bed with their new husband."

My grin is so big, it's probably blinding him. "You bring out the best in me, darling."

He rolls off me, chuckling.

Arlo walks in without knocking, wheeling a linen-covered cart. "Good morning!"

Horrified, I yank the covers over my head. "Arlo! What the hell do you have against announcing yourself before you barge into a room?"

"I brought breakfast," he says, as if that's a reasonable explanation.

He must be getting to know me well, because he starts to tick off a list of goodies that makes my anger dissipate and my mouth water.

"We've got bacon, sausages, scrambled eggs, chocolate croissants, fresh fruit with cream, yogurt parfait, and coffee. I'll set everything up for you."

Callum lifts the sheet and grins down at me hiding beneath. "I told him we'd be hungry."

I mutter, "I bet you did."

"You're cute when you're mortified."

"And you're insufferable when you're smug."

"It's not as if he hasn't seen a pair of breasts before."

"So you'd like me to start parading around stark naked in front of him and the chef?"

His smug smile disappears, replaced by a scowl.

"That's what I thought." Folding the sheet down to my chin, I peer at Arlo setting up our breakfast on the coffee table in the sitting area across from the bed. He catches me looking and smiles at me.

"Can we please make an agreement that you'll at least *try* to learn how to knock?"

"Of course. I beg your pardon."

I can tell by the way his smile deepened as he looked away that he'll do no such thing.

When he's finished setting up the table and leaves the room, Callum strips the covers off us both, stands, and swaggers naked over to the table.

Which is when I notice his huge new tattoo.

Spanning the width of his muscular back from shoulder to shoulder and accented with a twining vine adorned with thorns, roses, snakes, and skulls, my first name is spelled out in thick black Gothic style lettering at least five inches high.

I sit up and stare at him in shock, my heart pounding.

He plucks a strawberry from the tray on the table, then turns and gazes at me, smiling.

"Would you like a piece of fruit, darling?"

"Don't talk to me about fruit. Talk to me about that thing on your back."

He pops the strawberry into his mouth, chews it leisurely, and swallows. "That thing is my wife's name. Croissant?"

"Hold on a second, please. The tattoo? Hello?"

He selects a croissant from the tray and strolls back to the bed. Standing over me, he tears off a piece and holds it out.

"Open your mouth."

"Callum, please tell—"

He slides the piece of torn croissant between my lips, cutting me off.

I consider spitting it back onto his hand, but chew and swallow instead.

No argument is worth wasting pastries over.

He tears off another piece and holds it to my closed lips. Gazing up at him, I shake my head. It makes him smirk.

"So stubborn. I guess you don't want to hear about my tattoo after all."

I close my eyes, count to ten, then open my eyes and my mouth at the same time.

"Good girl," he murmurs, eyes alight. "Fuck, how I love it when you're obedient."

He feeds me another piece, sliding his thumb over my lips as I chew.

"You have such a gorgeous mouth, wife."

I can't be sure, but think he's testing my patience. He expects me to make a smart remark so he can pivot to another subject, but he was right about me being stubborn. I want to hear what the hell he was thinking by getting that ink on his back, and if I have to sit here and let him hand-feed me an entire bag of croissants, so be it.

Besides, it's a win-win.

"You look like a cat that can't decide if it's going to purr or claw me to shreds."

I accept another bite from his fingers, batting my lashes coyly.

As I chew, he reaches down and fondles my bare breast, thumbing over my nipple until it hardens.

"Such a responsive little kitty," he whispers.

Hanging long and thick against his thigh, his cock stiffens.

Setting the croissant on the nightstand, he draws me to my feet, leads me over to the sofa, and settles me on it, pushing me back so I'm reclining against the arm with my legs stretched out. Kneeling on the floor between the sofa and coffee table, he turns back to the tray of food. Pursing his lips, he looks over the assortment of items, smiling when his gaze alights on the dish of fresh berries.

"Berries and cream," he murmurs, slanting me a hot look. "Sounds yummy."

His gaze travels slowly down my body. When it settles between my thighs, he licks his lips and plucks a plump strawberry from the dish.

"Spread your legs."

"Whatever you're thinking of doing with that berry, you can forget it."

Holding my gaze, he deliberately places the strawberry into the V between my closed thighs.

"Callum. I'm serious. I don't want fruit stored in my vadge. It's not Tupperware."

Ignoring me completely, he turns back to the berry dish and picks out a selection of blueberries, blackberries, and raspberries, then arranges them around the strawberry between my legs, carefully placing them as if he's setting up a still life drawing until there's a lovely little mound of blues and reds covering my mons.

Sitting back on his heels to admire his handiwork, he says softly, "The tattoo is the first of many I'll get with your name all over my body."

My breath catches. I study his profile as my pulse begins to race. "But...why?"

His expression contemplative now, he reaches for the small silver cream server on the tray. "Because I'm yours. You've tattooed your name on everything inside me. The least I can do is make the outside match."

His words blast through me like a hurricane, stealing my breath and knocking me senseless.

He tips the silver server, pouring a thin stream of cream over the berries between my legs. Then he moves it up my body, baptizing my belly, ribs, and breasts, his eyes hungry and his concentration acute.

The sensation of the cool cream sliding over my bare skin makes me shiver. The adoration in his gaze makes my heart ache.

I whisper, "I don't understand. We barely know each other. How can you say that?"

Setting the silver server aside, he turns back and gazes deeply into my eyes.

"You wear my ring. You sleep in my bed. You made a promise in front of witnesses to have and to hold me for the rest of your life. You *chose* me, Emery. And because you chose me, you own me, now and forever, come what may."

I feel as if somebody pushed me out of an airplane and I'm pinwheeling through space, tumbling over and around with no sense of direction, my pulse screaming through my veins and my entire life flashing through my eyes as I hurtle toward the ground at a thousand miles per hour with no chance of rescue or survival.

I don't know how we got here so suddenly. I don't understand what it all means. All I know is that he's electrocuted me with his words. My blood is lightning and wildfire. My heart pumps nuclear power through my veins.

He dips his head and licks cream from one nipple, lapping it up with gentle strokes of his tongue until the nub is taut and flushed.

Struggling to control my breathing, fraught with emotion, I watch him and try not to cry.

He moves to my other breast, licks it clean, then makes his way down my belly, tenderly kissing my flesh, cleaning it of the cream, sweeping his tongue over every hill and valley until he reaches the V between my legs.

Grasping my hips, he closes his eyes, nuzzles his face into the mound of berries, and starts to feast on it, making his way through the fruit to my skin as I lie there in a stunned sort of bliss, speechless and panting.

When his tongue strokes lazily over my clit, I moan helplessly.

He squeezes my hips and keeps eating.

The sounds he makes. The husky little chest-deep grunts. The way he's holding me. The feel of his tongue, hot and wet, of his hands, rough and strong, of his beard scratching my sensitive skin and the silken sofa cushions beneath my back and the heat blooming all over my body. I'm overwhelmed by sensation, caught in a rising tide of emotion that's beginning to swell like the crest of a wave.

Elation battles with panic for dominance. Battered by too many sensations at once, I close my eyes and let it all wash over me. I let go and allow myself to be swept away.

A deep sigh of release shudders past my lips.

Callum parts my thighs and shoves his tongue inside me.

My soft cry is lost under the sound of his heavy breathing. He grips my hips so hard, I know I'll be bruised. I sink my hands into the thick mess of his hair and arch into his mouth, rocking my hips eagerly as he makes a meal of me.

He slides a finger inside me and sucks hard on my throbbing clit, rubbing his tongue back and forth over it until I orgasm.

When I do, it's his name I scream. It tears from my throat and into the stillness of the room, echoing back into my ears like a hymn chanted over and over in church.

Callum.

Callum.

Callum.

Hallowed be thy name.

He sits on the sofa and drags me on top of him, spreading my legs over his hips and guiding his engorged cock into me as I grip his shoulders for balance. He shoves inside my pussy with a possessive growl.

"Ride me, wife. I need to hear you scream my name again."

Frantic with pleasure, I bounce up and down on his erection as he sucks on my nipples, roughly squeezing my breasts, his cheeks hollowed and his eyes closed.

I drop my head back and give myself over to another orgasm, stronger than the first.

He slaps my ass as I sob my way through it, grunting his approval against my skin.

Then he puts his mouth next to my ear and closes his arms hard around me.

Crushing me against his chest, he says gruffly, "I know you think we should've gone slow. But I know nothing of slowness. I dove into you like the ocean, headfirst, not caring if I'd drown."

He jerks, groaning. Then he kisses me passionately as he spills himself inside me, claiming me body and soul.

Thirty

We shower together in silence. I want to speak, but don't know what to say.

How do you tell the stranger you married for his money that he's becoming your center of gravity? That his magnetic field is so strong, the compass needle in your heart is swinging around to point to him as true north?

It feels like a fairy tale.

What worries me is that the flip side of every sweet fairy tale reveals something much darker lurking underneath.

After the shower, Callum dresses, kisses me goodbye, and leaves for work. I linger over the breakfast, which has grown cold, attempting to reorient my balance to this strange new landscape I find myself in.

I didn't want an emotional connection with him. I didn't want to feel anything for him at all. But he's so much more than I expected. More sensitive and thoughtful. More generous and kind. There's a depth to him that has me enamored.

And as a lover, he's unmatched. He makes my previous partners look like bumbling amateurs. No one has ever had the effect on me that he does.

Resolving to let it be whatever it is and not overthink things for once, I finish breakfast and dress, looking forward to the day. For now, at least, everything seems right with the world.

Then the housekeepers arrive and knock me askew again.

I'm in the kitchen with Arlo when the first one walks in. Young, brunette, and curvy, she smiles at me and says hello.

"Hi. I'm Emery."

"Pleased to meet you."

"Sarah, this is Mr. McCord's wife," says Arlo, looking up from the newspaper he's reading at the big center island. "They were recently married."

"Oh, congratulations!" says Sarah warmly.

"Thank you."

My reply is less than enthusiastic, because two more young women have walked into the kitchen to join us. They're all dressed in white, carrying bags of cleaning supplies as Sarah is, a trio of lovely brunettes who all look just like me.

Right down to the red lipstick.

Sarah says, "This is Kelly and Michelle." The two murmur demure hellos.

After a moment, I manage to reply, "Hi there."

"Do you have any areas in particular you'd like us to focus on today?"

They stare at me with an air of professional expectation. I realize I'm supposed to provide them with some sort of instruction. Never having had to direct domestic workers before, I find myself at a loss.

I don't even know where the washing machine is in this place, for fuck's sake.

"Maybe just do the usual?"

"Of course." Sarah, who apparently is the leader, turns to the other ladies and says, "Let's get started." They nod and set about bustling around the kitchen, their movements quick and efficient.

In addition to feeling unsettled, I also feel in the way. So I say goodbye to everyone and head to the garage, where I stand staring at the rows of luxury cars for several long minutes in a daze, questioning my own sanity.

It can't be a coincidence that we all look alike, can it?

And Callum's secretary too?

Frustrated with myself, I shake my head to clear it.

Of course it's a coincidence. I'm being ridiculous. I'm letting the emotion from this morning go to my head. There are millions of short brunettes in this city. Literally millions. I'm acting like I'm an eight-foot-tall redhead with a rainbow unicorn horn for a nose.

Besides, Konrad said his son had a preference for blondes. If anything, I should be worried if all his employees looked like Sabine.

By the time I arrive at work, I've gaslighted myself into believing it.

When I hear the knock on my office door, I look up from the computer. "Hi, Murph."

He stands in the doorway, jerking his thumb toward the front of the store. "There's a young man here to see you. Says his name is Cole."

Oh God. It's Callum's crabby brother. My stomach drops. "Does he look angry?"

"Not at all. Seems a friendly sort. Should I tell him you're unavailable?"

I rise, smoothing my hands down the front of my skirt. "No, send him back, please."

I force myself to take a few deep breaths to calm my jittery nerves. I have no idea why Cole would want to see me, but I can't help but think this unexpected visit won't be good.

Then he walks through the door, and I rethink it.

He's not wearing the glower from his family photo, nor does he have the dark, crackling intensity he had that day in Callum's office. Dressed in black slacks and a white dress shirt, he looks serious but not severe.

He walks toward me, extending his hand.

"Hello, Emery. I'm sorry I didn't call first. Is this a good time?"

I shake his hand, trying not to wince when he crushes all the little bones in mine. The man has the grip of a hydraulic press. "This is fine. Though I have to admit, it's unexpected. Is something wrong?"

My question makes him smile. Well, not smile, exactly, but his lips do something that looks as if they'd curve up if only they weren't afraid he'd rip them off for the audacity.

"You sound like me."

"Oh? How so?"

"Your first thought is always a negative one."

I'm not sure how to take that, so I bypass it. "Would you like to have a seat?"

"No, no, I won't take up too much of your time. I just wanted to talk to you about Callum."

His expression makes me nervous all over again. "Does he know you're here?"

"No. And I'd appreciate it if you didn't tell him I was."

We stand in uncomfortable silence for a moment, until I say, "I don't want to be rude, but you're putting me in kind of a bad spot by asking that."

"I'm not asking you to lie. Just don't offer the information."

"Is there some reason you don't want me to tell him I saw you?"

He gazes at me for a beat, his dark eyes assessing and his handsome face somber. "May I be blunt with you?"

"I prefer if you are."

"My brother..." Glancing away, Cole clears his throat as if he might choke on whatever it is he's about to say. His voice an octave lower, he says, "This is hard for me to tell you."

I sink into my desk chair and pass a shaky hand over my face. "Please don't say he has a secret family somewhere."

Cole looks back at me with an expression of horror. "No. Jesus, of course not. Why would you think that?"

I close my eyes and sigh. "Because I'm the queen of awfulizing, that's why. Here's where I'd like to throw myself out the window, except we're on the first floor." I open my eyes and meet his startled gaze. "Sorry. You were saying?"

It takes him a moment to regroup from being hit over the head by the blunt force of my stupidity. Then he says, "What I was going to say is that my brother and I aren't close."

When he doesn't continue and only stands there in obvious discomfort, I try a gentle prompt to get him talking. "He hasn't mentioned that to me, but it did seem like there was some tension between the two of you the day we met."

"He didn't tell you we don't get along?"

He seems surprised by that. I can't help but wonder what's behind it.

"No. To be honest, Cole, he hasn't told me much about your family at all. Though he's tight-lipped about pretty much everything, including himself. I wouldn't have known if you two were best friends or complete enemies. He acts like his personal life is a government secret."

It takes him a good thirty seconds of inspecting my face with narrowed eyes to decide how to respond. Then he sinks into the chair across from my desk, drags his hands through his hair, and sighs.

"I thought for sure he'd told you what an idiot he thinks I am."

I startle him again when I laugh. He looks up at me in confusion.

"I apologize for laughing. It's just that he thinks everyone is an idiot but him. I wouldn't take it personally if I were you. He's got the ego of a Rothschild."

Cole frowns. "We're richer than the Rothschilds."

This is what happens when a poor person tries to make rich person jokes.

Seeing my crestfallen face, Cole tries to be helpful. "Maybe you meant the Waltons?"

"Who are they?"

"The family who owns Walmart."

"They're richer than your family?"

"No."

"Then why did you offer them as an example?"

"I didn't think you'd ask."

I'm beginning to see why Callum might have a problem with his brother. "Maybe you should just tell me what this is all about."

He sits back in his chair and levels me with a steely look, then says ominously, "You're in for a lot with him."

I wait, knowing there will be more, but I'm not expecting what he comes out with.

"If you want the truth, he's an asshole."

Irritated, I hold up a hand to cut him off. "Let me stop you right there. I have no idea what your beef is with him, and to be honest, it's none of my business. But what I do know is that I'm married to him, asshole or not, and I won't sit here and let you talk shit about my husband."

Apparently unprepared for the force with which I delivered that speech, Cole stares at me in open surprise.

When he recovers, he says, "I wasn't finished. What I was leading up to is that he's an asshole, but I'm glad he found someone who could put up with him. I didn't get a chance to say it at the office, but I hope you'll be very happy together."

"Oh." I feel silly that I scolded him for all of one second, then I'm irritated with him again. "Why didn't you say that in the first place?"

His glower is even worse than Callum's, if that's possible. "You didn't give me a chance."

I swear to God, these McCord men could give a woman a stroke.

"Is there some reason you wouldn't want me to tell Callum you came by to say something so supportive?"

He chuffs out a dark little grunt. "Because he'd blow a goddamn gasket if he knew we were in a room alone together. After you left that day at the office, we got into our usual bullshit. I won't go into all the details, but I said I was surprised someone so nice would go for a dick like him, and he almost killed me."

I say drily, "Gee, I wonder why he'd be offended by such a lovely compliment?"

"Probably because I didn't say nice. I said sexy."

Heat rises in my cheeks, but I sit there like it's no big deal.

He can tell I'm mortified, because he says, "I promise I'm not trying to hit on you."

"That's good. It's maybe the only way this conversation could get more awkward. Can we please get to the part where you tell me why you don't want him to know you were here?"

"My point is that I've never seen him jealous over a woman before. Hell, I've never seen him exhibit any emotion toward the women he's dated before you. But I said you were sexy, and he had me up against the wall with his hand curled around my throat before I could even blink, spitting death threats into my face like a crazy man."

I know I should probably make a sound of disapproval or produce some kind of supportive comment about how horrible that was of Callum, but I find myself curiously pleased.

I really do need to book that therapist.

Lacking even a marginally coherent response, I simply say, "Oh."

"Yeah."

"In that case, I won't tell him."

His mouth does that almost-smile thing again. "I appreciate it."

"Since I've got you here, would you mind if I asked you a

personal question? And you don't have to answer. I won't be offended."

Looking curious, he says, "Go ahead."

"It's about your family's business."

I was expecting him to tense up or look guarded the way Callum would, but he simply waits for me to continue with no change of expression. Encouraged, I continue. "Is everything okay with that?"

The question earns me a frown. "How do you mean?"

"I mean is there ever any danger involved in what you do?"

He couldn't look more baffled if he tried. "*Danger?* Of course not. What would make you think that?"

"Just something Callum said. Maybe I misinterpreted it."

"You must have. The only thing dangerous in the media business is that you might die of boredom. I spend all day behind a desk, shuffling paperwork. It's hell."

That makes me smile. "If you're looking for a career change, I could put you to work here cleaning cat boxes."

A faint look of disgust crosses his handsome features.

"That was a joke."

Judging by his expression, he's unfamiliar with the word.

He rescues us from more scintillating back-and-forth by rising and saying he has to go. I walk him to the door, second-guessing myself about that conversation I overheard with Callum and his father in the kitchen. I can tell Cole's confused reaction to my question was genuine, which means either I didn't hear what I thought I heard or Konrad and his eldest son are up to something Cole doesn't know about.

He pauses on his way out the door to shake my hand again.

"Hopefully, you'll be able to convince Callum to have dinner at my parents' house soon. My mother is dying to meet you. With three sons, she's thrilled to have another female in the family."

That gives me the warm and fuzzies. I had no idea what to expect from my new mother-in-law, but from the sound of it, we might get along.

"That's a relief," I say softly.

Cole cocks his head, frowning. "What do you mean? Are you worried she wouldn't like you for some reason?"

My laugh is self-conscious. "I mean, it's an unusual situation."

"She's not a snob about things like that."

"Things like what?"

"You being in a different social circle."

Me being poor, he means. What an elegant way to put it. I suppose having billions means having to learn genteel ways of insulting the unmoneyed population of the planet.

"No, I meant because of why Callum had to get married."

He stares at me as if I'm speaking Dutch. "Had to? What do you mean *had* to?" His gaze drops to my stomach, and he blanches. "Oh God. You're pregnant."

It's plain as day that Cole doesn't know anything about his father's ultimatum to Callum that he had to marry or lose his inheritance.

I've just stuck my foot in my big stupid mouth.

Trying to backpedal, I laugh and hope it sounds authentic. "No! God, no, I'm not pregnant. I just meant that he had to get married...so quickly...because he was...I mean we were—*are*—so in love!"

He buys my act, brushing it off with a dismissive wave of his hand. "My parents knew each other two weeks before they eloped. Stupidly, love at first sight runs in the family."

I almost collapse at his feet in relief. I can imagine how Callum would react if he found out I'd spilled the beans on something so important. It wouldn't be pretty.

Then I find myself backpedaling again, but this time it's to something Cole just said. "Love at first sight? Is that how Callum described it?"

Cole studies me for a moment, hesitating. "Not exactly."

"Now you've got me curious. What did he say? I promise I won't repeat it."

With obvious scorn at the sentiment, he says, "He said he saw his whole future the first time he looked into your eyes."

My breath whooshes out of me with such unexpected force, I lift a hand to cover my mouth. Overwhelmed, I stare at Cole, my eyes beginning to water.

"I wouldn't have believed it if I didn't hear it with my own ears," he says, shaking his head. "But good for you guys. Like I said, I'm happy for you."

"Thank you," I say, my voice shaky. To cover my sudden onslaught of emotion, I force a smile. "Let me walk you out."

We head to the front of the shop together with me in a daze, thinking that maybe everything bad that ever happened to me had been leading up to this.

"He said he saw his whole future the first time he looked into your eyes."

Not even Jamie Fraser could compete with that.

I'm all misty-eyed and sentimental until Cole and I reach the front door of the store. That's when he looks out the window to the view of the shopping center beyond and sticks a pin into my happy little bubble, popping it to smithereens.

Gesturing toward ValUBooks, he says, "I'll never know why we opened a location here instead of downtown."

We?

Opened a location?

Feeling as if he just kicked me in the gut, I manage to croak, "What?"

"We acquired them a few years ago. Overpaid, if you ask me, but Callum insisted it was a good addition to the portfolio. It was all supposed to be a big secret for some reason I could never figure out." He glances at me. "Has it affected your business much, having such a big competitor right next door?"

I want to answer, but I can't. My mouth is unable to form words because my mind has gone blank.

McCord Media owns ValUBooks.

They acquired the company a few years ago.

It was supposed to be a secret.

My husband insisted they buy it.

My husband insisted they buy it.

My stomach turns over. I'm sure I'm about to be sick.

"No," I whisper, feeling everything inside me begin to give way like the unstable edge of a cliff right before it crumbles and turns into a landslide.

"No, it hasn't affected us at all."

Thirty-One

The moment the door closes behind Cole, I dash into my office and get on the computer, running a search on ValUBooks and McCord Media to find any information I can.

It takes a few minutes of frantic link clicking and article scanning before I finally find a clue. Buried in the depths of a story about the future of brick-and-mortar bookstores in the digital age is a mention of ValUBooks being acquired four years ago by a company called Dolos Inc.

That name doesn't ring a bell.

When I run a search of public corporate records, it reveals the corporation is no longer active. I try to find more information, but other than the corporate listing, I can't find anything. No website, no press releases, no social media profiles.

It's like they never existed at all.

I stare at the computer screen, my mind moving at the speed of light, until I realize Dolos must be a shell corporation. An entity created solely for the purpose of acquiring ValUBooks, keeping the name McCord out of the transaction and thereby the public domain.

A secret indeed.

Hands trembling, I pick up the desk phone and call Dani.

"Hello?"

"Dani, it's me. I need you to do something for me."

"Sure. You okay?"

"I don't think so."

"What's wrong?"

"We'll talk about it later. Just listen. I need you to call Ryan at work and ask him to get on the company computer and see if he can find anything about a corporation called Dolos."

Without further questions or argument, she says, "You got it. Spell it for me, babe."

I love this woman.

After I give her the spelling, she says, "Anything in particular he should be looking for?"

"I don't know. Just whatever he can find. And call me back as soon as you hear anything. I'm at the shop."

After we hang up, I sit and hyperventilate, sweating through my blouse and staring blankly at the wall as cognitive dissonance fucks my perception of reality right up the ass.

When the phone rings again, I jump, startled out of my wits. Snatching up the receiver, I say a breathless hello.

"Babe, it's me."

"Did he find anything?"

"No. There was nothing on the company computer about a Dolos Inc."

I blow out a hard breath, feeling deflated. Until Dani says, "But there was on the county property assessor's site," and my heartbeat takes off like a rocket.

"Tell me."

"So corporations have to file annual statements with the county if they own any property there, right? Ryan uses the site all the time for research in his assessments. Your Dolos Inc. owned a building in Venice—the address is right near you—but they sold it to some other corporation overseas about three and a half years ago."

"What's the name of the other corporation?"

"Let me check. I wrote it down."

I wait with my heart palpitating until she comes back on.

"I'm not sure if I'm pronouncing it right, but it's called Sassenach. They're based in Prague."

My eyes widen. My lungs seize. My entire body goes cold.

Prague. It can't be. This can't be happening.

"Em? You still there?"

"I'll call you back. Thank you, Dani."

Carefully placing the receiver back in the cradle, I inhale a series of deep breaths until I can breathe again. Then I search the internet for a company named Sassenach in Prague.

Like Dolos, Sassenach doesn't have any social media profiles. There isn't a single press release, no corporate website, no digital footprint at all.

The only evidence it exists is a listing in the Czech business register for the limited liability company. A listing that reveals the company is owned by a man named James Fraser.

The same name of the hero in *Outlander*, my all-time favorite novel.

And sassenach, which means foreigner or outlander in Scottish Gaelic, is the nickname Jamie calls Claire, his time-traveling love in the book.

My heart pounding and my stomach in knots, I stare at the poster on the wall across from my desk at the actor Sam Heughan in his role as Jamie Fraser in the TV drama based on the novel. Then I turn my focus back to the computer for one final search.

This time, I don't include the word "corporation." I type only Dolos and wait for the results.

According to Wikipedia, Dolos is the Greek god of trickery, treachery, and deceit.

A chill in my blood, I recall the way Callum looked at me the first day I met him when he walked into the store, so handsome and charismatic with his air of mystery and his dark, burning eyes.

Eyes that always seem so cloaked in secrets.

Shaking badly now, I open my desk drawer, remove the letter from David Montgomery informing me that my business tax account has a zero balance, and dial the number on the letterhead.

When it goes straight to voicemail, I pull up the CDTFA website and call the main number I find there. I spend five minutes fighting through a maze of prompts until finally I get a live human on the phone.

"I'd like to speak with David Montgomery, please."

The woman on the other end of the line sounds as if she's chewing gum. "Do you have an extension?"

"No. I only have his name."

"I'll look him up by last name. Give me a moment while I check the computer." After a brief pause, she says, "We don't have a David Montgomery here."

Swallowing down the bile rising in the back of my throat, I say, "Are you sure?"

"I'm sure. Unless it's a different spelling?"

She spells out Montgomery for me, but I already know there's no employee listed with that name at the tax board.

He isn't listed because he doesn't exist.

I hang up and use the online white pages to search the 800 number listed on the letter I received, which reveals the number is owned by none other than Dolos Incorporated.

They must have paid a few years' phone bills in advance before they went defunct.

Which indicates an extraordinary amount of preplanning.

As I sit there frozen in shock, it's as if my life flashes before my eyes. A series of memories form a kaleidoscope flying past at warp speed.

The grand opening of ValUBooks.

The landlord calling to double my rent.

The bank, credit union, and Small Business Administration all denying my applications for loans.

The dinner where Dani told me Ryan was laid off.

The tax fine.

The lawsuit.

The signed copy of *Outlander*.

The way Cole knew nothing about his brother having to marry to keep his inheritance.

The way Callum told no one in his family he'd wed.

The lunch where Callum smiled a beautiful, enigmatic smile and said, "Hello, little lamb. Welcome to the lion's den."

And finally, what Callum's father said to him in the conversation I overheard in the kitchen: "Not everyone's as mercenary as you."

If this is what I think it is, mercenary doesn't even begin to scratch the surface. Machiavellian is more like it.

I make one more phone call, my fingers trembling as I dial. When my landlord answers, I say, "Hi, Bill. This is Emery Eastwood. I have a question for you. When I told you on our last call that I recently came into a bunch of money, why didn't you ask how?"

When that's met with dead silence, I've got my answer.

The god of deceit, indeed.

Sitting back into my chair, I exhale, close my eyes, and gather my strength.

"Okay. Let's talk about your deal with Callum McCord. How much of a bribe did he give you to make you double my rent?"

The line goes dead as he hangs up on me.

Son of a bitch.

I guess Callum didn't instruct him how to answer.

Thirty-Two

I slowly replace the receiver and sit at my desk until all my shaking has stopped and the dust has settled on my chaotic thoughts. Then I pull the batphone from my handbag, set it on the floor, and stomp on it until it's nothing but bits of smashed metal.

I find the main number for McCord Media on their website and dial it from the desk phone, telling the operator to put me through to the CEO.

"Tell him his wife is calling," I say, my voice hollow. "It's an emergency."

Callum comes on the line sounding convincingly concerned. "Emery? What's wrong? What's the emergency?"

"No, Callum. I'm the one asking the questions. Number one: who did you hire to pretend to be David Montgomery from the tax board?"

When his pause draws out too long, I warn, "If you ever want to see me again, you'll tell me the truth."

There's a sound on the other end of the line. Footsteps. He's started to pace. When he speaks, his voice is tense. "An old acquaintance. Someone who owed me a favor."

Oh fuck.

Adrenaline floods my body. I start to shake again, and I can't catch my breath.

Until this moment, there was still a tiny possibility it was all a misunderstanding. Some terrible, but explainable, mistake. But with his admission, everything has become painfully, horribly real.

I have to moisten my lips before I can speak again. Trying desperately to keep the tremor from my voice, I say, "And the bogus lawsuit? Was that the same acquaintance?"

"Listen to me, Emery. Let me explain."

"Not one more word from you unless it's an answer," I say hotly, unable to control my anger from filling my voice. "Who filed the lawsuit?"

When he speaks, it sounds as if it's through a clenched jaw. "A junior clerk at William's firm filed it."

"On behalf of?"

"No one. The plaintiff doesn't exist. I made him up."

My God. The treachery is staggering.

Unable to stay seated any longer, I stand and start to pace too, going as far as the cord on the desk phone will allow before spinning around and walking the other direction. "And Ryan? You had him fired from his job, didn't you? You knew I'd ask you to hire him at your company so you could look generous when you agreed."

"Yes."

He didn't even hesitate that time. The adrenaline running through me turns to fury. My hands shake so hard, it's difficult to keep my grip on the phone.

"What about my apartment building being condemned? Did you arrange that so you could swoop in like a superhero and save the day?"

"No, but I wish I'd thought of it. You might have moved in with me sooner."

His utter lack of shame in that admission makes me stop dead in my tracks and stare at the wall with my mouth hanging open. When I've recovered, I start to pace again.

"Your inheritance," I snap. "Let's talk about that. The thing that got this whole shit show on the road in the first place. Your father never gave you an ultimatum that you had to marry or lose everything, did he?"

"No. He's much too sensible to disinherit his eldest son."

"Okay, Callum. One final question." This part I holler. "*What the actual fuck?*"

"You're not prepared for the answer."

"You better goddamn give it to me anyway!"

"We should talk about this in person."

"How are you so fucking calm? You're admitting you sabotaged my entire life to get me to marry you, you asshole!"

"I assure you, I'm not calm. But shouting won't change anything."

My chest heaving and my eyes filling with tears, I take a moment to catch my breath. "Why? Just tell me why. Why the hell would you go to all that trouble when you could've just asked me out on a date like a normal person?"

"I did ask you out on a date. You told me you'd rather be forced to do a naked shame walk through crowded streets while onlookers screamed curses at you and threw rotten cabbages in your face like Cersei Lannister in *Game of Thrones* than go out with a smug rich prick like me."

I take that in, the whole preposterous story and the way he so matter-of-factly recounted it, and have to laugh.

It's a sick laugh, a demented one, but a laugh just the same.

"You're mixing me up with someone else, billionaire. I never laid eyes on you before the day you walked into my store with your insane proposition."

"Yes, you did. It was at a Halloween party in the Hollywood Hills. You were dressed as Catwoman, and I was the Big Bad Wolf."

I stand with my mouth open and my heart hammering like mad.

I remember that party. I remember it very clearly. My outfit, shoes, what I had to drink, who I went with, everything.

And yes, I remember the Big Bad Wolf. How could I not?

He was utterly unforgettable.

A black fur wolf mask covered most of his face. Only his chin and eyes were exposed, eyes that gazed out from behind the mask with the feral hunger of a nighttime predator peering out from the woods. The mask was accented with gold paint across the cheekbones and bridge of the nose like some Egyptian pharaoh. Its big pricked ears resembled demon horns.

The wolf wore tight black jeans that showcased the size of his muscular thighs. He was shirtless, his incredible chest and biceps on plain display for every female in attendance to ogle. He had no tattoos or identifying marks of any kind then, other than those piercing nocturnal eyes that kept following me.

The house belonged to a friend of a friend of a friend, some guy Ryan knew from work. I don't know how we wound up with an invitation, but I clearly recall being impressed by the size of the home and the obvious wealth of its occupants.

Until the homeowner made a drunken pass at me and called me a cheap little piece of trailer trash when I refused to kiss him.

The way I felt when he sneered that at me...I'll never forget it.

He made me feel worthless, like I had no right to even exist because I clearly wasn't of his social position.

If he was a king, I was a cockroach.

I think it was my shoes that gave me away.

Rich people don't wear clothing with designer logos because they consider it in bad taste, so lacking other more obvious status symbols like your car or house, they look at your watch, your handbag, or your shoes. None of which will bear obvious logos, either, but when you've been brought up to know the difference between a Patek Philippe and a Vacheron Constantin, you can spot a person in the lowest tax bracket a mile away.

Only a few minutes after that humiliating encounter, I stumbled across the Big Bad Wolf. Literally stumbled across him when

I rounded a corner and bumped into him, catching my foot on one of his giant black shoes.

A big hand shot out and grabbed my arm, steadying me before I could fall flat on my face in front of everyone.

He stared down at me with perfect dark focus, his eyes locked onto mine. He didn't let go of my arm.

The first thing he said to me, in a low, gruff voice that sent a tingle up my spine, was, "Who are you?"

It sounded like an accusation. Like a demand. Like he knew I didn't belong in that house with its grand piano, art collection, and sliding walls of glass that opened to the spectacular view of Los Angeles sparkling like jewels strewn across black velvet far below.

Even if he didn't mean it that way, that's how I took it. Having just been called a piece of trailer trash, my temper was high.

I yanked my arm from his grip, propped my hands on my hips, and stuck out my chin belligerently. "I'm the one your mother warned you about, that's who."

Heat flared in his eyes. He leaned closer. "In that case, I need to get to know you better. I'm taking you out."

I remember how arrogant that seemed. Not "Will you go out with me?" but "I'm taking you out." As if I had no choice in the matter. As if I were already a foregone conclusion.

Which is when I decided he was another rich asshole who felt entitled to something he didn't deserve. Namely, me.

"Not a chance in hell," I said.

Then I proceeded to make the melodramatic declaration about Cersei Lannister in *Game of Thrones* and stormed off like a diva.

I was twenty-five when I attended that Halloween party with Dani and Ryan. It was five years ago.

Five years.

"Do you remember now?" Callum asks, his gruff voice an echo of the one in my memory.

I whisper, "Yes."

"That was the beginning for me."

"The beginning of what?"

"My obsession with you."

I close my eyes, swallow, and decide that if a single tear escapes my eyes, I'll never forgive myself. "You don't sound the least bit ashamed."

"I'm not."

I cry, "Jesus Christ, Callum. What's the *matter* with you?"

His voice drops an octave. "You. You're what's the matter with me. You have been since the first time I laid eyes on you and every day since."

My pulse crashing in my ears, I say, "You spied on me."

"Yes."

"You set this whole thing up so I'd have to marry you."

"Yes."

"You manipulated me! You lied to me and manipulated me and you somehow think that's okay?"

"I would have killed to have you if it had come to that."

"Oh my God! Are you even listening to yourself? You're insane!"

"No, I'm in love. There's a difference. And let's not get too dramatic about it. You're in a much better position now than you were a few months ago. And so are all your friends. Because of me."

"My friends?" I repeat, brand-new alarm bells ringing in my head. "What about my friends?"

"Ryan is the obvious example. Dani benefitted from his salary increase, too, as did their daughter. Then there's all your employees, who you so generously gave raises to. Now Vivienne can move out of her awful apartment someone was always vandalizing, Taylor doesn't have to follow her mother to Florida to live with her grandparents in Sunnyside Retirement Village, Harper can afford to hire a good attorney to take her deadbeat ex back to court for more child support, and Mr. Murphy can afford all that expensive medication he's on."

My body can't decide if it wants to freeze or drench me in sweat, so it does both.

Stunned almost speechless, I manage to say, "You were behind the vandalism at Vivienne's apartment?"

"Don't sound so upset. She was never in any danger. It was just a few broken windows."

I sputter, "And...and Taylor? Her parents' divorce?"

"I might have given that piece-of-shit stepfather of hers a little incentive to leave his wife and stepdaughter alone."

My head is spinning. I can barely stand up. The scope of what he's done is mind-boggling. Something else occurs to me, and I gasp.

"Ben."

That's all I can get out, but it's enough. Callum knows exactly what I'm talking about.

His tone disgusted, he says, "Yes, your worthless ex-boyfriend. Speaking of pieces of shit, he takes the cake, that one. He didn't deserve you."

Nearing hysteria, I demand, "What did you do? Did you threaten him? Did you *hurt* him?"

"I showed him pictures of him and the girl he was fucking behind your back and told him if he ever spoke to you again, I'd slit his throat. I was holding a rather large knife to his jugular at the time, so he wisely decided to believe me."

Stars burst in the corners of my vision. The room starts to spin. "Oh my God. Oh my God. You're...you're..."

"Your husband," he finishes, making it sound like a death sentence.

"I was going to say evil!"

There's a pause, then he comes back on sounding exactly like what he is: a ruthless, charismatic liar.

"There are a million shades of gray between good and evil, love. Am I on the darker end of the spectrum? Yes. Am I a bad man who does good things or a good man who does bad things? Both. But you made this monster your slave. All of what I am, good and bad, light and dark, belongs to you."

My brain has had enough of attempting to deal with this rationally and finally allows my temper to take the helm. I shout, "Well, whoopdie-fucking-do for me! I won the psychopath lottery!"

He chuckles. "I might have ambiguous morality, but I'm hardly a psychopath. What time will you be home?"

"Never!"

I slam down the phone, seething. Then I bring up the trust account balance on the computer.

It's all there. Twenty million minus what I've paid in bills and operating costs since I wed my darling husband.

My face burning and my heart in shreds, I fax a copy of the marriage contract to my lawyer with a note asking him for a recommendation for a good divorce attorney.

On my way out of the office, I remove my wedding band and throw it into the trash.

Thirty-Three

I drive to the castle as if I'm competing for first place in the Indy 500, running red lights and screaming at people to get out of my way. Pulling into the garage, I shut off the car and hurry inside, hoping I won't encounter Arlo.

I only need a few things, then I'll never have to set foot in this place again.

In the master bedroom, I head straight for the closet, where I pull a few outfits from hangers and underwear from drawers. I throw it all into a leather Tumi bag I pulled down from a shelf, then turn to leave. I'll buy myself a new wardrobe later.

A glint of silver catches my eye.

On the floor under Callum's row of suits, a small key is caught between the baseboard and the carpet. It must've fallen out of one of his pockets.

Remembering the last time he left for Prague, how he seemed to be searching for something in his drawers that he couldn't find, my heart starts to beat faster.

I set the Tumi bag down and get on my hands and knees to retrieve the key. It's actually a pair of keys, both small, hooked together on a tiny loop. They look almost like the keys Arlo used to unlock my handcuffs, but aren't identical.

I stand in the middle of the closet, staring at them, wondering what they might be for.

Then I remember the rope.

I turn and look at the bottom drawer of the dresser where I found the unlocked case of colored rope, remembering how I told Dani about it over dinner. How she laughed and said I wasn't that clueless when I wondered what Callum used it for.

I assumed then that it was a bondage thing.

Only he never used that rope on me.

Kneeling on the floor, I open the bottom drawer and look inside. All the black cases are still there, in various sizes and shapes, except the one that held the rope is now locked.

I fit the key into the lock, and it opens.

Yep. Still rope.

I close that case, pull another out, balance it on my knees, and use the key to open it.

Staring down at the contents, I feel my stomach flip. My pulse accelerates until my hands are shaking.

I'm looking at a big black semiautomatic handgun with a cylindrical extension on the barrel.

A silencer.

Hyperventilating, I carefully close the cover of the case and return it to its place in the drawer. I stare at the other cases in growing fear, trying to decide whether or not to open them.

I'm not sure I want to know what I'll see inside.

But after a few moments of internal debate, I pull another case from the drawer and open that one too.

It's full of cash. Paper money in foreign currencies banded together in neat stacks. The only ones I recognize are the euro notes. Everything else is printed in languages I can't understand.

I close that case, put it away, and pull out another. That one reveals a stash of USB drives and batphones like the one Callum gave me, dozens of them rubber banded together in stacks.

The final case I open is stuffed with passports.

Russian, Czech, Canadian, American, plus dozens more. All

of them have a picture of the same man, but with different names, matching the nationalities of the passports.

It's not Callum, but I think I recognize him.

Even without the mirrored aviators, the man in black is hard to forget.

I don't know why I do it, but I grab one of the passports and keep it, stuffing it into the Tumi bag. Then I throw the case back into the drawer, toss the keys inside, and slam it shut.

The final thing I do before running out the door is grab the signed copy of *Outlander* from the armoire.

Then I drive straight over to Dani's and have a breakdown.

Thirty-Four

"Here. Drink this."

Dani hands me a glass of white wine filled to the brim. I'm lying on her sofa with a washcloth on my forehead that she soaked in ice water. My bare feet are propped up on a pillow. An open bag of Cool Ranch Doritos rests on my chest. I take the glass from her, lift my head, and guzzle half of it in one go.

Sitting on the other side of the room in a recliner, her father-in-law stares at me with an expression of extreme suspicion, as if I'm an IRS agent who's here to auction off the house.

Apparently, he doesn't remember me.

I wish I could borrow some of that.

Ignoring him, I hand the glass back to Dani. She sits on the wooden coffee table and puts the glass down beside her. Clasping her hands between her thighs, she says, "Let's go over this again. You're telling me Callum saw you in your Catwoman costume at that Halloween party and became so obsessed with you after you rejected him that he spent the next five years orchestrating an elaborate scheme to ruin your life so you'd agree to marry him?"

"That's it in a nutshell."

"Wow."

I narrow my eyes at her. "What do you mean wow? And why do you sound impressed?"

She pulls a face. "You have to admit it is kind of impressive."

"No, I don't have to admit any such thing. It's insane is what it is!"

She hands me the glass of wine, which is probably just to get me to stop shouting. It works, anyway. I finish the rest of the wine, then stuff a few Doritos in my mouth to wash them down with.

Taking the empty glass from me, she says in a soothing tone, "I'm not disagreeing that it's crazy. The man is definitely certifiable. I'm just saying that it took an impressive amount of dedication to pull it off."

"If you say the word impressive one more time, I will grind the rest of this bag of Doritos into your white carpeting."

"I can't believe what he said about Ben, though. He cheated on you? What a sleazebag."

"It was just another lie." I groan, remembering the look of terror on Ben's face when he saw my wedding ring the day I ran into him at ValUBooks. "Oh my God, Callum put a knife to his throat! The poor guy!"

Dani's father-in-law grunts. "What a pussy."

Dani says, "Dad!"

He waves her off with a grumble. "If a man tucks his tail between his legs and runs when another man threatens him, he's a pussy. Good riddance. Count your blessings you didn't end up with that nincompoop, girl."

I stare at him. "I thought you were supposed to be deaf?"

He blinks, squints at me, and raises a hand to cup one ear. "Eh?"

"Never mind him, Em, let's focus on you." Dani pats my hand. "What happens now?"

Sighing, I close my eyes. "Now I divorce him."

When the silence stretches on too long, I glance over at Dani. She's looking back at me with her lips pulled between her teeth.

"What's that face?"

"I'm so sorry, and please forgive me for being selfish when your entire life is a dumpster fire, but..."

"But what?"

"I guess Ryan will have to start looking for another job now."

"No, because I'm going to tell Callum that if he fires Ryan, I'll go to the media and expose him for the manipulative con artist that he is."

"You said you were never going to speak to him again."

"You're right. I'll send him a text message."

We stare at each other until I say, "Why do I get the feeling you're trying to be a supportive friend, but you really have a bunch of stuff to say that you think I won't like so you're not saying it?"

"Because I am. And I do. And you won't."

"I'm going to need more wine for this."

She rises, heads to the kitchen, refills my wineglass, and returns. Handing it to me, she says, "Okay, keep an open mind now."

I mutter, "This should be interesting."

"Drink your wine and be quiet. I'm going to throw a bunch of different things out there that might not make sense, but you know I think by talking, so hang in there. Here we go. The giant tattoo of your name on Callum's back."

She makes googly eyes at me.

I sigh and drink more wine.

"The signed copy of your favorite book. All the priceless first editions. The enormous engagement ring. What he said to his brother about seeing his future in your eyes. What he said to you about diving into your ocean. Twenty million dollars. *Twenty million dollars.*"

"You said that last one twice. And I regret telling you about the lovey-dovey BS he spewed, because you're too much of a romantic."

"You want to talk about all the amazing sex you two had instead?"

"I never told you anything about our sex life."

"So it was awful? No connection there, huh? You didn't feel a thing?"

"What the hell is wrong with you, Dani? Did he pay you to be on his side or something? The man lied to me—*to my face*—about everything!"

Her father-in-law cackles. "For twenty million bucks, I'd let him lie to me too."

Dani scolds, "Dad."

He clucks his tongue. "He's a man. He did what he had to do to get what he wanted. You're just mad you found out."

I glare at him. "Excuse me for not taking life advice from a man who shouts obscenities at Vanna White for a hobby. And for the record, if it wasn't for him having all that money, everyone would agree he should be in jail for stalking."

"The money and the face. And the body too," says Dani, as if that's at all helpful.

This is when I remember all the nice things I said to him about his character, and wish I could go back in time and punch myself in the nose.

Dani's house phone rings. She goes into the kitchen to answer it. When she turns and looks at me with wide eyes, I know who it is.

"I'm not here!" I sit upright, dislodging the bag of Doritos so it falls to the floor and sprays chips everywhere. The washcloth falls off my forehead and lands on top of the chips.

"Uh, she's not here. Uh-huh. Okay. Thank you too. Bye."

She hangs up and looks at me with an expression of guilt.

"That was the shittiest lie-telling I've ever witnessed. Was it Callum?"

"Yes."

"What did he say?"

"He thanked me for taking care of you."

"I can tell that's not it by that puppy-dog face you're making. What else?"

"You won't like it."

"Dani!"

"He said to tell you that he was going to confess everything eventually but he wanted to give you time to fall in love with him first. Also that he adores you, and he'll do anything you want to make up for it."

The look on her face makes me glower. "Don't you dare think this is romantic."

"I didn't say a word."

"You didn't have to. I can see you swooning from over here. He *lied* to me."

"I know."

"You don't look like you know."

Sighing, she returns to sit on the coffee table. "He was wrong. I get that. You can't trust him now, and without trust, you can't have a relationship."

"Exactly!"

"But if I had a rich, gorgeous husband who bent himself into a pretzel because he was so madly in love with me, he couldn't think of anything else, I'd probably take a minute to evaluate the situation to see how I could benefit from it before I threw the baby out with the bath water."

Dani's father-in-law says, "Amen."

We both turn to him and say, "Be quiet!"

The house phone rings again. Before I can give her a stern warning, Dani holds up her hands. "I know, I know, you're not here."

But when she answers the phone, it's not Callum. It's Murph, calling from the shop.

Dani hands me the cordless receiver. I take it, terrified of what he might be about to say.

It turns out, it's worse than I could have ever expected.

"Emery, your attorney called. He says you need to call him back immediately."

"I will. Wait, how did you know I was here?"

"Callum called the shop to tell me that I could find you at Dani's today in case of an emergency."

Grinding my molars, I hang up on him and curse Callum's name. He probably had a tracker installed on my car, the maniac.

Then I call the lawyer and listen in growing shock as he delivers his news.

"When I received your fax, the first thing I did was visit the LA County Registrar-Recorder's website to get the date of your marriage so I could forward that to the family law attorney I was going to refer you to. But there was no record of any marriage for either you or Mr. McCord."

He pauses, giving me a chance to speak, but I'm speechless. I don't know where this is going, only that it will be bad.

"So then I had my assistant check the registrar databases for the other forty-nine states and US territories. No hits there either. Then we went internationally through the Department of State website."

He pauses. I want to scream *And!* but my mouth has gone dry.

"And that's how we found what we were looking for."

I must make some sort of sound of acknowledgement, because the attorney continues.

"Your marriage was recorded in Rome. Vatican City, to be specific."

I find the will to speak and say, "But we weren't married there. I don't understand."

"I don't understand it either, but the documents were correctly filled out and filed. A local official signed off on the paperwork. Everything is in order."

I remember what a blur the wedding ceremony in the store was that day, how Callum rushed me and that I barely glimpsed the paperwork I signed, and my stomach turns over.

"So that means I have to get a divorce attorney over there to handle it?"

"No. There aren't any divorce attorneys in Vatican City."

"Why not?"

"Because divorce is prohibited there by law."

Oh my God. The irrevocability clause in the wedding contract.

All that wine I drank is about to make a dramatic reappearance.

I jolt to my feet and shout into the phone, "*You're telling me I have to stay married to him?*"

"For the time being, yes. I'll have to find an expert in international matrimonial law to unravel this, but most likely, it will take a while."

"How long is a while?"

"If it can be done at all, which is a big if...years."

Years.

"We'll have to claim fraud and prove it. You should prepare yourself for a long and ugly fight. And considering the financial resources of your husband, if he decides to contest it..."

He doesn't have to finish that statement.

We both know I'm fucked.

That bastard checkmated me before I even knew the game we were playing.

Thirty-Five

I call back Murph at the shop and put him in charge of operations indefinitely. Then I order a taxi to pick me up from Dani's. I have the driver make a stop by my bank, where I withdraw enough cash to live on for a month, then I tell him to get on Pacific Coast Highway and drive north until I say to stop.

"How you gonna pay, lady?"

I throw a wad of cash onto the passenger seat. He counts it, whistles, and turns the radio to a soft rock station.

I lie down on the back seat of the sedan and stare at the roof, replaying every moment in my memory as the miles fly by, hearing Callum's words from the day we met in my head as if he were right here whispering them into my ear.

"I have a proposition for you."

"I want you to marry me."

"Let's just say I find you interesting."

When I let out a frustrated yell, the driver turns up the volume on the stereo, but otherwise ignores me.

Money buys a lot of leeway for bad behavior.

As I'm sure my lying, manipulative, scoundrel of a husband knows all too well.

I'm hurt, yes. I'm in shock, yes. And almost all of me hates him.

But there's a part of me—a small, stupid part—that doesn't.

I'm going to spend the next month beating that stupid part of me to death.

When the sun is setting, I finally sit up in the back seat and take a look around. "Where are we?"

The driver says over his shoulder, "Montecito. Rich people heaven. Prince Harry and Meghan Markle live here. Oprah too."

Okay. Why not?

"Is there a Four Seasons Hotel?"

"Yep. Big one."

"Good. Take me there."

I've never stayed in a five-star hotel in my life, but today I discovered the man I married is an evil mastermind, so I'm thinking I deserve a nice long vacation.

The first few days are rough. Emotionally rough, that is. Not physically rough, because the hotel is the most beautiful place I've stayed in my entire life.

The suite is bright, spacious, and overlooks the ocean. Housekeeping places handmade chocolates on my pillow with the turndown service every night. The bed is huge and the linens are decadent, and I think I could spend the rest of my days here, if only to hide.

It's not the days that are the worst, however.

It's the nights.

I lie wide awake in that giant sumptuous bed staring at the ceiling, wondering why I can't hate Callum. I *want* to hate him. But I don't.

It makes no sense.

I check in with the shop every day to see what's happening

there. The answer is always "nothing." Callum hasn't gone in looking for me. It's business as usual.

By the end of the week, I've cycled through the five stages of grief about a dozen times and have settled on anger. Denial is useless, bargaining won't do any good, and acceptance is out of the question. I'm probably depressed, but am too pissed off to admit it.

I have more questions than answers, which I hate.

Overthinkers are tortured by unanswered questions. It's our own personal version of hell.

When I can't stand being cooped up in the suite any longer, I head down to the pool, where I float on my back and stare listlessly at the clouds as the occasional tear leaks from the corner of my eye like some Victorian heiress with a wasting illness sent off to recuperate away from polite society.

On day six, I realize with a jolt of horror that I miss him.

A bottle of rosé consumed poolside takes care of that.

On day seven, I decide that I'll use the millions my deceitful spouse gave me to open a shelter for stray cats. I'll live in the back, avoiding humanity, until I grow old and die, whereupon the cats will eat my shriveled corpse, allowing me to exist inside my furry friends for eternity.

On day eight, realizing my state of mind has dangerously deteriorated if I'm dreaming of being ingested by cats, I call around to local therapists.

Day nine is when I see the man in black.

I'm sprawled on a lounge chair by the pool. It's late in the afternoon. I've been drinking mai tais since ten o'clock in the morning, so at first, I'm not sure it's him because things are a little fuzzy. From my peripheral vision, I spot a figure in black leaning casually against the wall of the cocktail shack, one foot kicked up against it.

My brain sends me a ping of alarm. I ignore it at first, but then do a double-take and look closer.

Cowboy boots, leather jacket, mirrored shades. Check.

Arms folded over a massive chest. Check.

Palpable air of danger. Check.

It's interesting how, even standing still, he exudes violence.

I suppose it's all the mai tais that make it interesting rather than terrifying, but I'll take it.

We stare at each other across the distance until I decide to go see what he wants. Standing, I wrap a towel around my waist. Then I pick up my drink and walk over to him.

He doesn't move a muscle as I approach.

Even with sunglasses on, I can tell how good-looking this guy is. His dark wavy hair brushes his shoulders. His angular jaw is covered in scruff. Tattoos decorate his knuckles. He could be a movie star, except for that aggressive, dangerous energy of his that suggests something more along the lines of contract killer.

Stopping in front of him, I say, "Hi."

His lips curve into a smile. "Hullo, lass."

He's Irish? God, that's hot. Stop gawking at him, he's probably here to murder you.

"Could you please take off your sunglasses? I'd hate to be strangled and thrown off a cliff by a guy wearing sunglasses. It seems so impersonal."

He chuckles, surprising me. He removes his mirrored aviators and gazes at me with a pair of gorgeous dark eyes that remind me of Callum's. They have the same piercing sharpness, a way of looking through you as if they can see straight down into your soul.

"Hi. I'm Emery. But you already know that."

"I do. Pleased to meet you. And I'm not here to throw you off a cliff, so you can rest easy."

"Are you the detective Callum has had spying on me?"

He curls his upper lip. "Detective? Bloody hell. Do I look like I'm on a police payroll?"

"Actually, no. You do not. I apologize. I wasn't trying to be insulting."

He chuckles again. For such a big, intimidating guy, his tendency to do that is pretty disarming.

"How many of those cocktails have you had, lass?"

"About forty-seven, but it's still early. Who are you?"

"The name's Killian. Killian Black."

When he doesn't reveal anything more, I say, "That's it?"

"That's it."

"I have to apologize again, Killian, but you're kind of irritating."

He presses his lips together to keep from laughing out loud. Dark eyes sparkling, he says, "Callum was right. You are a handful."

"I don't want to talk about him. I want to talk about you. You were at the grand opening of ValUBooks a while back, weren't you? And standing outside again the other day?"

"Aye."

"Why?"

"To make sure you were all right, lass."

I make a face at him and sip my mai tai.

Clearly amused by my state of gentle intoxication, he says, "I've been watching over you every time your man's had to go away on business for years now."

"He's not my man. And back up. Years?"

"Aye."

Oh fuck. That's right. I saw this guy at my father's funeral.

"Wait, what do you mean watching over me?"

The humor fades from his gaze, and his smile dies. "Making sure you're safe."

Despite the heat of the day, a chill washes over my skin. "Why wouldn't I be safe?"

"Because life is full of unexpected dangers."

"Very true, but not an answer to my question."

"That's all the answer you'll get."

I was wrong. He's not kind of irritating, he's extremely irritating. I demand, "Are you a hitman?"

"No. But if you're asking if I kill people, then yes. Sometimes. Not if I can avoid it, but when necessary, it's part of the job."

"What's the job?"

A hint of humor creeps back into his eyes. "Saving the world."

"Ah, yes. Saving the world! So you're one of those good bad guys Callum thinks he is. Or was it a bad good guy? Morally ambiguous? I can't remember, I was traumatized at the time, but my point is that..."

Something occurs to me that makes me stop and gape at him in horror. "Oh God. Does Callum kill people too? Did I marry a *murderer*?"

"Callum doesn't kill people. He's on the administrative side of things. And murderer sounds a bit judgmental, don't you think?"

"No, I don't think. When you kill people, you're a murderer. Like, by default."

"Or maybe you're a social engineer. Or a vigilante, righting the scales of justice. Or a man who chooses to do unsavory things for the greater good."

I say flatly, "That's called rationalizing."

Killian shrugs. "Either way. Murderer brings to mind images of a rampaging sociopath with no self-control running around with a chainsaw."

"Uh-huh. And you're a sociopath with excellent self-control, is that it?"

He grins. "Precisely."

I look down at my empty drink and sigh. "I'm gonna need another one of these."

"Listen to me, lass. I've got something important to say."

I peer at him suspiciously.

Gazing straight into my eyes, he says, "Callum loves you."

"Oh, for fuck's sake, he does not."

"He does. I've known the man for years, and he absolutely does."

"No. He lied to me. He manipulated me. He set me up!"

"His methods might be unorthodox, but..." Killian shrugs again. "Love is madness."

For a killer, he's awfully nonchalant. I might bash this empty glass against his nice straight nose and break it. "I notice you're wearing a wedding ring. What would your wife do if you did to her what Callum did to me?"

This time when he smiles, it transforms his face. Light beams from it, as if he's lit from within. "Ah, my sweet Juliet," he says softly. "She'd probably chop off a body part of little importance. A pinky toe, maybe. But she'd soon forgive me."

"She'd forgive you," I repeat doubtfully.

"How could she not?" He makes spokesmodel hands at himself. "I'm me."

"You sound exactly like Callum. Smug overload and cockiness galore."

"Thank you."

"It wasn't a compliment."

Still smiling, Killian pushes off the wall, puts his sunglasses back on, and gazes down at me from behind them. Bright sunlight glints off the mirrored lenses, blinding me.

"I've kept him away for over a week now, lass, to give you some time to think things over, but I can't keep him away any longer. He's going bloody mad. I came to let you know that he'll soon be darkening your doorstep."

The thought of seeing Callum again makes my stomach tighten and my breath catch. "Then I'm packing up and leaving."

"There's nowhere on earth you could run that I couldn't find you."

He says that as a matter of fact, without a trace of his former cockiness. For whatever reason, I believe him.

"Have it out with him. Make him beg if it makes you feel better. But don't leave him hanging. Don't punish him with silence. Despite what you think, that man worships you. You'd do well to give him a chance."

He turns to go, but then turns back. "Oh, and I left you

something in your suite. Something that might make your decision about him a little easier."

I say crossly, "How'd you get into my suite?"

Ignoring that, he withdraws from a pocket inside his jacket the passport I stole from Callum's dresser. Waving it at me, he says, "I took this back too. Sticky fingers you've got there, little book lover. That might come in handy if you decide to join the cause."

"What cause?"

"Your man will tell you if you ask him to." He turns and ambles away, disappearing around the corner of the cocktail shack.

"Hey! Wait!"

I run after him, but stop in my tracks when I round the corner and discover that Killian has vanished into thin air.

Thirty-Six

I rush back to the suite, sobering up along the way from all the adrenaline flooding through my body. When I get inside, I lock the bolt and security latch, then back away from the door, expecting Callum to burst through any second.

When he doesn't, I spin around and run into the bedroom.

Which is where I find the manila file of photos on the bed.

There are dozens of them. Full color close-ups and distance shots. In every picture, the subjects are the same.

My ex, Ben, and a pretty blonde girl I recognize because he introduced me to her once at his company's July barbecue. Her name is Bethany. They worked together.

Apparently, they did lots of other stuff together too.

All over the place.

Inside and outdoors, in hotel rooms and parked cars, they had sex with a reckless passion that appears to have overtaken them anywhere.

Killian sure wasn't concerned with sparing my feelings when he took these.

Or was it Callum? Or someone related to their mysterious "cause"?

Whoever it was, I suppose I owe him my thanks. I might have

tried finding Ben and getting back together with him if it weren't for this harsh evidence of his betrayal. And I know these pictures aren't fabricated or digitally altered, because I recognize certain details that couldn't be faked.

The worst is the Christmas tree in my apartment with the James Fraser-dressed-as-Santa-Claus topper I bought online. Ben kissed Bethany next to that tree in front of the open window.

In my apartment.

I wonder if he fucked her in my bed?

Remembering how Callum said he held a knife to Ben's throat makes me smile.

"Oh God. I'm sick!" I let the folder slip from my hands as I cover my face, groaning. When the room tilts sideways, I groan again, then crawl up the bed and bury my face in a pillow.

I'll just rest for a minute, then I'll pack.

I have no idea how long I'm passed out, but I wake up sometime later after the sun has set. I'm lying on my side, facing the sliding glass doors, which are open. A gentle ocean breeze stirs the gauzy white drapes. It's quiet and dark in the suite, except for a single lamp burning in the living room.

A large, heavy arm is draped over my waist. Another one cradles my neck. Warm breath tickles my nape. A heartbeat thuds steadily in the space between my shoulder blades.

Callum murmurs, "Don't scream."

I consider it, lying there as my pulse accelerates. Then I draw a deep breath and close my eyes. "I want you to leave."

"No, you don't."

The ego on him. Unbelievable.

It's also incredibly unfortunate that he's right.

Sighing heavily, I snuggle down into the bedding. I hate to admit it, but his big arm makes a pretty great pillow. If I wasn't so mad at him, I might go back to sleep.

He brushes the gentlest of kisses on my nape, making me shiver involuntarily. Then he whispers, "What do you want me to do?"

"Jump off a bridge."

"No, you don't."

"Fine. Tie a rope to one ankle, then jump off a bridge and dangle over the side for a few days until somebody notices you hanging there and rescues you."

When he kisses the back of my neck again, I say, "I swear on all things holy, if you try to fuck me right now, I will end your penis's life."

That muffled sound behind me is laughter. Then he composes himself and says seriously, "I promise I won't try to fuck you right now."

I say with withering scorn, "Oh, you *promise*? How reassuring."

After a moment, he sighs. "If I say I'm sorry, will you believe me?"

"I don't know. Try it."

"I'm sorry."

"I don't believe you."

He sighs again. "Good. Because it was a lie."

I pound a fist on the mattress in frustration. Now I'm wide awake, vibrating with anger, wishing I had the strength to rip off his head and throw it over the balcony into the sea.

"I'm sorry that I hurt you. That part is true. But I'm not sorry that you're my wife."

"Or that I can apparently never divorce you either, huh? How the hell did you arrange that, anyway?"

"Our family is tight with the Pope. We called in a favor."

"*The Pope* owed you a favor?"

"We kept a potentially embarrassing personal story out of the news."

I can't believe this is my life.

Callum starts to massage the tension from my neck and shoulder, kneading his strong fingers into my muscles until I hate him a little less.

"I have questions."

"Ask me anything. I'll tell you the truth."

"Don't throw that word around so recklessly, billionaire. I'm not sure you understand the definition."

"I'll never lie to you again. I'd rather die than hurt you. I swear on my life."

I want to accuse him of being melodramatic and ridiculous, but he sounded convincingly contrite, so I just growl a little in the back of my throat instead.

Then I say, "Do you think I'm so stupid that I'd never find out?"

"No. I know how intelligent you are. I just thought I'd have a little more time before you did."

"Time for what?"

"To make you fall in love with me."

This again. The man needs more therapy than I do. "You do realize that manipulating someone into having feelings for you is unethical, right?"

There's a long pause.

"Forget it. Next question. What would you have done if I didn't agree to the contract?"

Another pause, this one more fraught. "Maybe we should leave this until the end."

"You better start talking before I start screaming."

"You'll probably start screaming when I give you the answer, though."

I growl again. He says, "Okay. Here's the truth. Don't say I didn't warn you. My backup plan was to kidnap you and hold you hostage until you fell in love with me from Stockholm Syndrome."

I gasp in disbelief. "*What?*"

"I'm confident you would've eventually come around. As you know, I can be very charming when I need to be."

"You should leave now."

"You can't hold it against me that I did exactly what you asked me to."

"No, but I can hold it against you that you're insane!"

His tone turns reasonable. "I'm not insane. I'm perfectly rational. My ethics are just a little more bendy than other people's."

"*Bendy?*"

"No, don't try to turn over. This conversation is going pretty well so far, so let's keep you on your side facing away from me. That way you can't claw out my eyes."

"You'd be surprised what I can do when I'm upset." I huff out a hard, angry breath, then start again. "My other two boyfriends I've had over the past four years, Chris and Brandon. Did you run them off with a knife to their throats too?"

"Not Chris. He left you on his own."

When he doesn't continue, I turn my head, craning it to try to see his face. "What about Brandon?"

"He was the one who stole your Visa and racked up all those charges."

"No!"

"Yes."

"How did you find out?"

"I'm not sure you want to know that. But I did have a chat with him to let him know it was in his best interests to disappear from your life."

A chat. Picturing him holding Brandon by his ankles upside down off the side of a building, I sigh. "What about the gun in your dresser and all that other stuff in the cases?"

"Killian keeps stashes of his supplies all over the world. My home is one of probably dozens. Hundreds even, I'm not sure, but what I do know is that he hasn't asked me to hold anything too egregious yet, so I accommodate him."

"Egregious like what?"

"A suitcase nuke."

My eyes widen. "You're joking."

"No."

"So he's an arms dealer?"

"No, but he occasionally has to remove weapons of mass destruction from the possession of certain people who shouldn't have them. Dictators, for instance. Despots. They're overly fond of suitcase nukes for some reason."

My head reeling, I say faintly, "Sure. Why wouldn't they be? They're so portable."

Callum's lips brush my cheek, raising all the hair on my arms. He whispers into my ear, "Ask me why I'm so obsessed with you."

Nervous now, I swallow and turn my head. "No. Let's not go there. I'm not ready for you to turn on the charm yet. I'm probably still tipsy from all the mai tais. Here's another question: what's the unresolved father-son shit you mentioned between you and your dad? And that stuff I overheard you talking about that night in the kitchen, what was that all about?"

He sighs, stirring my hair. Then he smooths a hand down my arm, threading his fingers through mine.

I allow it, though I know I shouldn't.

"My father's been involved with Killian's organization for years, long before I knew anything about it. When he was diagnosed with diabetes six years ago, he decided I should step in for him and take his place. I didn't want to. I'm not the world-saving type by nature, but I wasn't given a choice."

I remember how Arlo slipped and said Callum was inducted into something. That must've been what he meant.

"What's Killian's organization?"

"It's a thirteen-member cabal of powerful people. Connected people. Heads of families like mine whose reach extends globally, or individuals like Killian who know everyone and everything and can get anything done. We work around the law, doing what law enforcement often can't."

I recall Killian saying his job was saving the world and marvel at the hubris.

"So...God, I don't even know what to ask next. Does this organization have a name?"

"The Thirteen."

I ponder that for a moment. "What if you add more members? Would it then become the Fourteen or the Fifteen? The name changes could be never ending."

He chuckles. "That's exactly what Reyna said."

"Who's Reyna?"

"Someone you should definitely meet."

"No, do better than that."

"All right. She's the head of the Italian crime syndicate."

I frown, then sit up, turn, and look down at him. "Crime syndicate? Meaning *Mafia*? I thought Killian's thing was saving the world. Isn't the Mafia the bad guys?"

Gazing at me with soft eyes, Callum reaches up and cups my jaw gently in his big rough hand.

"Questions of good and bad are never simple. Nothing is purely black, just as nothing is purely white. It's the intention that matters, even if blood gets spilled along the way."

"The road to hell is paved with good intentions. Ever heard that saying?"

"Of course. But it's bullshit. The road to hell is actually paved with the prayers of cowards who think sitting on a church bench once a week is sufficient. If there is a god, he doesn't give a shit about prayers. He wants to see if you're willing to put skin in the game, not just give Him lip service with a few pretty hymns on Sunday, then go home and hide while evil runs rampant through the streets."

I stare at him for a moment until I can't stand to look at his handsome face anymore because it's making me want to kiss him. Then I lie down facing the sliding doors again, heaving a sigh.

Callum squeezes my shoulder. He kisses my neck. He slides his palm down my arm and threads his fingers through mine again, which is when I notice his new tattoos.

Below the first knuckle, every finger on his right hand has a letter, inked in black, of my name.

I close my eyes and whisper, "You tattooed my name on your hand?"

"I wanted to get 'I Love My Wife,' but I didn't have enough fingers."

"Oh God, Callum."

"Wait until you see what I have on my chest."

"Please don't tell me it's an image of my face."

After a pause, he says, "Okay. I won't tell you."

I bury my face in the pillow and groan. "This is crazy. *You're* crazy."

"Sometimes love doesn't make any sense. But it doesn't have to. When you find someone who makes your soul sing, all that matters is joining in the song."

Oh, my heart. My poor, tender heart wasn't made for such things.

"You could have just walked into my shop like a normal person and asked me out, you know. You didn't have to concoct such an elaborate scheme to trap me."

Squeezing me closer, he whispers, "If I had, you would've rejected me again. You would've looked at my suit and my watch and my car and told me to get lost, because you have a thing against wealth."

"That's ridiculous."

"Is it? Why don't you carry billionaire romance in your shop?"

"Because I like all the other tropes more!"

"No, because you think men with too much money are deficient in character. And before you lie to me and deny it, I've heard you say it more than once."

"Wait. You've *heard* me say it?"

"I bugged your shop."

Outraged, I demand, "You've been listening in on me too?"

"Yes. Not all the time, only when the yearning gets really bad and I need to hear your voice. I love your voice, by the way. It's beautiful."

Now I'm mad all over again. "You know what? You're right. I do think men with too much money are deficient in character, and you're proof. Now get the hell out. I never want to see you again."

I try to rise from the bed, but he pulls me closer against his body and keeps me there, his strong arms like a vise. His mouth next to my ear, he growls, "No more lies. From now on, it's truth between us only. You *do* want to see me again. Admit it."

So angry, I'm shaking, I say through gritted teeth, "I'd rather be boiled alive than see you again."

"Wife. Don't make me punish you."

I should scream some clever epithet at him for that, but his words send a little thrill through me, making me shiver. I say nothing, clamping my mouth shut.

"Now listen to me. No, I'm not a knight in shining armor. I'm the bad guy. I'm the dragon the prince tries to slay in fairy tales. But this dragon is your slave whether you like it or not, and I always will be. We made a vow that included the words until death do us part'."

"Under duress!" I exclaim. "Because you tricked me!"

"Nobody forced you to sign the contract. You did that all on your own, little lamb."

"Yes, and if I hadn't, you admitted you'd have kidnapped me!"

His voice loses the intensity of before and turns pragmatic. "Well, you can't blame a man for trying."

"Gah!" I squirm, trying to escape, but it's useless. He's too strong.

He rolls me onto my back and flattens me by lying on top of me and taking my face in his hands. Gazing down at me with blazing intensity, he says, "Do you remember that night in your apartment when I said you were something much better than beautiful?"

I do, but won't admit it. I glare at him instead.

He says, "You are beautiful, Emery, but that's the least interesting thing about you. What I meant then is that you're the only thing that's ever made me feel alive. I was dead before I met you, but I looked into your eyes, and you brought me back to life.

What you are is my reason for being. My center of gravity. The fixed point around which everything else turns. You feel like sunlight to me. You feel like a sky full of stars. I loved you before I even knew your name, when you were wearing cat ears and spitting fire at me. You ripped my heart out of my chest the first time we met, and you've been carrying it around with you ever since, bloody and beating in your hands. If you truly want me to leave you alone, I'll do it. But be prepared to have a ghost for the rest of your life, because I'll never stop haunting you. Which is only fair, considering you'll always haunt me."

My heart pounds so hard, I can't catch my breath. My eyes are full of water. I hate him, but I also don't, and I despise myself for this wretched ambivalence.

Turning my head, I close my eyes and sniffle.

He kisses my throat. His voice husky, he says, "I know I'm damaged. But all my broken pieces belong to you."

I don't understand how he can be so wrong, but feel so right.

I don't understand any of this.

"Final questions," I whisper, trembling all over. "Prague?"

"Headquarters of the Thirteen is there."

"And so are the headquarters of Sassenach. That's a shell corporation?"

"Yes."

"Like Dolos, the one you used to buy ValUBooks."

"Yes, but Sassenach isn't defunct. I use it occasionally for Thirteen business."

"Do your brothers know about the Thirteen?"

"No. And I want to keep them out of it. It's too dangerous."

That's why Cole had no idea what I was talking about when I asked him if McCord Media was involved in anything dangerous. He has no idea what his father and big brother are up to.

Talk about weaving tangled webs.

"Why is the head of Sassenach named James Fraser?"

"He's your hero. Something I know I'll never be. So, since I couldn't list myself as CEO for obvious reasons, I gave him the position." He chuckles. "Considering the position is fictional and so is the character, it seemed fitting."

This is so fucked up, I can't even begin to wrap my brain around it.

"Okay. My clones—the three housekeepers and your secretary. What's that about?"

His voice wistful, he says, "I like having people around who remind me of you."

Where do I go with that? It's strangely sweet, in a completely wrong sort of way. I decide to just keep asking questions.

"Why is your house decorated in French country style?"

"I had it redone when you posted on your shop's blog how much you loved the novel *Madame Bovary* and wished you had a house like hers in the French countryside."

"Oh God," I whisper, rocked. "That was right after my dad's funeral."

Knowing I'm freaking out all over again about how long he's been watching me, Callum wisely remains silent. He rolls off me, rolls me onto my side, and positions himself so I'm tucked into him, back to front, cradled in his arms.

"Thank you for not throwing me out," he murmurs into my ear.

"I tried. You didn't listen."

"Go back to sleep now. You'll feel better in the morning."

"Or I'll fling myself off the balcony."

"Don't be so dramatic."

"Considering the situation, it's an appropriate response."

We lie in silence for a while. I try to unfuck my brain and ignore the hard length of Callum's cock, which is poking into my ass. He makes no move to do anything about it, however, earning him the tiniest of gold stars.

I don't think there's any possibility I'll be able to sleep, but suddenly I find myself opening my eyes to brightness and blinking into a sunny room.

A sunny, empty room. Callum is gone.

His huge diamond engagement ring sparkles on my left ring finger.

A note lies on the pillow beside me. I pick it up and read.

> NOT ALL HAPPILY-EVER-AFTERS ARE FOR WHITE KNIGHTS, DARLING. SOMETIMES THE VILLAIN GETS THE GIRL. AND ISN'T THAT A MUCH MORE INTERESTING ENDING TO THE STORY?
>
> WITH ALL MY BLACK HEART,
>
> YOUR MONSTER

I read it over and over until I realize I'm smiling.

Then I rip the note into pieces, flush it down the toilet, and pack my bag.

Thirty-Seven

"He's still out there."

"I know. Ignore him."

Gazing out the front window of the shop, Vivienne grimaces. "He makes it kinda hard."

And how.

In a posture he must have stolen from his buddy Killian Black, Callum leans against the wall of ValUBooks, one leg propped up against it, arms crossed over his chest. He's not wearing mirrored sunglasses, however, and is making no attempt to disguise how he's staring openly in our direction.

He's been doing that every day for the past six weeks.

He said he'd haunt me, but I had no idea he'd be doing it this closely.

"Just don't look over there. We're only indulging his nonsense. Here, unpack this for me."

I slide an unopened box of books across the counter toward her, purposely avoiding allowing my gaze to stray anywhere near the front window. Sighing, Viv turns her attention to the box.

I look at her expression, a mix of sadness and longing, and know she's upset. "What's wrong?"

"Oh, nothing."

Unlike someone I know, Viv is a terrible liar.

"Viv, look at me." When she does, I ask again, "What's wrong?"

Making a face, she flattens her hands on the countertop. "I feel bad for him."

"You've gotta be kidding me."

"I know, I know, he's a weenie, but..."

"But what?"

"But look at him. He's miserable."

I prop a hand on my hip and snort. "You're the one who told me I shouldn't marry the guy!"

"Yeah, but that's when I thought you'd only be marrying him for his money."

"Newsflash, genius: I *did* only marry him for his money."

"I know, but now it's different."

"How the hell is it different now?"

"Because *he* married *you* for love."

When I sigh and roll my eyes, she adds, "Plus, I know you actually married him for more than his money. You like the guy."

"If I had melanoma, I'd like it more than him."

"You're just mad."

"Oh, how wrong of me!"

My sarcasm isn't lost on her. She sighs again, shaking her head. "I can't tell you what to do, obviously, but if it were me, I'd forgive him."

"Yeah, but you're the hopeless romantic around here, not the one who was wooed under false pretenses. I'll be in my office if you need me. I can't stand the view out here anymore."

I head to the back of the shop, feeling the weight of Callum's gaze on me as I go. Even across distance and through glass, the man's focus is palpable. If I have to endure this for the rest of my life, I'll go mad.

Which is probably all part of his evil plan.

I sit at my desk, rub my eyes, and force myself not to look at the signed copy of *Outlander* lying next to the computer. I keep meaning to put it out of sight, but haven't found the time.

Yes, I'm aware that I'm fibbing to myself. I'm not sure if this is the denial or the bargaining stage, but whatever it is, I'm smack in the middle of it.

I've been sleeping on Dani's living room sofa, unable to commit to finding myself a place to live. Every morning, I wake up determined to go house hunting, but by noon, I've decided to wait another day, telling myself that times of turmoil are bad for making big decisions.

Which of course has nothing to do with seeing Callum loitering like a broody, hot vagrant in front of ValUBooks every day.

Nothing at all.

I'd take a swig of whiskey, but have been on the wagon since returning from the Four Seasons. Though I'm loath to admit it, Callum was correct when he said liquor hasn't been helping me deal with my problems. I've started taking long runs after work instead, ignoring the jogger who always follows at a comfortable distance behind me, stopping when I pause to catch my breath, sprinting when I sprint, and generally making it obvious that he's stalking me.

Several times, I've considered running into traffic to see if he'd follow. I never do it because I know I'd be devastated if he were to get hit.

I mean if he got hit and *died*, I'd be devastated. It would be fine if he only got banged up. A few broken bones would serve him right, the obsessive jerk. And maybe knock some sense into him.

My desk phone rings. "Lit Happens, how may I help you?"

"Hey, babe. It's Dani."

"Hey. What's up?"

"I wanted to see if you'd go with me and Ryan to a party tonight. We got a babysitter."

"What kind of party?"

"A Halloween party."

"Ha! That would be a no."

"Oh, come on. You need to get off the sofa. I have a costume you can wear and everything. It will be a good distraction for you."

"You know what happened the last time I went to a Halloween party, right?"

"Yes, but are you determined to live your life in the past or what?"

She has a point. I heave a sigh and relent. "Okay, I'll go."

"Yay!"

"But if I'm having a horrible time, I'm taking an Uber home."

"Deal. See you later."

She hangs up, a little too gleeful for my mood. But I owe it to her not to be a drag tonight. She and poor Ryan have been putting up with me moping around their house for weeks. The least I can do is fake a smile for one night.

When I leave the shop that afternoon, I notice that Callum has left his usual spot against the wall of ValUBooks. Surprised by that, I tell myself it's a good omen. Maybe he's finally getting the hint that I'll never speak to him again.

Back at Dani's, I find her in her bedroom, trying on a giant black witch's hat.

"What do you think?"

"I think you won't be able to walk through the door in that thing. Where did you get it?"

"Amazon. Should I wear that purple one instead?"

She points to her bed, which is strewn with witch hats in various colors and sizes. "I like the crooked one with the green band. What am I wearing?"

"Here." She goes into the closet, then returns holding a flowing white gossamer gown on a hanger and a pair of iridescent wings that sparkle blue and green under the ceiling lights. Draped around the neck of the hanger is a crystal-covered crown.

"What am I supposed to be? A fairy?"

"An elf queen! Like what's-her-face in *Lord of the Rings*."

"Galadriel," I say, pleased by the choice. I've always wanted to be tall and immortal. This is as close as I'll ever get.

Dani holds the gown up against me and gestures to the mirror on the back of the closet door. "Look how pretty. I have fake pointy ear tips you can stick on too. I've got a bunch of makeup out on the bathroom counter if you want to play around with it."

She returns to her witch hat collection, and I head into the bathroom to get changed. Half an hour later, I emerge with a full face of makeup, wings, a crown, and a pair of pointy ears that Mr. Spock would be super jealous of.

When Dani sees me, she jumps up and down, clapping. She's in full witch regalia, including a slinky black dress and a fake nose with a big wart on the end.

"Oh my God! You look amazing!"

"Thank you. Shouldn't I be wearing a blonde wig?"

"You'd look all washed out with blonde hair. You'll be a brunette Galadriel. Wow, that gown is low-cut. Your boobs are practically waving hello to me."

"Thanks for making me self-conscious."

Grabbing my arm, she says, "Never mind. The babysitter just got here, so we're gonna hit the road. Ryan's waiting in the living room."

When we walk into the living room, we find Ryan—dressed as one of those flying monkeys from *The Wizard of Oz*—chatting up the babysitter, a smiling gray-haired lady who seems like she'd be a really nice grandma. We say our goodbyes, pile into Ryan's Jeep, and hit the road.

"So where is this party, anyway?" I ask from the back seat.

"Pacific Palisades," answers Ryan. "If we don't hit traffic, we should be there in half an hour or so. Dani's in charge of the music."

She finds a Reggae station, and we all sing along to Bob Marley. The drive goes by quickly. I was expecting the party to be at a club or restaurant for some reason, but we park on a lovely, tree-lined street in a residential area overlooking the Pacific Ocean. The sun is starting to set, and the sky is awash in a blaze of color.

"Who's house is this?" I ask as we approach a large Mediterranean-style home with a sprawling front lawn. Other people walk down the street toward us, dressed in colorful costumes, talking and laughing as they come.

"A friend of a friend," says Ryan. "I got the invitation secondhand, but my buddy said everyone was welcome. This house is awesome, right?"

As we walk through the open front door, Dani and I murmur in agreement.

The main foyer opens to a living room that has an unobstructed view of the ocean. The house is decorated in tasteful earth tones. The furnishings are contemporary, but not cold, and there are plants of various sizes and varieties everywhere, lending a subtle lush, tropical atmosphere.

It's already crowded.

We make our way through the living room to the patio outside, where Dani and Ryan get in line for the bar. Impressed by the grounds and not wanting a drink, I wander down past the pool to the far end of the yard where an incredible thicket of scarlet bougainvillea spills over a stone wall. The view beyond the wall is spectacular. For miles in each direction, the sea shimmers cobalt under the sunset sky.

I feel oddly at home here. This is exactly the sort of place I'd buy for myself.

Wondering if the owner would sell, I turn and head back toward the bar. Dani and Ryan are nowhere to be seen, so I go back inside, looking for them.

When I round a corner from the living room to the hallway, I trip over something in my way.

It's a foot.

A big foot, clad in a black shoe.

I catch only a glimpse of it before I teeter and start to topple forward, a strangled cry escaping my lips.

A hand shoots out and grabs my upper arm, preventing me from falling. Then I'm dragged against a hard chest. A low voice growls in my ear.

"Careful, little elf. You don't want to break that pretty crown of yours."

My pulse surges. I look up into a hard, handsome face with burning dark eyes, and I can't help the small gasp that slips out of me.

Callum stares at me like I'm the rising sun and it's the first time he's ever seen daylight.

I don't pull away. I should, but I'm too busy drinking in his scent and drowning in his eyes to coordinate a retreat. Like always, he short-circuits my brain and plugs directly into my central nervous system.

Being this close to him after so many weeks apart sets my whole body on fire. I could burn the house down with this heat I'm generating.

Breathless, my heart pounding like mad, I say, "How gallant. Thank you for saving me, Mister…?"

"Snape." His gaze drops to my mouth. "Severus Snape."

This man is truly unbelievable. He couldn't have chosen a more fitting costume to represent the antihero he is than the cunning and complicated professor of wizardry at Hogwarts in the *Harry Potter* series, an expert in the Dark Arts whom nobody knows is good or evil until the end, where he proves his loyalty by sacrificing himself and gaining redemption for seven books' worth of assholery.

I don't know if this is an astonishing display of self-awareness or a calculated ploy to give the impression that he's got a good side lurking under all his shortcomings, but I'm impressed nonetheless.

If nothing else, at least he's a *Harry Potter* fan.

"Ah. That would explain the cape and the air of foreboding."

Releasing my arm, he adjusts my crown, then gently brushes his knuckles across my cheek. He murmurs, "I'm only foreboding on the outside, elf queen. On the inside, for you, it's all mush."

Swallowing around the lump that has formed in my throat, I gaze up at him and wish I could summon a little more anger and a lot less longing to feel his mouth on mine.

We stare into each other's eyes, the party forgotten, the crowd disappeared. There's nobody but the two of us in our own small bubble of dysfunction.

I whisper, "Is that a tattoo of my name on your forearm?"

"You can read. You know it is."

"Just checking. I didn't tell anyone about the Thirteen."

"I know."

"How do you know?"

The emotion in his eyes is overwhelming. "Because you're everything good and true, and I trust you. With my heart, with my life, with everything I am, I trust you, Emery. And I've never loved anyone more."

"Callum. Goddammit." I can barely get the words out, I'm so choked up.

He takes my face in his hands and presses his forehead to mine. His voice low and urgent, he says, "Let's start over. Give me another chance."

"Why should I?"

"Because you made a vow to never leave me. Because despite all my faults, you know we're good together." He presses the softest of kisses to my lips. "And because you're in love with me, sweet little elf, even if you don't want to be."

I really fucking hate it when he's right.

But because we're a couple of big fat liars, I swipe the water from my eyes, straighten my shoulders, and lift my chin. Looking him in the eye, I say coldly, "I'm not in love with you. Not even a little bit."

There's a pause where the world spins silently, and my heartbeat thrums.

Then he smiles at the same time I do and crushes his mouth to mine.

The kiss is long and passionate. I hear catcalls from somewhere in the background but ignore them. When we draw apart, both of us panting, I say, "You own this house, don't you?"

"Yes. I thought you might like it better than the Bel Air place."

"And you're the one who invited Dani and Ryan to this party, aren't you?"

"Don't blame them. They felt obligated."

"Why?"

"Because I set up a college trust fund for Mia and bought a condo for Ryan's father."

"Callum?"

"Yes, darling?"

"Don't ever do something like that again."

"I won't. I promise."

When I narrow my eyes at him, he grins.

It's going to be a disaster. I already know it will be. When liars like us fall in love, everything else falls apart.

But, for now at least, we're falling together.

Epilogue

Two months later

The Four Seasons Resort in Maui is even more beautiful than the one in Montecito. Not that I've seen much of it, because Callum and I have spent most of the time since we arrived a week ago in our suite.

In bed in our suite, to be exact.

"Stop squirming."

"I can't help it."

"Yes, you can. And you will, or else I won't let you come."

"Why do you always get to be the one in charge?"

"Because I'm your master."

"No, you're my *monster*."

"Same thing. Speak again, and I'll turn you over and spank your ass."

I glare up at him but don't say another word.

His smile is the definition of smug. "Good girl."

Lying on my back in bed, I exhale and try to relax. I'm bound by my ankles and wrists, with my arms overhead and my legs spread. I made the mistake of mentioning to Callum that I thought Killian's rope stash was some kind of bondage gear, and he's been tying me to furniture ever since.

He checks the tension on the tie binding my right ankle to the bedpost. Satisfied, he trails his fingertips up my calf to my inner thigh.

His touch leaves sparks in its wake. When I shiver, his smile deepens.

He murmurs, "I love how responsive you are to me. Stay silent, or you'll be punished." He slides a finger inside me, his eyes flaring with desire when I tilt my hips and bite my lip.

As a reward for following instructions, he gives me his mouth.

Leaning over, he slides his tongue back and forth over my clit until it's throbbing, and I'm trembling with need.

"Not a sound," he whispers, knowing I'm close to breaking into loud moans.

I bite my lip so hard, I probably draw blood. But I obey him. The only noise that escapes me is the sound of my ragged breathing.

He adds another finger to the first and finger-fucks me as he eats me, feasting on my pussy with that wonderful hot mouth. My nipples are hard and my pulse is wild. Though the patio doors are open and a lovely cool breeze is blowing through the room, my skin mists with sweat.

When his teeth scrape my engorged clit, I tense, sucking in a breath. It feels so good, but if I let go too soon, he won't be pleased.

I try not to think about how much I love pleasing him. When I do, it makes me want to bash him over the head.

"You need to come, baby?"

I nod frantically, rocking my hips, desperate for it.

"Hold it for me."

He rises. Standing naked next to the bed, he gazes down at me as he strokes his thick shaft. My hungry gaze devours him from head to toe, those muscles and those burning eyes, the tattoos of my name on his knuckles and forearm, the image of my face surrounded by thorns on his pec. And that gorgeous erection, jutting out proudly from his hand.

I lick my lips, wanting to taste that small drop glistening in the slit of the crown.

"You're so beautiful. Look at you. You need my cock in your mouth, don't you, sweet girl?"

I nod again. At this point, anything he asks me will be answered with an enthusiastic yes.

"Take it."

He guides the head of his cock past my lips, hissing when I start to suck. Slowly pressing his hips forward, he sinks deeper into my mouth. Then he wraps a hand around my throat and commands darkly, "Don't come."

He gives my pussy a bracing slap.

I jerk and moan as pleasure blasts through my body. My pussy tingles, aching with need.

Between gritted teeth, he says, "So fucking good. You're my good girl, aren't you, wife?"

I make a small sound of agreement and suck harder on his cock. His low groan lets me know how much he likes it.

He runs his open palm all over my naked body, pinching my nipples and fondling my belly and thighs. Writhing under his touch, I struggle to breathe through my nose as he fucks my mouth, holding my head steady with that hand under my jaw.

When he tweaks my clit between two fingers, I moan involuntarily, my eyes rolling back in my head. I flex my hips desperately, needing him to fill me.

"She's so good for her master," he whispers, a thrill in his voice. "I think this pretty wet cunt deserves a reward."

He withdraws from my mouth and opens the drawer in the nightstand next to the bed. Panting, I watch as he takes out a vibrator. It's pink and is curved into a shape that vaguely resembles a saxophone, with one large head at the top and a smaller one atop the U on the bottom.

My eyes widen. I want to ask where he got that, but don't say a word.

He takes a small bottle of lube from the drawer and drips a clear stream of it between my legs, spreading it around my clit and through my soaked pussy down to my ass. Then he flicks a switch on the vibrator and slants me a dangerous look.

"Scream my name when you come for me, wife."

He works the vibrator into me, chuckling when I shudder as the smaller end breaches my ass. When the larger end is seated deep inside my pussy, he leans over and licks my engorged clit.

I orgasm almost instantly, sobbing his name. My back arches off the bed.

He makes sounds of approval deep in his throat as I rock helplessly against his face, straining against my bindings as wave after wave of pleasure surge through my core.

When the contractions have subsided and I'm lying there sated and sweating, he pulls the vibrator out of me, unties the binds on my ankles, and kneels on the bed between my legs. Pulling my thighs up around his hips, he says, "Let's see if you can scream louder."

He shoves inside me with a dominant grunt.

My breasts bounce. My pussy clenches. I tip my head back on the pillow and moan.

He starts to fuck me with short, hard strokes, driving his cock inside as I cry out in pleasure underneath him. Gripping my hips, he thrusts harder and faster until we're both moaning and the headboard is banging loudly against the wall.

"Get ready to take my cum," he rasps, fingers digging into my flesh. "Open that sweet pussy wide for me, baby."

His entire body jerks. He falls still and throws his head back. Then he climaxes, shuddering, rocking gently into me as he spills himself inside.

My own climax hits seconds after. My pussy contracts around the long, hard length of him, over and over until I can barely breathe.

I gaze up at him in hazy wonder, thinking how beautiful he is and how lucky I am, even though our journey to this moment belongs in the fucked-up hall of fame.

He collapses on top of me, breathing hard. Bracing himself on his elbows, he takes my face in his hands and kisses me deeply. I wrap my legs around his waist and kiss him back.

When we've both caught our breath, he murmurs, "You didn't scream my name."

"I didn't come again."

He rears back and stares at me, eyes wide.

My smile is as smug as his was earlier. "Or am I lying?"

Narrowing his eyes, he growls at me.

I laugh. Euphoria blazes through my body, making me feel as light as air, as if I could float right off the bed.

Later, lying in his arms as the sun begins to descend over the horizon and the breeze coming in through the open lanai doors stirs my hair, I whisper, "You told me once that you didn't want kids. Was that the truth?"

He stirs, pressing a kiss to the top of my head. His chest rises as he inhales a breath. "Yes."

"Can I ask why?"

"You won't like the answer."

"You can't see it, but I'm making a face at you."

"All right. The answer is because I don't want to share you."

"You're right. I don't like the answer."

"Told you."

I push up to an elbow and look at him. "Are you being serious?"

"Yes."

"Interesting. Guess what?"

"What?"

I smile sweetly at him. "You're going to rethink your position.

Because being a father doesn't mean you have to share me, it just means you'll have more people in your life who will aggravate you the way I do."

His look is dour. "Just what I need."

"It is, actually. You're still too bossy and arrogant for your own good."

Tucking myself into his side again, I snuggle close to him and breathe him in. "I'd also like to throw it out there that for someone who doesn't want children, you sure spread your seed around willy-nilly. Our condom use isn't what you'd call methodical."

His voice turns dry. "Half the time my 'seed,' as you so eloquently put it, doesn't wind up anywhere near your ovaries, darling."

I smile, thinking of all the lovely ways he uses my body. "Yeah, but it only takes once."

After a long moment, he says quietly, "I know."

Something in his tone makes me look up at his face. He's gazing down at me with warm, soft eyes. The expression in them makes my heart skip a beat.

"You're worried you won't be a good father, aren't you?"

"You know me better than anyone does. It's a valid concern."

My heart expands, filling with love for him. Most men never take the time to think of how their faults would affect a child. But then again, most men aren't Callum.

"I think you'd be a great dad, if that counts for anything."

Eyes shining, he swallows. Stroking a hand over my hair, he says gruffly, "It counts for everything, wife. But there's also my work to think about. What my family is involved in with Killian. If anything were to happen to me—"

"Happen to you?" I interrupt, alarmed. "What could happen to you? He told me you were on the administrative side of things!"

"The bad guys don't recognize sides."

We stare at each other for a beat until I say, "You need to let me help you."

He replies with a flat "No."

"Callum—"

"Absolutely not, Emery. I won't allow it."

"There must be something I can do."

His eyes flash with anger. "I said no. Drop it."

This stubborn man. He'll never learn.

"We'll circle back to this topic later. In the meantime, let's order dinner from room service. I'm starving."

He gazes at me suspiciously, lips thinned and nostrils flaring.

"What?"

"You're going to try to talk to Killian about letting you help with the Thirteen, aren't you?"

"Who, me?" I bat my lashes innocently. "I wouldn't even know how to contact him, silly."

When I smile, a growl of displeasure rumbles through his chest.

I tap him on the sternum and smile wider. "Dearest, darling husband. You're such a grump."

Then I roll over and hop out of bed, whistling *The Pink Panther* theme as I swagger into the bathroom.

Callum shouts after me, "No, Emery. The answer is fucking *no*!"

I call over my shoulder, "Okay, honey!" and change my tune to "London Bridge Is Falling Down."

When I hear him mutter, "Goddammit. This woman," I start to laugh.

I stop laughing abruptly when I see the small black velvet box sitting in the middle of the marble vanity counter. My heart skips a beat, then doubles its pace.

I stand frozen, staring at the box, until a soft voice behind me says, "I realized that I never asked you properly to marry me."

I spin around and stare up at him. He's smiling now, his face so handsome, it hurts.

Then, as I watch in disbelief, he sinks to one knee and takes my hands in his.

"Emery Eastwood. I love you with all my broken pieces and will until the day I die. Will you do me the honor of being my wife?"

Water wells in my eyes. My heart decides it's time to do some calisthenics. My voice cracking, I say, "I'm already your wife, dummy. Just ask the Pope."

"Is that a yes?"

Because my throat has closed, I can only nod.

He stands and picks me up, crushing me against his chest and burying his face in my neck. I feel his heart pounding against mine, their frantic beats in sync, and wonder how I ever thought I was happy before I met him.

"Oh, wait. Before I say yes, I should see the ring. Make sure it isn't another gaudy monstrosity."

"You already said yes."

"I could take it back."

"And I could lock you in a basement."

My arms wrapped around his broad shoulders, I lift my head and gaze up into his loving eyes. "And you say I'm a handful."

"At least I don't think baby shit makes a nice sandwich spread."

"Callum?"

"Yes, darling?"

"Time to shut up and kiss me."

Eyes aglow, he bends his head and does as he's told.

Against his mouth, I murmur, "Oh, one more thing. You're giving me ValUBooks as a wedding present."

"Of course I am."

"Good answer."

Acknowledgments

If you've been reading my work for any length of time, you might be starting to see what I'm doing.

If not, zoom out to a bird's-eye view and look at my contemporary series, starting with the Bad Habit books and working forward in order of date of publication to this novel (skip the Slow Burn series because they're actually standalones). What you'll find is that all sixteen of those novels and novellas are, in big ways or small, connected.

Characters from one series make cameos in another.

Plotlines converge, then disconnect.

There are bodyguards and mercenaries and Mafia kingpins, spies and thieves and hackers, heroes and villains, lovers and haters, and the morally ambiguous of every shade of gray.

At some point in the future, all these universes (and ones yet to be created) will converge.

Big things will happen.

I won't spoil anything by telling you which of your favorite characters will survive.

If you're a new-to-me reader and this is your first book of mine, *hellllooo*! And please don't worry. Forget about all that stuff I just said and enjoy the scenery. I've arranged things so you can jump onto this carnival ride anytime. (For the reading order of my books, visit my website at www.jtgeissinger.com.)

Thank you to Jay, for always telling the truth.

Thanks to Linda Ingmanson for catching all my mistakes, for the fast turnaround, and for the encouraging words when I send you half a manuscript and you think the story is about a vampire when it's not because it's all so confusing.

Thank you, Lori Jackson, for creating the beautiful cover and being so wonderful to work with.

Thanks to Michelle Lancaster for your talent, humor, and artistic eye. You're simply the best in the business and a badass to boot.

Thank you to Troy Duran for being a genius and a damn good human.

Thank you to Marnye Young (and Denise!) at AudioSorceress for your partnership and professionalism.

Thank you to Jenny Bent at the Bent Agency for being awesome.

Big thanks to the crew at Valentine PR for supporting my releases and helping me pimp my books in between. I so appreciate the effort you put in.

Geissinger's Gang, I love you. It's a rare honor to have friends who have my back and make me feel special even on the days when all I want to do is run away to Cabo and hide.

And to my readers, a special thanks for allowing me into your lives for a while. I'm honored and grateful that you picked up this book. All my life, I've loved to read and write, and I thank you for letting me tell you my stories.

Mom and Dad, I miss you every day.

About the Author

J.T. Geissinger is a #1 international and Amazon Charts bestselling author of thirty-one novels. Ranging from funny, feisty romcoms to intense erotic thrillers, her books have sold over ten million copies worldwide and been translated into more than twenty languages.

She is a three-time finalist in both contemporary and paranormal romance for the RITA® Award, the highest distinction in romance fiction from the Romance Writers of America®. She is also a recipient of the Prism Award for Best First Book, the Golden Quill Award for Best Paranormal/Urban Fantasy, and the HOLT Medallion for Best Erotic Romance.

Connect with her online in her Facebook reader group, Geissinger's Gang.

Also by J.T. Geissinger

Queens & Monsters Series

Ruthless Creatures

Carnal Urges

Savage Hearts

Brutal Vows

Beautifully Cruel Series

Beautifully Cruel

Cruel Paradise

Dangerous Beauty Series

Dangerous Beauty

Dangerous Desires

Dangerous Games

Slow Burn Series

Burn for You

Melt for You

Ache for You

Wicked Games Series

Wicked Beautiful

Wicked Sexy

Wicked Intentions

Bad Habit Series

Sweet As Sin

Make Me Sin

Sin With Me

Hot As Sin

STANDALONE NOVELS

Pen Pal

Perfect Strangers

Midnight Valentine

Rules of Engagement

Made in United States
Orlando, FL
23 May 2023

33400751R00212